The Holts: An American Dynasty

PACIFIC DESTINY

WAR FEVER SCORCHES A TROPICAL ISLAND, DREAMS OF UNTOLD WEALTH TURN TO DEATH AND DESPERATION IN THE FROZEN NORTH, A YOUNG NATION SEEKING A FOOT-HOLD ON THE PACIFIC RIM FOMENTS REVO-LUTION . . . THE HOLTS LEAD THE WAY TO THE FUTURE AS AMERICA PURSUES ITS MANI-FEST DESTINY.

TIM HOLT

Owner of the San Francisco *Clarion*, he is outraged by the incendiary headlines, masterminded by rivals such as William Randolph Hearst, that are stirring the nation's passion for bloodshed. Rushing south, directly into the line of fire, he is about to bear witness to the terrifying reality of America's "splendid little war" in Cuba.

ELIZABETH HOLT

Her honeymoon with Tim in Europe cut short, this feminist and freethinker has moved from the front lines of the suffragist movement to the front lines of a bloody invasion. The war will shake her faith not only in her country but in her husband as well, exposing the shocking secret in his past.

ROSEBAY WARE

Her marriage to Hugo Ware, reporter and artist for the *Clarion,* is bound to lead to tragedy and sorrow. For she lives with the haunting memory of a night of reckless passion with another man—a night she will never forget . . . or forgive.

MICHAEL HOLT

His childhood bout with rheumatic fever has left him with a weak heart, but nothing can stop him from seizing a once-in-a-lifetime opportunity. Moving-picture camera in hand, he is determined to record for posterity the exploits of Teddy Roosevelt and his Rough Riders—a vow that may exact the highest price of all.

HENRY BLAKE

A spy for the federal government, he is the agent of an expanding American empire in the Pacific. Reporting directly to Admiral Dewey in the Philippines, he has been ordered to set in motion the kind of operation he knows all too well—a mission requiring diversion, deception, and betrayal. And this time his greatest enemy is himself.

PAUL KIRCHNER

He is an irreverent drifter who has abandoned his prosperous family business to pursue adventure in the Philippine jungle. With his quick intelligence, his unfailing courage, and his contacts among the Filipino insurrectionists, he could prove to be a powerful ally—or a formidable enemy.

FRANK BLAKE

He staked his claim to a gold mine in the Yukon wilderness and won the love of a woman. But now the small outpost of his dreams has turned into a boomtown . . . and her love has turned bitter as the Arctic cold. Not yet twenty, he is ready to undertake the greatest challenge of his young life: a return home.

PEGGY DELANEY

She taught Frank Blake the power of passion and gave him comfort when he needed it most. But the world is changing and so are her needs and desires. Although her love for Frank may last forever, her future rests in the arms of another man.

THE HOLTS: AN AMERICAN DYNASTY
VOLUME EIGHT

PACIFIC DESTINY

DANA FULLER ROSS

 Producers of **The First Americans,**
White Indian, and **The Robber Barons.**

Book Creations Inc., Canaan, NY • *Lyle Kenyon Engel, Founder*

BANTAM BOOKS
NEW YORK • TORONTO • LONDON • SYDNEY • AUCKLAND

PACIFIC DESTINY

*A Bantam Book / published by arrangement with
Book Creations Inc.*

Bantam edition / February 1994

*Produced by Book Creations Inc.
Lyle Kenyon Engel, Founder*

ISBN 0-553-56149-9

Published simultaneously in the United States and Canada

Bantam Books are published by Bantam Books, a division of Bantam
Doubleday Dell Publishing Group, Inc. Its trademark, consisting of the
words "Bantam Books" and the portrayal of a rooster, is Registered in
U.S. Patent and Trademark Office and in other countries. Marca
Registrada. Bantam Books, 1540 Broadway, New York, New York
10036.

PRINTED IN THE UNITED STATES OF AMERICA

OPM   0 9 8 7 6 5 4 3 2 1

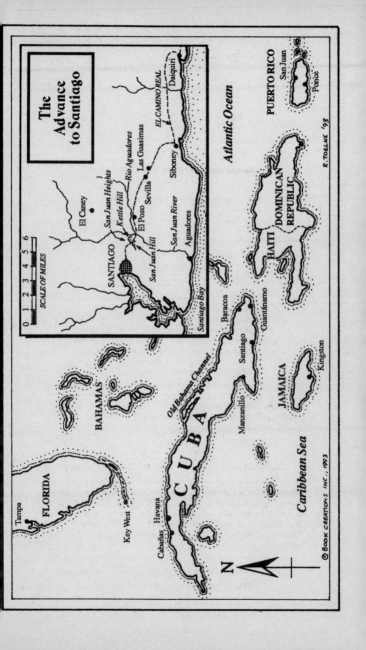

N

The
Advance
to Santiago

SCALE OF MILES
0 1 2 3 4 5 6

El Caney

San Juan Heights
Kettle Hill
Rio Aguadores

SANTIAGO
El Pozo
San Juan Hill
San Juan River

San Juan Hill
Aguadores

Santiago Bay

Sevilla
Las Guasimas

EL CAMINO REAL

Siboney
Daiquiri

Atlantic Ocean

R. TOELKE '93

Baracoa

Guantánamo

PUERTO RICO
San Juan

Ponce

DOMINICAN
REPUBLIC

HAITI

Manzanillo

Santiago

Old Bahama Channel

C U B A

JAMAICA

Kingston

Caribbean Sea

BAHAMAS

Tampa

FLORIDA

Key West

Cabañas
Havana

© BOOK CREATIONS INC., 1993

PROLOGUE

Havana Harbor, February 15, 1898

The *whump* of the explosion came first, allowing the American sailors only a split second to ask, "What was that?" before their battleship heaved herself upward through the black water. She came walloping down in a hail of blazing debris and the sharp metal shards of a broken smokestack.

Lights in the city above the harbor began to go on, and frightened citizens peered out through windows that had been shattered by the blast. The *Maine* was on fire, banging and shuddering as small-arms magazines below-deck exploded. A watery red glow bathed the harbor while the battleship, sent by Washington to protect American citizens and property in Cuba, settled bow first in the dark, rolling swells.

I

New York

"Spanish atrocities! *Maine* blown up!" A newsboy waved his papers at the arriving passengers as Tim and Elizabeth Holt came arm in arm down the gangplank. Tim detached his arm from his wife's and bought a newspaper. Elizabeth, eyes widening, read it over his shoulder. All around them the Cunard liner's passengers, who had just disembarked in New York City, were snatching up papers.

Tim ground his teeth as he read. He and Elizabeth had cut short their honeymoon, a year's tour of the Continent, because of the situation in Cuba. Nevertheless, he had not gotten home in time. Home was San Francisco, where his newspaper business was—where he ought to be right now.

Tim pulled Elizabeth out of the bottleneck that the newspaper-reading passengers were creating and found a relatively quiet corner in which to read. The *Maine* had been blown up four days before, but Spain and America were not at war yet, it seemed. Spanish sailors had helped pull survivors from the water, and Cuban hospitals had been opened to the wounded. The *Maine* was a smoldering wreck, her bow buried in the muck of Havana Harbor, her mast still jutting like an accusation above the water.

According to the article, the captain of the *Maine* suggested that the American public refrain from making any hasty judgment as to who or what might have been

2

responsible for the explosion, but Tim could have told him that Americans would exert no such self-control. Two hundred fifty-four men had been killed, and it was America's destiny to avenge them—and to free Cuba from Spanish oppression while they were at it. *Remember the* Maine!

Diplomats bustled back and forth, and Destiny with a capital *D* was invoked. Tim cabled San Francisco and booked railway tickets.

He and Elizabeth paused long enough in New York to have dinner at the home of Tim's sister Janessa and her husband, Charley Lawrence. Charley had just returned from London. He said that the English considered America too much an upstart to get into a war all on her own.

"I don't think much good came of the last war," Charley, who was from Richmond, Virginia, drawled wryly.

"I don't like the idea much, either," Tim said. "But we've painted ourselves into a corner. We've asked the Spanish to initiate a cease-fire by laying down their guns before the rebels do." He shook his head. "I can't believe that the imbeciles in Washington could hope the Spanish would do any such thing."

"It might be difficult to persuade the *insurrectos* to stop shooting first," Elizabeth said, "since no one can *find* them. Besides, Washington hasn't officially recognized them."

"That might have occurred to someone before the notion of a cease-fire came up at all," Tim said grumpily. "Initiating a cease-fire would be impossible for Spain. The Spanish populace would interpret it as a call for mercy, and it might even lead to mutiny in the army and revolution at home."

"I still can't understand why Fitzhugh Lee yelled for a battleship to rescue him," Charley said. "The old fool thinks he's still leading the cavalry."

Fitzhugh Lee was the American consul general in Havana. He was one of *the* Lees of Virginia, a dapper dresser with a fondness for liquor and cigars. Charley, as a

Virginian, tended to take the man's shortcomings personally.

"If it hadn't been old Fitz, it would have been somebody else," Tim said. "This fight's been brewing for years, and everybody over here has been yammering for it. You can't blame it on poor Fitz Lee. He didn't know they were going to blow up the *Maine*."

"We still don't know that Spain was responsible," Janessa said. "We've managed to get hysterical over what may have been an internal explosion." She sniffed. "Not that your fellow journalists care to put on their brakes till they learn the truth."

The *New York Journal* and the *New York World,* the papers of Hearst and Pulitzer, were publishing imaginative drawings purporting to show exactly how the submarine mine fastened to the bow of the *Maine* had been set off by an electrical signal from Havana—despite the fact that their reporters and artists had never been allowed near the wreck. Meanwhile, navy investigators were diving in murky waters and looking for clues. No one with half a brain could believe that the Spanish would deliberately blow up the *Maine*. Spain had wined and dined the battleship's officers. Surely the last thing Spain wanted was to bring America into a war on the insurrectos' side. Despite all that, Hearst and Pulitzer were trumpeting for vengeance in banner headlines.

"The *Clarion* has printed more inches than I can count on exactly why we should *not* get mixed up in Cuba," Tim informed Janessa. "Hearst actually called me a lily-livered blackguard in print."

"Your efforts don't appear to have done any good," Janessa said crossly. "I have a very clear picture of the human toll a war would take on both sides."

Charley reached over and patted his wife's knee. "She is also convinced that the Hospital Service will send me down there." Charley and Janessa were both doctors. Janessa had recently founded the Brentwood Hospital, for women and children, in New York City, while Charley was a doctor with the Hospital Service and had been assigned to the Immigration Department on Ellis Island.

Janessa did not dispute Charley's statement. Instead, she glanced at Elizabeth, whom she did not know very well. "Do you think that if we get the vote we'll be able to put a stop to war?" Janessa asked seriously.

Tim was pleasantly surprised by his sister's question. His wife came from a radical family of freethinkers and feminists, which, for some reason, made Janessa uneasy. Elizabeth was active in the women's movement that Janessa had spurned. Janessa's politics were more personal.

"I used to think so," Elizabeth said. "Unfortunately, I listened to the war talk at a suffrage meeting here just this morning—"

"Some women go shopping," Tim commented to Charley. "Elizabeth goes to rallies."

"I listened to the talk about this war," Elizabeth said, ignoring him, "and I'm afraid I didn't hear any evidence that we're smarter than men."

"That must have been depressing for you," Tim said.

"Extremely," Elizabeth said serenely, "given the intelligence level of men. Of course we aren't any stupider, either."

"That would be particularly difficult to achieve just now," Tim agreed.

Elizabeth looked at him shrewdly. "But if war starts, you'll be in the thick of it, won't you? Cuba would be a journalist's paradise."

Tim flushed slightly. "War's always an opportunity for a correspondent," he said stiffly.

"Mmmm," said Elizabeth.

"If we do have a war, don't think for a second that I'd stay away from it as a form of protest," he informed her.

"The idea never occurred to me," Elizabeth said fondly. She smiled at Charley and Janessa. "Every other idiot on his staff is rabid to go. Rafe Murray keeps sending us telegrams pleading for assignment."

Janessa studied the woman who had married her brother. "Don't you mind his going?" she asked. "It's not as if he was in the army and wouldn't have a choice."

"I'd mind it more if he *were* in the army," Elizabeth said. "I prefer that people be able to make their own decisions. After all, that's the whole goal of our movement." She eyed Janessa thoughtfully.

"Oh." Janessa seemed unable to find any other suitable answer. "Let's take our coffee in the parlor," she said abruptly. "It's more comfortable."

As opposed to what? Tim wondered. *As opposed to the dentist's chair, or sitting on a flagpole?* He could feel the undercurrents rippling between Elizabeth and Janessa. He supposed Elizabeth was proprietary of him; as his wife, she would naturally feel that way. It was up to Janessa, he decided, to loosen her reins on him. That would come with time, he knew. She had been his older sister for a lot longer than Elizabeth had been his wife.

"We can't stay late," he said to everyone's unspoken relief. "We have to catch an early train."

In the morning they were seen off at the depot by Tim's brother, Michael Holt, and Michael's wife, Eden. Michael made moving pictures, and he and Eden lived at the Chelsea Hotel, in an apartment down the hall from a composer and his python. Mike and Eden disapproved of nothing, were interested in everything, and despite an air of permanent artistic distraction, were actually extremely well-informed.

"We're in for it," Mike predicted. "Even money I'll see you again before the end of April."

Tim grabbed him by the collar. "You wouldn't enlist!" Mike had a weak heart, the legacy of rheumatic fever.

"The army wouldn't take me, you dimwit," Mike said. "But what an opportunity!" He rubbed his hands together. "I'm bringing the camera, of course."

Opportunity seemed to be the way that everyone thought of it. John Hay, the ambassador to Great Britain, called it a "splendid little war," and Theodore Roosevelt, assistant secretary of the navy, said what a bully thing it would be for the navy. No one took any particular notice that while the navy might be well prepared for war, the army had not been ready for an all-out mobilization in the last forty years. It certainly was not ready for a conflict in the tropics. Resolutions were passed, and theater orchestras played "Rally 'Round the Flag, Boys" and "Johnny, Get Your Gun." Roosevelt and his friend Senator Henry Cabot Lodge took advantage of the fortuitous absence from Washington of the navy's secretary, John D. Long, to wire a number of cables to the fleet, including one that sent Commodore George Dewey and the Asiatic squadron to Hong Kong to prepare to strike the Spanish fleet in the Philippines in the event of war.

In the face of popular and congressional enthusiasm, President McKinley finally abandoned his antiwar policy and sent Spain what amounted to an ultimatum for political and military concessions. Congress appropriated fifty million dollars for "national defense," and the battleship *Oregon* steamed out of San Francisco for Key West. Spain, which couldn't afford war, offered the rebels armistice and agreed to negotiate Cuban independence. It was too late. McKinley, having been pushed to war, was going through with it. All hell was about to break loose.

Portland

When Tim returned to San Francisco, he immediately conferred with his editors and hired a railroad car to stand by for the mountains of baggage he would need. Meanwhile, his father, Toby Holt, was home in Portland, Oregon. After years of working in Washington, first as a senator, then as a lobbyist for a world peace organization, Toby was watching the political drama unfold with what appeared to his wife, Alexandra, and his sister, Cindy Blake, to be the same mild interest he might give a yacht race or tennis match.

"They'll do very nicely without me," he said, pushing Alex away when she appeared to be about to take his temperature. "This whole country has become determined to have a war. Who am I to stop it?"

Alex studied him. Toby's graying sandy hair was immaculately brushed, his spectacles polished, his handsome, stubborn, square-jawed face serene. He didn't look like a man whose faculties were failing. "It isn't like you to be so placid," she said.

Toby looked up at her from his reading chair. He put his newspaper, the *Oregonian,* on the floor. Their cat came along and sat on it. "I beat my head against the wall long enough. I can't stop the war, so there's no point in tying myself in knots. Theodore Roosevelt says that what this country needs is a war, and he and his playmates are going to see that we get it. I think Theodore's dead wrong on this, but there's nothing I can do."

"You might have found something if you'd stayed in Washington," Alexandra said. She knew that Toby had returned to Oregon because of her, and she felt guilty about it.

Toby's hand shot out, and he grabbed Alex by the wrist before she could back away. "Let's get something straight right now." He pulled her very carefully down onto his lap, then traced a fingertip along her forehead, twining the stray tendrils of red hair, which she had tied up in a scarf for spring cleaning. "Washington was making you sick. You are more important to me than my work. And Sally was becoming a spoiled belle. What's she doing this morning?"

"She and Midge went fishing," Alex said.

"You see? A marked improvement."

Alex sighed. "She'll probably make Midge bait the hooks."

"It's preferable to being a spoiled flirt and wearing clothes that are four years too old for her," Toby said.

Alex snuggled closer to him. He sneezed at the dusty scarf but hugged her anyway. "And it's good for the Madrona to have me back," Toby continued. "Mother's too old to run a working ranch, and Cindy's too distracted. I'm expecting her to leave for Washington any minute. When there's war, Henry's going to be in it."

"I know," Alex said. "Do you think she'll go back to him? She's said she won't."

"She may not, but she won't let him get sent God knows where while she sits here, either. Until he gets his assignment, she'll probably follow him around the house and glare at him, but at least she'll know he's safe."

"Oh, Lord. Life is so complicated," Alex said. "Just think of how deeply in love those two were."

Cindy had come home to the Madrona with her younger child, Midge, leaving her husband, Henry, in Alexandria, Virginia. She was furious at him for his dictatorial ways. Their son, Frank, had run away after a terrible argument with Henry, and no one knew exactly where Frank was now. Henry considered the argument to have been Frank's fault. Cindy, with ironclad certainty and venomous fury, set the blame at Henry's feet.

"I don't like the way Cindy looks," Alex remarked.

"Hmmm?" Toby's thoughts had drifted.

"She looks . . . old, as if she's settling into being a battle-ax. It's not like her."

Cindy came in on the heels of Alexandra's observation, and Toby studied her unobtrusively over his wife's shoulder. "Don't mind us," he said. "We're just keeping each other's old bones warm."

"Good idea," Cindy said brusquely. She looked around Toby's study. "Have you got the morning paper?"

Toby pointed downward. "Under the cat." He watched her move the cat, pick up the paper, and scrutinize the front page. There was some truth in what Alex had said, he decided. Cindy's hair, the same graying sandy blond as his own, was yanked back into a severe bun, and her bangs were curled with tongs into an unbecoming frizz better suited to a woman of seventy than forty-eight—or at least Cindy at forty-eight. Other women might gray into dowagers at forty, but not Cindy. Trim, pretty, with an artist's flair for design and a passion for Paris fashions, Cindy had routinely turned younger men's heads on the street—until recently. Now her face was lined with anger, two hard creases on either side of her mouth, and her eyes were dark-circled and dull. Further-more, she didn't seem to care. She read the front page of the *Oregonian* and, unaware, tapped her foot on the study floor.

"What does Tim say?" she demanded.

Tim, as the family journalist, was popularly believed to know whatever there was to know.

"He says we're going to be at war with Spain inside a month," Toby answered. "Which any damn fool could tell. When are you going to quit pacing like a penned wolf and go home?"

"I can't leave Frank," Cindy said.

It was her stock answer. "You don't know where Frank is," Toby told her. "You just think he's up north some-where. You can't go off to the Klondike to find him, so you might just as well be in Washington."

"I have no reason to be in Washington," Cindy replied curtly, still reading. "But I suppose I'll have to take care of the house there, since Henry isn't going to."

Toby ignored these contradictory statements. "What about Midge?"

"Would you like to leave her here with us?" Alex asked. "You know we'd love to have her, and she's happy in school. If you think she might feel more secure . . ."

"To be without her mother?" Cindy asked, exasper-ated. "After her father has already abandoned her?"

"Her father was thrown off this place by you," Toby pointed out. "Almost with your bare hands, I'm told. Will

you forget how angry you are with Henry for a minute
and—"

"I don't think I can do that." Cindy went back to the
paper and its account of the battleship dispatched for Key
West. "It will take two months for the *Oregon* to get there
from San Francisco, around the Horn. Why haven't we
opened a Central American canal yet? That's what I want
to know." She glared at Toby as if he might be responsible.

Toby gave up. He felt relieved that Cindy hadn't
taken Alex up on her offer to keep Midge. Midge was a
very nice girl and undoubtedly a good influence on Sally,
but Midge was no match for her cousin. Sally was fifteen
going on twenty. It seemed hard on Midge to have to put
up with being overshadowed by Sally, along with everything else. Toby was not certain that Sally meant to be
condescending, but he wasn't at all confident that she
didn't, either.

Midge was fourteen and having trouble adjusting to
adolescence. She had felt grateful to come to the Madrona
with her mother. In Washington she never felt pretty
enough or fashionable enough, not quite in the know, like
the other girls. When her father had come to the ranch,
she had had visions of the whole family living happily
there, with her grandmother. But then her father had gone
back to Washington, estranged, and her uncle Toby and
aunt Alexandra had come home instead—with her cousin
Sally. The Madrona was Sally's, not Midge's; Sally had let
her know that quite clearly.

Midge turned, careful not to disturb her fishing line,
which stretched taut to the deep current in the middle of
the stream. She drew one knee up higher on her rock and
contemplated her beautiful, rebellious cousin. Sally's hair
was a mass of rose-gold curls, and her blue eyes and
delicate mouth looked like those of a Botticelli angel—but
one with a temper. Sally didn't really like to fish; she had
only come along because she couldn't stand for Midge to
do anything that she didn't. Right now her line was drifting

in the water, unattended, snagged in the reeds, while Sally plaited a chain of flowers with deft fingers.

Sally turned the chain of bachelor's buttons into a crown, which she placed on her head. "Isn't it pretty? Do you want me to make you one?"

Midge looked away and shook her head.

"Well, let's go back, then. This is boring." Sally stood up and smoothed her skirts.

Midge shook her head again, and Sally looked at her with interest. "You haven't caught anything," she observed. "Who wants to sit on an old wet rock and swat bugs?"

"I *have* caught something," Midge said. She opened her creel. "While you were playing with flowers," she added.

"Oh. Oh, well, you can have my line, too. I think maybe the bait's still on it." Sally wrinkled her nose at the water. The streambed was dank with the smell of rotting vegetation from the last flood.

"I don't want your line," Midge said. "It's all tangled in the reeds."

Sally shrugged, perfectly prepared to abandon it, when a movement on the other bank caught her eye. A towheaded boy a few years older than the girls was picking his way along the opposite side. Sally sat down again and began to try, without much success, to retrieve her line.

The boy turned toward them, hopping with agility from rock to rock.

"Oh, Finney, I've made such a mess." Sally fluttered her hands at the line.

The boy waded into the water and began to untangle it. He shook his head. "You trying to catch fish or mud turtles?" He grinned and tossed her the line, then let his eyes slide toward Midge.

Midge looked at her lap. She couldn't talk to him with Sally there. Sally talked easily to boys, flirting with them with a skill beyond her fifteen years. Midge only grew tongue-tied and watched them with wistful eyes, drawn to and a little frightened by their coltish power and the quick hunch of their shoulders, the restless tossing of their heads. Finney, who was nearly as shy as she was, had seemed different, until Sally had come home.

"Show me how to throw this silly line, Finney," Sally said, laughing, "so I don't get it snarled in the reeds again."

"You don't throw a line, you cast it," Finney said. His eyes slid toward Midge again. "And I ain't got time to teach girls to fish. I got work to do."

"You work for my daddy," Sally said. "So it's all right."

Finney looked uncomfortable, but he took Sally's rod and cast the line for her out into the center of the stream, while she stood next to him in a cloud of lilac scent and asked how to hold the pole and whether he thought she would ever be good enough to catch anything.

"I reckon you could probably catch just about anything you wanted," Finney said. Sally smiled at him, and his face flushed.

Midge's line tightened. "I've got a bite!" she said loudly. She pulled her fish in, wishing Finney would watch her and not her cousin.

Finney edged away from them both. "That's a fine one," he said. "I got to get back now, or White Elk'll skin me." White Elk was the Madrona foreman. He wouldn't count fishing with the girls as working. "I got branding to do, and then a loose box to patch up in the north barn." He looked at Midge. "I got to git," he said again and took off through the woods.

Sally peered after him thoughtfully. "He's kind of cute, but sometimes I think the poor thing's just scared to death of girls."

"Why don't you leave him alone?" Midge blurted out. "You don't want him, you're just—just practicing on him. Why don't you leave him alone?"

"Why, Midge honey." Sally blinked golden lashes. "Don't tell me *you* want him? Finney Williams?" She burst into joyous laughter.

"You be quiet," Midge hissed.

Sally reeled her line in. "My goodness, you should

have told me. I wouldn't have said boo to him if I'd known *you* were sweet on him."

"I'm *not* sweet on him." Midge glared at Sally, miserably contemplating their differences—her schoolgirl clothes and Sally's elegant ones, far more grown-up than the year's difference in their ages warranted; her straight brown hair in its plain braid and Sally's knot of pale curls. She rubbed a hand across her nose as if that would wipe away the freckles she hated, while Sally's china-doll face looked back at her with elaborate sympathy.

"Well, it's a good thing you're not," Sally said practically. "Since you're going back to Washington."

"Back to Washington?" Midge's eyes widened.

"That's what Dad says." Sally tucked her fishing rod under her arm and picked up her straw hat. "He says Aunt Cindy won't stay here now that we're going to have a war."

"You don't know!" Midge shouted. "You don't know, and I don't believe you. I'm not going!"

"My goodness, Midge, he's just a ranch hand." Sally's eyes narrowed, intrigued. "Aunt Cindy wouldn't like it if you got interested in a ranch hand."

"There's nothing wrong with him," Midge muttered.

"Well, *I* wouldn't want Coot Williams for a papa-in-law," Sally said airily. "Not that I'm not fond of him—he's been with the Madrona forever—but honestly, just imagine. And nobody knows where Finney came from. He just showed up one day, I hear, and said Coot was his dad, so Gran let him stay. I bet she wouldn't have if she thought you—"

Midge snatched up her rod and creel. "You shut your mouth, Sally Holt!" She marched away, tears sliding down her cheeks. "And I'm not going back to Washington!" she snapped over her shoulder.

When she was out of sight of Sally, Midge sat down on a rock and cried. Everything in the world was unraveling. It had all started when Frank left, and then her parents had decided to hate each other, and now her father was gone, too. She had thought that at least she had the

Madrona. But it wasn't really hers; it was her uncle Toby's. And now he and her aunt and Sally had come home, and she had to leave. *Sally doesn't even like the Madrona,* Midge thought with a flash of jealousy so sharp that it stung. *Sally would rather be in Washington.*

And now Midge would never get to know about Finney Williams. He had told White Elk's wife, Mai, that he thought she was pretty, but he had never told her. Maybe he didn't even think so now, with Sally home. Midge thought of Finney, and an odd feeling came over her. He made her feel strange. He made her feel things she didn't want to tell anybody about, and the way she saw him look at Sally made her feel stranger still.

Tears slid down Midge's face. Everybody did what they wanted to and just dragged her along with them, she thought. Nobody asked her what *she* wanted. Everybody thought she was a baby.

"I'm not a baby," Midge said aloud. "I'm fourteen, but nobody notices it."

She got up quite deliberately and walked back toward the house. The trees were just beginning to leaf out, and they unfurled delicate fans of green, as pale and strange as the inner hearts of flowers. Midge came out of the misty damp of the woods and let herself through the gate and into the north meadow, into buttery sun, with the house sailing like a ship on its hill. Her heart squeezed tightly in her chest at the thought of leaving this beautiful haven, but she had decided not to cry. Babies cried.

Midge hurried to the house. She left her creel in the kitchen and went up to her room, up the familiar stairs and down the hallway with its Turkish runner, past her grandmother's room, where the woman was taking her afternoon nap, and into the old nursery that had been turned into a room for Midge.

An ancient stuffed rabbit sat on the windowsill, and Midge picked it up and stared out through the window at the madrone trees that circled the house. In the field beyond, the hands were branding new foals. She could almost feel the iron come down on skin, burning it through. She saw Finney's pale head among the men around the fire.

Midge drew the shade down and pulled off the old gingham dress she had worn to fish in. She put on a clean plaid shirtwaist and the black sateen skirt that was her longest one, then combed out her hair. She rebraided it, tucked the braid under into its usual neat club, then anchored it with a black bow at the nape of her neck. Arms still raised, she turned sideways to the mirror, seeing how her body was changing. She wore a corset now, stays laced not too tight. And she had begun to have her monthly two years before. Midge began to count these signs upon her fingers. She touched her left breast with a fingertip, uncertainly.

"Midge? Did I hear you come in, darling?"

Midge spun around. Her grandmother, Eulalia Blake, stood with her hand on the knob, the door a little open. She leaned carefully on her cane.

"I'm sorry, dear. I should have knocked."

"It's all right, Gran. I just finished dressing." Midge's face was flushed.

Eulalia looked at her more closely. "Child, are you all right?"

"I'm fine," Midge muttered.

"You jumped like someone hearing a firecracker go off," her grandmother observed. She came in and sat down on the white iron bed. "I hope I'm invited. It's difficult for me to stand for very long these days."

"Of course," Midge said, contrite. "Sally says we're going back to Washington," she offered. "I don't want to leave."

Eulalia made an irritated noise, then sighed. "Sally says too many things she doesn't know anything about. But in this case, I'm afraid she's right. I talked with your mother earlier. With this awful war brewing, she feels she may need to go."

"I hate Washington." Midge groaned. "I thought we were going to live here forever."

"*I* hoped you were both going to live in Washington with your father," Eulalia said. "Since it doesn't seem as if that is about to happen, I wanted you to live here, too, darling. But your father's sure to be in this war, and your mother doesn't want to leave the house empty."

"The house has been empty for months," Midge pointed out.

"I think she wants to be where she can get news of your father," Eulalia said gently. "Don't you, darling?"

"I don't want news, I want *him,*" Midge wailed. "Him and Frank. Everybody goes away. How do you make people stay?"

"Oh, dear, I wish I knew." Eulalia stood up and put an arm around Midge and kissed her cheek. "That's a very becoming shirtwaist."

"Thank you," Midge said gravely.

"I suppose dinner's nearly on the table."

"I'll be down in a minute."

After her grandmother had gone, Midge raised the shade and looked through the window again at the men in the field. Finney wrestled the last colt to the ground, snubbed the rope around its legs, and one of the men quickly branded it. As soon as they let go of it, the colt shrieked and rocketed away. The men set off across the field, cooling irons balanced carelessly on their shoulders. They walked easily, unperturbed by the job. Behind them, the blackened ring of turf, charred by the fire, faded in the deepening dusk, leaving its mark on the earth.

After dinner, Midge slipped away from the table while the four adults lingered over coffee. Sally sat down in the parlor to write letters to her friends in Washington. No one had said anything yet about going back there, and Midge wanted to get away before they did. To hear it spoken about—especially by her mother—would make it true, and Midge wasn't ready to deal with it.

Not wanting to talk to Abby Givens, the cook, who was in the kitchen, Midge avoided the back door and went through the front instead, skipping down the porch steps and into the shadows of the madrone trees. They were just beginning to bloom, and their white clouds of flowers shone above her in the darkness. From the back of the house she could see the north barn, where her aunt's show horses were stabled.

The air smelled of flowers and the coarse, wet scent of green hay. Midge noticed a faint glow shining through the barn window, and she walked toward it. She matched her steps to the rhythmic sound of hammering coming from inside the barn and remembered that Finney was going to repair a loose box. She headed in that direction and stopped just inside the barn door.

Midge smelled the sharp aroma of straw and horses. Finney looked up from the corner of the loose box, hammer in hand. The lantern on the floor beside him illuminated his bony face and the wide, questioning line of his mouth. He stood up slowly.

"Hello," Midge said.

"Hello." Finney looked at her, uncertainty overlaying the eagerness in his pale eyes. "Were you looking for—? Did you—?"

"I saw the light," Midge said. "I came to see what you were doing. I mean, I just happened to be outside, and I remembered you said you were . . ." She stumbled to a halt. "Are you mending Jezebel's box again?"

"Yeah. I put her in an empty box at the end." Finney swung the hammer casually. "She kicks it down every time she gets fractious. I don't know what would keep that devil in. I just nail up another board every so often. See?" Midge came forward, and he pointed to the splintered sides of the box. "See? Printed her shoes right in that one."

Midge traced her fingertips over the semicircular imprints. Finney stood close to her, holding the lantern. He smelled salty like the horses, and the faint odor of burned hair clung to him from the branding. He set the hammer down, and Midge felt his shoulder shift against hers. He was thin; the arms under his flannel shirt were bony. His hands were thick with calluses, and there were dark lines of dirt under the nails.

Finney saw her looking at his nails and hid his hands behind his back. "I'm all dirty," he mumbled.

"You've been working." Midge reached for one of his hands. "It's all right."

Finney looked down at her, hopeful. "You're so clean. You'll get dirty out here."

"It's all right," Midge said again. She didn't know what she wanted, but she wanted something. Something that she would have and Sally wouldn't. Something before her mother made her go away.

Finney put his fingertips on her shoulder. "You're so pretty."

Midge smiled, heart thumping. "Am I?" She wanted to hear him say it again.

"Oh, God, you're pretty," Finney breathed. "I wish I could kiss you."

Midge wanted desperately for him to kiss her. Without saying a word, she lifted her face to his and closed her eyes. His mouth came down on hers. It was a delicious feeling. But even more extraordinary was the way his body felt pressed against hers. It made her head swim, the way the champagne at her cousin Tim's wedding had. She wrapped her arms around his back to make it last longer. His mouth pressed hard against hers.

When she thought she would pass out, he lifted his mouth and stepped back a little. He was breathing hard. They looked at each other in terror and excitement.

"I hadn't ought to—" Finney said.

Midge touched his face with her fingertips. The hand on her rib cage trembled, and he covered her mouth with his again, this time parting her lips with his tongue. Midge pressed herself against him, and they stumbled in the straw but kept their balance. Finney's hand moved up over her breast. Midge stiffened, more embarrassed than outraged, and then relaxed and let him play with her because it felt so good. This couldn't be bad if it felt so good, she thought.

They fumbled and, managing to stay upright, kissed in the loose box. His lips were nuzzling her ear while his fingers unbuttoned her shirtwaist. His hands slid into her chemise above her corset, and quivering fingers touched bare nipples. Midge closed her eyes and thought, *I am going to remember exactly how this feels.* She swayed against him, happy to let him go on doing this forever.

That was when Alexandra, holding a lantern, opened the door. She had an apple for Jezebel. Finney saw her first. He jerked back so quickly that Midge nearly fell over.

Startled, Midge turned in the direction Finney was staring. She looked at her aunt in horror, then jerked her eyes away and worked frantically to refasten her buttons.

"It—it was all my fault, Mrs. Holt," Finney said haltingly.

"I don't doubt it!" Alexandra snapped.

"It *wasn't* Finney's fault," Midge blurted. She put her face to her hands, wishing the ground would open up under her.

Alex advanced on Finney. "Get back to the bunk-house, you *depraved* boy!" He took to his heels.

"As for you, go back to the house!" Alexandra said furiously. "And you'd better tell your mother what you did, young lady, because if you don't, I'm going to."

"Oh, no! Please don't!" Midge whimpered.

"You have until I get back," Alex said coldly, and Midge fled.

"I didn't do anything but let him kiss me," Midge wailed. She was flattened into an armchair.

Cindy glared at her daughter with the foreboding expression that the avenging angel might have worn when he appeared with his flaming sword.

"He had his hand inside the front of her shirtwaist," Alex informed Cindy. Midge, her mother, and her aunt were gathered in the parlor, Eulalia having dragged Sally out of the room by force when the fireworks began. Toby had been banished, too, for delicacy's sake, but not before Alex had informed him that he was to fire Finney Williams.

"Don't take it out on Finney." Midge groaned. "It wasn't his fault. I—I let him!"

"You let him!" Cindy shouted. "Whatever possessed you to do such a terrible thing?"

"I wanted to," Midge said defiantly.

"Do you know what happens to girls who let boys do things like that?" Cindy asked ominously.

"They have babies?" Midge asked, puzzled. "I didn't—"

"Certainly not!" Cindy said, aghast. "No nice boy ever speaks to them again, that's what. And some of them"— she lowered her voice meaningfully—"*do* have babies if they go *too far*."

"Mother, I wouldn't—"

"If you let a boy treat you like that, he won't have any respect for you, and he may do anything," Cindy said. "Men have no restraint," she added darkly.

"No *nice* boy wants to marry a girl who would let him *do* a thing like that," Alexandra informed her.

The parlor door opened a crack. Toby stuck his head in. "Since I can hear you out in the hall, I thought I'd stop by and tell you Coot gave Finney the tanning of his life, so I think female virtue is safe around here for a while." He looked at Midge. "You look done in, honey. You go to bed. I want to talk to the ladies here."

Cindy started to protest, but Midge was gone before her mother could speak. Cindy, Toby, and Alexandra heard the girl's footsteps pounding up the stairs, the door to her room slamming, and the lock clicking. Sally's inquiries through her cousin's bedroom door were clearly audible even in the parlor, but apparently Midge did not reply. Then they heard Eulalia shooing Sally away from the door.

In the parlor, Cindy and Alexandra glared at Toby.

"Do you mean to tell me you are going to allow that young man to stay on at the Madrona?" Cindy demanded.

"Coot beat the tar out of him," Toby said. "I don't think the poor boy will so much as look at a girl for at least a month."

"And what about after that?" Alexandra put her hands on her hips. "Who's going to protect our girls?"

"A boy like that might do anything." Cindy's gaze skewered him as if *he* were the offender.

"That boy's a viper," Alexandra said.

"A debauched, immoral libertine!"

Toby envisioned Finney Williams's thin form and hangdog face and barely managed not to chuckle. "You two are having hysterics," he said. "If you think Finney Williams is a libertine, you've led mighty sheltered lives. Come on, girls, he's just a kid." Toby's eyes gleamed. "Hell, I remember being that age. I had a few outings in the barn myself."

"Indeed?" Cindy said icily. "I intensely dislike being addressed as 'girls.'"

"Hell, yes," Toby said, unrepentant. "In fact, I nearly had to marry one of them."

"Dear—" Alex was diverted from Finney's depravity by Toby's lack of tact.

"I suppose you're going to tell me that it's all the girl's fault?" Cindy exploded. "'Boys will be boys'? I suppose you think *Midge* is to blame? Men always do!"

"Hell, no," Toby said. "Will you calm down? She's just a kid, too. They were just doing what comes naturally, and they got a mite carried away. I expect they're both embarrassed to death right now."

"Toby," Alexandra said solemnly, "you don't know what he *did*."

"Yeah, I know what he did. He told Coot. Now why don't you ladies back off and get some perspective?"

Alexandra held her back straight to indicate unbending morality where her niece was concerned. "How can you possibly excuse—"

"Alex, think a minute. Do you mean to tell me that in your whole life, you never let any boy put his hand on your tit?"

"Tobias Holt!"

"Alex, I'm your husband. I've been putting my hands on them for years, and I'm not going to mince words with you."

"Well . . . I can't remember." Alex turned away, but not before Toby saw her mouth twitching into a half smile.

"Ah-ha!"

Alex turned back to Toby. "That has nothing to do with this."

"Of course it does." He pointed his finger at Cindy. "And don't you act all pious with me, either. You used to have a fine time with Henry behind the barn. I caught you at it once, remember?"

Cindy narrowed her blue eyes at him. "I do not wish to hear any more of this."

"She had to give me her desserts for a week," Toby said cheerfully. "Hush money."

Alexandra burst out laughing, but Cindy exploded. She jumped up and whirled on her brother. "You're just like all men! You don't care about anyone but yourselves. You behave like insensitive billy goats and all defend one another. You and Henry and Frank and that awful boy and—"

"Cindy—" Alex held out her hand.

"I'm taking Midge back to Washington!" Cindy snapped, ignoring her. "And I don't want you to so much as speak to me between now and then, do you hear me, Toby? I don't want to *speak* to you!" She turned on her heel and slammed the parlor door behind her. They could hear her sobbing as she ran up the stairs.

"Oh, Lord," Alexandra said. "Now what do we do?"

"Nothing. Cindy's mad at every male on the face of the earth," Toby said. "I'm tired of being held personally accountable for Henry and Frank. And I'm tired of her acting like an old-maid schoolteacher." He cocked his head at her. "You, too, Alex. You overreacted. That wasn't like you, honey."

Alex bit her thumbnail. "I know. But *I'm* worried about Sally."

"There *is* that," Toby admitted. "Sally's another kettle of fish. But firing poor Finney won't solve that. Maybe we should just tie her to the bedpost."

"Toby!"

He put an arm around her. "You're getting as literal-minded as Cindy. It's driving me crazy."

"I see," Alex said. "Is that why you provoked her into going home?"

"Was it that obvious?" Toby asked. "I already want to strangle Henry, and now my fingers are itching when I talk to Cindy—or rather, when she talks to me. The two of them have to work out their problems, and they won't do it with Cindy hiding out here. Somebody had to get her moving."

"She was already planning to go," Alex said.

"But she wasn't doing it. We're about to have a war. If she doesn't get off her bustle before there's a general call-up, she'll never get a railway ticket."

"You're so thoughtful," Alex muttered.

"I plan ahead." He slipped an arm around her. "Now come on to bed. You can tell me about this young man."

"What young man?"

"The one you allowed to take such indecent liberties."

"Oh, him." Alex turned to look at Toby and kissed his cheek. "Not on your life."

II

Cindy and Midge left two days later, with a polite exchange of kisses and farewells all around. But Cindy made it clear that she had not forgiven Toby and that he needn't think she had. Finney Williams kept out of sight, although Sally, who liked to be a key player in anyone's drama, smuggled a note from him to Midge. *I'm awful sorry,* it said.

"I feel so *bad* for him," Midge said. She wrote *It was worth it* on a piece of her best stationery. "You take him this."

Sally eyed Midge with new respect. As soon as Midge left, Sally took the note to Finney in the barn. To her disappointment, he didn't read it in front of her; she had wanted to see his reaction.

As soon as Sally was gone, Finney read the note. Then he went back to his room, reread it with a certain sense of wonder, and put it in the cigar box where he kept his few treasures.

Alexandra sat Sally down, and they had a mother-daughter chat about why what Midge had done was ill-advised. Sally assured her mother that she understood entirely, but Alexandra watched her blossoming daughter with the same trepidation with which she read the morning headlines. The stately and conservative *Oregonian* was demanding war now, and even Tim's *Clarion* spoke as if it was inevitable.

On April 19 Congress adopted a war resolution,

25

somewhat more calmly thought-out than its previous cease-fire demand. The newer resolution recognized Cuba's independence from Spain, called for Spanish withdrawal, and authorized the use of United States forces to enforce it. Before this document could be delivered to Spain, however, the U.S. minister to Madrid had had his passport handed to him, and the Spanish chargé d'affaires in Washington had been asked for his. On April 25 the United States formally declared that a state of war had existed as of April 21, when Spain had broken off diplomatic relations.

"Interesting how the government thinks it can make something have happened yesterday by announcing today that it did," Toby commented from the depths of his overstuffed reading chair in the parlor. "An exciting concept."

"They like the dates to match," Alexandra said. "What difference does it make?"

"It irritates me," Toby said. "It argues an attitude that we can fix anything by going back and saying it didn't happen."

"They've done just the opposite," Alexandra said. "They've said it *did* happen. Why do you get worked up about these things?"

Toby smiled ruefully. "Because I'm not in charge, and, as usual, I'm certain I could do a better job. I'm even too old to enlist."

"Well, thank goodness," Alexandra told him. "You probably would, too."

"Of course I would. If we're going to have this stupid war, we'd better do it right."

"Well, then, persuade Finney to enlist," Alex said practically.

Finney showed no interest in enlisting, but two of the Madrona's best hands signed up, to Alex's annoyance. Volunteer regiments were forming everywhere. Anyone could recruit a regiment and be its colonel. Young men wishing to be officers had only to bring the prospective colonel enough men for a platoon and thereby become lieutenants. Enough for a company would make you a captain. Theodore Roosevelt had resigned from the navy and was recruiting a cavalry regiment.

Red flannel bellybands were believed to prevent tropical diseases by containing the body's heat and warding off the dangerous miasmas of the night. Patriotic young ladies sewed the bands by the dozens, and it was a rare volunteer who didn't have at least two of these talismans.

As Toby had predicted, every available railway car overflowed with recruits, some hopelessly confused by conflicting orders as to where they should report. But they climbed aboard anyway, and in optimistic chaos, an army began to pull itself together.

The journalists who would glorify their efforts were somewhat better organized, having been preparing for years for war with Spain; but now that it was here, they were scrambling, too, trying to outguess an army that from all appearances had no idea what it was doing.

The newsroom and loading dock of Tim Holt's *Clarion* were only marginally less chaotic than the army camps. The dock was filled with tents, suitcases, artists' easels, paintboxes, sidearms and ammunition, sacks of coffee and flour, and medical kits packed for the tropics— nux vomica, rhubarb pills, sun cholera drops, acetate of lead, vaseline, talcum powder, calomel, morphine, mosquito nets, and quinine—all to be stored on the press boat and removed to the front as needed. "You'll get sick anyway," had been Janessa's parting shot.

Rafe Murray had already been sent in February to Key West to arrange for a press boat for the *Clarion* staff. Just now Rafe was in Tampa, where the army was gathering. The navy had snagged Key West and claimed, quite correctly, that there wasn't any more room. Rafe had wired from Tampa that everything was in the biggest snarl he had ever seen and mules were $130 apiece—if you could find one. Untrained men were arriving in droves and camping in the sand.

Tim's contingent was to consist of himself and Hugo Ware, who could sketch as well as write, and Rafe, who would run the dispatch boat. The plan was that Tim and Hugo would be on the front line in Cuba, with Rafe just offshore, waiting for their news stories. He would grab their articles and run them to the nearest telegraph office, to be wired to the *Clarion* in San Francisco, while Tim and Hugo returned to battle.

A new process had come out only the year before, to turn actual photographs into what the *New York Tribune,* which had developed it, called halftones. They could be run on a press; but the process was prohibitively expensive and confined to the Sunday feature and magazine sections. The bulk of the *Clarion's* illustrations were line etchings made from an artist's drawing or from a photograph printed directly on a zinc plate as a guide for the engraver. Both would have to be shipped from Tampa, and Tim, stewing about the time delay, had an extra wire installed in the *Clarion's* office for another new process called phototelegraphy. It didn't send photographs; it sent drawings, but it sent them in half an hour.

Rafe wired again to say that the Spanish fleet was reportedly sailing from Cadiz, and until it was destroyed, the army wasn't going anywhere. He advised his employer and colleague to be prepared to spend some time in Tampa or Key West. Although nothing much was organized militarily, he reported that the journalists ran a terrific poker game.

Half the army's wives were in Tampa, too, Rafe added. That being the case, Elizabeth could find no reason to stay in San Francisco and worry about Tim when she could worry in Tampa and learn of any bad news sooner. She told him so when she came to the Clarion Building to watch the phototelegraphy wire being tested. Rosebay Ware, Hugo's wife and the *Clarion's* bookkeeper, marched into Tim's office minutes later, nodded a greeting to

Elizabeth, then announced her own intention of escorting
Hugo.

"And what is the newspaper supposed to do for a
bookkeeper while you're gone?" Tim demanded.

"You'll hire a new one," Rosebay said. "Tim Holt, if
you think I'm going to let Hugo gallivant off to Cuba while
I stay here, you can think again. And I already hired a
housekeeper to see to my boarders and feed the cat."

"I expect the cat would understand," Tim said. "But
the last time someone went off and left this paper with no
bookkeeper, Waldo nearly folded it." Waldo Howard was
the managing editor, a journalistic asset but a walking
financial disaster.

"I already found a replacement," Rosebay said. "And
I told him not to let Waldo buy anything over a hundred
dollars while you're gone. He's also agreed to serve as a
kind of quartermaster whenever you think of something
else that you want shipped to Florida." She stuck her chin
out. "Hugo may be gone a right long time, and I'm goin' to
Tampa." The more passionately Rosebay felt about something, the more her Appalachian Mountains accent crept
back into her voice.

Elizabeth stood with her back half-turned and pretended to peruse the books on Tim's shelf. Elizabeth didn't
blame Rosebay for wanting to go to Tampa, and she knew
that Tim was going to give in and let her. But listening to
the conversation made Elizabeth feel odd for some reason,
as if she were intruding. What history lay between Tim and
Rosebay Ware? she wondered, not for the first time.
Something had gone on between them, she thought. It was
that feeling that made her feel like an eavesdropper.

She looked sideways at their profiles as the two
argued. Tim looked a great deal like his father, with wavy
sandy hair that refused to lie flat and the square chin that
was a dominant trait in all of the Holts. He was looking at
Rosebay with a kind of exasperated familiarity that argued
old acquaintance on more than a platonic level.

Elizabeth did not know Rosebay very well, but Tim

had known her for years. She and Hugo Ware and Tim had met during the Oklahoma land rush in eighty-nine. Elizabeth didn't see how Rosebay could have aged since then, because she still looked twenty. She had pale, corn-silk hair, large blue eyes set under feathery brows, and a delicate, heart-shaped face. Beauty like Rosebay's caused more problems than it solved; her mouth probably made kissing the first thought to cross the mind of every man who met her. Half the *Clarion*'s staff were in love with her, despite the fact that she remained businesslike and wasn't a flirt. Elizabeth thought that Rosebay knew the effect she had on men and that her life had not been untroubled by it.

And what was her effect on Tim? *Am I jealous?* Elizabeth wondered. She had been slightly acquainted with the Wares before the wedding, although she had sensed Tim's reluctance in introducing her to Rosebay. Once, when Elizabeth had visited Tim at his office to show him a sketch of her wedding dress, Rosebay had given them both a kind of beseeching look from under her green eyeshade. Then Rosebay had stepped with Tim to the door, and Elizabeth had heard her whisper, "Are you *happy?*"

Elizabeth caught sight of her own reflection in the glass of Tim's bookcase—dark eyes, dark hair, an oval face with the faint look of a Renaissance portrait. She had always been considered a "handsome" woman—not a beauty, but she had never wanted to be.

She was wondering uneasily how she could slip out of the office past Tim and Rosebay when Tim wound up the argument.

"All right, come on if you want to. But I warn you, it's hotter than Hades, and with all those horses, there are going to be more flies than in a cowshed. Tampa's always full of bugs, but you aren't going to believe what it'll be like now." He went off down the hall, muttering, "Centipedes, millipedes, cockroaches . . . don't say I didn't warn you."

Rosebay ignored him. Satisfied with victory, she told

Elizabeth good-bye and said she was going back to her office to confer with her replacement.

Elizabeth drifted down the hall in Tim's wake. His leaving her behind bespoke his level of irritated distraction.

The newspaper world was new to her. As a feminist and a veteran of several suffrage campaigns, she was used to finding herself in the news, not always flatteringly depicted; but she had never had the opportunity to inspect the inner workings before.

Waldo Howard, Stu Abrams, the city editor, and Sid Appleton, the national news editor, were gathered with Tim around the phototelegraphy wire. The receiving machine looked much like a miniature printing press, with a telegrapher's table set up beside it. The wire ran to the main San Francisco office of Western Union, then across the continent to Florida, and finally, by 150 miles of cable at the bottom of the Gulf of Mexico, to Key West, the closest uncensored cable office to whatever was going on in Havana.

American reporters had been in and out of Cuba for two years now. Some were there officially, but the majority slipped into rebel territory on arms-running filibuster boats. "Filibuster" came from the Spanish *filibustero*, which meant "freebooter." At least one journalist had been drowned and another executed by the Spanish. Several had done time in cells in Morro Castle for being where they should not have been. Rafe had gone to Cuba once since the *Maine* blew up. Now he was safely back in Key West and tailing the fleet in his dispatch boat.

The telegraph key began to click with a message from the main office at Western Union: "We have Key West and will connect you."

Everyone gathered closer to peer at the phototelegraphy receiver. The picture being sent from Key West had been drawn on a sheet of tin, with the lines traced over in shellac. A clockwork mechanism in the sender moved an arm with a platinum-pointed stylus over the drawing. The

electrical circuit was broken every time the point touched
a shellacked line. On the receiving end, a stylus with a
sharp steel point hovered above two sheets of paper with
carbon between them. When the circuit was broken at the
sending end, it closed at the receiving end, and the stylus
was pressed down.

It made perfect sense to Elizabeth, who was familiar
with basic electromagnetic principles; but when the stylus
began to move, it looked like magic anyway. The tip of
something that might have been an inverted Christmas
tree appeared, then slowly resolved itself into a beard and
finally into a bushy gray mustache, drooping beneath a
hawkish nose. It was obviously drawn from a photograph.
The stylus moved higher, and by the time it got to the eyes,
Sid Appleton said, "Gómez."

The stylus moved up through bushy eyebrows, a
rounded skull, and a receding hairline. The rebel general
Máximo Gómez y Báez was a veteran of a previous
revolution, the Ten Years War of 1868–78. He was considered to be a tough old bird, but he looked more like an
elderly peasant farmer than a man who had nearly driven
the Spaniards crazy. The stylus ran to the top of the
picture, then stopped. The telegraph began to click again.
"Latest portrait of Gómez, taken in the field," Rafe sent.
No one asked by whom. If Rafe hadn't taken it himself, he
had probably stolen it. The man's ingenuity was legendary.

Tim breathed a sigh of relief. "It works."

"It worked once," Stu Abrams said.

Sid Appleton glared at him. He was miffed at
Abrams's refusal to be impressed at the national desk's new
marvel and aggravated because he was staying home while
Rafe Murray, of whom he did not approve, was enjoying all
the adventures.

Waldo Howard looked wistfully at the portrait of
Gómez and the message from Rafe, insouciant in its lack
of detail. "Dang! If I were ten years younger . . ."

"Well, you aren't," Tim said. He couldn't blame
Waldo for being so hot to go. All the Cuban correspon-

dents were becoming famous for their exploits. But war reporting was a young man's game. "You'd get malaria and die." Tim looked at the telegrapher. "You treat this thing with respect. It's going to let us walk all over Hearst." He winked at Elizabeth. "Ready to go?"

"In just a minute. I'll meet you in your office."

He went off whistling, while Waldo watched him, eyes still envious. Then he shrugged and grinned. "Hell, the Hearst papers can't say *their* boss is in the field, or Pulitzer, either."

"What if he gets shot?" Abrams demanded.

"Hell of a story," Waldo said happily. "Circulation would go sky-high." He flushed. "Pardon, Mrs. Holt. I expect you know not to take me seriously."

"Of course not," Elizabeth said gravely. If the *Clarion* men were trying to take her measure, she couldn't blame them. She had gone from being the subject of a front-page story—"Suffragist Arrested While Attempting to Vote"— and an unnatural female, to the wife of the owner. The *Clarion* staff was accustomed to associating with upstanding wives and mothers—or opera dancers and chorus girls. Mrs. Holt belonged in neither category, and except for Rafe Murray, who knew her family, they didn't know what to make of her. Even Rosebay Ware, who was doing a man's job as bookkeeper, was more fathomable to them.

The railroad trip from San Francisco to Tampa provided the first opportunity Elizabeth had had to get to know the Wares. A three-day journey in adjoining compartments in a Pullman car made it impossible to continue any sort of superficial relationship. If they weren't friends by the end of the journey, they would at least be thoroughly acquainted.

Hugo Ware, as fair-complexioned as his wife, was tall and bony, with an upper-crust British accent. Elizabeth had known that his father was a member of England's royalty, but she now discovered that Hugo was what was popularly called a remittance man—someone who was

packed off to the States by his family for sins that usually
went unmentioned, then was paid regularly to keep his
disgraceful self on that side of the Atlantic.

"To tell the truth, I haven't had any correspondence
with them in seven or eight years," Hugo said, looking
untroubled. "I sent no forwarding address when I left
Oklahoma for San Francisco, so I imagine they stopped
sending checks after a while. One supposes that they are
fondly hoping I'm dead."

"You didn't want the money?" Elizabeth asked. Hugo
was reasonably well paid, but he wasn't going to get rich in
the newspaper business.

"It exacted too high a price on my pride," Hugo said.
"Rosebay's always been a hard worker, and after we got
engaged, I decided I couldn't just sit around anymore and
take money." He smiled fondly at Rosebay.

Rosebay looked indignant on Hugo's behalf. "You
make a good living, and you don't need to take a thing
from kin that treated you like they did."

"They did have their reasons, my darling," Hugo told
her.

Rosebay was hearing none of it. "That was when you
were young—and right foolish, I expect."

Elizabeth expected so, too, but she doubted that
Rosebay would ever be shocked by anything that Hugo
chose to confess; she would simply find reasons why it
hadn't been his fault. For a childless woman, Rosebay's
maternal instinct seemed to be amazingly well developed—
and nearly indiscriminate, Elizabeth decided, remembering
that the same impulse had been extended to Tim. *Are you
happy, indeed!*

At every stop Hugo and Tim leapt off the train to
check the cable office. Now that war had been declared,
Tim was convinced that their arrival would be too late and
they would miss the invasion. It was a groundless fear.
Rafe, after several days of trailing the fleet in his dispatch
boat, wired that the navy was still blockading the Cuban

coast and had managed to capture several unarmed merchant ships. No one knew where Admiral Cervera y Topete and the Spanish fleet were. There would be no invasion by land until Cervera had been dealt with.

"Easy for Rafe to say," Tim muttered, climbing between the sheets of Elizabeth's narrow lower berth. He periodically referred to Rafe's wire and assumed that everyone would understand what he was talking about. "He's out there in the middle of it."

"You'll get your chance." Elizabeth watched the lights of some unknown city flash by the window. She was perfectly aware that correspondents were just as likely as soldiers to get shot in battle. She hugged him a little closer.

"What I want to know is where Uncle Henry is," Tim said.

"Would your aunt Cindy know?" Elizabeth asked.

"Probably not, if it's anywhere interesting. Anyway, she claims she doesn't care."

"Why do you?" The couple's split had resulted in Henry's vitriolic estrangement from Cindy's brother and his children. Henry had made that clear at Tim and Elizabeth's wedding, and Elizabeth frankly hoped that she would never see him again.

"Because secret military operations are Uncle Henry's specialty. That's a family secret, you understand. I don't want to socialize with him, but I do want to know what he's doing."

The train rattled into the night, and the town dissipated into scattered lights.

The car rocked from side to side. There was only a curtain between their berth and the aisle. Elizabeth heard a low murmur of voices from the next berth.

"Tell me about Rosebay Ware," she said on impulse. Even though she and Tim had been married a year now, she felt uncomfortable asking him about Rosebay.

"Oh, hell," Tim grumbled.

Elizabeth waited.

"Well, I didn't want to make you anxious," Tim muttered.

"Yes, dear." Elizabeth waited some more.

"We got drunk together one night and made love," Tim whispered. "Before she married Hugo. I don't think Hugo knows about it. Those were wild times, boomtown days. She's not—"

"I know she's not," Elizabeth said.

"I think she was interested in me," Tim went on, whispering into Elizabeth's ear. "But I was too thick to notice. Anyway, she married Hugo."

"I see." Elizabeth wondered what had happened when Tim finally noticed. Whatever it was, it felt like past tense. She kissed the top of his head. It was odd, in a coincidental sort of way, that she would wait in Florida with Rosebay Ware while Tim, with Hugo, went to Cuba.

III

Tampa

Tim and Hugo took a look at the chaos in Tampa and presented themselves and their wives to Major General William R. Shafter, who was in command there. The man was not glad to see them. General Shafter weighed three hundred pounds, and in a blue wool uniform he suffered visibly from the heat, which was over one hundred degrees. Two privates had to hoist him onto his horse—a spectacle beyond the resistance of irreverent reporters and cartoonists. Despite his bulk, he was most known for his energy and the vileness of his temper.

Army headquarters was the Tampa Bay Hotel, where the correspondents, nearly outnumbering the command staff, were also staying, in unpleasantly intimate proximity. The hotel, a fanciful concoction of Moorish arches, domes, and silver minarets, had been built as a resort. Wide verandas graced its ornamental brick façade, and peacocks strolled among palmettos and white-flowering oleander trees. As Hugo and Tim registered at the front desk, two regimental bands were playing waltzes and patriotic airs. The rotunda was crowded with dapper correspondents, uniformed officers, and women in evening dresses.

But nothing much was going on. The navy was still hunting for Cervera and his Spanish fleet, and the civilians along the Atlantic coast were terrified that marauding Spaniards were about to murder them in their beds. Every port city was screaming to the War Department for a battleship to protect it.

Cervera appeared at the Cape Verde Islands to take on coal; then he vanished. Shafter's orders to land a force protected by a convoy of navy vessels on the south coast of Cuba were withdrawn because the navy was after Cervera again. The War Office was flooded with conflicting information—the Spanish were about to launch an attack on defenseless citizens along the seacoast! They had made it undetected to Havana and were lying in wait there to intercept U.S. shipping! They were sailing south to Brazil to meet the *Oregon*, which was coming around the Horn, and blow her up! The navy alternated between standing off the Virginia capes and steaming back and forth across the northern shore of Cuba. It stuck its nose into the harbor at San Juan, Puerto Rico, and got fired upon from the fort but found no fleet.

Tim conducted a reconnaissance among old acquaintances, among them Felix Runyon of the Associated Press, and decided that they didn't know anything that he didn't. He presented Elizabeth to them and stood smugly while they congratulated him on his good fortune. But Tim had an itchy foot. He left Hugo and Rosebay in Tampa, and the next morning Elizabeth and he went down to Key West to look at naval headquarters.

Key West was a somnolent and sunbaked town with a hotel far less grand than the Tampa Bay and overcrowded into the bargain. Beyond the hotel was the customhouse, sweltering under motionless palms. Despite its sleepy appearance, Key West was the jumping-off point for adventurers, smugglers, and the arms and blockade runners' filibuster boats.

Those who couldn't get hotel rooms slept on iron cots in the corridors for an outrageous five dollars a day. Tim bribed the desk clerk to set someone's bags in the hall to provide a room for Elizabeth and him. The evicted correspondent protested loudly. Then, finding that he had made way for a lady, the displaced gentleman relented somewhat. Tim treated the fellow to dinner, and all was forgiven.

With the navy in residence, there was already a severe water shortage. All water not shipped in came from cisterns and rain barrels, and in two months the cost of a gallon had jumped from one and a half cents to ten cents. Bottled water sold for a dollar a gallon, affordable only to officers and newspaper correspondents.

But there were other things to drink, at such establishments as the Eagle Bird, which offered a roulette wheel and claimed the patronage of visiting correspondents, including Stephen Crane and Richard Harding Davis. Davis was the epitome of the dapper "special" and reputed to be the model for Charles Dana Gibson's "Gibson man." Crane, a raffish and hardworking, hard-living man, was already famous for his Civil War book, *The Red Badge of Courage.* He had written a poem about the Eagle Bird, Rafe said. No one knew what it meant, but it had a dreamy and fatalistic air that Rafe liked:

> *Oh, five white mice of chance,*
> *Shirts of wool and corduroy pants,*
> *Gold and wine, women and sin,*
> *All for you if you let me come in—*
> *Into the house of chance.*

Raphael Murray was a thin man, just over thirty, with wavy, dark hair and a mouth that was slightly off kilter, so that he possessed a perpetually quizzical expression. As he welcomed Elizabeth and Tim aboard his dispatch boat, he explained that he had christened it the *Chance* in admiration of the poem, despite the fact that Crane wrote for the abhorred Joseph Pulitzer's *New York World.*

The *Chance* was an elderly tug that had been outfitted as a filibuster boat and had made several arms-running expeditions financed by the Cuban junta in New York. She could get up a top speed of twelve knots and in a heavy sea was always sloshing wet. But, as Rafe cheerfully pointed out, the tug hadn't sunk yet, although she had come close to being run down in the darkness by the navy's warships.

Rafe kissed Elizabeth on the cheek with the privilege of an old acquaintance and showed her to a seat in the chart room.

"Leon's making turtle soup," he said. "And I have a fine bottle of wine here, bought for an exorbitant price—guaranteed to be at least six months old. So, Liz, how's your dad?"

"He's presenting a paper on municipal reform to the Association of Nationalist Clubs," Elizabeth said. "He says Jack's gone north to the gold fields, and you're down here running guns, and he doesn't approve of either of you."

"I wasn't running guns," Rafe protested. "They just happened to be on board. And as for Jack London, you can't keep him to anything for more than six months at a stretch. I guarantee he'll be down here, too, if the war lasts long enough."

"What's it been like for you?" Tim asked.

"Never dull." Rafe poked an ink-stained finger at the chart-room map, which Tim had already been examining. "If you imagine these straits pretty well clogged with anything that'll float, you'll have the idea. We can't run lights at night because they pinpoint the American fleet for the Spanish. But if we don't use lights, the navy can't see us, and they run us down."

Tim gave a low whistle.

"But it's thrilling, too. Havana Harbor is about a hundred miles from Key West. When something exciting happens, we all race back here to fight for the use of the cable. Then we go tearing out again. Yesterday the *World*'s boat and the AP's got back here neck and neck, and their men nearly had a brawl at the cable office." Rafe chuckled. "And Davis got thrown off the flagship, just when he thought he was going to have a box seat. Admiral Sampson decided no one but one AP man could stay, so now the illustrious master correspondent has to slog it out with the rest of us." Rafe didn't sound sympathetic.

"Mmmph." Tim was squinting at the map. "Where were you when Davis filed a dispatch about the fleet firing on the shore batteries at Matanzas?"

"Hanging around the fleet in Havana Harbor, O my captain . . . where it was rumored we were about to begin bombardment." Rafe sighed. "We didn't, of course."

A tall black man in a chef's hat and apron appeared in the chart-room door. "Luncheon served, Mr. Murray."

"Thank you, Leon. Shall we?"

They settled down to turtle soup and grilled fish with fresh mayonnaise. Leon filled their glasses with wine, and the sea obliged by maintaining a gentle rocking.

"War certainly is hell," Elizabeth murmured.

"Isn't it just?" Rafe said. "If you will look out the starboard porthole, you will observe the *New York*. That's the fleet flagship, now devoid of correspondents. And to the left, you will observe the *Journal*'s yacht, *Anita*. They have another yacht, too, and a tug. They are very important boys."

Since nothing in particular seemed to be happening, after lunch Rafe took them on a tour of the Florida Straits. The *Chance* dodged in and out among the slate-colored hulls of the fleet and the ragtag flotilla of press boats. With immense dignity the fleet made its patrols, lumbering like distant, moving islands while the press boats chased after them, funnels belching smoke, trying to keep up.

In the distance lay Havana, enigmatic and unresponsive in the sharp sun. Gulls wheeled and *awk*ed overhead, swooping on the scraps that Leon tossed overboard. It might have been a pleasure cruise except that Tim constantly surveyed the area through his field glasses.

Toward the end of the afternoon, when they were heading back, Tim noticed a commotion on the dock.

Rafe picked up his own glasses and looked around. Across the water other boats were beginning to turn toward Key West. "Do you suppose Shafter's got his marching orders at last?" he wondered.

"There's a signalman on the dock," Tim said. "I can't make him out yet."

The captain of the *Chance* put on more steam, and the tug plowed her way in. Tim kept the field glasses riveted on the signalman while Elizabeth looked distressed. If the navy was being given orders to escort Shafter, then the army was going out, and Tim would go with them. Of course it had to come sometime, she thought, but she hadn't been ready for it that afternoon, not after wine and turtle soup.

The signalman waved his flags again.

"I'll be damned!" Tim shouted. He focused the glasses intently. Then he spun around, slapping his thigh. "Dewey's sunk Spain's Pacific fleet in Manila Bay! Wherever Cervera is, he's on his own now!"

IV

Even after the first headlines announced Dewey's victory, nobody knew exactly what had happened or might happen next. Half the population was uncertain as to where the Philippines were, so newspapers printed maps.

Bands played in the streets, and fireworks went off. A fashion started for gowns of red, white, and blue and for gold epaulettes. Songwriters produced such ballads as "Dewey's Duty Done" and "How Did Dewey Do It?" Dewey was promptly promoted to admiral, and popular verse made further play with his name:

> *Oh, dewy was the morning*
> *Upon the first of May.*
> *And Dewey was the admiral*
> *Down in Manila Bay.*
>
> *And dewy were the Spaniards' eyes,*
> *Them orbs of black and blue.*
> *And dew we feel discouraged?*
> *I dew not think we dew!*

Dewey lost no vessels. Only eight men were wounded, and there was but one casualty—an engineer who had died of heatstroke. A shore party had taken over the battery at Sangley Point, and the land guns in the city of Manila had stopped firing when the admiral threatened to turn his eight-inch guns on them. Still, no one knew what to do next. Dewey didn't attempt to take the city because he had no men for such a military maneuver. The admiral reported that to capture Manila, he required five thousand men.

On a wave of enthusiasm and with very little thought as to what the United States government would do with the Philippines once it had them, the soldiers began to be sent. There was an overwhelming rush to join the army. It was a "glorious opportunity." Ten thousand men sailed from San Francisco to liberate the Philippines. On the way they stopped at Guam and fired a five-inch gun across Apra Harbor to show the Spanish they meant business. The Spanish governor came out in a launch and apologized for not returning the salute, but, he explained, he had no gunpowder. Guam had no cable, either; the governor had been blissfully unaware of the war. The American soldiers gave him the news, left a troop of marines to hold the fort, and sailed on for Manila.

Word spread slowly. At first even Washington had thought that Dewey had taken the entire Philippine archipelago. When it found out that he had not—and, in fact, that the Spanish were still in Manila—it seemed, to the navy, halfhearted not to finish the job. The newspapers proudly reported further triumphs.

The business of gathering news—of sending it faster than anybody else, or sending more of it than anybody else—became an entirely new enterprise. The telegraph, the telephone, and now the phototelegraph made scooping the competition imperative. Being first with the story was more important than being accurate. Fresh news had become a commodity, like fresh eggs.

Competition for the cable at Key West became fiercer. Underwater transmission was slower than the overland wires, and the man who got there first might manage an exclusive story if he could tie up the cable long enough. Three thousand words filed at midnight were pretty sure to guarantee that no other paper would get anything out of Key West that night. Runyon of the AP was said to have been challenged to a duel over wire use by a hot-tempered Creole from New Orleans. He fled to Tampa to let things blow over.

Tim thought Runyon had probably gone to Tampa because nothing was going on at Key West . . . pretty much the same reason Tim had come to Key West—nothing was happening in Tampa. Journalists played poker, waited, trailed the navy, and loafed in the street until they would have been a public nuisance had they not been spending so much money. Restless, Tim decided to go back to Tampa to see how the army was doing.

He and Elizabeth set off again—Elizabeth seemed fascinated by this process—and found Tampa still in upheaval. Volunteers were arriving by the thousands, their tents strung out along the sandy wastes beyond crumbling wooden houses, their paint scoured by the wind. . . . These were all that comprised the rest of Tampa. An occasional palmetto enlivened the view, when one could keep one's eyes open long enough, and the wind-driven sand blew everywhere. A single railroad track connected the town with the harbor nine miles away, and there was only one pier. Until now Tampa had not needed more, since its population consisted almost entirely of exiled Cuban cigar makers. What these workers and their families thought of the situation, Elizabeth had no idea.

As more soldiers and militia arrived, everything ran out, broke down, or backed up. The militia did not get along with the regular army, and neither group had enough supplies. What items they did have were generally missing some vital part or had one that was designed for a different model. Sidetracked supplies continued to rot upstate, and no one could figure out the artillery—gun mounts had been shipped to one destination, guns to another, and ammunition, none of it the right caliber, was stashed anywhere. The weather was sweltering, and the campground sandy and overrun with mosquitoes and sand fleas. To add insult to injury, because the army had yet to go anywhere, it was becoming known as the Rocking Chair Brigade.

Men began getting sick. Improperly prepared meat rotted before it could be eaten, there was not enough water, and everyone wrote outraged letters home. Theodore Roosevelt arrived from San Antonio with his Rough Riders and fired off cables that raised hell in Washington. President McKinley had been advised not to invade Cuba until the middle of September and the end of the rainy season, due to the prevalence of tropical diseases, but it seemed that the troops could get just as sick staying in Tampa.

Tim wondered if the exiled Cubans in Tampa were pinning their hopes for a free homeland on the sweating, cursing, floundering mass of men encamped on their doorstep. Or did they just shrug their shoulders at the gringos drilling self-importantly in the sand and trying to find all the pieces of their guns? The Cuban junta in New York, the men with the money and the ambition, most certainly had their agenda. But these exiles? How did they feel? Tim wondered. Elizabeth told him that they might be more concerned with keeping their daughters at home as the town filled up with soldiers.

Meanwhile, the officers were comfortably encamped at the Tampa Bay Hotel. Men who had not seen one another since West Point days embraced and bought rounds of drinks. Foreign military observers arrived, resplendent in exotic uniforms and speaking with fascinating accents. There were dances in the evening, and the army's wives and sisters and daughters were introduced to fellow officers and cautioned to steer clear of the unsuitable newspaper correspondents, although socially acceptable men such as Richard Davis and Sylvester Scovel were much in demand. There still weren't enough women to go around, and Elizabeth and Rosebay, under their husbands' noses, were asked to dance by importunate young officers.

Then, fed up with hearing the praises of the navy sung in all the papers, the army prepared to mount its first

expedition—to land supplies for the hard-pressed insurrectos at a point near Mariel, about twenty miles west of
Havana. They were totally unprepared to do so, but they
were getting tired of being called the Rocking Chair
Brigade. They fitted up a ship called the *Gussie,* the only
vessel on the Gulf Coast that had not already been
snapped up by the navy or the newspapers. The *Gussie*
was a fat, old-fashioned, red side-wheeler that was unmistakable in her profile and well-known in Havana. And not
even the pleas of the correspondents could persuade the
army to change her name.

To go to war in a boat called *Gussie*—Felix Runyon
groaned and put his head in his hands.

"Maybe it's just to distract us," Tim said. "Maybe
they're actually mounting a real invasion elsewhere."

Elizabeth giggled. She couldn't help it. They were
standing with Rosebay and Hugo on the Tampa pier,
waiting for the *Gussie* to put out. Tim had wangled a spot
aboard and been told that he would be the only noncom-
batant except for the distinguished war artist Rufus Zogbaum of *Harper's Weekly.* He had been sworn to absolute
secrecy, which, given the *Gussie's* silhouette and the army's
ponderous machinations, was a hopeless cause. The *Gussie's* departure was about as secret as a brass band.

A skiff put up to the pier, and Tim dropped his bag
into it. Elizabeth bit her lip, worried. The *Gussie* looked so
silly! How could they go off to war in her? She had green
shutters, and she blazed with lights like a floating hotel.
She had been delayed in leaving and now, at ten o'clock at
night, was being towed to sea by a helpful tug belonging to
Sylvester Scovel's *New York World.* A further flotilla of
press boats awaited her outside the harbor. Tim had cabled
Rafe to pick her up as she passed Key West and follow her
to Tampa.

A few hours later Rafe cabled back that the U.S. fleet
had fired on the *Gussie,* not believing that this apparition
might actually belong to them.

"She made it through all right," Hugo said. His lip twitched, but he took note of Elizabeth's taut face. "The navy gunners didn't hit anything."

On board the *Gussie*, Tim had discovered to his chagrin that there were five other correspondents from various papers as well as Zogbaum. Besides the *Chance*, two other tugs stuck like glue to her wake, and Tim estimated that approximately twenty-five publications were represented. Since Captain Dorst had announced his plans in detail before leaving Tampa, Tim remarked that the correspondents' presence on the boat was superfluous— they could simply have read about the invasion in the papers in Madrid.

That was before the U.S. fleet started shooting at them. No one had thought to inform the warships block- ading Havana Harbor of the *Gussie's* expedition. When they got a look at her, the U.S. fleet shot first and then hauled alongside to see what she was. The scenario was repeated several times. . . .

"You there—heave to! My God, what the hell is it?"

Irritated explanation was offered from the *Gussie*.

"All right, then, go on."

"Heave to—"

By dawn the crew was eager for its first sight of Cuba and relieved to have picked up a second escort ship. Thus bracketed, the *Gussie* made her way toward Mariel.

Because nobody seemed to be shooting at them at the moment, Tim leaned on the rail and watched the shore- line. The deck was crowded with soldiers staring at Havana. No effort had been made to conceal the *Gussie's* movements from the shore, so Tim presumed that the Spanish soldiers in Havana were staring back at the big red tub.

"Why don't we just fire a salute?" Tim demanded in disgust. "Just to make sure Blanco notices us."

When the *Gussie* made Mariel at noon, it was obvious

that General Blanco had needed no help. Not surprisingly, several hundred Spanish soldiers occupied the hill. As the *Gussie* dithered, a small troop of cavalry detached itself and swept down the beach to fire at the boats. One of the escort ships lost its temper and shot back. The Spaniards dispersed but were certainly lying in wait.

The *Gussie* and her 120 soldiers were to land a cargo of food and ammunition for the hard-pressed Cuban rebels, along with three Cuban scouts who were to make contact with the interior. The scouts' horses, brought on deck, snorted down their noses and looked no more eager than the *Gussie*'s crew to land in the middle of the Spanish. After a hurried conference, the *Gussie* sailed on. As she neared the bay at Cabañas, her officers made the decision to go ashore there.

Poultney Bigelow of *Harper's Weekly* raised an eyebrow. "An excellent choice," he said sarcastically. "There are two thousand troops in the fortress at Cabañas. That makes it a natural spot to put three horses and a tubful of supplies ashore."

They were immediately distracted by furious cursing aft.

"God *damn* it!"

"Watch your language, Sailor!"

"They appear to be having some trouble with the anchor," Tim commented.

He and Bigelow strolled over and found an infuriated Captain Dorst, Lieutenant Stock, and members of the *Gussie*'s crew attempting to get the ship's anchor to catch and hold. The bottom of the bay proved to be as receptive as a flat rock, so the correspondents all retired to a poker game below deck. Three hours later, after a sullen cheer announced that the anchor had been secured, the journalists went back up in a pouring rain to watch as two boats were lowered.

Tim got into one without being asked, and Lieutenant Stock, in charge, gave him a look that said he didn't much

care—Tim could come along and drown or get shot if he
wanted to.

Up until that point, the whole *Gussie* expedition had
had a comic opera flavor that made it impossible for Tim
to believe that someone might actually get killed. It was as
if the Cuban shoreline were a painted backdrop, and its
Spanish soldiers were firing wooden guns. This false
security vanished entirely as soon as the boats hit the
water, however.

There were certainly Spanish troops in the woods, for
they opened fire on the invaders. Tim felt a bullet *zing*
past his ear, whining through the pelting rain and the roar
of the surf. He looked back and saw men on the *Gussie's*
upper deck flatten themselves behind hay bales brought
for that purpose.

Another bullet returned Tim's attention to the shore,
and then the boat jarred to a stop.

"What is it?"

"Reef!"

"Aw, Gawd!"

The Cuban scouts had failed to mention that a sunken
coral reef ran two hundred feet from shore across the
entire bay. Cursing, the soldiers stumbled into the water
and dragged the boat across it while bullets continued to
fly by. Miraculously no one was hit. Leaving his notepad,
weapon, and ammunition in the boat, Tim sloshed through
the surf and thought the Spaniards probably couldn't see
through the rain any better than he could.

The Cuban couriers' three horses had been lowered
with some difficulty into the surf from aboard the *Gussie*
and had been encouraged to swim for the shore. Tim saw
Ralph Paine of the *New York Journal* in a small boat with
two sailors, trying to pull a bay gelding in the right
direction by the halter rope. The horse rolled its eyes and
tried to swim back to the ship. A roan mare plunged
hysterically and aimed her nose for the open sea. Tim had
lived on a ranch long enough to know what to do. He dove
after her and caught the flying end of the halter rope. The

mare shrieked in terror. Tim floundered hand over hand along the rope, cursing. "This way, you thick-headed bitch."

He got one leg over her back, hauled her head around with the rope, then headed her for shore. She seemed to settle, the man on her back a comforting presence. Through the spray, Tim could see Paine's boat go bow over keel as the bay upended it in the shallows. The roan mare swam toward the boat, buffeted by the surf. Tim wound his hands in her mane and prayed she wouldn't panic and throw him. As they stumbled into the shallows, the gelding went down, hooves flailing, knocked flat by the surf, and landed on Paine. The man extricated himself from beneath the animal, and Tim, still on the mare, reached down a hand and hauled the man upright. He staggered onto the beach, and Tim slipped from his mount and turned her loose. Where the Cuban couriers were, he had no idea. The rowboat was on the sand, and he retrieved his belongings.

The jungle beyond the shore was too thick to see more than ten feet into it. The captain from the second boat ordered a skirmish line twenty paces apart, and Tim fitted himself into it beside Lieutenant Stock. Stock was a square-headed Kansan with the look of a man who knew how things ought to be done. Just then his expression proclaimed his opinion that nobody else did. Tim didn't bother getting his notepad from its waterproof case. There was no time to write anything, and he thought his revolver would be more useful than his pen.

They hacked and wriggled their way through the undergrowth, and within moments the Spanish were firing on them. Tim flattened himself on the ground and fired back, hardly able to see what he was shooting at. Some enormous insect crawled down the neck of his flannel shirt, past the barrier of his scarf. Tim ignored it, sighting down his pistol barrel at a Spanish trooper who unexpectedly popped out from the jungle and then withdrew. Tim fired after him anyway.

A flurry of hoofbeats announced that the Cuban scouts had caught up with their mounts. One was sent to "ascertain the landing party's location" and returned with the news that it was less than two miles from the fortress of Cabañas. Tim heard the word passed down the line. He stared, unnerved, into the jungle. How many Spaniards were in there?

The captain gave a hasty order to retreat. Tim began to wriggle backward with a sick sensation in his stomach. He had been trapped inside a coal mine once, waiting for the rest of it to fall in on him. The jungle with its unseen Spanish troopers gave him much the same sensation. He emerged onto the beach with an intense feeling of relief and joined the run for the boats. The *Gussie's* naval escorts lobbed shells into the jungle, and the Spanish pulled back, too. The landing party rowed out unmolested, leaving the Cuban scouts ashore, presumably to make contact with the interior.

Because no one had been killed, the excursion was considered a victory by everyone involved. In fact, only one man had been shot, James F. Archibald, a reporter for the *San Francisco Post*, who had taken a bullet through his arm. The other correspondents gathered around Archibald on the *Gussie* and, a little envious, offered sympathy and whiskey. The gunshot was a badge of honor, Paine said, lamenting that all he had to show for his battle with the horse were lacerations and bruises. Tim displayed a millipede, fished out of his shirtfront, to appreciative shudders.

None of this changed the fact that the *Gussie's* mission had not been carried out. The Cuban insurrectos did not have their supplies, and no one knew how to get them to the rebels. No word or signal had come from the scouts on shore. Furthermore, the anchor, which had been so reluctant to stick to the bottom, now refused to come up. Red-faced and enraged, Captain Dorst finally ordered the boat to sail without it.

The *Gussie* spent the night cruising the coast and

getting in the way of the fleet's blockade. The next day a white flag appeared in broad daylight atop a palm tree near Baracoa, and Captain Dorst ordered the *Gussie* into the bay.

"How does he know it's our boys?" Paine asked.

"Maybe it's the Spanish," Tim said. "Maybe they just want to surrender."

"Yeah, we must be scaring them to death," Poultney Bigelow offered.

The line of correspondents chuckled and continued to lean on the upper-deck railing. A few moments later they were facedown on the deck as two Spanish field batteries opened up at close range. The captain beat a hasty retreat. Thereafter, the Spanish didn't bother to conceal anything much. The *Gussie*'s crew could read their heliographs from the water.

The Americans had one more opportunity to get the supplies to the insurrectos. They sailed to a point near Matanzas and put another scout ashore.

"Our last Cuban," Tim said. "They'll use the correspondents next."

"They bloody well ought to," Bigelow growled. "*We* got more information out of Cuba than the army ever managed."

"Nobody's going to find a place to land during this trip," Tim said. "It's like riding in on an elephant and trying to sneak through the back door. Hell, the Spanish knew we were coming before we set out."

"Of course they did," Lieutenant Stock snarled in passing. "Every damn newspaper in the country published it."

The correspondents shrugged. "You made your plans pretty plain," Tim told Stock. "Seems to me the captain got a little tired of the navy getting all the glory."

The lieutenant glowered at him. "You watch how you talk, or I'll have you put off this ship."

Tim looked around him. "Where?"

"Let's all calm down," Bigelow said before Stock

could suggest overboard. "The press didn't report anything that wasn't common knowledge. If you want secrecy, Lieutenant, don't go to sea in something that looks like an oversize birthday cake."

"That's not the army's fault!" Stock snapped. "The navy's commissioned every vessel available."

"Of course they have," Bigelow said soothingly.

They waited all night for their Cuban scout to come back, and when he did, he reported that the whole coast was too well patrolled now to risk a landing. Very short of coal, the *Gussie* steamed sheepishly back to Tampa.

Tim, shaking his head over what he had witnessed, stepped from the *Gussie*'s deck. Elizabeth hurled herself into his arms, surprising him a little. She said he looked wonderful—tanned and even quite dashing in his flannel shirt and khaki breeches and slouch hat. Best yet, he was in one piece.

"Thank goodness you're all right!"

"I'm fine." He peered at her. "You were scared, weren't you? My poor darling, I didn't encounter anything more dangerous than some bugs and ridicule."

"Rafe said you were fired on," Elizabeth informed him.

"Oh. Well, yes, but not very much." That sounded silly, even to him. "Archibald's our hero. He got a bullet in the arm. I suppose Hugo's been letting you read the dispatches."

"Of course he has. Oh, you don't know—Sylvester Scovel thought he could do a better job than your group, so he landed two of his men from one of his newspaper's boats. The Spanish got them first thing. Now there's a big diplomatic hullabaloo, trying to exchange them for Spanish prisoners." Elizabeth tucked her arm through Tim's.

"Ha!" Tim cackled happily. "That takes some of the sting out of it."

Negotiations over the *World*'s imprisoned journalists provided nearly all the action there was, except for

Richard Davis's running quarrel with Poultney Bigelow over how much of the chaotic situation in Tampa ought to be revealed to the American public. Davis felt it unpatriotic not to keep a good face on the news, while the acerbic Bigelow made enormous trouble for himself by telling the whole truth in as inflammatory a manner as possible. Tim and the other *Clarion* men walked a kind of middle line and managed not to get themselves thrown out of camp, as General Shafter had threatened.

Settling in to wait until the next military or political development, the men nonchalantly went back to their poker game. They seemed to Elizabeth to have an inner gyroscope for maintaining their equilibrium while reality shifted and slid around them.

Elizabeth, however, was without that knack. She alternated between perplexity and outrage at life in Tampa. The country was at war, yet she was living in a kind of cosmopolitan house party at a resort hotel built in the middle of a desert for winter tourists who had never materialized. Beyond the brilliant flowers of the hotel gardens and the shrieking of the peacocks who lived on the grounds, the mostly Cuban civilians and the soldiers seemed like an impoverished peasantry with their noses pressed against the glass of the luxurious hotel's windows. Steeping in a bathtub of perfumed water with her returned husband, she felt uncomfortably like Marie Antoinette.

The next morning, Tim went out to trail General Shafter again, and Elizabeth put on walking shoes and went into town, trying to walk away the sensation of living in a hothouse. The streets were crowded and sandy, thick with flies and soldiers. The Cuban shopkeepers were doing a landslide business selling cigars and rum to bored men. Elizabeth contemplated the results with disgust and wondered if her own husband would be inclined to stagger down the street if he were there without her. Probably not, she decided. Tim had a job to do. These boys—most of them weren't more than twenty, if that—had nothing to do but wait. A number of them had girls on their arms, while others, there not being enough girls to go around, sat on the shop stoops and played cards. They eyed Elizabeth appreciatively, and there were a few whistles and entreaties; but an outraged expression was enough to keep them at bay. Of course she didn't look like a village girl and was considerably older than the young women hanging on the soldiers' arms for promises of chocolates and silk sashes. Elizabeth flinched. That had always seemed to her a bad bargain.

A sudden commotion inside a tobacconist's shop made her abandon speculation. Drawn by the shrieks of outrage inside, Elizabeth ran through the open door, with a handful of soldiers on her heels.

"Fornicator! Viper! Toad! I'll cut your liver out!" The shrieks proved to come not from a ravished damsel, as Elizabeth had expected, but from a woman who was apparently the damsel's mother. A middle-aged Cuban woman had a soldier backed at knife point into the corner of her shop, bent as far backward as he could get over a glass case of cigars and humidors. She berated him in furious English, lapsing occasionally into Spanish while his eyes crossed as he tried to focus on the stiletto blade under his chin.

A weeping girl of about sixteen was huddled in the opposite corner with a younger girl, who looked to be about twelve. "Mama, no!" the elder one said plaintively.

"Christ!" one soldier said to another. "Grab her!"

"No, wait," Elizabeth told them.

They turned and stared at her. "Lady, she's got a knife."

"I know she has a knife," Elizabeth said with some asperity. "And she's threatening to cut his liver out with it, but she hasn't done it yet. You boys are wearing the same uniform that he is. Do you think she's going to feel any more kindly about you?"

"You got a better idea?" one of them demanded.

"Maybe." Elizabeth eased up to the weeping girls. "What's happened?"

"Mama catch me with him," the elder one said, sobbing. "She say not to go with the soldiers, but he promise to take me to ride in a buggy, out to the beach."

"I see," Elizabeth said. "And would you get in a buggy with any man who asked you?"

"Nooooo!" The girl wept.

Elizabeth thought that the girl probably would. She was beautiful, with golden skin and huge eyes, and she didn't look as if she had any sense at all.

"Rapist! I carve your gizzard out!" the mother threatened.

The soldier looked as if he were about to faint. Elizabeth was afraid that the woman might do it by accident if he did.

"My Lupita, she don't go with soldiers!" She pressed the point of her knife into his Adam's apple.

"Señora." Elizabeth got herself in the woman's view by wedging herself between the soldier's petrified fingers and the glass cabinet, which he kept trying to clutch. He grabbed a handful of Elizabeth's skirt instead. He didn't even look eighteen.

"Señora, let me help." Elizabeth spoke as evenly as she could. "Let the soldier go, señora."

The woman shot her a dark glance. "I'll cut his liver out."

"You can't do that. You will make much trouble for yourself. Did he actually hurt your daughter?"

"Not yet," the woman said angrily. "I catch him with Lupita, he don't get no chance. They're always coming here, hanging round the girls. Their captains don't do nothing, so I will!"

"I promise you the captains will do something," Elizabeth said. She eased a little farther between the woman and her captive, until the woman pulled the knife back a bit. "If you kill him—and I certainly don't blame you a bit for wanting to. An admirable idea, in fact." She looked at the white-faced soldier with an utter lack of sympathy. "But if you kill him, the authorities will lock you up, and then who will protect the girls?"

"Hmmph!" Lupita's mother stood back a pace, and Elizabeth peeled the woman's fingers gently away from the knife.

"Go," Elizabeth said to the soldier. She turned to the girls as he tottered to the door. "Now, then." She looked back again at the knot of soldiers still loitering in the doorway. "Get him out of here," she suggested, "or *I'll* cut his liver out. Next time you go prowling, just remember what happened here." She turned back to the girls and smiled at the younger one. "What's your name?"

"Rosie. Rosalita."

"All right, Rosalita, put this knife back where it belongs."

"That's Mama's fish knife," Rosie volunteered.

Now Elizabeth looked to the mother. "Señora . . ." She paused, eyebrows raised, waiting for a name.

"Verdugo," Mama said. "And you?" She eyed Elizabeth suspiciously.

"Señora Holt," Elizabeth said. "My husband is a journalist."

"They are as bad as the soldiers," Señora Verdugo said.

"Not my husband," Elizabeth promised her. "Have you had much trouble with the soldiers?"

"Plenty," Señora Verdugo said. "That's why I'm ready to cut one up, teach them to stay away. Why don't they go to Cuba, if they are going? There is not enough water, not enough food, for all you people. Nobody feeds the soldiers, so they steal from us. They follow our girls around, make promises. After our girls disgrace themselves with the soldiers, what are the generals going to do with all the babies born next year, I ask you that. I tell you, my Lupita she don't get in trouble, if I have to stick a knife in every soldier who shows his face here!"

"I don't, Mama." Lupita sniffled. "I just want to go on a buggy ride."

"You bad girl! Don't the nuns teach you nothing? You stay away from those Americano boys. They just want one thing."

"Mama chased one off with a bread knife yesterday," Rosie said. "He come to the house, Mama chased him all the way around it. That's when she brought the fish knife to the shop."

Elizabeth's mouth twitched. She thought Lupita's virginity was safe. She didn't know about the other town girls, though. No one could stop a girl who was determined the presents were worth it. The thought of the others troubled her. "I'm going to talk to General Shafter," she said. "I don't think he knows what's been going on." Of course he did, as she knew perfectly well, but she was going to point out to him that he couldn't afford to ignore it any longer.

"You really going to talk to the general?" Señora Verdugo looked both suspicious and startled.

"You bet I am," Elizabeth said. "I'm staying at the hotel. I'll just make a nuisance of myself until he sees me, that's all."

Señora Verdugo's eyes filled with tears. "The Blessed Virgin bless you. People like me, we got no power, just a fish knife. He will hear an Americana."

Elizabeth wasn't entirely sure of that, but she was going to make a fuss with somebody, and if possible, it was going to be Shafter.

Elizabeth set up camp outside Shafter's hotel office and prepared to dig in.

"Name, please?" a bored secretary asked her.

"Mrs. Holt. I am staying in the hotel, and I witnessed a scene in Tampa today involving some of your soldiers that I think the general should know about. Some of your soldiers and a sixteen-year-old girl. I should tell you," she added grimly, "that I write for a number of women's magazines."

The secretary blanched. Elizabeth saw no point in telling him that she wrote for these magazines sporadically and on suffrage issues. Besides, she thought, she might take it into her head to write an article on the conduct of soldiers in a war, if the army gave her any trouble.

General Shafter did not receive her, but an adjutant did. The aide was young and round-faced, going prematurely bald, probably from working for Shafter, Elizabeth thought. He introduced himself as Lieutenant Morris.

"The general is unavailable?" she inquired icily.

"Yes, ma'am," the adjutant said.

"When will he be able to speak with me?"

"Never, I'm afraid, ma'am. The general is a busy man. After all, we're getting ready for a war," the aide said condescendingly.

"A fact that must have escaped my notice," Elizabeth said, her tone sarcastic. "However, it has not escaped the notice of the women in this town, particularly the ones who are young and pretty, or have young and pretty daughters."

"Well, now, ma'am, boys will be boys. Those girls need to stay at home and out of trouble."

Elizabeth glared at him. "The daughters should hide in their houses? Whom are we invading here, Cuba or Tampa?"

The aide sighed. "I'll mention it to the general."

"Mention it to the commanders in the encampment!" Elizabeth snapped. She lost her temper and did what she had sworn she would never do. "Did I mention to *you* that besides my work for women's magazines, my husband is the owner of the *San Francisco Clarion*? I expect he will also be interested in the disgraceful behavior of your men!"

The aide groaned under his breath. "I'm sure the matter will be taken care of."

Departing, Elizabeth met Tim coming up the stairs to the general's quarters.

"What are you doing here?" he inquired.

Elizabeth laughed suddenly. "Trading on your name," she said. "I lost my head."

She told him the entire story over dinner. In their subsequent outings into the town, and according to the journalists' scuttlebutt, it did seem as if the troops had been warned to leave Tampa's girls alone. But how long it would last, if the troops were cooped up in their camp much longer, was another matter.

In the meantime, the privileged continued to dance or organize musical evenings in the ballrooms and piazzas of the hotel. Periodically General Shafter stalked through the festivities, trailing cigar smoke and a queue of adjutants. A tide of correspondents would customarily rise from the lobby chairs and flow after him for several paces, protesting the army's policy of censoring their dispatches since the *Gussie* venture, then ebb back again after he shut the door in their faces.

Mike Holt arrived from New York with his moving-picture camera and provoked Shafter to incoherent rage by filming a militiaman protesting the insufficient rations by angrily shaking an empty tin plate at the lens. Eden was with Mike, and Tim found his beguiling sister-in-law leading the general toward the hotel before the man could think to order the camera opened and the film exposed. Intrigued, Tim followed within earshot.

"So delightful to meet you, General." Eden slipped her arm through Shafter's and gave him her most angelic smile. She was dressed in a pale pink linen walking suit, and her straw hat was tied under her chin with a rose-colored ribbon. She tipped a white lace parasol prettily over one shoulder so as not to poke the general in the eye. "I believe you were acquainted with my husband's grandfather, General. General Leland Blake. Didn't we meet at his funeral?"

"General Blake?" Shafter looked startled. "Yes, indeed, he was a fine man. One of the best." Shafter shook his head. "Wish we had him now."

"I'm sure he would appreciate the job you're doing here," Eden said.

Shafter became almost avuncular. "You couldn't have been more than a child when he died."

"I was fourteen," Eden said modestly. "But I do remember you."

A man that size is hard to forget, Tim thought.

"I believe he spoke very warmly of you," she went on, slipping into outright fiction.

Now Shafter looked amazed. "Did he indeed? I wouldn't have thought—"

"I expect he knew you by reputation," Eden said demurely.

By this time they were nearly to the hotel piazza. Tim stopped and watched them ascend the steps, Shafter gallantly huffing along. Tim wondered if he should suggest to Elizabeth that she adopt Eden's technique.

Mike joined his brother. "She'll have him eating cream puffs off her fork in another minute or two." He grinned. "Of course, it will only last till he notices me again."

"You might have stopped in to say hello before you started a riot," Tim remarked. "Shafter hates journalists. It's a shame we've got the same last name."

"You could change yours," Mike suggested. "You could be Richard Harding Davis, and I'll still be Leland's grandson."

"I don't have the wardrobe to be Davis," Tim said. "He's the complete correspondent. He has a Norfolk jacket with twenty-four pockets."

"What are the chances of Shafter's letting me on one of the troop ships?" Mike asked.

"After this morning? Thinner than smoke."

"What if I let Eden work on him for a while?"

"He won't let any of us on," Tim said. "Why should he give *you* the time of day?"

"Because my heart is pure," Mike said. "Besides, I'll eat my hat if those troop ships don't have newspapermen all over them by the time they sail. When is that, by the way?"

"Nobody knows," Tim said.

"You wouldn't hold out on a brother?"

"Not unless you go to work for Hearst. Come on in and say hello to Elizabeth. She seems to like you, God knows why. She had a run-in with Shafter, too. Actually not a run-in. He wouldn't see her, and she was furious," Tim explained as they strolled up to the hotel and found that Eden had been left in the lurch by her general— "Although in the nicest way," she said. She'd been scooped up by Elizabeth and Rosebay Ware, and they were having tea in the cavernous palm-dotted lobby.

Tim and Mike turned up their noses at tea and hailed a passing waiter for gin rickeys. They settled themselves in wicker armchairs beside their wives and stretched long legs out on the marble floor. It struck Elizabeth for the first time how alike they were despite their physical differences. Whereas Tim was muscular, Mike was lanky, and even his hands seemed attenuated. He had Alexandra's green eyes and russet hair, and a red mustache, which was totally out of fashion and which Eden swore he had grown for that very reason. He looked as if he might be consumptive but wasn't, while Tim was solid and, at thirty-one, had an ever so slightly expanding waistline. But there was a similar cock to both their heads, and a look in their eyes, and something very pronounced about the shape of their chins that made the family resemblance noticeable.

"This is the oddest place I've ever seen," Eden said, peering around her.

Elizabeth chuckled. For a young woman who had grown up on a sugar plantation in Hawaii and now lived in the bohemian splendor of New York's artists' colony, that was saying something. "It's the location," Elizabeth said.

"It really wouldn't be any sillier than any spa if it hadn't been abandoned in the middle of the desert."

"No, it isn't that. It's the feeling of waiting," Eden said. "Like being stuck in a train station and having your train never come."

"It will pep up enough when it does get here," Tim said. "Charley's coming down, have you heard?"

"Yes, Janessa telephoned us before we left," Eden said. "I suppose they think there will be yellow fever."

They chatted idly, immobilized in the train station of Eden's imagining. They had more tea, another round of gin rickeys, then drifted in to dinner. Mike found a cavalry officer he had gone to school with in Washington. He ambled over to his table and after much backslapping and inquiring after relatives, came back grinning.

"He's going to let me ship out with his troops—he's to be with Roosevelt. I'll be sure to get something good."

The days dragged on with false alarms, finally punctuated by one genuine report: Commodore Schley and the U.S. flying squadron had found Admiral Cervera at last. The Spanish fleet was bottled up in Santiago Harbor. That ought to kick things loose, everyone said.

But for several days nothing happened. Everyone seemed to think that General Shafter knew something. His temper grew shorter daily, which was a reliable sign. Mike set up his camera to record scenes of Theodore Roosevelt's Rough Riders and accidentally captured General Shafter being helped onto his horse. That evening Mike's cavalry crony informed him that he was terribly sorry, but he couldn't give him a spot on the troopship after all.

Pleading for a place on the *Chance* did no good. The next day Shafter ordered all the press boats seized to prevent them from following the invasion fleet. Rafe telegraphed furiously from Key West that the *Chance* had been grabbed before he could hide her. All the journalists were treading very carefully now. Everyone feared that the boats were going to be held until the action was completely over.

Although no sailing date had been announced, Tampa had erupted into activity. The army, finally, was managing to keep a secret, but it was obvious that it was going somewhere soon and was frantically trying to unsnarl its provisions in time. Three hundred boxcars still sat on tracks twenty-five miles outside Tampa and contained God knew what because they had no invoices accompanying them. Some of the volunteer regiments still pouring into town had neither guns nor blankets nor tents. And when everything was all assembled, the men and supplies would have to be funneled down that single track nine miles to the pier.

Finally, on the night of June 7, General Shafter was seen at the telegraph, and rumor held he was conferring with the President. Word went out that the expedition force would sail at daybreak.

The hotel lobby filled immediately with correspondents' luggage. Piles of canteens, blanket rolls, binoculars, and cartridge belts littered the floor. The press was notified that it would be allowed to embark on the troop transports, and a list had been circulated of those favored, along with their assignments. Tim and Hugo had berths on the *Olivette,* Shafter's hospital ship, Tim's secured only after he had sworn that his brother Michael was not in his employ or vice versa.

Tim and Hugo kissed their wives and caught the train for the pier at five the next morning, with Mike disconsolately trailing them, dragging his camera and gear—a good sixty pounds' worth. Throughout the train ride, Mike groused about having to haul his equipment down the pier and to the ships.

"Why don't you just set up and shoot the embarkation?" Tim asked him at their destination. "Nobody else will have footage of it. You've got no business going into a battle anyway."

"Oh, stow it," Mike said irritably. "My heart hasn't given out on me thus far."

"What does Eden think?" Mike had contracted rheumatic fever as a child. There had been a time when his family was firmly of the opinion that he shouldn't even marry.

"Unlike the rest of you, Eden has sense enough to know that being given the freedom to pursue my career is better for my heart than having my relatives chasing me with stethoscopes whenever I go outdoors."

"Getting shot at isn't exactly a stroll in the park. What does Janessa say?"

Mike grinned. "Who asked Janessa?"

Mike set off down the pier. He heard someone behind him shouting for the press to get a move on if they wanted to come. He had been personally barred by Shafter, but in the confusion on the pier, no one paid much attention to him. No use in trying his friend with the Rough Riders again. Still, there was their ship. . . .

There was no mistaking Roosevelt's toothy smile. He seemed to be arguing with the officers of the Seventy-first Militia from New York over possession of the vessel.

"We're supposed to have the *Yucatán!*" a captain said, outraged.

"Well, *we* seem to have it," Roosevelt retorted. "Not my fault if they put us both down for it. The early bird gets the worm."

The officers of the Seventy-first departed in search of other transport, and Roosevelt inspected Mike and his camera. "What are you up to? And don't I know you?"

"I'm Michael Holt, sir," Mike said. "Toby Holt's son. You haven't seen me since I was a kid."

Roosevelt chuckled. "That hasn't been that long. What the devil is that thing?"

"It's a moving-picture camera. I want to record the landing."

Roosevelt scratched his chin.

Mike came a little closer. "The trouble is," he said confidentially, "the old man's barred me from going. I caught him by accident being hoisted onto his horse. No one's got the nerve to take me on board."

Roosevelt chortled. "Oh, my. No one has the nerve, eh? You must be a desperate character." He chuckled again, eyes twinkling behind his spectacles. "I don't think I could tell old Toby I left his boy behind on the dock. Make it quick, before the old man spots you."

V

Dawson City, Yukon Territory

The country was ravenous for information on the war. The newspapers trumpeted success with every headline, whether there had been a victory or not. Better to pretend that your paper knew every skirmish as it happened than to be found wanting. Headlines in Wednesday's papers often contradicted stories in Tuesday's, with the real story appearing on Friday. This was the newspapers' war—they had begun it, and they would give the public what it wanted: Dashing correspondents, danger, daring raids, heartrending "color."

Information was doubly valuable where it was hard to come by. In the north, in the goldfields where another set of American adventurers had gone to try to dig their fortunes out of holes in the ground, the knowledge that their country had gone to war made a newspaper worth anything you could get for it.

A copy of the *Seattle Post-Intelligencer*, a month old, had arrived in Dawson City on the Yukon River in early June, with an entrepreneur who announced that it could be had for the highest bid, the auction to commence immediately. He stood on the deck of his moored boat and displayed the prize, held aloft so everyone could see the headline: "Dewey Takes Manila."

"Five dollars!"

"Who's Dewey?"

"Ten dollars!"

Klondikers crowded the riverbank and jostled one another to peer at the newspaper. It was the first news they had seen since the sinking of the *Maine*. The auction was punctuated with war whoops and the crack of pistols, and several enthusiasts announced their immediate intention of going home to enlist.

Frank Blake leaned morosely against a telephone pole, watching to make sure nobody was shot by accident. The pole was still wireless, just erected the day before for the newest enterprise to come to the boomtown of Dawson. As sheriff, Frank supposed he ought to take a certain civic pride in that, but he could not. He had to hang a man at five o'clock.

Frank, six weeks short of his twentieth birthday, was sheriff of Dawson because nobody else would take the job and Dawson needed some kind of law. He had been elected to the position against his will, and he didn't feel old enough to hang a man. He suspected that right afterward he was going to feel a lot older.

The auction was up to twenty-five dollars for the paper.

"Thirty!"

"I'll give you five if you'll let me be next to see it." Side deals began to emerge.

"Forty! And I got plans for it."

"Forty-five!"

"Fifty!"

No one wanted to go higher. The paper was sold for fifty, and its owner promptly announced that it would be read aloud that night in the town hall—the roof had been finished only the month before—admission, one dollar.

Frank watched glumly as the crowd dispersed. He supposed he'd go with the rest and hear the news, if he still had the stomach for it.

"See you at the hanging, Sheriff!" someone shouted, and Frank snapped his head around.

"It's not a party!" he retorted.

But he knew it might as well be. Dawson was full of bored men who had arrived after months of hardship to find that they were too late. Every decent claim had been taken the year before. A few took jobs in the sawmills or worked other men's diggings, but most milled in the streets, gossiped in the saloons, or drank. Anything was an event—a hanging or a newspaper, it didn't matter.

The town was bursting at the seams. A flood of hopeful miners had rafted downriver from Lake Bennett into Dawson with the spring thaw, and more were coming every day. The whine of the sawmill couldn't keep up with the demand for lumber, and yet the new buildings were being financed by the men who had been there for a year or two. They were the lucky ones, for they had actually found gold. The swelling population found nothing here for them. They moved aimlessly, in enforced idleness, their interest sparked now and again by some happening or by the fierce homesickness that assailed them when they found that after all their struggle, they had come for nothing. Occasionally they killed one another.

The Canadian government was growing concerned and said that the Mounties were being sent out in force to set up a post in Dawson. Frank wished they would get there by five o'clock.

Up the street, in front of the jail, a temporary gallows was waiting for Arvin Garst. Frank stared at it, feeling miserable. Garst had shot his unarmed partner in the back in a drunken fit of temper. He had done it in the Daybreak Saloon in front of ten witnesses. There wasn't any possible doubt, and if turned loose, he would inevitably shoot someone else; but Frank didn't want to hang him. He didn't actually have to do it personally—he had said he wouldn't, so the town had voted a fund to hire a hangman—but Frank was in charge of it.

His dogs at his heels, he walked past the gallows, deliberately giving it a long stare, hoping he could desensitize himself to it. He turned down toward Peggy Delaney's laundry. He didn't know what he thought he'd get from Peg that would help with Arvin Garst, but being with her was better than being alone.

"Fellow came in with a Seattle paper," he announced as he walked in. He took off his coat and hung it over the back of a chair.

Peggy, red hair curling in a cloud of steam, was bent over her new wringer washing machine. "War news?" She tugged a pair of denim pants through the mangle and threw them in a basket.

"Seems like it. We just sank a Spanish fleet in Manila Bay."

"And where might that be?"

"In the Philippine Islands. They're in the Pacific Ocean, sort of southeast of China."

"What were we doing over there? I thought it was Cuba."

"I haven't the faintest idea," Frank said. "Some sourdough bought the paper for fifty dollars. He's going to charge a dollar a head to hear it read tonight. You want to go?"

"Of course," Peggy said. "I like to know what's going on, 'specially the way men get hysterical over a war. You aren't going to go and enlist, are you?"

"Not planning on it," he said. "Not unless I can do it before five."

Peggy paid him closer attention. "You look plain awful. Why'n't you just go home and let that hangman take care of Arvin Garst?"

"Can't," Frank said. "My responsibility."

She gave him a pitying look. "You pull yourself open over stuff. You always did. Maybe it's just because you're so young. You better grow some calluses."

"I don't *want* calluses," Frank snapped. "I don't want to be able to pretend things aren't real, just by saying they aren't. I don't want to see things the way my old man wanted me to."

"Your old man." Peggy looked thoughtful. "He's in the

army, isn't he? He'll be in this war, sure. That what's got you so riled?"

"No!" Frank snapped again.

"Aren't you worried about him?"

Frank prodded a laundry tub with his toe. "He'll do fine. He's got lots of calluses."

"I expect they aren't bulletproof," Peggy murmured.

"Get off it, Peg."

Peggy nodded. "There isn't going to be any right thing to say to you till after the hanging." She looked at her watch.

Frank looked at his. Four-thirty. He shrugged his coat back on. "I'd like to leave my dogs here. You coming to see the spectacle?"

"Do you want me to?"

"No."

"I'll wait here, then. Hangings aren't my cup of tea."

Most of Dawson thought otherwise. When Frank got there, a crowd was already jockeying for position around the gallows, and the hired hangman was waiting. Frank went inside the one-room jail and unlocked Arvin Garst's cell. Garst was pasty looking, and sweat beaded on his forehead. He looked at Frank with fear.

"Time to go."

Garst shook his head. A miner deputized for the occasion held a gun on the prisoner while Frank tied a rope around the man's hands behind his back. Then the lawmen dragged him out of the cell and walked him to the platform steps.

A preacher was waiting, and Garst fastened his eyes in terror on the man. "God has a place for you, my son, if you repent," the preacher said.

Garst nodded, babbling unintelligibly, and the hangman and the deputy dragged him up the steps. Frank watched, arms folded, refusing to look away, while they knotted the noose around Garst's neck. If he was going to preside at this, Frank thought, then he was going to see it.

He wasn't going to look away and tell himself later that it hadn't really happened.

The hangman, turning to Frank, raised his eyebrows in question. The crowd leaned forward expectantly. Frank nodded. The hangman pulled the lever that worked the trap, and Garst dropped through it. The rope snapped taut, and the crowd let out a long sibilant breath.

Frank allowed himself to look away. The hangman appeared a little green, too. He wasn't a professional. "How long we supposed to leave him?" he asked Frank.

"Oh, Christ, I don't know! Two hours." Frank invented a number, a rule for the *Hangman's Handbook*. "That'll leave enough daylight to get him out of there and that gallows dismantled. That's part of your job. You don't get paid till that's done."

The crowd had already lost interest in the event. They shifted down the street, into the saloons or toward the boats where many of them were camped. When the miner who had bought the newspaper began to shout for an audience outside the town hall, they thronged to give him their dollars. News from home drew them in until the hall was full, the gallows already forgotten. Peggy met Frank at the door.

"I was supposed to come get you, wasn't I?" Frank asked contritely.

"I heard them shouting," Peggy said easily, "so I came along." They put their dollars into the miner's hat and found seats among the last of the folding chairs in the hall. These had been augmented with packing crates, and by the time everyone was inside, men stood three deep along the walls.

The newspaper reported victory in Manila Bay and the dispatch of U.S. troops to take the city. Invasion of Cuba was held to be imminent, and there was a call for volunteers.

Afterward, Frank walked Peggy home in the lingering northern daylight, to the sound of the gallows being dismantled. The weather was still cold, but the mosquitoes were beginning to wake up, to hatch in the puddles in the thawing muskegs and swarm around any breathing body. Peggy brushed them away from her face with gloved fingers. When Frank pulled her into his arms just inside her door, she smelled of citronella and pennyroyal.

Peggy peered at him, startled, as he pulled her scarf off and unbuttoned her cloak. She hadn't thought he would be interested in making love right after the hanging, but it seemed that he was. Without saying much, he dropped the bar on the door and tugged her with him around the screens that made a bedroom of one corner of the cabin. His dogs—a pile of silver fur beside the stove—yawned, decided that no one was going anywhere, and went back to sleep.

Hungrily Frank unbuttoned Peggy's dress and kissed her throat. She could feel him pressed against her, feel the urgency with which he wanted her. Under a woolen dress she wore a flannel bodice, petticoat, and flannel drawers. "Undressing you is like peeling an onion," he murmured, folding layers away from the body underneath. He did it deliberately, as if letting the desire build, to blot out the memory of the hanging.

Peggy's skin was white and freckled, and from doing laundry her arms were almost as muscular as his. Her thick red hair was tangled around her shoulders. Frank stuck his hands into it as if it would warm them.

Peggy's blue eyes rested on him uncertainly, but she didn't protest. They were old friends and old lovers; she was past demanding that he flirt and court her first. Anyway, he usually did. She crawled under the blankets and the fox-skin coverlet and watched while Frank stripped his own clothes off. He was broad-shouldered and muscular, with straight, straw-colored hair, pale eyes, and a wide mouth. Over the past year his face had lost the softness of his teens and become more angular.

Frank slid under the covers with her and closed his mouth around a breast. He ran his hands down her soft body, and she felt the spark leap between them. Peggy twisted her legs around his, letting him take comfort, letting him hang on. He had known this urge before, when other demons had been on his trail, to bury himself in her, to hide under her blankets.

After he was spent, he pulled Peggy heavily toward him. She rested her cheek on his shoulder. He looked into the twilight that hovered under the roof beams and let his breath flow deeply until his racing heart began to slow down, slower and slower like a locomotive braking.

"Men are a mystery," Peggy said into the dusk. It was a pronouncement she seemed to have given some thought to.

Frank blinked and detached his stare from the ceiling. "How so?"

"Well, I was thinking anyone who'd been to a hanging, and was as wrought up about it as you, he wouldn't have the stomach for anything like this, not right after."

"*Au contraire,*" Frank said. He was grinning. However he had done it, he seemed to have chased the devils out. "I'll tell you a secret." He propped himself up on one elbow and fluffed the pillow for her. "Death makes us think about sex."

"Oh, go on." Peggy gave him a scornful look.

"It's true," Frank said. "Whenever we get good and scared or we come too close to somebody else's death, we get the urge. It's how nature makes sure there'll always be more people to replace the ones that get killed."

"Sounds daft to me," Peggy said.

"Think," Frank said. "Remember when we ran the rapids last year. Remember you and I sneaked off after?"

"Mmm," said Peggy.

"Well?"

She chuckled. "You've always got some half-baked theory. And I'm not ever knowing for sure which ones you read somewhere and which ones you're making up off the top of your head."

"It doesn't mean I'm wrong just because I thought it up," Frank said indignantly. "I'll tell you this: All the fellows at my school knew it. If they wanted to spark with a girl, they'd take her up to the graveyard. Scare her to death with stories about a cadet who was supposed to have hanged himself. Worked every time. Girls who ordinarily wouldn't let you kiss them—"

"I would never want to do anything with anybody in a graveyard," Peggy said firmly.

"How do you know? Anybody ever court you in a graveyard?"

"No, and they're not going to." Peggy started to laugh. "In case you might have ideas."

"I'm right all the same," Frank said. "Look how people get married in droves during a war. I bet it's going on right now. I bet the marriage rate's gone up fifty percent, with all the damn fools enlisting in the army."

"You aren't thinking about it?" Peggy asked him again.

"I'm not." Frank wondered if the question of marriage had anything to do with her asking. There were times when he thought he ought to settle down and marry Peg. "I'll join the army if raving Spaniards with cutlasses in their teeth actually attack the United States. And provided I can be sent to a regiment as far away from my father as possible. Otherwise, I would sooner dig ditches."

"You don't think the Cubans need help?"

"I don't think they need us to help ourselves to Cuba."

"That war declaration the fellow read out of the paper—it said right out the President wasn't planning to take over Cuba for the United States—he was going to turn it right over to the Cubans."

"If we don't keep a hold on it somehow, I'll eat my hat," Frank said. "It's too close to Florida. And then there's the question of what we're going to do with the Philippine Islands. Care to take any bets on our turning *them* back over to the Filipinos?"

"I don't know," Peggy said. "It all makes my head ache. Don't you think it's our duty, being a civilized country and a democracy, to give other countries a chance to be free, too? Isn't that what we fought the revolution for? It's what my relatives came over for, from Ireland, I can tell you that."

"It's what they all come over for, sweetie," Frank said. "But I don't know that that gives us the right to go out and run the world. 'Take up the white man's burden,' as Kipling says. My guess is that the black man and the brown man would just as soon be left alone."

"Not if Spain got hold of them, instead," Peggy pointed out.

"No, I suppose not. I just wonder if we'll make things any better, blundering in and lumbering about."

"You always wonder," Peggy said. "I never knew a man that wondered so much. It's no surprise you can't make up your mind what you want to do."

"I haven't any trouble at all," Frank said airily. He crossed his hands behind his head.

"You don't want to be sheriff, but you won't chuck it," Peggy said.

"I can't chuck it. Nobody else will do it."

"You insisted there's gold in the hole you dug, but you only work it about half the time."

"It's only about half the time that I think there's gold. The other half of the time it's a skunk."

"Well, there. You see? You're worried sick about your dad, but you won't write home to see if he's been shipped out."

"I am not. I don't care if he's been shipped out to Timbuktu or the moon."

"You don't have any idea what you want to do with your life, Frank Blake," Peggy said. "You got a good family and an education, and so far you've been an oil-field roughneck and a railroad bum."

"And a snake charmer. Don't forget the snake charmer."

"I wouldn't call that a recommendation."

"Maybe I'll be a nabob." Frank sighed. "Just as soon

as I find more gold. Hell, Peg, I don't know. Maybe you're right."

"You got an itchy foot," Peggy said sleepily.

"I want to see things. I can't help feeling like I've seen the Klondike. Aren't you getting tired of it up here?"

"I am not," Peggy said. "This laundry's making good money. I'm getting ready to expand, order me two more machines, hire some girls. I'm not going anywhere. You go, and you're on your own." She pulled the covers up to her chin, then wriggled down, digging in.

"And you better see about your old man." Her voice emanated from a tangle of red hair and fox fur, as if disembodied. "You won't forgive yourself if you don't."

It was light again by the time they woke up. It was practically always light during the summer. And by now it was getting warm, time to shed some layers. Peggy yawned and slid out of bed, pulling her wool wrapper from under Frank's dogs. They were on the bed again. She looked at the red flannel underwear that Frank had dropped on the floor and decided that today she'd switch to cotton.

Frank was lying on his back, his face endearingly youthful, mouth slightly open, a lock of hair curling on his forehead. Peggy looked at him and shook her head slightly. What on earth was she doing with a nineteen-year-old kid? She stuck her feet into her slippers and padded around the partition to poke up the fire. There was water in the kettle, and for a change it wasn't frozen. Peggy put some kindling in the firebox and closed the door. She set the kettle on the stovetop and whistled softly under her breath. The air felt new that morning, fragrant with some kind of change.

What was she going to do about Frank? She supposed she could talk him into marrying her, but she'd be a candidate for the loony doctors if she did.

Peggy spooned coffee into the pot and set it out, ready. The dogs got off the bed and came to see if she was fixing breakfast. Peggy never fed them—Frank did—but they always came to see anyway. They yawned, showing curling pink tongues and snowdrop teeth, and sat down by the stove.

"Go wake him up," she told them. "I'm not giving you anything." She heard Frank stirring, so she put the coffee on. He was fine company, there was no denying that. He read her poetry in bed and told her stories, and he was a wonderful lover. Peggy felt proud of that, since she had been his first woman, back in Sierra, California. He never bragged about it in the saloon, either, the way some men would. Peggy liked to live privately, and Frank respected that. There wasn't anybody in Dawson who could call her a loose woman. Up in the Yukon, if a woman stuck by one man, it didn't matter so much if they were married or not.

Peggy listened to Frank stretching and cracking his knuckles behind the partition. She wasn't crazy about the sound, but it didn't annoy her that much. She had invested a lot of time in not letting herself work up the kind of feeling for Frank Blake that would be affected by knuckle cracking. That was the kind of thing that would bother her if she knew it was going to be permanent.

Peggy got the skillet down and sliced some bacon into it. She knew that one of these days Frank was going to go home to his folks, no matter what he thought now. He wasn't the kind to be estranged all his life. She could see the separation eating at him already, with this war. And if she married him in the meantime, there'd be hell to pay. Peggy tried to envision herself being introduced to Frank's parents, trying to act right but not knowing how, trying to be something she'd never been raised to be. The thought opened up a big queasy place in her stomach. They'd hate her; they'd just flat right out hate her, she thought. She knew that perfectly well.

The bacon started popping, and she stirred it around in the skillet with a fork. Besides that, the man was supposed to do the proposing. Peggy didn't hold with women bringing it up, not even if the man gave her the chance. That wasn't how it was supposed to be. She looked exasperatedly at Frank, in his long johns, hair sticking up in spikes, as he came around the partition. How could a man who looked so beautiful asleep look like that when he woke up?

Frank ran his fingers through his hair. He grabbed Peggy around the waist and kissed her ear.

"They were up on the bed again," she said.

Frank kissed the other ear. "Let's get romantic."

"How can I be romantic with the dogs watching me?" she asked. "And I don't hold with dogs on the bed."

"They're mighty nice in the winter."

"Well, it's not winter. And they've got fleas, and I don't know what all."

"I can't teach them the difference between winter and summer," Frank said. "If you can figure out how to do it, I'll be glad to explain it to them."

"It would be simpler to just shut them in the bathhouse, which is what you were supposed to do. Frank, if you don't quit pawing me, I'm going to burn this bacon. You want breakfast or you want to canoodle around?"

"I want both."

"Well, eat first. It's nearly done." She couldn't help smiling at him. She couldn't help letting him talk her back into bed again, either. The things that had been deviling him the night before seemed forgotten entirely.

Peggy threw him out before her customers started coming. Frank stood in the cabin doorway and stretched again, just enjoying the feel of his body and the soft summer air. He twitched his nose like the dogs, sorting out smells—the hot sawdust smell from the mill that ran twenty-four hours a day now, the yeasty odor of the brewery, the smell of last year's vegetation, thawed out and rotting, while this year's grew up through it.

He whistled the dogs to heel, to keep them out of Peggy's hair, and started up toward Front Street to make sure they had torn down the gallows. He wasn't going to have a thing like that sitting in the middle of town.

Front Street had undergone a substantial change

during the last year. There were four churches now, nowhere near enough to shepherd a town like Dawson onto the Upward Way, but they did lend a lot of respectability and permanence, as if the residents might be undergoing some kind of metamorphosis. If you watched carefully, Frank thought, you might see a sourdough walk inside a church and emerge a banker in a fine gray worsted suit. There were halls for the Masons and the Odd Fellows, too, and down the street an entrepreneur was tacking up a pasteboard sign on one of the still-bare telephone poles: COMING SOON! MOTION PICTURES FROM THE AMAZING VITAGRAPH CAMERA! CHILLS, THRILLS, AND DARING!

Frank strolled over. It looked as if Mike had been right. Motion pictures had come to Dawson in the two years since Frank had listened to his cousin expound on the process; Mike had said they were the wave of the future. What else had been going on in the States since he'd left?

"Mornin', Sheriff." The man with the sign paused, his hammer in midair. "Top of the morning to you. That was a fine hanging yesterday."

"What the hell's the matter with people?" Frank demanded. "It's not entertainment. It's not one of your Vitagraph shows."

"That's why I figure this is a sure bet," the man confided. "All the excitement of a hanging, none of the emotions that distress the ladies. I figure it'll make me rich in a year."

"Take it in at the ticket booth," Frank advised him. "Don't try to dig it out of the ground."

He looked at the dismal array of miners' outfits for sale along Front Street: *$50 Takes It All, Best Offer, Gone Bust, Going Home*. Nevertheless, they arrived every day, unaware, ever hopeful. The Canadian government had laid down some regulations that were being enforced by Mounties at the top of Chilkoot Pass. From now on, every man allowed over the pass had to bring with him one thousand pounds of food and supplies and five hundred dollars in cash.

But after they got here and failed, Frank thought, they ended up selling their equipment at fifty cents on the dollar. Frank decided he wasn't quite that desperate yet, but he sure as hell was bored with trying to wash gold out of a marginal claim. He felt restless and decided to be stern with himself. *I'm going to give it one more shot*, he thought. *I'll stay with it for the summer, no coming into town every week. Learn to pay attention to the claim, learn to read the vein. . . .*

Peggy didn't complain when Frank explained this plan to her. "That's a fine notion," was her sole comment. He rode out of town relieved, eager now to start washing the rest of the dirt that he had piled up over the winter outside his cabin on Caribou Creek. You could dig the frozen ground if you set a fire in the shaft at night, but as soon as it was dug, the dirt solidified again and couldn't be washed until thaw. There was plenty to do.

Frank felt very virtuous as he rode along. His horse trotted through a field of flowers with the dogs loping at his side, gamboling through white anemones and raspberry-colored alpine rhododendron, blooming amid patches of snow. It was an amazing country, and it still made him gawk like a greenhorn. There was too much out here to see to spend his time in Dawson, watching telephone poles go up or lolling around in bed with Peg, although that was fun. With luck, nobody in Dawson would shoot anyone else, and the hard-luck cases lining Front Street would stay out of trouble.

Frank watched his dogs streak after a snowshoe hare, dun-colored for the summer and as fast as lightning. They never caught one. The dogs weren't a lot of use in the summer, but in winter they were hooked up to a sled for transportation, since the snow got so thick that a horse just floundered in it.

Frank stretched his arms again, fingers laced together, cracking them backward. It felt good to be alive.

He might even whistle as he worked his way through the mountain of dirt outside his door, forget that his country was fighting Spain, let his father go his own way . . . Colonel Henry Blake, of the Army of Self-Righteousness, aide-de-camp to God. To hell with him. He didn't have a moose in his backyard. He didn't have anemones and buttercups and arctic poppies bending on supple stems, flowing like a river of sun.

Frank leaned forward. He let the horse have its head, and it galloped joyfully, face to the warm wind. The dogs gave up on the hare and came circling back from the horizon, shooting through the anemones. They overshot, and Frank reined in and turned in the saddle to see what they were after now. He saw a horseman on the opposite horizon, dark against a blue-gray sky. The man raised an arm.

"Hey, Blake!"

Frank reined his horse to a slow trot, half tempted to whistle back the dogs and kick the horse into a gallop instead.

The man raised his arm again and this time made himself known with a gunshot. "Hey, Sheriff!"

Frank drew his horse to a halt and waited, leaning back in the saddle, arms crossed on his chest. Let whoever it was come to him. Frank was blasted if he'd turn back to meet him.

Heartache Johnson, mayor of Dawson City, came into view. He had the morose countenance of an earnest moose, and muttonchop side-whiskers. Frank's dogs ran around him, acting as if they had fetched the man.

Frank groaned. "What do you want?"

"Some dang fool robbed the bank," Heartache said. "He shot a teller and got clean away with two hundred thousand dollars."

"In gold dust?" Frank asked. "Was he hauling a pack train?"

"Naw, in folding money," Heartache said. "Another ten minutes and he'd have the Daybreak's deposit." Heartache owned the Daybreak Saloon, the setting and source of solace for his perpetual string of punctured love affairs; but that day he was in his mayoral mode. "You got to come on back."

"Like hell I do. I just left."

"As sheriff you got a responsibility to the citizenry. You can't just go off and leave 'em unprotected."

"I just hung a man for the citizenry. Can't the citizenry stay out of trouble for two days so I can work my claim?"

"It wasn't any of our boys," Heartache said, as if that made the crime more deplorable. "Not anybody we know. Some dang *cheechako,* the teller said, in city clothes."

Cheechakos were newcomers, greenhorns. Frank thought about the outfits offered for sale on Front Street. Some poor bastard had just gone over the edge, he imagined. "Did you send a posse out?"

"Some of the boys took off after him," Heartache said. "But they kind of lost the trail. So we figured we better send for you."

"Heartache," Frank said wearily, "I resign. I'm not going to chase down some poor tenderfoot who's likely to be scared to death and ready to shoot anything that moves. And not when your boys have churned up the trail to shit. I have a claim to dig."

"You can't resign," Heartache said. "We took a vote that whoever won the job of sheriff had to take it for a year. Now you've been duly elected, and you aren't going to weasel out of it."

"Yeah, but I thought *you'd* win. Damn it, Heartache—"

"What about all those poor souls who lost their money?"

"You mean the ones who run the bank?" Frank inquired. "How come they aren't chasing him?"

"Because they aren't the sheriff," Heartache said. "They tried to chase him, but like you said, all they did was muck up the trail. They were mostly three sheets to the wind to start with, being over at the Daybreak having lunch when it happened."

"Doesn't anybody in this town ever stay sober?" Frank demanded. He knew the answer to that. Usually there weren't more than two or three men who were actually falling down in the street, but most of the men, and a number of the women, drank to cut the boredom and the loneliness. It didn't matter anyway. It wasn't their job to chase him; it was Frank's.

"All right," he growled. "Let's go. But I'm taking this one to the Mounties at Fort Constantine if I catch him. I'm not hanging anybody else."

VI

Tampa

When Tim and Hugo boarded the *Olivette*, they found Charley Lawrence there, muttering and reading a dog-eared treatise on field surgery.

"I heard you were supposed to be aboard," Charley grunted when he saw his brother-in-law.

"That's a nice welcome," Tim said. "What's got you in such an uproar?"

"I'm petrified," Charley admitted. "I'm not a surgeon, I'm an epidemiologist. I don't know what I'm doing here."

"I thought you were supposed to set up a hospital at Tampa."

"They changed my orders," Charley said. "Damned fools."

"Can't you treat fever here as well as on land?"

"I suppose," Charley said. "There'll be plenty to go around. The President must be crazy, ordering an invasion in the rainy season."

"We can hardly sit around until fall," Hugo said practically.

"We're going to wish we had," Charley retorted. "The summer is bad enough for the Cubans, and they're used to it. We poor gringos are going to drop like flies."

"My God, you're cheerful."

"I sat up two nights in a row in railroad cars," Charley said, "trying to get here in time. And now we haven't budged."

"We will." Tim was determinedly cheerful. "We'll be off any moment now."

But they weren't. By late afternoon the transports were fully loaded. Cheering men hung from the rigging, and a regimental band played the send-off. General Shafter went on board his flagship, the *Seguranca*, and then, to everyone's bewilderment, ordered all remaining transports back to cluster around the wharf, and anchor. The gunboats waiting in the harbor took off with great speed and purpose, and rumors began flying nearly as fast: Spanish destroyers were in the channel, the transports that had already left had been sunk, the Spanish had mined the harbor. . . . Nobody knew what was happening, but everyone had theories.

By morning the endangered transports, including the poor old *Gussie*, came steaming back, shepherded by the gunboats, and the correspondents learned that Spanish warships had been seen above Cuba in the Old Bahama Channel and that General Shafter was ordered not to sail until the warships had been dealt with.

The army, cooped up in steaming transports, sat off Port Tampa for five days. The army unloaded its horses and mules when fifteen animals died of the heat below-decks; but the men stayed on board. Tim remained on the *Olivette*, afraid to get off, even though his ship was the last in line. He thought it would take at least a day to reload the animals, but Shafter might sail without some of them.

Finally it was learned that the alarm had been false. What ships might actually have been seen, and by whom, was not made known to the press. The horses and mules were reloaded, the water supplies refilled. Tim and Hugo stood fuming on the deck with Charley, while indistinct figures that might have been Rosebay and Elizabeth waved to them from the pier.

Finally, late on June 14, the *Olivette* set out, ten hours behind the rest, while her correspondents gave a ragged cheer that was half aggravation and half relief. By ten the next night she had caught up with the convoy and put on steam to draw up next to the *Seguranca*. The ships were sailing east along the north coast of Cuba. The island lay to the starboard. Wrapped in rain clouds, it provided a wet and almost inviting contrast to the glassy seas and marble-blue heaven the flotilla made its way between. There was no word as to their landing place. Even in the middle of the sea, Shafter was telling the press nothing.

"What would we do with information if we had it?" one of the journalists complained. "He's motivated by pure spite, I tell you."

"Maybe he thinks we'll file it by heliograph."

"We were bad boys," Tim said lazily. "Don't you know the *Gussie* disaster was our fault?"

"So where do *you* think we're going, Holt? Santiago or San Juan?"

Among the possible battle plans speculated on by the newspapers was the option of attacking Puerto Rico first.

"I'm betting Santiago," Tim said. "If we land in Puerto Rico, we could bite the Spanish on the tail, but we'd still have Cuba to take."

They placed bets to alleviate the boredom, which was broken only for several frantic minutes during the next few days when everyone mistook a loose water barge for a torpedo boat.

As they rounded the eastern tip of Cuba, it eventually became evident that they were steaming for Santiago, where the American fleet had the Spanish boxed in. By this time the press boats had gotten loose from their baby-sitters in Tampa and Key West and were bobbing around the convoy. The naval escort was disinclined to obey Shafter's tirades to seize them, so there they stayed, getting in the way and in some cases nearly run down, all the way to Santiago Harbor.

The *Chance* came up beside the hospital ship, and Rafe climbed up a rope ladder to confer with his boss.

"Did you know your brother's on the *Yucatán* with Roosevelt?" Rafe asked him.

"*What?*"

"You don't suppose Roosevelt would turn down that kind of publicity, do you?" Rafe asked. "Pity he hasn't got his horses with him, though. Cavalry always looks more dashing on horses, but only the officers' mounts were brought along."

"What's the navy doing?" Tim asked.

"They put some marines ashore at Guantánamo," Rafe said. "Got in a fight with the Spaniards and drove them off. Crane was there."

While they talked, Tim lifted his binoculars to the coastline. No one knew much about Santiago—nothing like the detailed information they had about the fortifications and defenses of Havana. Santiago's harbor was entered through a narrow channel, which led to a bay some six miles long and two miles wide. Steep hills, studded with gun emplacements, dropped to the shoreline at the entrance to the bay, and the highly forbidding fortress of Morro Castle dominated the eastern side. To get into the bay, it would first be necessary to take out the guns of Morro Castle and then clear the mines that were almost certain to be guarding it.

"Something's up," Hugo said, and Tim and Rafe peered through the scattered convoy at the flagship. The unmistakable figure of General Shafter was seen with an officer of the fleet on the deck of the *Seguranca*. Then the *Seguranca* peeled away from the transports and sidled through the fleet to Admiral Sampson's flagship. When it came back out again, Tim went down the ladder with Rafe into the *Chance*. Something *was* up, and he wasn't going to miss it.

The *Chance* dogged the *Seguranca* at a decent distance until it hove to three miles to the west. Three small boats put out from it, and Tim ordered the *Chance*'s boat lowered. No one had invited him, but he could see Davis and some others in the *Seguranca* boats and took that as an invitation.

The expedition proved to be a conference among Shafter, Sampson, and the venerable Cuban general

Calixto García y Iñigues. General García, a Cuban officer confided, was a martyr to seasickness and required his conferences to be held on dry land. Unfortunately, General García was a mile up the mountain. Everyone looked doubtfully at General Shafter, then at the trail, while Tim stayed carefully out of Shafter's sight, if not out of earshot. Conferences ensued. A Cuban officer produced a mule for the hefty general. It looked to Tim not much larger than a goat, but *"tiene mucho corazón,"* said the Cuban officer.

Shafter was placed on the mule's back, nearly concealing the unfortunate animal from view, and the party set off, the journalists stifling chortles.

The generals conferred upon a hilltop while the American army and naval aides looked dubiously at the Cubans. Plainly the adjutants had not expected them to be so dark or so ragged. Even General García was ancient and mummylike.

The journalists were held at bay and fuming over it. Finally Tim got tired of complaining—it was all they seemed to do lately—and slid quietly into the damp trees. A little reconnoitering brought him around to the far side of the hilltop clearing, where a thicket of vines recommended itself as cover. He wriggled and twisted into the tangle, hoping he could get out again, and found himself in earshot of the generals.

"Bring your men ashore and take Morro Castle," Sampson was saying to Shafter. "Only thing to be done." He smacked one palm against the other for emphasis.

"Don't be ridiculous." Shafter snorted. "With respect, if you want into the bay, you'll have to shoot your own way in. There's a much better approach farther up the coast. Then we can go around the back and take Santiago in one operation while you keep them pinned down in the castle."

García looked from one of the Americans to the other as if wondering why they had come to confer with him, only to argue among themselves.

A bug crawled up Tim's nose, and he sneezed. General Shafter's aides spun around, and one lifted his

pistol purposefully. Tim scuttled backward through the
vines. A shot went over his head. He hoped they mistook
him for a Spanish sniper. It would be unsettling if he had
actually provoked Shafter into shooting journalists. He
returned to the rest of the correspondents with as much
dignity as he could muster.

In half an hour, the generals signaled the end of their
conference, and the Americans departed, the journalists
still informationless and the adjutants casting one last,
apprehensive look at García's ragged Cubanos.

"You could tell what they were thinking," Tim reported to Hugo after he got back to the *Chance*. "'Where
are the heroes? These won't do.' Half of them didn't have
shoes, and there wasn't a uniform among them. They had
rifles, though."

Shafter had declined to take Sampson's suggestion to
storm Morro Castle. But Shafter and Sampson had agreed
upon another plan. Afterward, they would argue about it,
each accusing the other of changing the agreed-upon
orders. But for the moment events were unfolding. The
soldiers on the transports, stifling in the heat and already
suffering from bad water and typhoid, were begging to
land. They let out a jubilant cheer as the warships of the
fleet began to lob shells onto the coast. No Spanish fire
answered them.

The transports were going in opposite the village of
Daiquiri, east of Santiago Bay, with the landing to be
continued at Siboney, a little closer. Daiquiri had no
feasible landing place except the open beach and a single
iron pier that jutted into the water. Tim, waiting with Rafe
and Hugo on the *Chance,* thought how easy it would be for
the Spanish to cut through anything that landed on that
beach. The hills above were covered with brush and
ominously silent. They could easily hide a dozen Spanish
batteries.

Shafter issued orders that only soldiers would be
allowed in the boats for the first landing, and the press set

up a howl again. Tim could have sold space on the *Chance*
ten times over to the correspondents on the *Olivette*; he
declined to do so but took pity on Mike and plucked him
off the *Yucatán*.

Mike carefully lowered his sixty pounds of gear,
wrapped in a rubber sheet, onto the *Chance* and then
came down himself, grinning. They backed out of the way
and waited. Since Roosevelt seemed favorably inclined
toward them, Tim decided to try to take the *Chance* in
when the *Yucatán*'s Rough Riders landed.

The guns had stopped, and long strings of ships' boats
were filling with men. The sea was running high, and the
men, burdened with their rifles and bedrolls, dropped
from the gangplank ladder into boats that bumped and
tumbled below them. The sailors watched the soldiers'
difficulties with amazement.

The only way to land horses and mules was simply to
push the unfortunate animals into the water. A high
percentage of them headed in the wrong direction and had
to be pursued in boats. Terrified, the animals drowned or
were caught in the current and killed on the rocks. The
horses of one cavalry squad turned back in time when a
bugler on the shore had the presence of mind to sound
"right wheel." They came about and paddled for shore,
comforted with the certainty of familiar sound. Roosevelt's
horses were lowered over the side with a caution not
exercised with the common herd; but one of them
drowned anyway, and the colonel was in a fury.

Then a navy launch towed the boats in to shore, and
the *Chance* followed. The steel pier was too high to be of
any use, and the wooden jetty beside it was nearly rotted
through. Soldiers climbed from their heaving boats into
the waves that washed over the jetty.

The captain of the *Chance* maneuvered her next to
the jetty, and Tim and Hugo leapt for it, stumbling a bit
but not going under. Behind them, men with pants rolled
up and rifles held high were floundering from ships' boats
through the surf. The *Chance* bounced and thumped at

the pier as Mike, swearing, tried to pass his rubber-wrapped camera over the side.

"Don't drop it!" he shouted at Tim over the roar of the surf.

Tim staggered backward with the camera in his arms. The jetty was slimy with water and rot. If he fell through, he was sure as hell going to let go of the camera, he thought. Mike came off after him, soaking wet and lugging the rest of his gear. The captain began to back the *Chance* away from the jetty. Naval launches, having realized she had no business there, shouted at her to move, and Rafe waved good-bye jauntily from the deck.

The landing was to be continued at Siboney, five miles down the coast, as soon as the Spanish troops there had been cleared out. Rafe and the *Chance* were to sit off Siboney and wait for Hugo's signal to come in for a news dispatch.

The Rough Riders came ashore and spent most of the day helping other troops land. Even so, two men slipped off the pier and drowned in the roiling water. Despite that, the rest sang jubilantly as they came ashore. They danced naked around the campfires on the beach, taking joy in their first bath in a week.

Tim looked uneasily at a Spanish blockhouse, unscathed by the bombardment and looming against the sky. The thought that it might still be full of Spanish soldiers crossed his mind. But Shafter seemed to be leading a charmed life. The menacing blockhouse proved to be unaccountably empty—a troop of Rough Riders ascended the slope on its own with an American flag and fixed it to the pole. When the soldiers on the ships caught sight of it, whistles and drumrolls joined the tumult. The regimental band on the *Mattewan* played "The Star-Spangled Banner." For whatever reason, the Spanish had withdrawn inland and lost their best chance to stop the invasion.

The landing at Daiquiri was like no picture of war Tim had ever imagined. It went on for three days in utter disorganization. Mike immediately set up his camera and began filming it. On the first night someone found three casks of wine in the village, and the correspondents and Rough Rider officers had a party. It wasn't very good wine, but that didn't matter, sitting in the moonlight in a burned-out cantina. There was very little else left of the village of Daiquiri. What the Spanish had not burned, the American shells had splintered.

Tim tipped his head back and took a long swallow from a tin cup, his eyes on the wheeling stars overhead. Any vision of a welcome by delectable Cuban señoritas—the subject of much talk aboard ship—had faded. There were no Cubanos left in Daiquiri.

Hugo and a Rough Rider lieutenant were trying to race a pair of tarantulas on the scarred cantina floor. Tarantulas were plentiful, as were the land crabs of various hues that scuttled everywhere and had to be swatted out of bedrolls and dinner plates. Mike had drunk two cups of wine and apparently gone to sleep, his arms around his camera. Tim stood up, restless, and refilled his own cup. He wandered outside with it and walked across the shattered plaza. A pair of forlorn troopers were playing dice on the edge of a silent fountain.

"Evening, Captain," one of them said.

"I'm no captain, just a miserable journalist," Tim responded. "Lower than troopers on General Shafter's scale."

"Well, now, you got invited to the party," one of them said, pointing at Tim's tin cup. "More'n poor bastards like Horace and me got. Ain't it so, Horace?"

"Truer words," said Horace mournfully, "were never spoken."

Tim chuckled. "Here, you—what's your name?"

"Bill," the other man said.

"Give me your cup, Bill."

Bill handed it over, and Tim went back to the cantina. He refilled his own and then Bill's. "Friend outside," he murmured, but nobody paid him any attention. At the fountain he gave Bill back his cup, then emptied his own into Horace's.

"Gawdamighty," said Horace reverently.

"You're true blue," said Bill.

In the morning, in defiance of Shafter's orders, the correspondents aboard the *Seguranca* and other ships—the men who had been without dispatch boats—were finally permitted to land just so the army could get rid of them. They milled about, hooking up with whatever unit was handy and pumping those already on shore for information. Most of it proved to be inaccurate. The Rough Riders spent time improving their campsite and then received orders to abandon it and march to Siboney, which had been deserted by the Spanish. The rest of the troops were now being landed there, with the army's stores and ammunition. Tim and Hugo slogged along behind the Rough Riders and lost track of Mike along the way.

"He'll turn up," Hugo said as Tim swiveled his head around and muttered worriedly. "Nobody's shooting at us."

"They will be," Tim said. He trudged on, still concerned. The heat was unbearable, and the soldiers, in their impractical woolen uniforms, were beginning to drop from heatstroke. At ten o'clock at night they came up to the campfires at Siboney, a disheartened little village whose modern improvements included not much more than a set of railway tracks. There was no water for drinking or cooking. After the details sent to find some had come back, a rainstorm extinguished all the fires and turned the ground to mush.

The Rough Riders and the 1st and 10th cavalries, all horseless, were under the command of Major General Joseph Wheeler, a former Confederate officer known since Civil War days as Fighting Joe. At dawn Fighting Joe announced that they were to make a sortie to clear out the Spanish entrenched in the heights of the coastal range north of Siboney. His information had come from Cubans who were drifting into camp, and Wheeler was eager to make the first strike at the Spanish.

The weary camp pulled itself together. Colonel Leonard Wood, commander of the Rough Riders, looked worn, but Roosevelt, his second, was perky. Roosevelt hustled and cajoled the men out of bed and into line, and they caught his mood. They were ready to fight, and Tim and Hugo went along, marching behind Horace and Bill.

Two tracks led out of Siboney, which huddled in a gap between the hills: A wagon road went east and slowly swung north and west again, and a trail went straight up the mountains. They converged at a crossroads called Las Guasimas on the way to Santiago. This intersection was where the Spanish were said to be.

The Rough Riders, laughing and arguing, singing songs and pointing out the scenery, took the trail. Roosevelt had never been in the tropics and found the unfamiliar flora and exotic birds delightful, so he said. Tim found the call of the wood cuckoo in the thickets unsettling, since it was said to be a Spanish signal call. The happy chatter of the column began to unnerve him. He glanced at Hugo, but his friend seemed relatively untroubled. As the sun rose higher, the soldiers began to shed equipment. Tim stumbled over tents, blanket rolls, and discarded uniform blouses.

The Americans passed plantations deserted and burned out, the legacy of unending civil war, and areas where the trail closed in around them, a suffocating green corridor twenty feet high and as hot as an oven. They passed an abandoned Spanish blockhouse, silent save for the unseen animals that scuttled among the sweet potatoes and peppers of its kitchen garden.

Finally a halt was called, and the advance guard, under a captain named Capron, came back to confer with Colonel Wood. The men lolled gratefully by the trail, grousing and speculating, and to Tim's relief an order came down the line to keep silence in the ranks. A sergeant bawled, "Stop talking, damn it!" at the top of his lungs until they did so.

The ensuing quiet was eerie, punctuated by the increasingly ominous notes of the wood cuckoo. The order came in whispers to prepare for action. The Rough Riders fanned out into the jungle on both sides of the trail. Tim, itchy and uneasy, stood waiting, and then the silent jungle exploded in gunfire. He dived for cover, falling over the wire that edged the trail, and tried to figure out where the fire was coming from before it hit him.

Hugo flattened himself in the grass. "Guess the Spanish are here, after all," he muttered.

On either side of them, the Rough Riders were hacking their way through undergrowth so thick it had to be torn apart or cut before a man could pass. One moment Tim could see the trooper next to him, then suddenly he would be alone in the green maze. The Spanish were still firing, but their smokeless powder left nothing to fire back at. Somewhere across the valley, the regulars under General S.B.M. Young were moving along the wagon trail, but no one knew where they might be or whether they, too, were being fired upon.

VII

Mike, who had sixty pounds of gear to carry, had spent a lot of time stealing a mule, so he arrived at Siboney in the morning, just in time to hear that Wheeler had sent for reinforcements and that the Rough Riders had been caught in an ambush. Freshly landed army regulars were heading north in a cacophony of bugles and shouting. He found no sign of Tim or Hugo.

Mike fell in with the column, trudging steadily uphill and monitoring the beat of his heart, as he was used to doing. A couple of years had gone by since it had reacted badly under stress, but the habit of checking on it was ingrained. He thought he felt it skip, but he couldn't be sure. It was maddening to be so focused on one's body. He waited, but it didn't happen again.

The trail climbed sharply above Siboney, narrowing into a ridge that fell away on either side, so he could see the transport fleet and battleships offshore. After a mile, he ran into the wounded coming down out of the jungle, dazed men with puzzled faces. "You can't see 'em," one of them said wonderingly as he passed. "You can't see 'em at all."

Two Rough Riders, their trouser legs drenched with blood, rode by on an army mule. One of them, recognizing Mike, turned and shouted, "Your brother's up there. I saw him with the colonel."

"Was he okay?" Mike asked, but the man only shrugged and continued on his way. Tim was up there in the thick of it, getting all the excitement or getting shot, either one of which Mike took as a personal affront. Mike swore and towed his reluctant mule along as the order came to pick up the pace—double-time.

Ahead, General Young, having discerned the Spanish position, was firing with Hotchkiss guns, and the Spanish found themselves caught between two wings. The Rough Riders kept pushing forward despite the fact that they could actually *see* Spanish soldiers only after they fell over them.

Tim shoved his notebook in his pocket again and wriggled after the American soldiers. They traveled face-down most of the time, through suffocating heat, over ground that was slick with blood and littered with abandoned equipment. Tim was frequently and unnervingly eye-to-eye with the land crabs, which took full advantage whenever someone stopped moving. Tim found Horace, sitting propped against a tree trunk, swatting at the crabs. His leg was shattered, and he had tied his Rough Rider's blue polka-dot bandanna around it. Tim snatched up a canteen and held it to his lips.

"We got 'em on the run," Horace whispered.

"You need to get to the rear," Tim said.

"I'll be all right till the surgeons come. Can't leave Bill." He laid a protective hand on something in the tall grass, and Tim saw the other man. He lay very still, facedown, a blue-black hole through his head.

"Bill's dead," Tim said gently.

Horace lifted his hat and slapped it viciously at the grass. A crab scuttled backward, just out of reach. The Rough Rider shuddered with disgust. "I won't leave him for those things."

"Sure." Tim put the canteen in Horace's lap. "I'll let the surgeons know you're here."

He crawled on and, finding himself behind the action, picked himself up and ran, dodging through the trees on paths already tramped out. He found Hugo crouched behind a rock, finishing a sketch of the guidon bearer. Tim slid in beside him.

When they heard cheering ahead as Young's left wing connected with the Rough Riders, they ran toward the sound. The whole regiment was engaged now and advancing, pushing the Spanish back. Tim saw Colonel Wood, still unperturbed, in contrast to Roosevelt and General Joe Wheeler, who might have been appropriately cartooned with cutlasses clenched between their teeth. The order came for the final charge. Fighting Joe forgot what army he was in and shouted, "Come on, boys, we've got the damn Yankees on the run!"

Tim let out a howl of laughter and thundered after them. The Spanish were in full retreat, pursued by cheering, bleeding, horseless cavalrymen.

The reinforcements from Siboney arrived too late to help, and they marched somewhat sheepishly down the hill again, but Mike stayed and set up his camera at the field hospital and began filming the wounded. He and Tim were reunited there around noon.

Mike inspected his brother for bullet holes. "Is any of that blood yours?"

Tim's jacket and breeches were smeared with blood and soaked with sweat, but only the sweat was his own. He inspected Mike in turn. "How the hell did you get that camera up the hill?"

"Stole a mule," Mike said, then sang, "'I got a mule, and her name is Sal, fifteen miles on the Erie Canal.' I'm afraid to turn my back on her. I'll never get back down without her." Tim noted that Sal's lead was looped through the handle of Mike's equipment box. "Marshall of the *Journal* got shot, did you know?"

"Damn!"

"Crane and some others took him down on a stretcher. He was trying to finish his dispatches before he died."

Disheartened, Tim looked around the small dressing

station. According to the first count, sixteen men were dead and approximately fifty had been wounded. The surgeons were blood-soaked to the armpits, aprons grisly with blood, flesh, and shattered bone. A man in the row of stretchers, drifting in delirium, moaned over and over,

> "My country, 'tis of thee,
> Sweet land of liberty
> Of thee I sing. . . ."

Finally other voices took up the song, forcing the man to go on to the next verse. It seemed to give them comfort, and Mike swung the heavy camera around and filmed a man who raised one bandaged hand, swinging it back and forth to keep tempo.

Hugo left before dark with a group of wounded soldiers from the dressing station and the front lines. He carried Tim's dispatches and his own sketches of the battle. They went warily, with an armed escort. Spanish sharp-shooters had begun to fire into the hospital camp as well as on the stretchers being carried downhill to Siboney. The popular belief that the "garlics" were inept marksmen had proved to be anything but true, and their smokeless powder gave them the eerie air of ghosts, incorporeal except for the bullets.

Hugo felt his skin prickle as he eyed the surrounding jungle. It wasn't an unpleasant sensation, more a feeling of being exceptionally alive. Everyone's nerves were tightly strung, and the jungle seemed painted in brighter colors than it had when the troops landed. A bird that swooped overhead, shrieking at them, was bright red. It could almost have been painted with blood.

They stopped to rest at nightfall, propping themselves alongside the trail. Hugo found himself next to a Rough Rider with a shattered leg. "You know a fellow named Holt?" the trooper asked him, noting his sketch pad and dispatch case.

"He's my boss," Hugo said.

"Well, you tell him I made it. Name's Horace. Tell him I made them take Bill away, too, didn't leave him for the crabs. You tell him." Horace nodded his head wearily.

"I'll tell—" Hugo said, then suddenly shrieked. He flung something away from himself. "There are tarantulas in the grass," he said with elaborate calm. A bullet slapped through the leaves by his ear. Hugo raised his pistol and fired at ghosts.

They reached Siboney after dark and found it full of hysterical rumors. Rafe was pacing on the beach. He grabbed Hugo by the shirtfront.

"Did Roosevelt really get killed?"

"If there had been any justice, he would at least have been nicked," Hugo growled. "But he's in fine fettle."

"What about Wood? They're saying Wood was killed. They're saying the whole column was wiped out."

"Not for want of trying," Hugo retorted. "Wood's alive, too. I'm alive, Tim's alive, Mike's alive. I see you're alive. Bloody miracle."

"You can say that again," Rafe said. "Do you have time to eat? I've food on the *Chance*."

Hugo shook his head. "No time. Here." He handed over his sketches and the contents of his dispatch case. "Better run for it. You know how the boss feels about being first on the wire."

"Why don't you file them and let me go back in?" Rafe asked hopefully. "You don't look so good."

"I'm fine. Top-notch." Hugo looked at the smoking ruin of the town. "What the hell is going on here?"

"Shafter's follies," Rafe said shortly.

Hugo returned in the morning to report to Tim that Siboney looked like the sack of Rome and that General Shafter seemed to have a plan for taking Santiago if he could just get his supplies on shore.

The confusion within the army that had begun in Tampa was worsened by Cuban rainstorms. The first downpour was greeted with delight by the sweat-soaked soldiers, who peeled off their uniforms and performed a jig in the rain. They were less enthusiastic about the second cloudburst and markedly unhappy about the third. The torrential rains washed away blankets and rifles and flattened shelter tents. The water turned the roads to sludge and bogged down wagon and mule trains.

Between Las Guasimas and Santiago was jungle traversed by a single road, the optimistically christened Camino Real. It was crossed several times by the Rio Aguadores, a little stream that turned treacherous in the rain. Two miles northwest of Las Guasimas was the village of Sevilla, where Shafter set up his command headquarters. Two miles farther was a hill called El Pozo—the Well—from which the city of Santiago could be seen. The ground between El Pozo and Santiago provided admirable opportunities for ambush. It was broken by a series of ridges known as San Juan Hill and otherwise was rolling and covered with thicket. Worse, every hillock was dotted with a Spanish blockhouse, fortified with rifle pits and barbed wire.

The Americans had never encountered barbed wire used as a military device, and they were not equipped with wire cutters. Nor were they provided with field guns that could do any damage to the blockhouses.

While Shafter concentrated on solving these problems and getting his ammunition and supplies from the beach to the front lines, the men were on short rations. Whatever food was available quickly went bad after having been soaked by salt water, then rainwater, and finally steamed in the sun. Even so, it seemed like miraculous provisions to the ragged Cuban rebels, and because the rations were unfamiliar and thus exotic, they willingly traded anything they had for them, including mangoes, sugarcane, and plantains, a fruit that looked like huge green bananas and tasted like library paste.

The insurrectos were a curiosity to the soldiers, although the correspondents, Tim excepted, paid them scant attention. The journalists had expected noble heroes, with dark eyes flashing and strong arms pointing the way to liberty. Instead, they saw ragged, barefoot mulattos with Pillsbury flour sacks that held their possessions slung over their shoulders. They were armed with machetes and one or two cartridge bandoliers made of sacking. They carried their rifles any way they pleased, and it was difficult to distinguish the officers from the privates.

Tim, intrigued as usual by what others spurned, took to trying out his marginal Spanish on them and learned several interesting things: Although everyone coveted the Mausers that the Spanish carried, no ammunition was available except for what was in a dead Spaniard's cartridge belt. Fresh ammunition was supplied by the prostitutes of Havana, who charged the Spanish soldiers their fees in Mauser cartridges. This was a happy arrangement because the cartridges were free, supplied by the government. Other gentlemen who came later in the night would ride away with cartridges—exchanged with the ladies for wood, charcoal, or wine—sewn in their saddle blankets. It was a barter arrangement that suited everyone.

Tim also discovered that the Cubans, who had simple rawhide sandals or no shoes at all, could outmarch the Americans with ease. This was something the other journalists chose not to notice. Lacking the money and men necessary for a full-scale war, the insurrectos had nonetheless been driving the Spanish crazy for years. Because they haunted the jungles even more effectively than did the Spanish sharpshooters, duty in the blockhouses, where the jungle grew to the edge of the kitchen garden, was particularly feared by the Spanish troops.

Some rebels were Cuban émigrés, recruited to return for the revolution by the junta in New York, but most were peasants driven by sheer desperation. And their treatment of the Spanish was no more humanitarian than Spain's, whose excesses toward the enemy had been trumpeted in American newspapers. One of the returned émigrés confided to Tim over hardtack and a stolen keg of rum that the men under his command played football in the streets with the hacked-off heads of Spanish soldiers.

The Cubans were tough, too. Malnourished, they nonetheless proved resistant to the diseases that decimated Shafter's army. The invading Americans had discarded at least half of their woolen uniforms in the heat, and anything thrown away immediately became the property of a ragged Cuban insurrecto and was therefore gone for good. Now, with no change of clothing available, the Americans grew dirty, then filthy, and finally became sick. Cases of yellow fever and malaria outnumbered the wounded in the field hospital.

"Are you taking your quinine?" Tim demanded of Mike shortly after Hugo's return from Siboney.

"There is some debate over whether or not it works as a preventive," Mike said placidly.

"Are you sleeping under a mosquito net? You can't afford to get sick."

"Will you leave me alone?" Mike looked at the sky and dragged his camera a little farther under the edge of the shelter tent they were sharing with Hugo. Sal the mule, tethered at the door flap, stuck her head in and lipped at the rubber wrappings.

"Mike—"

"Rafe saw Charley Lawrence on the *Olivette*," said Hugo, who had heard the brothers' conversation numerous times and did not want to hear it again. "He says Marshall's still alive."

"Probably all due to quinine," Mike said, and Tim gave up.

The usual afternoon downpour fell on them suddenly, as it always did, like a bucket upended from the sky. When the rain stopped, the air was steamy, thick enough to grab hold of, and almost as hot as a Turkish bath. The bugs that had been momentarily silenced by the rain crawled up on the topsides of the leaves again and began to chatter. The thin hum of a mosquito went by Tim's ear, and he swatted at the insect.

Hugo began to scratch, idly at first, at the backs of his knees, and then more vigorously all over.

"Oh, don't do that," Tim groaned. He began to scratch, too.

They were bug bitten, filthy, and soaked with sweat. There was no place that did not itch. Mike held out a minute longer than Tim, then rolled onto his back and scraped his shoulders against the corner of his equipment case. "Dashing life of the special correspondent," he muttered, then made a snuffling pig noise, which Tim echoed as he rubbed his own back up and down on the tent pole.

"We're better off than the Spanish in Santiago," Tim said. "They're eating rats."

"So are we," Hugo said. "I think." The tins that the army supplied labeled Roasted Beef contained a gluey, stringy, gelatinous mess that no one could identify.

"Santiago's out of food," Tim said. "Has been for a while. The Spanish are trying to reinforce it from Manzanillo, and García's been sent out to turn them back. But Shafter had better get a move on. There were two more men sick today. The Cubans say that when yellow fever gets started, it spreads like fire." He looked at Mike again. "I wish you'd go down to Siboney."

"If you knew anything about yellow fever," Mike said, "you'd realize that Siboney isn't far enough away to be safe. It's full of fever itself, anyway. If you don't believe me, go out to the *Olivette* and ask Charley. It'll get you out of my hair."

"Nope, can't leave." Tim peered through the steamy air at the trail that led out of Sevilla to Santiago. "Something's coming."

"Tarantulas," Hugo said. "Hordes of them on the march."

"No, by God, it's Shafter on a horse."

They all stood up to investigate.

The general and an aide had been up to El Pozo to view the prospective battleground. The aide rode beside the general and was jotting orders in a notebook. Rumors began to fly again. While Tim went to trail Shafter, Hugo took a sketchbook and his pens and went out toward the front picket lines, where the Cubans were keeping an eye on things. Tim offered to pack Hugo's gear and take it along if the army decamped while Hugo was away. The men agreed to meet on the trail.

Hugo set out, then found a likely spot in a ruined old hacienda, which the Cubans had taken over. From its crumbling piazza he could see Santiago, still elegant at this distance, with its red tile roofs and blue, white, and yellow houses. Occasional church towers lifted themselves above the rooftops, and the sun cast a warm sparkle on the old city's yellow walls.

Somewhere behind those lovely walls, the population is eating rats, Hugo thought. If the Spanish did manage to get reinforcements through, there would be just that many more mouths to feed. There was no food to be found. The American blockade had taken care of that; there was hardly a plantation in Cuba that had not been burned out by either the Spanish or the insurrectos or both.

Hugo wrote *Santiago Before the Battle* at the top of his pad and began to draw while the Cuban pickets played dice in the corner, leaving one of their number to stand guard. The hacienda was slowly being eaten by the jungle. Creepers grew through cracks in the plaster walls, forcing them wider. White-trunked royal palms lifted their feathery heads over burned-out cane fields below. The jungle had reclaimed the fields already. It was like parts of India, Hugo thought, the way the jungle simply came and ate up the land. He had had some experience with India; his family had tried sending him there, to work for an uncle, before giving up and exiling him to America. What a circular life, he mused, to be sitting in the jungle again.

He cocked his head, half expecting to hear guns. It wouldn't be long now. His heart thumped a little faster as he stared at the walls of Santiago. It seemed to be an oddity in him that while Tim and Mike spent all their time worrying about the other's getting shot, Hugo viewed the prospect with a strange excitement. It wasn't that he wanted to get shot; it was just that the possibility of it made him feel more alive.

Hugo would never have stuck it out in the army— another of his father's suggestions for employment—but the independent acceptance of danger teased up an emotion in him that was highly pleasurable. It was a trait that possibly had something to do with the hell he had raised in his youth, before he met Rosebay and found an anchor in her. Certainly it was all right to revel in that old excitement. Hugo bent over his pad and sketched Santiago's gleaming towers across its surface.

He stayed until nearly sunset, then stood, stretched, and slid the sketch into his map case. The Cubans had been stirring some mess in a pot on a fire built in the middle of the veranda. Through the low insect hum that droned up the valley, Hugo heard another sound, the distant bang and crash of heavy equipment moving. He set his hands on the veranda wall and leaned out, looking toward Sevilla. The Cubans were already packing up their pots and picking out the contents with their fingers. The rumbling became clearer, and Hugo knew what it was now—approaching artillery. Through gaps in the trees he could see the low sun glint on the guns' shiny steel jackets.

Hugo packed up his equipment, slung the case across his back, and tore down the hill. Behind the guns the road was thick with marching men. Shafter had decided to do it at last!

Tim and Mike found him on the road. "We're to attack in the morning," Tim said. "That's the word I've got. Wheeler's gotten sick, and General Sumner's commanding the cavalry."

They slogged along, mainly uphill, through squashy black mud, to a cadence set by the sucking sound as the mud gave up each boot, and the splat as the next boot came down. There was no talking in ranks, and after that brief exchange the three men marched in silence, listening to the jingle of Sal's harness and the rhythmic click of swinging cups against bayonet scabbards. Both from behind and ahead they could hear the field guns and the snap of the muleteers' whips.

Half a mile beyond the Rio Aguadores, the horseless cavalry swung left and camped on a ridge at El Pozo. Near midnight the troops were still coming in, and General Sumner and his staff were making maps by candlelight. In the morning, July 1, they would go through the little villages of El Caney and San Juan and take the city of Santiago.

On board the *Olivette,* Charley peered through a porthole and watched the flickering lights from the shore at Siboney and tried to see up into the moonlit hills. He had more yellow fever patients aboard the *Olivette* than he did wounded, but that would change in a hurry. Ed Marshall of the *Journal* was still on board, stubbornly refusing to die despite having been shot in the spine. He was fretting for news and pestering Charley to know what was happening on shore.

"If I knew, damn it, I'd tell you," Charley said. "I'm not a general. Now go to sleep, or we'll be burying you at sea."

"I am writing my impressions of the experience," Marshall said with dignity, "since I don't seem to be going to die." He was flat on his back but had a notebook and was writing in it with a pencil.

Charley gave up. Too restless to sleep, he went on deck and stood by the rail. He stared at the hills, waiting for the sound of guns.

The main attack was to be made against San Juan Ridge, where the Spanish were well dug in. Sumner's dismounted cavalry planned to cross the San Juan River and deploy to the right, while an infantry division under General Kent was to deploy to the left and simultaneously charge the heights. Artillery bombardment from El Pozo was to facilitate the attack, as was the preliminary capture of El Caney, where there were believed to be about five hundred Spanish troops. General Lawton's infantry division would wipe them out before they could menace the main army's flank.

That was the strategy—and when it went wrong, the chaos was reminiscent of Tampa. The roads were muck, nothing fitted what it was supposed to, no one with General Shafter at El Pozo knew what was happening at El Caney. The odds there were ten to one against the Spaniards, but the fighting continued.

Shafter dithered, then sent his other two divisions forward anyway, through mud and intermittent rain and the confusion that can arise only when an entire army is funneled into a single, narrow, unpaved road. The Signal Corps observation balloon floated above them, despite howls of protest from the soldiers below. It exposed their position to the Spanish.

The wounded from El Caney and from the march on Santiago began to be brought in, and there were only three ambulances for them. The other vehicles were still on ships five miles out to sea at Siboney. The surgeons did what they could in a field hospital on the banks of the Aguadores, now running full with muddy water; but the muck, the dirt, and the incessant rain seeped through the roof and under the tent flaps. There weren't enough supplies, and what the doctors did have was often mud-soaked and contaminated.

When the rain stopped, those of the wounded who could walk were sent off, limping and hobbling, to Siboney, where there might at least be dry bandages and, eventually, a launch to take them to the *Olivette*. Those who couldn't walk lay in the field hospital by the Aguadores and watched the rain wash the blood off the surgeons' aprons until it ran like thin pink wine in runnels along the canvas floor.

"Where are you from, son?" a surgeon asked a dying

soldier. His parents would have to be written, some words said about a brave death for flag and country.

"El Caney," the boy whispered. It loomed larger in his mind than his hometown. "I came from El Caney. We can't kill 'em. . . ."

Mike and Sal the mule had gone with the artillery to film the bombardment of El Caney. By the time the infantry—wet, tired, and fed on hardtack, fatback, and lukewarm coffee—arrived at the base of the hill, the battery above was set up, and the officers were peering through their range finders, triangulating the solid-looking, tile-roofed blockhouse just outside the town. Beyond lay the village of El Caney, with its whitewashed walls and church tower.

Behind the American battery on the hill was gathered a laughing, chattering mass of soldiers, Cubans, and correspondents waiting to see the first shell launched. A white cloud bulged from the gun muzzle, and a cheer went up from the crowd as the shell hissed through the air.

It was almost like the opening of a boat race or some such silliness, Mike thought. But he kept his thoughts to himself and concentrated on cranking the film through his camera—no easy task with the *blam* and bellow of artillery exploding everywhere. The shells were falling all around the blockhouse now, kicking up fountains of dirt. Smoke, mortar dust, and brick blew off the surface of the building, but there simply wasn't enough firepower to knock it down. Mike could see the American infantry moving forward, under heavy fire from the Spanish. The sound of rifle fire rose to a crescendo that spread across the valley and caused an eerie echo in the hills.

Frustrated, Mike lifted his head from the viewfinder. He was too far away to see the infantry properly. Coughing from the smoke, he packed up the camera and heaved it onto Sal's back again. They slowly made their way down the hill toward El Caney, passing wounded men on the road. The rifle fire was more distinct now, each shot crisp and ominous. The soldiers looked at him curiously and limped by. The woods thinned, and then Mike came into a grove of mango trees on the outskirts of town. Beyond them was the battle. He could see the village and its earthworks and blockhouse plainly. He wondered what had possessed Shafter to think they could be taken easily. The stone fort was forty feet square, with loopholes for rifles, and surrounded by trenches protected by barbed wire.

The garrison inside was fighting with furious desperation. Artillery fire had battered it and torn away the flagstaff and colors, but the Spanish in the trenches below the fort poured volley after volley at the advancing Americans. Like machinery, row after row, the Spanish soldiers rose on command from their trenches, shot, knelt to reload, then rose and shot again. Their light blue jackets flowered with red when they were hit, and as soon as they were carried away, other men would take their places.

After tying Sal to a tree with a secure hitch, Mike set the camera up again. Slowly he cranked the film through, murmuring to himself to keep time, to keep the speed steady, sixteen frames per second. Meanwhile, bullets *ping*ed past his ear, rattling like a handful of pebbles flung at the trees.

The American troops were closer to the blockhouse now and still advancing. Mike saw a photographer with a still camera under his arm go by at a trot. Mike cursed his own camera for its size and cumbersomeness. He hauled the tripod farther out from the mango trees.

Sumner's cavalry division was moving toward San Juan, and Tim and Hugo were in its midst. The soldiers and journalists were clambering over one another, pushing through the mud that bogged the narrow, jungle-walled trail and mired wagons and gun carriages. Blanket rolls and woolen blouses were jettisoned once again by men who streamed with sweat and might already be sick with fever.

"How do you tell if it's the climate or malaria?" Tim grumbled to Hugo.

"You can't, till you leave," Hugo said. "Then, if you feel better, it was the climate."

He sounded intense and almost chipper to Tim, despite the fact that Spanish shells were falling all around them in the jungle. The trees had proved to be full of sharpshooters. Hugo spun around suddenly to his right. He aimed his pistol and fired, and a Spaniard dropped from a tree, tumbling with a thud at the feet of a startled trooper.

A ragged cheer went up, and someone shouted, "Shoot the goddamn balloon, why don't you?"

No one knew why the observation balloon was still there, but there it was, fat, yellow, and rubbery, visible through rain or shine. Towed by four privates, it continued to be the subject of furious outrage. Finally the Spanish scored a direct hit on it. The balloon sank gently, with stately grace, its occupants miraculously unharmed. The soldiers on the ground cheered the Spanish artillery.

Tim and Hugo came at last to the point where the road crossed the San Juan River. The forest ended, and the land opened into a meadow five hundred yards across, with the San Juan Heights on the opposite side. So far the only orders the field commanders had received were to march their troops to the river and deploy them in the forest on the meadow's edge.

Tim, with his nose in the grass, could see the Spanish rifle pits on the heights when he lifted his head; but lifting his head had drawn Spanish fire. He carefully stepped backward, and when he thought he was far enough into the trees to be safe, he moved among the waiting men.

"Get down, old man—sharpshooters!"

The *wheet* of a Mauser bullet went just over his head, and Tim dropped in the brush again, although not far enough back, it seemed to him. Two more shots went overhead and rattled into the trees.

There was no way to get out of the Spanish fire. They

shot constantly from the heights, into the border of the trees and at the road still crowded with troops. There was no way to retreat—the trail behind them was wedged with men. There was nowhere to go but forward . . . and still no orders came. It was one in the afternoon, and the men along the San Juan River were being cut to pieces by the Spanish fire, unable to go forward or fall back.

To charge the San Juan Heights, occupied by well-trained troops armed with the most modern rifles and artillery, was a foolhardy idea, and Tim knew it. Why the hell had they been sent in the first place, then? And where were the troops from El Caney, a third of Shafter's army? Finally, Lieutenant Miley, Shafter's aide at the front, decided that orders from El Pozo were unlikely to make it through the jam on the narrow trail. He took it upon himself to give the only possible order: Take the heights.

Theodore Roosevelt spurred his horse forward, and the Rough Riders and the Ninth Cavalry, a Negro regiment, followed him, advancing up the slope of a hill that was ahead and to the right of San Juan. Tim scrambled behind them, slipping in the smooth grass, trying to write as he ran. All around him men were pushing forward in short rushes, firing as they went, lumbering over the dead and dying. Tim saw Hugo loping ahead of him, paying no attention to bullets, and then saw him fall, entangled with a trooper of the Ninth Cavalry. Legs flying, Hugo rolled nearly halfway down the slope again. Tim scrambled toward him, flattening himself in the grass to turn Hugo over gently.

Hugo groaned and sat up. "He fell on me. Poor devil of a cavalryman took a Spanish bullet. He was right in front of me."

They wriggled into the cover of a scrubby bush and lay there panting. Tim pulled his notebook out again. The cavalrymen continued to climb the hill, through grass now blood-soaked and slick. A Rough Rider stopped and gasped for breath, and Tim heard the muffled *chonk* of a bullet hitting bone, and then the hiss announcing its coming. Because bullets travel ahead of their own sound, the army saying that you will never hear the bullet that gets you is accurate. The Rough Rider clutched his knee and toppled, and Tim and Hugo dragged him under their bush. Tim tied the man's spotted bandanna around his thigh above the wound.

Hugo tugged Tim's arm. "Come on. They're up to the top!" His eyes glittered.

They hurried after the Ninth to find the cavalry chasing the last of the Spanish from the hill, the top of which was crowned with a monstrous iron sugarcane kettle. Bullets from farther along the heights clanged off its fat black sides with a sound that was deafening, louder than the Gatling guns. The Rough Riders dropped down behind the kettle. Roosevelt, teeth and glasses shining, a sword in one fist and a pistol in the other, took stock of the situation. With the Spanish fire stopped from Kettle Hill—it would ever after be called by that name—the main line was advancing on the heights. The Rough Riders settled in behind the kettle to keep the Spanish pinned down.

Shafter had finally sent a message to Lawton at El Caney "not to bother about those little blockhouses" and to come and reinforce the main army. But it was too late. Lawton's forces were irrevocably launched on their attack. Mike saw them battling their way up to the Spanish trenches, with the Spanish line firing, kneeling, reloading, then firing again. As the Spanish rose, American bullets toppled them out of line, and finally, by sheer force of numbers, American bullets killed more Spanish than the Spanish could kill Americans. The firing slackened, and when the American front line finally cut the barbed wire and made its way clear to the trenches, they found them full of dead men. A few live ones huddled beside the corpses, waiting for the end. Inside the blockhouse the few survivors were willing to surrender. They stood among piled corpses. One clutched a white flag he had never managed to display. The intensity of the American fire had kept him from the windows.

Mike was willing to risk his own neck to Spanish fire, but not his precious camera. He had left Sal tied to the mango tree and run for the blockhouse, in time to discover that it was now being fired on not by the Americans but by the Spanish in the village. He dived inside and found a scene beyond words—despite the fact that it was description he had come for. An idea occurred to him: If he brought Tim something newsworthy, Tim would send his exposed film down to Siboney with Hugo, and Mike wouldn't have to worry about something happening to it—or have to carry it around, since the film was heavy.

Mike swallowed hard, trying not to vomit, when he got his first look around the blockhouse. The first dead soldier he saw was a young Spaniard, younger than Mike. One arm was doubled under his torso; he had been hit by shrapnel, and there was very little else to be seen except a red pile of flesh. There were dead Spaniards and Americans everywhere—in the pineapple fields and the trenches, in the corners and doorways of the blockhouse, and horribly, in the hammocks of their quarters, where the wounded Spaniards had crawled to die. The air smelled of smoke, of powdered lime and plaster, and of a horse's carcass that must have been in the road for two days.

Mike waited until he had an estimate of the casualties—235 Spanish dead and 441 Americans—and set out for San Juan. He didn't think Tim would want any more of a description than that.

The road that the main army had traveled along was littered with death and its debris, mired wagons abandoned where they had stuck. Mike led Sal over and around, trying to keep her out of the deepest of the mud holes. A mule, three legs stuck in the mud and cut loose from its gun carriage, waited balefully. When the mud dried up and they managed to free themselves, the abandoned mules would find freedom in the lush Cuban countryside.

At the San Juan River, Mike came to Bloody Ford, as it would be known forever after. The mud was churned with red muck, and the waters spilled around the bodies of dead horses. Dead men had been dragged to the edge and lay still, some with their feet still in the water. The wounded had been taken to the field hospital not far away. Sal flattened her ears back and didn't like it, and Mike thought uneasily of snipers.

VIII

Dawson City

Frank Blake reluctantly returned to town with Heartache Johnson after the bank robbery. He found that it would not be necessary to rebuild the gallows—the bank teller was still alive and furiously conscious of the fact. The ether that the doctor had administered while removing a bullet from his rib cage had worn off, and the teller was mad enough to chew nails.

"You find him, Sheriff, you hear me? You better find him before I do. I'm a law-abiding man, but I can be pushed just so far." The teller was small and would have been red in the face if he hadn't already bled so much. He tried to get up off the bed where his landlady had solicitously tucked him in, then howled when he realized again how much it hurt to move.

"Tell me exactly what happened," Frank said. "Had you ever seen the fellow before?"

"Not in my life. But if I see him again—"

"Yeah, I know. But what did he *do?*"

"He shot me! I was handing him the money like he said, and he shot me! You aren't supposed to do that—not when a fellow's handing you the money!"

"Well, he may have been new to bank robbing," Frank said. "I expect he doesn't know the rules. What kind of gun was it?"

"Just a cheap Sears, Roebuck revolver." The teller

sniffed. He hadn't even been shot with a proper outlaw's gun. "He was waving it all over the place."

It was lucky no one else had been shot, Frank thought later as he wandered down Front Street.

The bank manager, who had been waiting in his teller's boardinghouse parlor, tailed him. "Aren't you going after the man? He'll be heaven knows where by now."

"He'll be lying low," Frank said. "He's got to sleep sometime. And he's a cheechako—he doesn't know the country."

"When are you going to bring him in?" the manager demanded.

Frank felt as if he had a particularly insistent terrier on his heels. He half expected the manager to bark. "After I find out who he is and where he's likely to have gone," Frank said patiently.

"How are you going to do that? Time is a-wasting, Sheriff!"

"Well, I'm not going to do it with you in tow," Frank said. "Anybody who knows anything will light out the minute they see you. Why don't you go home and have dinner? Let me have mine."

"Dinner?" the manager yelled.

Frank abandoned him and splashed through the muck in the street. The usual idlers and disappointed new arrivals were perched morosely on their trunks across from the bank's imposing false front. Their wary eyes followed Frank's progress. His badge, the sole emblem of his office, was pinned to his shirtfront.

"Afternoon," Frank said. "You boys see all the ruckus?"

"Heard the shooting."

"See the fellow that did it?"

"Not to recognize."

"Don't believe I know him."

"Had a scarf over his face."

Frank tried again. "I understand he just came downriver. I thought maybe somebody might have traveled with him." He looked with hope at the row of faces.

"Lots of boats on the river." The men's expressions said plainly that they all thought they were in enough trouble without admitting to knowing bank robbers.

"You know it's mighty pretty up here right now," Frank said. "But it's not exactly a city park. You boys know that. This country eats greenhorns. I'd sure hate to think about some dumb bastard being out there on his own with nothing but a lot of paper money for protection. The inside of a jail might look mighty good after that."

They shifted uncomfortably.

"I think I heard he had a partner," someone muttered.

"Not for bank robbing," another man said. "Just a trail partner. I heard they quarreled coming over the pass and split up."

"You think they got back together in Dawson?" Frank asked, carefully ignoring the fact that these two had now admitted to knowing the culprit—or the partner. Probably the partner. "You know where I could find him?"

"Downriver, I reckon. Name's Bates." A round-faced young man with rimless spectacles looked earnestly at Frank. "Fellow I happened to know back in the States. He didn't have anything to do with it, but I think he's worried sick about—about his partner."

Frank nodded and went toward the river. Halfway there he stopped and put his badge in his pocket. It seemed like a target.

The river was completely free of the ice that had broken earlier that year, and its banks were lined with boats of every size and description, from the homemade craft on which optimistic Klondikers had shot the rapids down to Dawson, to the sizable river steamers from St. Michael on which they were leaving. It took him a while, asking questions of the loafers along the jetties and among the beached scows, to find Bates. When he did, Bates looked like a man who expected to hear no good news.

He was about thirty-five, by Frank's guess, with a flat cap of mouse-colored hair and pale blue eyes that kept flicking just past Frank's shoulder, as if looking for something he hoped wouldn't show up. Frank thought of a song that went back seventy-five years:

> *Oh, what was your name in the States?*
> *Was it Thompson or Johnson or Bates?*
> *Did you murder your wife,*
> *And fly for your life?*
> *Say, what was your name in the States?*

Whatever Bates had done wasn't Frank's business now. There were plenty of Bateses in the Klondike. Frank took the badge out of his pocket and balanced it on the palm of his hand. Bates blanched. "I understand you have a partner," Frank said conversationally.

"I didn't never—"

"I understand you have a partner who went and pulled a damned foolish stunt when he ran out of money," Frank went on. "I sure would like to find him before the wolves get him or he gets lost and starves to death. City boys, aren't you? Not much practice hunting?"

Bates licked his lips.

"The bank would like its money back, too," Frank said. "It might be willing to pay a reward."

"I don't sell out friends!" Bates said indignantly, finding his voice.

"I expect the reward money would pay to hire him a lawyer," Frank said. "Suppose you tell me why he went and did it."

"How would I know?" Bates grumbled. "He wasn't confiding in me. We had a fight on the trail and split up—not over anything important. It wears a man's nerves out, getting over the pass. Hailey got all huffy on me because he didn't think I was pulling my weight, and I quit him. I never saw him again till I bumped into him yesterday."

"How was he then?" Frank asked.

"Looked like hell," Bates said. "Stupid jerk got in a poker game and lost about everything."

"So he decided to mend his fortunes by robbing a bank?" Frank raised his eyebrows. "He do that kind of thing often?"

"Nothing *that* bad," Bates allowed. "It was Hailey talked me into coming up here after I left Joplin. I ought to let the wolves have him," he added morosely.

"Why'd you leave Joplin?" Frank inquired.

Bates flinched. "No reason," he muttered. "Just looking for work."

"Uh-huh. Well, that's not my business, thank God." Frank hooked his thumbs over his belt. "I've got to get him, you know. It'll be easier on him if it doesn't take me too long to find him."

"*I* don't know where he went," Bates protested.

"I can track him a ways," Frank said. "But he might feel easier about giving up if you were with me."

"He might just haul off and shoot me, too."

Frank grinned. "There *is* that. But he's more likely to shoot at *me* without your restraining influence. If he does that, he'll come in across the back of my horse."

Bates groaned. "Aw, God, this ain't fair. You don't even look old enough to be a sheriff."

"I'm older than I used to be," Frank informed him. "We're leaving as soon as I've had some dinner. I'll be back down here with a livery horse to get you. It would be a real good idea if you didn't go anywhere in the meantime. It would look sort of suspicious."

"Where do you think I'm going?" Bates asked dolefully. "I'll be here, if you think you can bring him in without killing him. If he takes a potshot at me, though, that's it. He's on his own."

"This has got to be the most half-assed bank robbery in the history of the goldfields," Frank told Peggy while he packed his bedroll. "It has all the elements of a farce, except that this guy is probably scared to death. That's going to make him unpredictable as hell."

"You never heard such a ruction," Peggy said. "I didn't see it, but I heard all the shouting and enough gunshots to have plugged any poor soul who happened to be out on the street. They're lucky they didn't hit anybody, firing after him that way."

"I take it they didn't hit *him*, either," Frank said.

"No. They chased him a ways, I heard, but he had a fast horse. And then they all decided it was your job, so they came back and sent Heartache after you."

Frank chuckled. "If I wasn't so mad, it would be pretty funny. Hand me that pack strap, will you?"

There was a loud knocking on the door. Peggy handed Frank the strap and went to see what late-night customer might be in search of his wash.

The nighttime sun revealed the largest Mountie she had ever seen. From the toes of his polished boots to the top of his peaked hat, he was at least six feet six inches. He swept the hat off, revealing a headful of blond curls, and said, "Evening, ma'am."

"Evening," Peggy said faintly.

"I'm looking for a Frank Blake?"

Peggy looked this apparition up and down while Frank tightened the strap on his bedroll. "That's me," he said finally. "What can I do for you?"

"I understand you've been serving as some kind of unofficial sheriff here," the Mountie said.

"I'm more official than anybody else," Frank said. "Being as nobody else wanted the job."

"Do come in," Peggy said. "Constable—?"

"MacKenzie, ma'am," the Mountie said. "Rory MacKenzie. Thank you." He gave her a breathtaking smile and crossed the threshold to loom over Frank, who was still fiddling with his bedroll. "I've been assigned to Dawson, Mr. Blake. I understand you've had a bank robbery, so I'll be taking over pursuit of the miscreant. You can rest easy now."

Frank stood up, hefting his bedroll. "We're grateful to the government," he commented. "But I kind of have a handle on the situation already."

The Mountie looked down at him with good humor, which annoyed Frank enormously. MacKenzie pointed a huge finger at Frank's badge. "You realize that thing is as likely to get you killed as it is to be any sort of protection."

"I could say the same about yours," Frank said, eyeing MacKenzie's official shield.

"Oh, no," MacKenzie said placidly. "Nobody shoots a Mountie. The government's very firm about that. Anyone who shoots a Mountie doesn't have much of a life expectancy." He shook his head solemnly. "I'm afraid we haven't the manpower to extend the policy to cover free-lance sheriffs."

"Where are my manners?" Peggy stammered and all but curtsied to the Mountie. "Won't you have a cup of tea, Constable MacKenzie? And maybe a bite of supper?"

Frank glared at her, but Constable MacKenzie took his hat off again and set it on a pile of clean, bagged laundry. "That's very kind of you, ma'am. I could use a bite before I set out. Something smells wonderful for certain."

"We were just sitting down to supper," Peggy said. "I'll fetch another plate."

"That's mighty kind of you, er, Mrs. Blake?"

Peggy flushed and stopped for an instant in midstride. "I'm not married," she said. "I'm Miss Delaney. Peggy Delaney." She bustled to the table and set out an extra plate and coffee cup.

The Mountie smiled broadly. "I'm pleased to meet you."

"Now, look here," Frank said. "As far as I'm concerned, if it's finally dawned on the Canadian government that we need some law and order out here, that's all to the good. But—"

"More of you Yanks coming in every day," MacKenzie said. "Had to."

"But I'm not letting you take over in the middle of a

crime. I got called in to handle this, and I'll see it through."
Frank looked MacKenzie in the eyes and held his ground.
"If you want to come along, you're welcome."

"Well, now, that would be fine." MacKenzie stood
solidly, planted with the gentle persistence of a young bull,
in the center of Peggy's cabin. "This is a mighty nice place
you've got here, ma'am." He cast an admiring eye on the
treasures she had dragged to the Yukon from California—a
blue willow soup tureen and a souvenir plate of a Hawaiian
maiden making obeisance to a volcano. On the opposite wall
was a picture of a fluffy kitten in a basket of roses. "I like to
see pictures on the walls. Makes it homelike. Takes a
woman's touch, I reckon, though."

Peggy blushed. "Why, thank you."

Frank, whose mother ran an art gallery, looked
balefully at MacKenzie's back and at the simpering kitten.
"I found the holdup man's partner," he announced. "He's
going out with us. He may be able to talk the robber into
coming back without trouble."

"I beg your pardon?" MacKenzie seemed to notice
Frank again. "Sure thing, Mr. Blake. You bring along
anybody you want to. It never hurts to have a few extra
hands on the trail."

"I wasn't asking your permission," Frank snapped.
"And I'm leaving in twenty minutes."

"Don't be silly, Frank," Peggy said. She was putting
her best napkins on the table. "You have your supper." She
smiled at MacKenzie. "I have a peach cobbler for dessert."

MacKenzie smiled back. "I reckon we can wait for the
peach cobbler, ma'am."

Frank yanked a chair out from the table and let Peggy
dish up the chicken fricassee she had been reheating in the
oven.

"It's not but leftovers," she said when MacKenzie
inhaled and beamed at her. "Don't they feed you fellows in
the Mounties?"

"Not this nice, ma'am."

"Well." Peggy sat down and spread her napkin in her lap.

"They have to catch it with their bare hands," Frank muttered. "Keeps them tough."

Peggy appeared not to hear him. "Where do you hail from, Mr. MacKenzie? That's a Scottish name, isn't it?"

"Indeed it is." MacKenzie winked at her, and his voice seemed to acquire just a touch of an accent. "We Gaels need to stick together. Me grandfather came over around the eighteen-thirties, and we've been Canadian ever since."

Peggy took a delicate bite of her chicken fricassee. "One of me granddads came then, too, or thereabouts, after the potato famine."

"The potato famine was in the late forties," Frank said.

"Oh, well, something like. And how did you join the Mounties, Mr. MacKenzie?"

"Looking for adventure, like any silly boy," MacKenzie said. "And found, of course, it was mostly mosquitoes and bad weather, and nobody to talk to but a moose now and then. There *have* been a few criminals I've tracked," he added modestly.

"Nice to know you're experienced," Frank said. He stabbed a piece of bread with his fork to mop up his gravy with and found Peggy staring pointedly at his shirtfront. It took him a moment to realize it was his napkin she was glaring at, tucked into his collar. He had let his table manners slide, into what his mother would have described as "country," in deference to Peggy, whose own were definitely of that style. It galled him that now she had apparently decided to be Queen Victoria. He pulled the napkin out of his collar and placed it with elaborate care in his lap.

"And have you been glad after all that you joined the force, Mr. MacKenzie?" Peggy asked, returning her gaze to the Mountie.

"Oh, aye. My family's not rich, you know, and I never

had a taste for farming. A man can retire from the mounted police with a decent pension and the knowledge that he's done some good in the world."

"A man should think about the future," Peggy agreed. "And have you family, Mr. MacKenzie? Children, I mean?"

"Oh, no, ma'am." MacKenzie swallowed his last bite of fricassee and beamed. "I'm not even married. There's just me and my horse and my dogs, and me mum on the farm. That's down toward Winnipeg." He hesitated, as if about to ask her something and not finding himself certain how to phrase it.

"We're just good friends," Frank said blandly.

Peggy glared at him. "Mr. Blake and I were acquainted in California," she said delicately. "It's always a treat up here to find a familiar face."

And if I leave my clothes here, you can pretend they're laundry, Frank thought sulkily, but he didn't say it. If Peggy wanted to pretend they weren't on a first-name basis, much less anything more intimate, she could go right ahead. If it salved her pride, it was fine with Frank. He didn't want to embarrass her. But he didn't think the Mountie was buying it. The Mountie couldn't possibly be as big a goof as he looked.

Frank tipped back in his chair. "If you really have peach cobbler, we'd better eat it and ride, before the bank robber has a chance to dig himself a hole clear to China."

"You'll bust that chair," Peggy said. "How many times I got to tell you?"

She flushed as soon as she'd said it, and Frank put his hand to his mouth to hide a smile as he sat forward in the chair. Peggy fetched the cobbler from the pie safe, then put clean plates out.

Rory MacKenzie watched her move around the table, and his face split into a grin. Frank saw with a faint unease that it wasn't the cobbler he was watching; it was Peggy. MacKenzie sat at parade rest, apparently his only posture, with his broad shoulders back and his immaculate red

jacket buttoned across a muscular chest. His hands rested
on the khaki expanse of his jodhpurs. Size thirteen feet, in
polished black boots, were planted firmly on the floor.

"This ride's likely to be pretty dirty," Frank commented, eyeing MacKenzie's spit and polish. "This time of
year, it's pretty much nothing but mud and muck and
muskeg."

Rory MacKenzie smiled. "I grew up in Canada, son."
He nodded his leonine head.

"You call me 'son' again," Frank said, "and I'll get up
and leave now, and you can try to track me when you finish
your tea and cobbler."

"No offense intended," MacKenzie said. "I don't
reckon I'm *that* much older than you are." He gave Frank
a bland smile.

Frank gritted his teeth. After he had finished his
dessert, he got up and went around the partition that
divided Peggy's bed from the rest of the cabin. The dogs
were on the bed again.

"Get down. You know you aren't allowed up there."
Frank came around the screen with his hat and gun belt in
his hand and the dogs at heel. Peggy glowered at him, but
there wasn't anything she could say that wouldn't make it
worse.

She shook MacKenzie's hand as the men left and gave
Frank a look that said that if he dared to kiss her in front
of MacKenzie, she would cut his liver out. So Frank shook
her hand, too, solemnly, and whispered in her ear, "Do not
worry, my dear. Your reputation is safe with me." He
hoped it annoyed the hell out of her. She had certainly
made him look like an idiot. Women were impossible to
figure out.

The Mountie's horse was tied outside, a sleek chest-
nut with a well-oiled regulation saddle and a clipped
mane. Frank swung into his own saddle and whistled the
dogs to heel. He had the livery animal on a lead. They set
off toward the river to find Bates and scare him to death.

◦   ◦   ◦

Bates saw them coming and dived around the other
side of his boat. "You're a liability," Frank said to the
Mountie. "Bates, come on out of there. This is Constable
MacKenzie of the Northwest Mounted Police, and he's not
after you. I brought you a horse," he added.

Bates skulked out from behind the boat, but he kept
a wary eye on MacKenzie. The river bums along the strand
had all scuttled into their cabins.

"I don't know where Hailey might have gone," Bates
protested as Frank handed him the horse's reins. "I been
thinking about it, I mean. And I don't think I'd be much
help, really, after all. That is, he could be anywhere, and
I—"

"Get on the horse!" Frank bellowed, and Bates
climbed up, still blathering. "*Ride!* That way, north, where
the vigilante committee started their expedition." He
smacked his hat down on the rump of Bates's horse, and
the animal leapt obligingly forward in the right direction,
snapping Bates's head back. MacKenzie looked at Frank
with respect. "I don't have time," Frank muttered. "And I
do not suffer fools gladly."

"Well, I'll make a note of that," said MacKenzie.

Frank found it hard to get used to the fact that it
never got dark. They rode in continuous sun, weirdly at
odds with his pocket watch. Tracking Hailey at first was
easy. They had only to follow the churned-up ground
where the self-appointed Dawson City Citizens' Posse had
galumphed across the tundra, obliterating any tracks
except their own but providing a path as obvious as a
highway. After a few miles Frank could see where the
posse had drawn rein and made several false casts into a
stand of woods. Frank could imagine them scratching their
heads and carrying on a conversation that would have been
surefire on vaudeville, replaying the motif of "Where did
he go?"

Certainly, as he said irritably to MacKenzie, the posse

had erased Hailey's trail beautifully for him. "Probably sitting in a tree over their heads the whole time," he grumbled.

MacKenzie's blue eyes opened innocently. "With his horse?" he asked.

Frank shot him a sideways glance and didn't answer. He was beginning to wonder if MacKenzie was as transparent as he seemed or if he was making fun of him some of the time.

He scouted the edges of the wood, looking for some sign, while Bates sat his horse morosely and waited. Frank's dogs snuffled briefly in the grass and then went back to Bates. Apparently they did not have any bloodhound in them. A low whistle from a clump of birches made Frank swing his horse toward MacKenzie.

"Looks as if he went north." MacKenzie was on foot, staring at some significant sign that escaped Frank entirely.

"Looks like he did," Frank said. How on earth could MacKenzie tell?

They rounded up Bates and headed out, and in a few minutes Frank saw the clear print of Hailey's horse in the mud. He looked at MacKenzie with grudging respect. They rode on, into the eerie gloom of a midsummer midnight.

"He's holed up in the mountains somewhere," MacKenzie said finally. He yawned. "Fool's probably lost. I thought sure he'd head for the border."

"Do we get to sleep now?" Frank inquired. "I'm falling off my horse."

"Law enforcement takes strong men," MacKenzie said.

Frank ignored him. He stared up at the mountains rising ahead, deceptively near. It was at least another day's ride, just to their foot. Hailey might have traveled that far, but no more. And it wasn't likely to snow and cover his tracks, even though it was getting cold again. Frank shivered. The upland slopes, where the permafrost was no more than eighteen inches below the surface, were sparse and thin of shelter, carpeted with dwarf birch trees, Labrador tea shrubs, and blueberry bushes. To find a place to hide, you would have to go up, into crevices in the rock and caves of ice. To build a fire, you had better have brought wood with you.

Bates hadn't said anything for the past two hours. He just hung on to the saddle, bumping miserably along. He looked dully at MacKenzie, and when the Mountie said, "All right, we'll stop," he climbed stiffly down.

They built a fire and spread their bedrolls in a stand of cottonwoods where the ground was relatively dry. The smoke from green wood was acrid and choking, but it drove the mosquitoes away. Frank emptied a can of beans and a can of tomatoes into a pot from his bedroll and set it in the fire. He rinsed out one of the cans in the cold stream that burbled just beyond the trees, filled it with water, then set it on the fire to boil for coffee. MacKenzie watched him without comment. Frank whistled under his breath. He peeled a potato and tossed it in, while Bates sniffed the air hungrily. Bates's nose was red, and he looked as if he were catching a cold. It was completely dark now, which meant that it was about one in the morning. It suddenly struck Frank as excruciatingly funny to be cooking a hobo's meal on an open fire in the middle of the night with a Canadian Mountie. Bates was a more plausible part of the picture; he was just another fellow on the run from somewhere, another wanderer—just like Frank, just like his pal Hailey up in the mountains somewhere, running from his own stupidity.

Bates shivered and scooted closer to the fire. "Are you sure he's gone up there?" The man looked northward through the darkness toward the high walls of ice.

"He's headed that way," MacKenzie said. "Maybe he'll get lucky."

"You mean he might get away?"

"He means we might find him before he freezes to death," Frank said.

"Or annoys a bear," MacKenzie put in.

"Or breaks his leg on the ice," Frank said.

"Aw, God." Bates put his head in his hands. "How could he go and do something like that? How could he make me come out here after him? I'm so cold. This whole damn country is cold. I ain't never going to get warm again."

"Here." Frank gave him a bowl of beans and tomatoes and a tin cup of coffee. He felt repentant. Bates sounded as if he was on the edge.

MacKenzie wolfed down the food. In the firelight he finally looked rumpled; the spit-and-polish Mountie who had graced Peggy's dinner table merged into someone who looked serious and businesslike. Frank watched him with interest, particularly when he noticed MacKenzie watching him back. Bates had begun to snore.

"You spend much time on the road?" MacKenzie asked after a while, as if the question were an idle one, of the utmost triviality.

"I hoboed for a year," Frank said. "After I left home. Off and on."

"You don't sound like a bum. You don't act like one, either."

"Any man's a bum when he can't get work," Frank said. "Just ask Bates here. Ask Hailey."

"Holding up a bank's a drastic solution," MacKenzie said. "You do that?"

"I worked the oil fields awhile. Trooped with a circus awhile. Did some jackleg carpentry. Stoked coal. No banks."

"You known Miss Delaney long?"

"I made her acquaintance in the oil fields," Frank said. "Where she ran a laundry." *And if that's your clumsy way of asking me if I have any claim on her, you can go boil your head.*

MacKenzie crawled into his bedroll beside the fire. "She's a mighty good cook."

"Yep." Frank slid into his own blankets, sandwiched between dogs.

"Mighty pretty, too."

"Yep."

"It's surprising she's not married."

"She has a wooden leg," Frank said. He pulled his coat collar up over his ears.

It was light again in a couple of hours, and they woke not long after sunup—or at least Frank and Rory Mac-Kenzie did, then shook Bates into consciousness.

Halfway to the first slopes of the mountain, the trail they followed grew erratic, as if the horse had been given its head. The tracks meandered through a field of pingos—conical mounds heaved upward by freezing water trapped between the surface and the permafrost. Once, the horse had stopped to crop a clump of stunted grass. Beyond that the trail grew more direct, as if Hailey had taken charge again, however tenuously.

"He's in bad shape," MacKenzie said.

"He's lucky it's not winter," Frank muttered. They shared a disdain for any moron who would rob a bank and then try to hide out in a country in which he was unfit to survive.

Bates heard it in their voices. "You don't know what it was like," he said, his voice quavering. "Packing all those goods over the pass, freezing half to death, near getting drowned in the rapids, being cold all the time—just to get here. And then to find there was nothing for us. Nothing to do but turn around and go home." His voice cracked. "Hailey couldn't take it. He said to me he'd just as soon be dead. It wasn't *fair*!"

"Life's not fair," Frank and MacKenzie said in unison. They looked at each other and chuckled.

The uneasy camaraderie achieved at Bates's expense lasted only until the subject of Peggy Delaney came up again. MacKenzie seemed unable to refrain from marveling at her beauty, her industry (running a laundry all by herself all the way up here), and her culinary talent (what more could a man want than chicken fricassee and cobbler?) and was stupefied when told that such a prize was not yet married.

He waxed eloquent until Frank clenched his teeth and informed MacKenzie that Peggy Delaney and he had an "arrangement." An "understanding."

MacKenzie nodded cheerfully. "But you aren't actually engaged to her?"

"No," Frank said shortly.

"Well, then," said MacKenzie.

In the foothills they lost the trail again, and Frank and MacKenzie left Bates to wait while they fanned out to look for it. They were riding over a scree of loose stone, difficult to leave a sign in. Frank found what he thought might be the track but lost it again. "Moose," said MacKenzie maddeningly when Frank showed him the marks.

Finally MacKenzie picked it up again—or said he did. Frank could see nothing.

The men stopped again for the night, and the temperature dropped suddenly so that the next morning they awoke with chattering teeth to find the previous night's coffee frozen solid. Bates looked uneasily at the gray and forbidding slope above them, studded with ice patches and twisted brush. The gnarled trunks clung like spiders to crevices in the rock, tormented almost beyond recognition. Above them a vulture rode the updraft, a reminder that the northern wilderness tore up the inexperienced.

"I expect we'll get the money back anyway," MacKenzie said. "If the critters haven't got in his pack yet."

Bates blanched.

"They like paper," MacKenzie explained. "They line their dens with it."

IX

Outside Santiago

Tim had followed the Rough Riders as they climbed San Juan Hill behind General Hawkins's infantry. The Spanish had been cleared from the heights, but they were by no means gone. Bullets ripped through the air from either side. The hill was steep, and the men scrambled diagonally, grabbing at the thick grass for handholds. They paused, breathing hard, in the lee of the crest, shielded from Spanish fire, and then made the final scramble for the blockhouse.

Its walls were pocked, hit by rifle fire and Gatling guns. The yellow hard-packed clay around the building was splotched with blood. The blockhouse was the commandeered villa of a rich Cuban, its walls now banked window-high with earth and revetments made of saplings. The red tile roof sagged around a hole blown by artillery shelling. Just to one side stood an open mess-hall shed with a roof of corrugated iron, sheltering two huge iron pots, one still warm and full of beans. Four soldiers had leaned a door against the pots and were firing their weapons from behind the makeshift shield. Nobody touched the beans—they knew better—there was no telling what the Spanish had put in them. Still, every so often a sergeant would come by and warn, "Don't eat the beans."

A battery came up but was driven back again by the

bigger Spanish guns outside Santiago. Its captain, unwilling to risk the horses, whose numbers were dwindling rapidly under Spanish fire, ordered the cannons dragged away by the soldiers.

Tim crawled to the edge of the heights to look at the Spanish trenches dug around the city. He noticed Lieutenant Stock, the big man from Kansas, and a row of journalists on the ridge near him. Tim scooted over to Stock's side.

"Keep your head down," the lieutenant said. And then the officer dropped, blood spouting from his neck, and bumped against Tim's shoulder. Tim recoiled but kept himself from jumping to his feet.

"Sit down!" someone shouted. "God damn it, Crane!"

Tim looked up and was infuriated to see a thin form in a long raincoat pacing up and down the ridge and giving away their presence. The elongated figure in the raincoat paid no attention.

"Get down!" A bullet whined past the heads on the ridge, and the speaker flattened himself, howling curses.

Tim scrambled forward. Another bullet zinged by him. Tim got to his feet and ran. He saw Richard Harding Davis coming toward Crane from the other side.

Tim grabbed Crane by the arm. "Get down!" he shouted. "You're drawing Spanish fire!"

"They won't hit me," said Crane. "I have a better view from up here."

"Yeah, but it's safer where we are," Davis said. "Unless, of course, someone is out in front of you, attracting fire."

"Oh! Sorry." Crane seemed to notice for the first time that he might get someone besides himself shot. He obediently accompanied Tim and Davis back to the huddled line of journalists.

The Spanish fire slowed to an occasional shot. Tim wriggled on hands and knees to the blockhouse, wondering what on earth Crane had been doing. Paying his dues to the House of Chance, maybe.

Inside the blockhouse, Tim propped himself against a corner and began to write, his first uninterrupted moments all day.

How could he describe the chaos? he wondered. How was it possible to put his readers in the midst of battle without nauseating them? Not being able to shoot back was beginning to make him twitch. He wanted to pick up a rifle and fire. Forget description; he wanted to kill someone to make up for all the good men who were dead. *Fine logic there,* he thought. *You really have a grip on things, Holt.*

Hugo came and flopped down beside him. He had a nick in his ear from a Mauser bullet, and it bled with a steady drip-drip on his sketchbook. Hugo swore and rummaged in his pockets for his first-aid kit. He put sticking plaster on his ear and went on drawing.

"Place is filling up with journalists," he said under his breath. "Nearly as many as there are troops. I saw you hauling Crane off that ridge. He's an odd bird."

"We're all odd birds," Tim muttered, "or we wouldn't be here. I can't even figure myself out, so I'm not going to start on Crane. This is a ridiculous life for a sane man."

Hugo began to whistle between his teeth. Tim wondered how odd a bird Hugo was, if it came to that. The war seemed to be bringing out something dormant and unstable in Hugo.

Tim concentrated on finishing his article, then got up and restlessly paced outside the blockhouse. Night was falling. The hills were slowly turning lavender. He stopped as many passing soldiers as he could and asked, "Have you seen a man with a moving-picture camera?"

All he got were the blank stares of dog-tired men. "A what?" they asked.

"He was at El Caney," one finally said.

The sun, hot and shimmering, dropped behind the western hills. The sky deepened from blue to purple. As if on some mutual signal, the Spanish firing stopped, and a bugle on the heights blew the "cease fire."

From the shadowy dusk a loaded mule came clambering up the crest from Bloody Ford, led by a thin figure with a slouch hat.

Tim let out a joyful hoot and a halloo, and the brothers danced in a circle, stamping their feet and yelling in relief.

"Where have you been?"

"El Caney. Some idiot thought we could take it in two hours. It looks like a slaughterhouse."

"We took this hill this afternoon," Tim said. "After lying out at the ford for an hour and letting the Spanish shoot us like fish in a barrel. I don't know if we can hold the position. I don't think the generals do, either."

Hugo came out straightening his jacket and carrying his dispatch case. He smiled when he saw Mike. "Glad you're in one piece, old man. I'm going down to Siboney, if the boss has finished his opus." He cocked an eye at Tim.

"It's as finished as it's going to get," Tim said. "Since I can't explain why we did it, I just reported it. You know the infantry that gave cover to that battery pulling out? They had twenty percent casualties."

Mike gave a low whistle. "Ten percent is supposed to be the point at which demoralization sets in."

"See if there are any supplies in Siboney yet," Tim said to Hugo. "If so, try to get us some. We're down to hardtack and green coffee." Behind them, two sergeants were pouring out the kettle of beans, just in case anyone felt tempted.

"And be careful, damn it. You're enjoying this too much."

Tim and Mike saw Hugo off down the hill, then they sank wearily beneath a battered tree. In the direct line of fire from the Gatlings and the Spanish rifles, it was nearly leafless. Broken branches hung at odd angles, and splintered ends pointed upward. They reminded Tim of human bones. He had seen enough of those. Surgeons in the field had been splinting bones with palm fronds for lack of anything better to work with.

There was a bird in the tree now, a fat sparrow,

feathers fluffed for the night. It sang sleepily to itself above their heads.

Tim chuckled. "He was hopping up and down earlier, when the Mauser fire was coming in, just having a fit and cursing out the bullets. It's a wonder he didn't get splattered."

"Too little to hit," Mike said. "Tim . . ." He paused. "There's a corpse over there. I can see its hand."

"Whose is it?" Tim asked.

"What difference does it make?" Mike said. "He's mostly under a bush. It was the hand that caught my eye."

"Well, just leave him there," Tim said. "The Spanish aren't going to come get him, and there won't be anybody here to bury him."

"I don't think I can," Mike said. "Now that I know he's here."

"Does he smell?"

"No, he's just . . . there."

"Well, I guess we'd better do something about him, then." Tim got up, his knees and elbows creaking, and he and Mike dragged the dead soldier out from the thornbush where he had died and peered at him in the deepening darkness. He was Spanish, so they rolled him down the hillside away from them, and somebody below shrieked into the night, then swore up at them.

They lay back down under the tree.

"There aren't any onions or potatoes," Mike said.

"There isn't any ammunition, either," Tim added.

"Or bacon."

None of this was news. Every man in camp knew the deficiencies.

"The Spanish guns are bigger than ours," Tim remarked. "Our big guns are all in pieces at Tampa or out on the boats."

"How would we get them up here anyway, through all that mud? The trail's full of mired mules as it is."

"Bad situation," Tim said. "I'm glad we aren't in charge. What do you suppose Shafter's going to do?"

They drifted off to restless sleep under the tree while the generals at El Pozo debated that. The road between the San Juan Heights and the command base was a bog. Wet, exhausted men were paying two dollars for an eight-cent plug of tobacco—when they could find one. The Spanish were well dug in along their inner line of defense before Santiago and were probably preparing for a counterattack.

Whether San Juan Heights could be held was debatable, and Shafter considered falling back five or six miles just to shorten his supply lines. He wired the War Department that he might do that, and the department was aghast. What would the American public think? the War Department wanted to know.

In the morning Shafter heaved his bulk off his cot and wrote to the Spanish commander inside Santiago, demanding a complete and immediate surrender.

Tim chuckled when he heard about it. "Shafter's got nerve."

"We had better hope the Spanish do it," Hugo said. His eyes were dark-smudged. He had been out all night, down to the coast and back in the darkness. But he had news. "Everything at headquarters is a bigger mess than it is here. Shafter's got heatstroke, and no bloody wonder with his weight. And Joe Wheeler's up here somewhere, fever and all, the stubborn old goat. The field hospitals have been working by candlelight all night. I watched a surgeon take a man's arm off by the light of an orderly's candle. There's fever at Siboney and El Pozo, too."

"Where was Rafe?" Tim asked.

"Right where he was supposed to be. He scooted in when I signaled. He took the dispatches to the cable at Jamaica. He said to tell you that you were a long-winded bastard and that the army would never let him put all that through from Guantánamo. He wired Elizabeth and wants you to know that the ladies are in good spirits. He'll wire again to let them know that *we* are."

"I wouldn't describe it that way," Tim murmured.

"He can describe it that way to your wife, you idiot," Mike said. "Worry her with the truth *after* the fact."

"Rafe went out to the *Olivette*," Hugo said, before the brothers could fall into one of the philosophical arguments they pursued when overtired and underfed. Some men hallucinated under those circumstances; the Holts tried to find the meaning of life. "Charley Lawrence says the ship's filling up with yellow-fever cases on top of the malaria, and they desperately need more doctors. That's what's got me worried. I'm afraid of its spreading to Tampa." Hugo's light mood faded, and he looked despairingly at Tim. "Why did you let Rosebay and Elizabeth come with us?"

"Because I'd sooner have lain under a freight train than tried to stop them," Tim retorted. "Why didn't *you* forbid Rosebay to come? Exert your husbandly authority?"

"Don't be an ass," Hugo rejoined, casting aside any deference due the boss. "After *you* said she could come?"

"I'm not married to her," Tim snapped.

"Sometimes I think you have more influence than I do, despite that." Hugo looked at him bleakly. "Sometimes I think you might as well be."

"Now look here!" Tim's voice had a note that made Mike look at him suspiciously. "If you wanted her to stay home, you should have made her stay home."

"I wish I had," Hugo said. "But I'm a selfish devil and wanted her with me." His mood shifted again suddenly, into penitence. "Now I'm worried sick." He looked it, too.

"Rafe says they're fine," Mike said, trying to put a stop to this conversation. "Worry about getting back to them in one piece."

Tampa

In Tampa, the women were not so much concerned about disease as they were about bullets, only because reports of malaria and yellow jack hadn't reached them.

Elizabeth, Rosebay, and Eden tried to reassure one another; with nothing to do but wait, it was impossible not to think about all the awful things that might befall one's beloved in wartime. The afternoon that they heard the first accounts of the battle for San Juan Hill, they went down to tea in the hotel lobby, and Elizabeth brought a flask of rum that she had acquired somewhere. They poured liberal doses of it into their iced tea to lend conviction to their repeated litany: "They'll be all right. You aren't supposed to shoot at correspondents."

"Who's not?" Eden asked, balking.

"Anyone," Rosebay said. "They're neutral. That's why they don't carry guns."

"They *all* have guns," Elizabeth said. "Pistols, anyway. I've been telling myself all afternoon that correspondents are neutral. But how can the Spanish respect that when our newspapers stirred up the war to begin with?"

"Well, the soldiers aren't supposed to shoot at them," Rosebay said. She took a drink of her tea and wrinkled her nose. "This stuff tastes awful."

"It needs sugar," Eden said, then waved at a waiter and had him bring them a sugar bowl and some mint. "Try that. It might be sort of like a mint julep."

"It might not. Anyway, I wouldn't drink one of those." Rosebay put some mint and sugar in the glass anyway.

"At least it'll kill the taste," Eden said.

Rosebay glanced at Elizabeth, who didn't seem to need the taste of hers killed. She took a long swallow and tucked her feet under her high-backed wicker chair. She was watching a peacock parade on the lawn in front of the oleander bushes. He fanned his tail for an admiring peahen.

"Isn't he pretty?" Eden said dreamily.

"He's practically brainless," Elizabeth pointed out.

"Mike would love him," Eden said. "He's such a wonderful counterpoint to the sand and the fleas and the dirt. He's just like this hotel."

"I think he'd be a better metaphor for this war," Elizabeth grumbled.

"Aren't you oversimplifying?" Eden asked. "I'll accept the peacock as a symbol for the sillier aspects of male rivalry, but I can't see the war as a mating dance."

"It's a contest for dominance," Elizabeth said.

"But the peacock's only interested in dominance over females." Eden poured more rum into her tea. "This isn't bad. And there were more important reasons for this war. The peacock isn't interested in democracy or the price of sugar."

"He isn't equipped to be," Elizabeth said. "But insofar as he's capable, what he wants is to run his world—be the head bird."

The peacock outside the window rattled his tail feathers. The sound reminded Rosebay of shaking a beaded curtain.

"That's because the head bird gets all the girls," Eden said. "I think birds are more interested in sex than people are. They haven't any other interests to distract them."

She and Elizabeth chuckled, and Rosebay watched them uncertainly. This was the kind of conversation that Tim and Hugo enjoyed with each other, and she never really minded being left out. But it felt strange when it was two other ladies, as if they had crossed somehow into some masculine world that no one had ever taught Rosebay to be interested in. She *wasn't* interested in it, to tell the truth. She worked all of her life because she had to, not because she wanted to be like a man. She supposed she wanted to vote, although now that she was safely married to Hugo, the necessity for it seemed less urgent than it once had.

Rosebay couldn't rid herself of the feeling that Tim had picked the wrong wife. Rosebay wanted to talk about women's things, and how nice it would be to have the men home, and how maybe this time, finally, she might manage to get in the family way. But she couldn't confide that in someone like Elizabeth. Why hadn't Tim picked a wife she could be *friends* with, trade recipes with, talk about their husbands with? Elizabeth never said anything intimate about Tim, and Rosebay longed for her to. It would have made her feel less as if she had completely lost him.

Elizabeth and Eden were looking at the peahen now, who seemed happy with the male's display.

"He's all feathers and no substance," Eden warned the peahen through the open window. "Has he got a job?"

"Does he have money in the bank?" Elizabeth asked. "Is he prepared to support your children? Will he sit on the eggs when you go to the dressmaker?"

The peahen cocked her head sideways as if listening to them. Elizabeth leaned out the open window and threw her a macaroon. The peahen picked it up, then shook it in her beak. She broke a piece off and swallowed it.

"What are his politics?" Elizabeth asked the peahen. "How does he stand on free silver and the tariff bill?"

The peacock noticed the rest of the macaroon and stole it.

"Oh, dear," Eden said. "I'm afraid he'll run off with an oriole and leave you and all the little babies to starve."

"When do you think we'll hear again?" Rosebay asked. She wanted to talk about how worried she was over the men, wanted to say it out loud enough times to make sure God knew how she felt, wanted to pick at the worry as a kind of catharsis.

Eden and Elizabeth turned back from the window. "I don't really know," Elizabeth said gently. "I'm sure we'll hear from Rafe again soon. He's being quite good, actually. I've known him to fail to mention far more critical intelligence."

"What could be more critical?" Rosebay demanded. She felt somewhat proprietary about Rafe Murray, also. He was one of her pet boarders, and when Tim had first taken up with Elizabeth, Rosebay had been annoyed to learn that Rafe had known Elizabeth for years.

"Well, there was the time he was supposed to get married," Elizabeth said. "The bride called it off by hitting

him with a waffle iron and throwing him out of the flat
they were already sharing. Rafe neglected to inform any of
the wedding guests—probably because he was on a
bender—so there we all were, in our Sunday hats, our
arms full of presents, prepared to launch him properly on
the sea of domestic bliss. The church door was locked.
Eventually we all went home."

Eden giggled appreciatively.

"I see," Rosebay said. She felt as if both the bender
and the unsuitable bride might be Elizabeth's fault, if only
for encouraging him. "I'm very fond of Rafe," she added
defensively.

"So are we all," Elizabeth said.

The peacocks outside the window exploded in a
sudden flurry of squawks and feathers, and the women
turned to see what was happening. A barefoot girl in a
faded gingham dress came at a dead run through the birds
and raced around the side of the hotel. Her two black
braids flew out behind her.

"That's Rosie!" Elizabeth said.

Before she could stand up, the child had rocketed
through the lobby, her eyes searching.

"You can't come in here." The headwaiter tried to
shoo her back out, flapping his hands as if she were a
chicken.

"I want to see Señora Holt!" The child dodged around
him. She saw Elizabeth and scooted around a potted palm
and past a startled trio of waiters. "Señora Holt! Mama's
got another one!"

"Another—?"

"She got another soldier! She caught him with Lupita,
kissing her behind the house. I remembered what you say
about if she kills him." Rosie looked at her imploringly.

"What is she doing with him now?" Elizabeth asked,
rising.

"She got him in the cellar, and she won't let him out."

"Good God," Elizabeth whispered. "Well, she can't
keep him there."

Eden shook out her skirts. "I'm coming with you," she announced. "I wouldn't miss this for worlds. Lead the way, Rosie."

They walked through the lobby with the child between them, leaving Rosebay looking uncertainly after them. She didn't follow.

"Can't you go any faster?" Rosie tugged at them.

"Not in these shoes," Elizabeth said firmly. She lifted a hand to the doorman on the veranda and signaled her desire for a carriage.

Rosie's eyes shone as it rolled around the circular drive from the stand at the side of the hotel. Once seated inside the carriage, Rosie surveyed the hotel grounds, the sandy road, and the decrepit town from its lofty heights. "I never rode in a carriage before. Lupita almost did, but that was when Mama tried to kill the soldier. The first soldier," she amended.

"Where on earth did she find another one to get in trouble with?" Elizabeth wondered. "Quartermaster's Corps, I suppose. They must still be left. Most of their supplies certainly are. It makes you wonder what the poor soldiers in Cuba are *eating*."

"He brought Lupita peas in a tin," Rosie said. "And coffee."

"Enterprising of him," Elizabeth said. She tapped the driver on the shoulder. "I think we had better go a little faster."

"Yes, ma'am." The driver touched his hat and flicked the whip, and the hotel's carriage horse picked up some speed. The set of the driver's back gave the ladies to understand that it was not his job to question why they were going downtown with an unsavory ragamuffin, but he did not approve.

"You wait," Elizabeth said firmly to him outside the shack that Rosie said was her home. "You wait however long it takes."

They went in apprehensively, half expecting the floor to be awash in blood, but nothing seemed to have happened yet. Lupita was sniffling on a bed in a corner of the one room. There was another bed, covered like the first in a worn quilt, plus a stove, a table and four chairs, and a crucifix on the wall. It was spotlessly clean despite the shabbiness. Small luxuries signaled that Señora Verdugo was a thrifty housekeeper—a rug on the wooden floor, a porcelain statue of the Blessed Virgin in a niche, a polished copper coffeepot. Señora herself sat firmly in an armchair over what looked like a trapdoor.

"They are at it again," was the first thing she said to Elizabeth. "For a while they are better, but now they are at it again."

"You cannot keep him down there," Elizabeth said firmly. "He'll suffocate." She wondered how Señora Verdugo had got a young and healthy man stuffed into a root cellar, but it was obvious she was a woman of determination. And there was the fish knife.

"I let him out, what will you do with him?" Señora demanded.

Elizabeth looked startled.

"If you save his life, you own him," Eden said to her. "Old Chinese custom."

"Nobody here is Chinese," Elizabeth pointed out. "Señora Verdugo, you really have to get off that door."

"Hmph," Mama said. But she slid her chair sideways.

Elizabeth bent down and lifted the iron handle. The trapdoor creaked up. She saw two panic-stricken eyes looking up at her. "Out," Elizabeth ordered.

The boy crawled out. Elizabeth didn't know whether to be dismayed or relieved that it wasn't the same boy as last time.

"Mi corazón!" Lupita jumped up from her bed and tried to fling her arms around him. The boy looked at her warily and backed away.

"Sit down!" Mama bellowed, and Lupita retreated to the bed again, pouting.

The soldier, appearing to notice for the first time that no one was holding a knife on him, hurled himself suddenly across the room and out the open window. He took to his heels up the street.

Lupita leaned out the window after him. "He is gone," she said. She glared at her mother. "See what you do? You make me a laughingstock. Now no boys will go with me."

"No Americano boys will go with you, that's right. You wait for a Cubano boy, and in the meantime I make sure you stay fit for him!" She looked at her younger daughter. "You be glad you're too young for all this foolishness."

Elizabeth and Eden fled, leaving Rosie waving at them from the front stoop. "We have to see the quartermaster," Elizabeth said.

"Absolutely," Eden agreed. "We'll give him an earful."

How much good the earful did, Elizabeth wasn't sure, when they finally alighted again at the hotel, but they had given it their best, taking turns protesting the outrages committed by the quartermaster's men in seducing the local damsels with tinned peas. He had seemed more upset about the peas than anything else, promising vengeance for thievery from the United States government.

"Oh, well," Eden said, "if they don't have presents to give them, the situation should improve some."

Elizabeth gripped her arm. "That's the boy from the cable office. He's coming our way."

They braced themselves for whatever the news from Tim might be, but the boy bypassed Elizabeth and gave the cable to Eden instead.

"It isn't from Tim," Eden said, her eyes widening. "It's from Janessa. She says they're calling for doctors with experience in tropical diseases. She'll be here in three days! I can't tell if they're setting up a hospital here or going on to Cuba. Nobody ever explains anything in a telegram."

X

North of Dawson

Frank and MacKenzie found the horse first, lying wedged in a crevice. One foreleg was folded under in the way that a stuffed toy bends when it is pushed into a space too small for it. Frank swore under his breath. The horse was still alive, and it watched them desolately as they scrambled up the rocks. The dogs sniffed curiously at it.

Frank knelt by the horse's head. They had left their own mounts below, having more sense than to try to take them up the mountain. Its nose and mouth were matted with ice and its eyes half glazed with pain. "Son of a bitch," Frank hissed. "Son of a son of a bitch." He pushed the dogs away and pulled out his pistol, then stroked the horse's forehead and scratched it between the ears. "Hush, then. Hush." He crooned softly to it and put the pistol against its head.

The shot reverberated in the battlements of rock and ice, flung itself far out across the valley floor where the pingos were growing—winter bulbs pushing through the earth. From here Frank could see that they were concave at the top, cupping clear water, snow goblets thrown on an arctic wheel. *What are we doing up here? Human beings don't belong here.* Quick tears slid down his face, and he angrily brushed them away.

MacKenzie didn't look any more cheerful when he scrambled up to Frank with Bates in tow. "I hate like hell to shoot a horse," he muttered.

149

"So did Hailey, apparently," Frank said with a vicious glance at Bates. "He probably didn't want us to hear the gunshot, the sniveling, weaseling coward."

Bates didn't say anything. He looked morosely at his toes, then turned his head away from the horse as they climbed past it. What they were following wasn't really a trail but merely a series of hand- and footholds among the rocks where MacKenzie, in the lead, said that Hailey had gone. Hailey was panicked now, the Mountie said, reading faint sign in broken twigs and tumbled stones. There was no point in going where he was headed; he was climbing blindly to reach nothing.

They kept moving upward. Frank's dogs lay down at noontime and declined to accompany the men any farther. MacKenzie stopped and stared upward. Frank felt uneasy, perceiving the presence of a terrified creature in the rocks above them. Fairly certain that Hailey was still alive, Frank wondered if the man was crazy enough with cold and exposure to shoot his only hope of rescue.

He tilted his head back and shouted, "Hailey!"

No answer. The name echoed among the rocks and lingered like the gunshot.

"Hailey!"

MacKenzie got a grip on Bates's shoulder. "All right, bud, this is what you came for. We've got to know where he is."

Bates twisted under MacKenzie's hand. "What if he starts shooting?"

MacKenzie tightened his grip. "He hasn't yet."

Bates took a deep breath. "Marcus! Marcus Hailey! It's Tom! Can you hear me?"

"We want to help you out of here!" Frank shouted. "Listen to Tom!"

Bates stared with rheumy eyes at the rocks. "Can you hear me, Marcus?" he yelled.

Frank thought he heard some faint noise from above. He flattened himself against the rock face, out of the line

of possible fire. MacKenzie grinned, but Frank noted that
the Mountie did the same thing.

MacKenzie cupped his hands around his mouth.
"Come on out and give up!" The words boomed up the
mountain.

"Go to hell!" The words came feebly down. There was
a crack in the voice.

"Give up now, and you won't get hurt," MacKenzie
shouted.

Frank, thinking of the horse, gritted his teeth. He
would have liked to tear the fugitive limb from limb.

MacKenzie jabbed Bates in the ribs. "Marcus," Bates
yelled, "let us come up."

"Go away, you damn fool," Hailey shouted down.

"I *can't* go away!" Bates complained. "They won't let
me. Come on down. You aren't going to make it if you
don't."

"I don't care anymore if I make it!"

"You will if we go off and leave you here," MacKenzie
shouted. "I'm Constable MacKenzie of the Northwest
Mounted Police, and I'm coming up. If you've got a gun,
you'd better not wave it around. There are three of us."

The Mountie started to climb, doggedly hauling
himself up precarious handholds, his boots slipping on the
cold stone. Bates sat down on an outcrop while Frank
followed MacKenzie up a track that only mountain goats
could have followed safely. Hailey must have been driven
by sheer desperation, Frank thought, to have gotten so
high.

He must have heard them coming. A bullet whined
past Frank's ear and ricocheted off the rock face beside
him, then zinged crazily off again. MacKenzie swore.

"You'd better put that gun down!" Frank yelled.

They inched upward, even more cautiously now.
Another bullet came down from above with a sharp crack
and knocked away a chunk of rock the size of a dinner
plate as it hit. Frank drew his own pistol and fired upward
to let Hailey know he had a gun. He was careful to aim into

the sky, though. He had no desire to have his own fire come back in his face.

"If you shoot us, you're going to die out here!" Frank shouted.

There was no more fire from above, after that.

They found Hailey crouched where he had stopped, trapped, walled in by rock on two sides and by a four-foot-wide chasm on the other. He had lost his hat, and his shirt was ribboned by the rock. Now he waited, cradling a pistol in both hands. The barrel wavered ominously, and Frank flinched when he saw that it was still cocked. Lichens on the rock showed where Hailey had gone to the precipice's edge and back, intending to jump but stopped by fear.

"You don't want to shoot us," Frank said in conversational tones. He loosened his own gun in its holster again.

"Give it here, son." MacKenzie held out his hand.

Hailey looked up at him, mouthing silent words. He might have been Bates's age, but just then he looked both older and younger. His terror and despair were that of a child lost and bewildered. His skin was stretched taut with fear, and there was a tic beside his left eye.

Hailey took in MacKenzie's scarlet jacket and the badge pinned to Frank's coat, then shook his head. Frank crept a little closer, and the man's gun wobbled around toward him.

"Hand it over," MacKenzie said again.

Hailey didn't speak. Frank was beginning to wonder if he could, now. He looked as if whatever thoughts were behind his eyes had turned inward, folded themselves around their own core. The North did that to people.

Hailey looked back toward MacKenzie. Frank edged a little closer. He didn't want to shoot Hailey. Frank had had enough of shooting, after the horse. And if he tried, Hailey would probably wing at least one of them—that pistol wasn't empty yet—and then where would they be? Frank waited, his tension building, building.

He waited an instant too long. Suddenly something snapped in Hailey, and he lifted the pistol and fired, the gun barrel wavering wildly. Frank felt the bullet pass by his cheek, heard its swift hum and then the splatter of rock below. Hailey *was* crazy enough to shoot them. Frank leapt on him, hoping Hailey couldn't make up his mind to pull the trigger again that quickly. The gun went off beside his ear, and they sprawled on the stone, Hailey momentarily on top.

"You bastard," Frank snarled into Hailey's collar. "You bastard! I shot your horse for you. I'm going to throw you right off that ledge, see how you like it."

Hailey's teeth sank into Frank's shoulder, and Frank kneed him in the groin. Hailey grunted. A huge hand reached down and plucked Hailey off him by the collar. The gun lay at Frank's elbow. He patted himself, feeling for bullet holes, and found none.

MacKenzie, businesslike, handcuffed the prisoner. "You're lucky you didn't kill yourself with a ricochet," he informed Hailey.

"Should have," Hailey said thickly. His tongue looked swollen, and the words came with effort. He sat where MacKenzie had put him, his back to the cold stones. "I thought about it. Couldn't find water once I got up here."

MacKenzie handed over his canteen without comment, but Frank looked ready to jump Hailey again. "You were ready to kill yourself and not the horse?"

"I thought maybe I could get him loose," Hailey said. Water dribbled down his chin.

"You dumb shit—his leg was broken!" Frank exploded.

"Oh."

MacKenzie and Frank looked at each other in shared disgust.

MacKenzie found Hailey's pack and riffled through it. The money was there. MacKenzie ran his fingers through the notes, stuffed loose into the pack, and shook his head with honest bewilderment. Frank had more sympathy for Hailey in that regard. He didn't suppose Constable Upright had ever stolen so much as an apple off a neighbor's tree. Frank's hobo days had taught him that theft might mean survival, and finding the notion repugnant didn't make a man less hungry. Robbing a bank was going too far, however.

MacKenzie slung Hailey's pack over his own shoulders. By mutual consent the Mountie and Frank each took the handcuffed prisoner by one arm and began leading him, none too gently, down the mountain. They stopped where they had left Bates, to see what would happen.

Bates was still sitting on his rock and looking as miserable as Hailey. "They swore they wouldn't hurt you," he offered.

Hailey didn't answer him. He gave MacKenzie an agonized look. "What are they going to do to me?"

Frank thought that the reality of the situation was beginning to sink into Hailey's consciousness for the first time.

"You'd better get ready to do some time, son," MacKenzie said equably. The fact that he was younger than Hailey seemed not to perturb him. MacKenzie's approach to law enforcement was paternal.

"Oh, God . . ." Hailey whimpered.

The dogs were waiting for them on the way down. They sniffed Hailey dubiously. Vultures were already beginning to feed on the dead horse.

The four men camped for the night in a forest of stunted spruce and hemlock contorted by wind and altitude—the timberline is low in the North. Hailey, handcuffed, had been riding behind Bates's saddle, with Frank ahead and MacKenzie in the rear. When they stopped and motioned him to get down, he looked at them dolefully. MacKenzie ignored him, but Frank, exasperated, blurted out, "What did you think was going to happen to you? You held up a bank!"

"I didn't know what else to do," Hailey said morosely.

MacKenzie, his back to them, snorted with amusement as he built a fire. Bates looked nearly as depressed as his erstwhile partner.

"And you shot the teller," Frank said, remembering that gentleman's grievances. "He's madder than hell, says he was already handing over the money. You better hope we get you in jail before *he* sees you."

"It was a mistake," Hailey said. "My hand slipped. I was nervous."

"Bank robbing's not a profession for the faint-hearted," MacKenzie said over his shoulder.

"I *told* you not to do it," Bates said.

"Fine for you, Tom," Hailey seethed. "*You* don't have any money. *You* don't have a way to get home, you know so much."

"I'm not going to jail, either!"

"If you have to slink back to Joplin and that girl's father catches you, you might."

Bates was indignant. "I never touched her!" He brooded a moment. "Anyway, it was *you* who said we ought to go to the Yukon."

"I've got some advice for you," Frank said. "Go back to Joplin and marry that poor girl. You'll be safer there than you will be here." He took a length of chain and a padlock out of his pack, slipped it through Hailey's handcuffs, and locked it around a small tree. He went over and sat by MacKenzie.

MacKenzie eyed the chain. "You figure they're planning a jailbreak?"

"I don't know what they're stupid enough to do," Frank said. "I don't want to chase him again. Where's that money?"

"In the pack," MacKenzie said. "Under my elbow. And if you think anybody can get it out without my noticing, you got another think coming."

Frank cut some bacon into a skillet. Hailey's eyes were fixed on it. Frank chuckled. "Dumb ass didn't take any food with him. I don't suppose it ever occurred to him you can't eat paper money."

"Funny what this country does to folks," MacKenzie said. "They go along just fine somewhere, then they take it into their heads to come up here and seem to lose all their good sense. Go off, get lost, freeze to death because they don't have any respect for the wilderness."

"It's not respect," Frank said while he punched open a can of beans. "It's ignorance. They figure it's like taking a hike in the countryside, ten miles out of town."

"Is it? And so where did you get all your vast experience, me boy?" MacKenzie was leaning back against a tree, hands laced behind his head, watching Frank stir the beans and bacon.

"I told you. I hoboed for a year. You get educated fast, or you die."

"And what was the gist of this vast education?"

Frank grinned. "Rob a henhouse if you're hungry. Don't rob a bank."

"Both are stealing," MacKenzie said stiffly.

"True, but one's in proportion to your problem, and the other's not. It's all mathematical," Frank continued with a straight face. "I can work it out for you on paper."

"I never had any head for figures," MacKenzie said with an equally straight face, although he seemed to know that Frank was having *him* on. "I just lock them up for chicken stealing same as bank robbery. That way I don't have to keep track of details."

"You could cook once in a while," Frank suggested, shifting the pan in the coals.

"No talent for it," MacKenzie said comfortably. "I probably ought to get married."

Frank looked at him suspiciously. "What's keeping you from it?" Any man as handsome as Rory MacKenzie could get married. Frank, aware of his own good looks, knew that from experience, even when he had been on the bum. "Shouldn't you be settled down by now?" That MacKenzie wasn't, by his age, might argue a wandering foot, a faithless nature, or something worse.

"That's what me mum says," MacKenzie said sunnily. "She'd be tickled if I brought home a bride. I just never found the right girl so far." He appeared to consider. "Of course, posted to Dawson now, I might have leisure to do some courting. Mostly I haven't been where females are, you know. I guess I'm love starved."

"I'll introduce you to some girls at the Daybreak Saloon," Frank offered. "They're love starved, too."

They rode into Dawson two days later with their prisoner and received a hero's welcome, which seemed to Frank absolutely ridiculous. The citizenry turned out to pump their hands and slap their backs and stare curiously at the dangerous outlaw in their charge. Frank had expected Peggy to be there, but she wasn't.

They took Hailey to the jail and told Bates to scram, to go home to Joplin. Frank saw MacKenzie slip Bates a folded bill on the quiet. "It'll get him downriver anyway," MacKenzie muttered when he saw that Frank had caught him at it.

There was no trial, to the disappointment of the citizenry, who had had a fine time holding citizens' courts up until the arrival of official law. There was an immediate hearing, presided over by Constable MacKenzie, at which the bank manager and the teller were asked to identify their money and Hailey's face, and Hailey was asked what in hell had possessed him.

"Of course that's our money," the bank manager said. "Whose else would it be, in that miscreant's pack?"

"Can you identify it by mark or serial number?" MacKenzie inquired.

"Well, of course I can't. We've never had a robbery, up till now."

The bank teller, very red in the face, couldn't conclusively identify the money, either, but he identified Hailey, over and over. "He's the one. He shot me! Do you think I'm going to forget a man who shot me?" He glared at Hailey. "I was handing him the money, and he shot me. You aren't supposed to do that!"

"Thank you," MacKenzie said. "You're excused." He

turned to Hailey. "You figured out any way to plead innocent to this?"

"I lost my head," Hailey said dolefully. "I couldn't find work, and I was out of money, and I lost my head."

"Well, you found work," MacKenzie said. "Two years at hard labor, but your meals will be free."

Hailey looked stupefied. "Don't I even get a jury?"

"Not out here, son," MacKenzie said. "I'm all there is." He looked around the room, letting his eyes rest on the spectators at the back of the hall. "The mounted police are the law for the Northwest, and being as I am now assigned to Dawson, you folks can lay off any free-lance law enforcement. Anyone taking the law into his own hands from now on will be subject to arrest."

The citizens—shopkeepers, bankers, the few prosperous miners, and unsuccessful cheechakos who were there just for something to do—mumbled among themselves and seemed to decide that Constable MacKenzie's massive frame and official scarlet jacket should be enough to do the trick.

Frank presented his badge to MacKenzie by way of resignation and demanded his last month's pay from Heartache Johnson, who was in attendance in his capacity as mayor, an office MacKenzie had assured him would continue for the supervision of all civic matters.

"You didn't work the full month," Heartache said.

"I got shot at," Frank said. "I got severely inconvenienced enough for *two* months. And if you short my pay, I'll turn you inside out."

"I can't arrest him until *after* he turns you inside out," MacKenzie commented.

"All right, I suppose the council will agree to it." Heartache dug into his pocket. Dawson operated on a cash basis.

Frank stuffed his pay into his denim trousers and tried to figure out how long it would last him. It looked as if he had better do what he had been planning on and put some work into his claim. It wasn't a complete skunk—it yielded enough gold to keep him fed and to have bought the dogs and the horse. But there wasn't anything to speak of left over afterward. For that kind of money, he could go back to the oil fields and not have cold toes all the time. He needed a summer's solid digging to see if he had a vein worth staying with.

"Well, good evening to you, Miss Delaney."

Frank, hearing MacKenzie's voice lilt happily, snapped his head around to see Peggy in the back row, looking like a Sunday-school teacher. Her red hair was fluffed into a fringe in the front under her new straw bonnet, and she had a bunch of silk violets pinned to her breast. She had just come in, despite the fact that she was trying to pretend she'd been there all along.

The bank manager was still in attendance, trying to get MacKenzie to turn over the money to him, but MacKenzie wasn't paying any particular attention to him.

"Miss Delaney, it's a fine thing to see you again."

"I'm relieved that you and Mr. Blake got back safely. I've been worrying and all."

The manager was red in the face. "Constable, I demand the return of the bank's funds. Nobody in their right mind would expect us to have serial numbers."

Frank stepped around him to Peggy. "I didn't see you when we rode in. Where were you?"

Peggy flushed. "I heard you were back, but I—well, I'd been in the washhouse and all, and I looked a fright. I wanted to freshen up."

Frank grinned lopsidedly. "The law appreciates your efforts on its behalf."

"I didn't!" Peggy said indignantly. "I just like to look nice. It's easy to let yourself go up here, get to looking like an old sourdough. And besides, I hoped—" She flushed again. "I hoped you'd stay for dinner with me and bring Constable MacKenzie with you," she finished in a hurry, looking at her toes.

"I'd be delighted," MacKenzie said joyfully.

"Since you look so nice already, and it's a shame to waste it on me?" Frank inquired in an undertone.

Peggy gave him a pleading look. "I just like nice company," she whispered.

"Sure," Frank said. "Maybe we can play pinochle."

"Constable MacKenzie—" The bank manager was losing his temper.

"You'll have to fill out forms," MacKenzie said. "In absence of proven identification." Frank thought the lawman was enjoying himself, taking his pay for having done the dirty work. MacKenzie winked at Peggy. "When I've returned this gentleman's funds, I'll take the time to clean meself up, and then I'll join you with pleasure, ma'am."

Frank took Peggy's hand and patted it. "I need to freshen meself up, too," he said, imitating MacKenzie's faint accent. "But unfortunately, me clothes are at your house."

MacKenzie arrived for dinner in an immaculate scarlet jacket, his blond, curly hair damp from his bath. He had a bottle of champagne under one arm.

Peggy let him in and flew around the partition, behind which Frank was still soaking in a tub. "I told you he'd be here before you were dressed," she hissed. "I *told* you to get out. I'm so mortified I can't look him in the eyes."

"I can't, either," Frank said. "I think maybe he's a little wall-eyed. Haven't you noticed it?"

"Get out of that tub!" She disappeared into the front room again.

When Frank emerged, Peggy was taking a pie out of the oven, and MacKenzie, smoking a pipe, was ensconced in the best chair. Frank's dogs were flopped at his feet.

Peggy had lit candles for the table, and she opened MacKenzie's champagne with dinner. Frank noted that she had just cleaned the house, too. Dust hadn't even had time to settle.

Peggy's face was flushed with the champagne and the heat from the stove, and her blue eyes shone brightly. Maybe she was just starved for a social life, Frank thought. Sourdoughs weren't the most scintillating conversationalists, and the only other women in town were the saloon girls and a minister's wife who never poked her nose outside the door so she wouldn't run into any sin. It wouldn't be a wonder if Peggy was lonesome; Frank was off at his diggings more often than he was in town.

Peggy hummed as she filled their glasses.

"I know that song!" MacKenzie said, delighted. "Me mum used to sing it to us." He joined her in song.

> *"'Tis of a fearless highwayman a story I'll tell*
> *His name was Willie Brennan, and in Ireland*
> *he did dwell."*

Peggy smiled. She started to sing, too, and Frank joined in. They made a fairly decent trio, or maybe it was just the champagne. Over champagne and roasted grouse Frank decided that MacKenzie was fine company. He couldn't fault the man for thinking Peggy was pretty. And after all, Frank thought, MacKenzie would go home, and he would stay.

They finished the grouse and picked the bones clean. Frank and MacKenzie were starved after a week on the trail, and Peggy had worked hard all day and ate accordingly. When they had eaten cherry pie with cream, they sang more old songs that they all remembered, "Cockles and Mussels" and "The Foggy, Foggy Dew."

"Do ye know 'Bonnie George Campbell'?" MacKenzie asked.

Frank noticed that the more they talked to each other, the more Gaelic MacKenzie and Peggy became.

"No, I've not heard that one," Peggy said. "Sing it for me. Sing it for us."

MacKenzie threw his head back. His voice, when he turned it loose, filled the cabin. Peggy's eyes shone. It was

a song a Scot or an Irishman could love—about war and
valor and untimely death. In short, romance.

> *"Saddled and bridled and booted rode he,*
> *A plume in his helmet, a sword at his knee.*
> *But hoom cam his saddle all bloody to see,*
> *Oh, hoom cam his guid horse, but never cam he!"*

"Ah, that's a fine song," Peggy breathed when Mac-
Kenzie had thundered to a close. Heartrending sentiment
appealed to her, in music as well as artwork.

Frank chuckled. Some devil within him that he
couldn't quite explain prompted him to end the evening
with "Careless Love." MacKenzie knew it, too, and Peggy
sang along with them; but she seemed to be uncomfortable.

Frank scratched his dogs' ears and tipped back in his
chair and waited for MacKenzie to go home.

"Don't tip in that chair," Peggy said automatically.

MacKenzie, who had been tipping in his, too, lowered
it. He didn't seem inclined to leave.

"Pity the champagne ran out," Frank said.

"You sound like a lush," Peggy said. "And I can have
a fine time without taking a drink."

"Drink to me only with thine eyes," MacKenzie said.

Frank yawned.

Peggy shifted uncomfortably in her chair.

MacKenzie stood up. "It's been a fine evening,
ma'am," he said to Peggy. "I thank you." He gave Frank a
nod of acknowledgment.

Frank got up lazily after MacKenzie had gone and put
his arms around Peggy's waist. "Good thing the champagne ran out," he said in her ear. "Too much makes you
sleepy."

"Frank, I'm not sure I—" She batted at his hands. "It's
not decent. He's hardly left."

"I know. I thought he never would. Kiss me, my little
plum blossom." Frank's lips tickled her ear.

She let him lead her into the bedroom behind the partition, but it seemed to Frank that she was thoughtful, distracted. She had a dreamy look on her face while he undressed her, and she didn't help much.

"Are you thinking about what to wear to church on Sunday?" Frank demanded, sliding into bed with her. "Or are you thinking about me?"

"Well, neither, I reckon," Peggy said, coming back to earth. Her eyes smiled up at him. "I guess I was woolgathering."

He cupped one bare breast with his hand and squeezed, and she accorded him her full attention. The whole time they made love, however, he had the impression that her attention was wandering.

"Frank, do you ever think about those bushes with the flowers that change colors?" she asked when they lay side by side, her head on his bare chest.

"Huh?" said Frank.

"The ones that are pink or blue—you know them. It depends on what's in the soil, I think."

Frank considered them, a vague memory of balls of blossoms outside a kitchen door. "I can't say I do." He twisted his neck to look at her. All he could see was the top of her head. "I can't say I have any idea what you're talking about."

"Well, about changing," Peggy said. "One day you're pink, and the next week you're blue. I wonder if people can change like that."

Frank chuckled. "They do it all the time. 'Say, what was your name in the States?'"

"I don't mean running off," Peggy said, "with the law after you."

"Or some woman," Frank murmured, thinking of Bates. "Besides"—he prodded her gently in the ribs—"the law's after you. The Northwest Mounted Police happen to think that you are very delectable."

"Oh?" Peggy said slowly. "What makes you think that?"

"I know it for a fact," Frank said. "Constable Mac-Kenzie bared his soul."

"Well, I can't imagine why you would be discussing me with Constable MacKenzie," Peggy said airily. "Anyway, he doesn't have anything to do with it. I was just thinking about life and all."

"Well, Lord knows life's nothing but a series of changes," Frank said. "Lots of them unexpected, not to say inadvertent. That what you mean?"

"I reckon." A long pause. "You going back up to Caribou Creek tomorrow?"

"I'd better," Frank said. "Summer's going fast. Got to wash that dirt before it all freezes up again."

"I think that's a good idea," Peggy said sleepily.

She was unflatteringly eager to see him go, Frank thought. He started to say so, but then he heard her faint, gentle snore as she lay with her head pillowed on his shoulder.

Frank and the dogs set off the next morning and this time made it to Frank's cabin on Caribou Creek without being summoned back. Any lawbreaking that was going on in Dawson was Constable MacKenzie's problem.

Frank went to work as soon as he arrived home and had fed his horse and dogs. Gold lay along the bedrock below the permafrost, the subsoil that never thawed—ten to fifty feet below. After a miner had mucked his way through the muskeg, which was over a foot deep and was frozen in winter and full of mosquitoes in summer, he came to the permafrost. The only way to dig through that, even in the hottest weather, was to set a fire in the shaft. Overnight about six inches of dirt would thaw and could be dug out. A lateral drift could be melted along a vein without timbering—the permafrost supported itself—but it was slow going, six inches a day. In winter the dirt was piled outside the miners' doors, until their cabins were overshadowed by mounds of frozen earth. When the creeks gushed in spring, the men washed the dirt in the running water and followed any faint glint of gold.

Frank washed the rest of the mud he had dug out of his claim during the winter, sluicing it in the now free-running stream. Maddeningly, he found just enough gold in it to lure him on, beckoning him to dig deeper into the creek bank. In the time since he had arrived in the Klondike, some miners had dug two or three skunked shafts and were embarking on yet another. Some had struck it rich and were hiring newcomers to do the digging. Others were still trying to reach bedrock and growing convinced that the permafrost went clear down to China.

Frank descended the twenty-foot ladder in his shaft and crawled into the drift he had started. The vein angled away from the streambed, tantalizingly possible, but the work was infuriatingly slow. He held his lantern up against the drift face. The last buckets he had hoisted up had been the most promising ever. But where did the main vein go? He still couldn't tell. The pay streak that floated on the bedrock, gold-bearing gravel of an ancient streambed, might wander anywhere. It might tease him on and then vanish, only to reappear elsewhere—or nowhere.

Frank slipped into the rhythm of the work with the elastic capacity of the young and healthy. He worked like a horse and ate like one, then fell into bed and into a deep sleep. His muscles grew harder, the calluses returned to his hands. Digging for gold kept a man in better shape than being responsible for upholding the law. He pictured MacKenzie lolling around the sheriff's office—now called the police station—all summer, possibly getting just the slightest bit paunchy.

The drawback was that Frank's work exercised everything but the brain. There was far too much time to think. Hauling buckets to the surface, Frank thought of the latest news from the States. Sluicing dirt in the creek, he reminded himself that he was uninterested in his father's whereabouts. Laying his fire at the end of the drift, he wondered what his mother and sister were doing about it all. Midge would be fourteen now, he realized. Did she miss him?

That was not a subject that Frank wanted to contemplate for long—it made him feel guilty—and to ease its maddening insistence, he told himself stories, recited poetry from memory, and sometimes presented for the dogs' edification the spiel he had learned to deliver with the circus: "Step right up and see the reptile show, vipers coiling a live . . ."

He decided that as soon as he ran out of coffee, he would quit talking to the dogs and make a run into town.

Front Street was as jammed with disappointed arrivals as it had been before. Some of them were being siphoned off on steamers headed downriver to St. Michael, but their numbers seemed to grow no fewer. They sat disconsolately beneath festoons of wire— telephone lines and electricity paid for with the boom they had missed. By the town hall Frank saw a hatless fellow in his undershirt, his brow dripping with sweat. He was chopping wood. Frank noted that he was chained to the foundation of the building by a ring about his ankle. Frank grinned. MacKenzie obviously believed in making a criminal earn his keep.

Frank asked for a five-pound sack of coffee in the dry-goods store and cupped his ear when the clerk told him the price. It was so low, Frank was afraid that talking to dogs all day had affected his hearing.

"You heard right," the clerk grumbled. "We're lucky if we can give it away. So many of these dang fools selling their goods on the street, an honest man can't make a living."

"The same honest men who were charging a three-hundred-percent markup last year?" Frank inquired, paying for the coffee.

"It's the dang Mounties' fault if you ask me," the clerk said. "They're making everyone bring in enough to live on for a year, claiming they'll starve otherwise. They've about put us out of business."

"They *would* have starved if they'd paid last year's prices," Frank said. He looked at the bins of multicolored candies that lined the counter front. "What else is slow on the market?" He thought maybe he'd buy Peggy a present. "A sweet tooth still looks pretty expensive."

The clerk sniffed. "Miners don't drag candy up Chilkoot. Only thing keeping us in sales, nearly."

"I'm sure if it wasn't for presents for the saloon girls, you'd starve," Frank said sarcastically. He inspected jaw-breakers and butterscotch, peppermint drops and rock candy.

"If you're courting a lady, you want chocolates," the clerk said.

"Who's courting?" Frank inquired.

"I figured you were," the clerk said. He chuckled. "If you ain't, you better be."

Frank gave the man a quizzical look, then bought a box of chocolates. He tucked them into his pack with the coffee and rode over to the laundry. Clouds of steam rolled out as he pushed the door open. It was hot enough inside to melt rocks. "Peg?" he shouted through the steam and soapsuds.

She was cranking shirts through the washing machine while a trio of irons heating on the stove added to the temperature. Her red hair hung in wet tendrils around her face. Before she could answer, the door swung open again, and Constable Rory MacKenzie appeared from the yard, incongruous in his red Mountie jacket and his jodhpurs, a copper kettle of water in each hand. He smiled at Frank with every evidence of pleasure, while Peggy looked uneasily from one to the other.

"What brings you to town?" MacKenzie said cheer-fully.

"I ran out of coffee," Frank said. "When did you take up washing for a living? Law enforcement slow these days?"

"Not a bit. I'm just picking up my shirts. Miss Delaney, me dear, I will be on me way."

"Thank you, Rory," Peggy said.

"'Rory'?" Frank raised his eyebrows as MacKenzie departed.

"He only left because you came barging in as if you owned the place," Peggy said, irritated. "You were rude."

"A thousand pardons. Next time I shall do better. I shall listen to you and Mr. MacKenzie speak in Celtic accents to each other all afternoon without complaining. You won't mind if I crawl into the corner and throw up now and again?"

Peggy put her hands on her hips, a gesture that never failed to annoy him. "Frank Blake, you don't have any claim on me, and you know it. I'm right fond of you, but I haven't noticed you trying to sew up the deal."

"I don't go with any other girls," Frank said, indignant.

"And maybe there's more to life than just going with somebody," Peggy retorted. "Frank, you give me one reason I should tie myself down to somebody that's got a wandering foot and a boatload of devilment left to work out."

"I don't really know." Frank felt baffled and hurt in spite of himself. "Are you sharing that bed with him, too?"

"No!" Peggy said. She bit her tongue. "And if I was, it wouldn't be your business." She looked from the wash in the machine to the irons covering the stove. "I got about an hour's work left to do. Are you staying for supper?"

"I guess," Frank said. "I brought you chocolates."

He spent the night with Peggy, but it was hard not to envision Rory MacKenzie's ghost on the other side of her bed and wonder if, and when, it was going to come to that. Annoyingly, Frank couldn't think of any reason why she should be faithful to him, but he had always assumed she would be. He was confused and angry.

He stayed four days in town, but everywhere he went he seemed to encounter Constable MacKenzie. MacKen-

zie was unfailingly friendly, which depressed Frank. When
he strolled down Front Street, there would be MacKenzie
instructing some minor lawbreaker in the proper way to
split logs for the municipal woodpile. None of them ever
just took the ax to MacKenzie instead. When Frank
stopped in the Daybreak for a drink, there would be
MacKenzie, discussing rumors of a new gold find in Nome
with Heartache Johnson. When he took Peggy to the
moving-picture show, MacKenzie would be there, too.

There was more war news, still out-of-date but
unsettling. Some of the Klondikers were going back home
to enlist. By the time they got there, the war would
probably be over, Frank thought. But maybe that didn't
matter. There would be pieces to pick up. Peggy's statement that he had better find out where the army had sent
his father recurred in his thoughts, whether he liked it or
not. She never mentioned it now. She was all talk about
expanding the laundry, hiring a girl to help. She pooh-
poohed the notion of gold in Nome. She said she wasn't
interested in what people she didn't know were doing in
Nome. Or Cuba or the Philippines, which she couldn't
even find on a map.

MacKenzie seemed to be over there all the time—
Frank never knew a man to have so many dirty shirts. He
watched, embarrassed, as Peggy's eyes met MacKenzie's
over the washing machine. And he bit his tongue before he
fought with Peggy over it. It really wasn't his business.

To keep his mind off that, he let himself think about
the war. Increasingly, he found that he envisioned his
father dead. He bought a world map and found the
Philippines. He spent one whole evening staring at it while
Peggy and MacKenzie played backgammon. MacKenzie
went home at midnight. Peggy went around the partition
to bed. Frank didn't follow her. The night felt strange, as
if there were too many people abroad in its lingering
twilight.

New York

Janessa, in New York, was packing her trunk with the fine unconcern of one who has so much to do in so little time that she has given up all hope of doing it properly or of worrying about the final outcome. When the call went out for current and past Hospital Service doctors, the army neglected to specify that they should be male. Janessa intended to be in Tampa before the issue came up.

She threw camisoles and petticoats into the trunk. They were tattered and full of holes. She had learned long before not to take new clothes into the field because they had to be boiled after each wearing. Gingham dresses, faded to smoky colors, were placed on top of the camisoles, keeping company with starched aprons and her old blue-serge Hospital Service uniform with brass buttons, gold braid, and a matching cap. Janessa had always felt that it made her look vaguely like a Cunard liner's captain, but at least it let people know that she wasn't a nurse or the scrubwoman, a misapprehension that female doctors encountered regularly.

The door banged open, and Janessa's three-year-old twins bustled through it. "Bye-bye?" asked Lally, and she attempted to upend herself in the trunk.

"Bye-bye," Janessa confirmed, "but only as far as Washington and Aunt Cindy. What have you done with Kathleen?"

"Kathleen won't feed us," Brandon announced. Being too young to wear pants, he looked almost exactly like his sister. His honey-colored curls twined over the collar of his white lawn dress. He had jam in his hair.

Kathleen Riley, the twins' nursemaid, appeared on the heels of his complaint. "I fed you both not half an hour ago, me darlings, and I'll not be feeding you again till suppertime." She looked at Janessa's trunk. "And you should be letting me pack that. All your things will be wrinkled."

Janessa inspected a faded calico housedress. "I can't do them much damage. You can pack my good dresses— but no more than four, just enough to look respectable at my aunt's house."

Kathleen began to repack the trunk anyway, nodding and muttering to herself.

"Are we going to see Daddy?" asked Brandon.

"Not now, darling," Janessa said. "But soon. You're going to see Aunt Cindy."

"Why?"

"Because your mother's going to go off risking her health with nasty foreign boys," Kathleen said. "It's not enough she had made herself a byword and a hissing at home."

"That will do, Kathleen," Janessa said. "My activities as a doctor are not your affair."

"Tell that to me friends," Kathleen said, her face flaming. "And Father Reilly stopping me after mass on Sunday. I was mortified. And high time to be leaving town, before you get in the papers again, teaching women not to have babies and who knows what sinful notions."

Janessa grinned, but she didn't let Kathleen see her. She knew she was a trial to her children's nursemaid. She was a trial to her hospital, too, and they hadn't complained at all over her taking leave to go to Tampa. Only the fact that Janessa had founded the Brentwood Hospital for Women and Children had saved her from being fired.

"My patients will be entirely male," Janessa said. "So I should manage to keep myself out of the public eye."

Kathleen nodded. Her cheeks were still flushed, but she looked satisfied with that notion. If she hadn't been, she would have mentioned it. Kathleen had been with Janessa for three years, and she had not been reticent to start with. Janessa allowed Kathleen license that her friends' servants would never have been permitted, but it seemed like too much trouble to change her; and Charley, who was used to Southern servants who *always* spoke their mind, didn't find anything odd about her.

They caught the train for Washington late the next morning at Grand Central Station. The women were carrying the equipment necessary to clothe and amuse a pair of three-year-olds for eight hours: two changes apiece, a satchel of toys and books, and the stuffed rabbit without which Brandon refused to go anywhere. Once, they had left the rabbit in a streetcar, and Charley had had to telephone the head office to get it back. Janessa was grateful that the twins had outgrown diapers, although they were not yet ready to give up their pram. When they were tired, their knees simply buckled, and they went no farther unless carried or pushed.

Janessa and Kathleen settled themselves into the parlor car with a child apiece. After the train had started up, the two women pointed out scenes of passing interest. The wheels groaned, turning slowly, then picked up speed, and the train chuffed through the outskirts of New York through the backside of the city that one always saw from the tracks—slum children playing in grassless yards, garbage cans overturned, bits of newspaper fluttering in the engine's wake, a man in overalls hoeing in a tiny garden under the shadow of the elevated tracks, a glimpse of a hobo jungle through the dusty trees. Janessa saw a man with a bindle on his back, crouching in the dry grass by the tracks. He would jump for one of the boxcars and pull himself up to the roof if a brakeman didn't spot him. These were hard times. Men were out of work everywhere. Maybe that was why so many rushed to join the army. Janessa cuddled Lally, guiltily feeling cocooned from the poverty through which the railroad tracks sliced their way.

Cindy met them at Union Station in Washington and appeared to Janessa startlingly older than at their last visit. Midge was with her, and mother and daughter kissed the children and exclaimed over them in properly doting fashion; but as soon as they were through, their faces fell again into an expression that Janessa could only describe to herself as flat—as if they were pasteboard faces, posed perhaps for postcards.

There was no sign of Janessa's uncle, Henry. She decided against asking about him. The carriage horses *clip-clopp*ed through the city and across the bridge into the cobblestoned streets of Alexandria, Virginia. It was nearly nine o'clock at night. The light was almost gone, and the sky turned inky once the travelers were out of Washington.

The Blakes' big stone house looked inviting from the street. Its windows spilled yellow pools of light onto a flower bed of lilies and roses that swayed gracefully in the warm night. As the women got out of the carriage, a squirrel came down the side of the house and chattered at them briefly before he dashed up his walnut tree.

Janessa laughed. "I beg your pardon?"

"Who are you talking to, Mama?" Lally was balanced on one hip, her face on Janessa's shoulder.

"A squirrel, darling."

They took the children upstairs and put them to bed, and they were asleep before the door was closed.

"They ought to be bathed," Janessa said, thinking of it too late. "They're covered with soot."

"Sure they've had a long day, the poor darlin's," Kathleen said, yawning. "Same as we all have." Brandon had stood up in her lap for most of the railway journey, and she showed no inclination to wake him up again. She yawned again and disappeared into the room next to the twins'.

There was still no sign of Henry Blake. Although Janessa was well aware of the Blakes' estrangement, she was always hopeful there might be a reconciliation, especially since her aunt had returned to Virginia. Janessa peered down the hall as if expecting her uncle to emerge from one of the other doors. Midge had vanished to her own bedroom, and Cindy was going down the stairs with a muttered invitation to join her in the parlor.

"Nobody here but us chickens?" Janessa asked. She followed her aunt into the parlor and sat down in the armchair on the opposite side of the hearth. Ordinarily in the summer, Cindy would have had a fan of magnolia branches in the fireplace, but that night it was bare. In fact, the hearth didn't look as if it had even been swept out since winter.

Janessa propped her feet on a hassock, ankles crossed, and considered that fact. Cindy looked worse than ever. Maybe it was only the dim light—she hadn't bothered to light anything but the table lamp—but Janessa didn't think so. That should make Cindy look better, if anything. Nor did her aunt have much to say once she had told Janessa that she had very pretty children and it was nice to see her. Janessa gathered her courage and inquired, "What did you do with his body?"

Cindy's eyes widened in surprise, then she laughed humorlessly. "Since the entire family knows all my business, for everyone's information, I have no idea where Henry is. He was not here when we arrived."

"And the War Office?" Janessa asked.

Cindy sniffed. "It never provided any information when your uncle and I were on good terms, so I doubt they'll start now. In any case, I don't give a damn where he is!"

Janessa decided to take another tack. "How is Midge liking it, being back in Washington?"

"She doesn't like it at all," Cindy said. "I suppose she'll come around." She twisted her fingers together, knuckles cracking, her eyes on the oil portrait over the mantel—Frank in his military academy greatcoat.

Janessa eyed the portrait dubiously. Cindy would turn the house into a shrine to her quarrel with Henry if she wasn't careful. And where would that leave Midge?

Cindy seemed to divine her thoughts. "I have plans for Midge," she said firmly. "When the war is over, as soon as Henry is here to take over responsibility for this house, she and I are going to travel. Midge needs to see a broader life than she had been afforded here in Washington or on the Madrona."

Janessa thought that, judging by Alexandra's last letter, Midge had seen a slightly too broad view already. "She seems to like the twins," Janessa ventured.

Cindy's eyes lit, this time with genuine pleasure. "Who could help it? It's been far too long since we had babies in the house. I promise you we'll take good care of them."

"I know you will. That's why I brought them," Janessa said comfortably. Maybe the twins would do Cindy good. She had always enjoyed playing with her own children.

"How long do you think the war will last?" Cindy asked. Her offhand tone appeared to be meant to indicate that she didn't particularly care; she was merely curious.

"I'll know more after I get down there," Janessa said. "All I know is what I read in the papers every morning, and half of that always turns out to have been wrong the next day."

"What does Charley say?"

Janessa coughed. "Well, nothing much. He really doesn't. . . . Uh, he's on a hospital ship, I believe. . . ."

Cindy leaned forward in her chair, focused now. She looked at Janessa over her spectacles. "Does Charley know you are going down there?"

"Not exactly," Janessa conceded.

"And what does that mean?" Cindy had raised Janessa since she was nine years old. Now, she gave her niece the same look with which she had once elicited confessions of homework undone or the whereabouts of missing pieces of pie.

Janessa chuckled and stood her ground. "It means I don't intend to tell him until I get there. Because of the twins, he has strong feelings about our both being in the field at the same time."

"And so he should," Cindy said.

"Charley's immune to yellow fever," Janessa said. "And with all due respect, Aunt Cindy, you can tell me how to deal with my husband after you settle affairs with yours."

Cindy's eyes narrowed, and she balled her hands into fists. "My relations with Henry are no one's business except my own! I will thank you and your father and Alexandra to keep yourselves out of it. I'm sure you've heard *all* about it from Toby and Alex, but let me add this: Midge came to more harm in their house than she ever had with me, with or without her father. So just remember that!"

"I beg your pardon," Janessa said, startled. "I apologize for being rude, and I—"

"Everyone's afraid I'll divorce him," she said bitterly. "That's what it is. No one in our family has ever had a divorce, and I'm getting tired of all of you watching me to be sure I'm not going to make a disgrace of myself."

"I'm not watching you at all," Janessa said hastily. "Anyway," she added with more practicality than tact, "you can't divorce him. You can't find him."

"Maybe," Cindy snapped, "I should tell the War Office I don't care where he is as long as they'll swear he isn't coming back!" Her mood shifted rapidly again. Her face was flushed now, and her eyes were bright behind her gold-rimmed spectacles; but it was the uneasy brightness that Janessa usually associated with fever.

Janessa wasn't at all sure what was going on. "I think," she said carefully, "that you shouldn't do anything until you are quite certain."

"Life is uncertain," Cindy said abruptly.

In the morning Janessa went on to Tampa, leaving the twins and Kathleen with Cindy. She felt oddly naked to be climbing alone into the railway carriage. She had never been away from the twins before.

Shipments were still being made to Tampa. When the train paused at a siding, Janessa would crane her neck out the open window and see boxcars being loaded with crates and bales and feel the jolt as the boxcars were coupled to the train. Going south through Florida, she could see other boxcars, waylaid on sidings. She wondered if anybody had any idea that they were still there, solitary on their tracks in the pine barrens. There were a few soldiers, in uniforms and red bandannas, in the Pullman cars and a few more camped outside Tampa, amid the jumbled piles of unlabeled crates and dismantled field guns.

Janessa found an old Hospital Service friend, Steve Jurgen, with whom she had gone to medical school, on the train, and Steve didn't know whether or not they were to stay in Tampa, either.

"Charley's on a hospital ship that went with the troop transports," Janessa said. "That was the last I heard of him."

"There'll be enough here to keep us busy," Steve muttered, looking out the window at the outskirts of Tampa. The air was hot and wet and felt unclean, a faint breath of swamp. "Damn unhealthy hole, but it's where the supplies are. I expect they'll ship the casualties here."

"There are civilians here," Janessa said uneasily. "I don't like that idea, not if there's disease."

"I feel quite certain the army will do whatever proves to be most inefficient and inadvisable," Steve said. "It's practically a tradition." He pulled his uniform cap down over his eyes. "Wake me when we get to Tampa," he said, then fell asleep.

XI

Eden met Janessa at the Tampa depot with a hired carriage and graciously invited Steve Jurgen to share it. He was introduced to Elizabeth and Rosebay and found himself having dinner with an escort of four women.

Rosebay, Elizabeth, and Janessa silently blessed his presence as an excellent diversion. As far as they were concerned, there was far too much tension among them, caused by past and present relationships with one Timothy Holt.

In the morning the two doctors went to the army headquarters and tried to get sent to Cuba. They found several other physicians demanding to speak with an officer and trying to accomplish the same thing. The harried major had not the least idea what to do with them.

"Then why did a call go out for doctors?" Janessa demanded in as reasonable a voice as she could manage.

"*I* didn't send for you," the major grumbled.

"You have men dying of yellow fever in Cuba, and you've got doctors trained to treat yellow fever in Tampa. Now what seems to you the logical thing to do?" Janessa straightened her cap and glared at him. The weather was intensely hot and humid, and she longed to put on one of her old gingham dresses.

"I don't have any orders," the major said.

"Well, we do, damn it!" Steve said. "They say to report to Tampa."

"Well, you have, haven't you?" the major pointed out. "You've done your duty."

"What the hell do we do now?" Steve bellowed.

"Wait for more orders," the major said. "That's regulations."

Janessa grabbed Steve's arm and towed him toward the door.

"Except for you," the major said to Janessa. "You can't go anywhere. You're a female."

Janessa raised her brows at him. "Ha." She pulled Steve the rest of the way out of the tent, assisted by one of the other doctors, who said he had been waiting there for four days.

"Nobody in this godforsaken outpost knows what he's doing," he reported darkly.

"No, but *there's* someone who does." Janessa pointed at a boxcar in the distance. The red cross on its side was plain. "I'd put my money on the Red Cross over the army."

Janessa, Steve, and several other doctors hiked through the ankle-deep sand and found a businesslike woman with a clipboard in her hand, ticking off supplies as they were hauled off the car. Janessa noted Rosebay Ware converging on the worker from the opposite direction. Because she never knew what to say to Rosebay, Janessa gave her a bright smile. Rosebay returned an uncertain one. The woman with the clipboard introduced herself as Miss Wheeler, daughter of old Fighting Joe.

"Are you sailing for Cuba with these?" Janessa asked.

"Quite soon, my dear." Miss Wheeler noted Janessa's Hospital Service insignia. She cocked her head politely, waiting.

"We'd like to sail with you," Janessa said.

"Strictly speaking, I believe you Hospital Service doctors are assigned to the army."

"The army has no transport," Janessa said firmly. "And the army doesn't want to take *me* because I'm female, which is ridiculous. The Red Cross is sending female nurses. I don't know what kind of idiotic reason they have, but—"

Miss Wheeler smiled. "I see. Well, I shouldn't like to

annoy the major, but he *doesn't* seem to be putting you to use, does he? If you were to be on the pier when we sailed, it *would* be foolish to leave you behind. It will take us about four days, though, to have all our supplies loaded and accounted for." She tapped her clipboard. Unlike the army, the Red Cross appeared to keep track of its stores.

"We'll be here," Janessa said. "I, uh—I don't suppose you have any news from the *Olivette*? My husband's aboard as a doctor."

"Then he has his hands full," Miss Wheeler said. "And so do I, so if you will excuse me—?" Politely but firmly, she turned back to her list.

Rosebay tapped the woman on the shoulder. "I can help," she said.

". . . seven, eight," Miss Wheeler said. "What, dear?" She took in Rosebay's elegant linen suit and her beautiful face.

"I can help," Rosebay repeated. "I'm a bookkeeper when I'm not holed up here going crazy. You give me something to do, I'll help you out."

Miss Wheeler managed to look appreciative and harried at the same time. "That's very nice of you, but I'm afraid we don't really need office help. Strong backs are more what we're in the need of."

"You don't understand," Rosebay said stubbornly. "I know how to keep track of things. I run a boardinghouse, too. If there's one thing I know how to do, it's sort supplies. Here, give me that." She took a crate from the man handing it down from the car. "You got two different kinds of bandages here," she told his assistant. "You want to keep them separate." Rosebay set the crate to one side and then inspected the stack for mismatched labels. "See, there's another." She began separating the pile into two stacks. "You let me help," she told Miss Wheeler. "You check them off, I'll set them where they go. Afterward, you boys can take the handcart and put these where Miss Wheeler tells you," she added.

Miss Wheeler smiled. "I believe we can use you after all."

"Time was," Rosebay said, "when a strong back was about all I had to keep me going. It might be a blessing to work like that again. I reckon it takes your mind off a lot of things."

Steve took Janessa's elbow and steered her away. "The hospitals won't be protected, you know," he said as they caught up with the other doctors. "The Spanish will be firing on them."

"On *hospitals*?" Janessa was outraged.

"They fired on casualties being carried down on stretchers after the fighting at San Juan," one of the other physicians said. "I heard it from one of the newspaper fellows."

"Fired on the newspaper fellows, too," another said. "Fired on anybody."

"My two brothers are over there," Janessa said faintly. "Their wives are here in Tampa. They didn't say anything to me about—"

"Of course not," Steve said. "Why would they want to get you all worked up? Of course if you're always such a cold fish to Tim's wife, she just may not want to discourage you from going, too."

"I am not!" Janessa said indignantly. "I was perfectly polite."

Steve shrugged. "Whatever you say . . . but I watched you at dinner. You acted like a missionary who has to be polite while dining with a Hottentot."

"I did not!" Janessa said. The other doctors were strolling a short distance away, studiously not eavesdropping. "I just don't know what to do with her. She doesn't like me," she added defensively.

"How do you know? Have you ever asked her?"

"Of course not."

"I'll ask her if you like," Steve volunteered.

"Don't you dare!" Janessa put a hand on his arm. "I—I just can't understand what my brother sees in her."

She looked back to see Rosebay determinedly stacking boxes. "And something about her makes me uncomfortable, too."

Steve nodded knowingly. "It seems to me, and my opinion may possibly be shared by Elizabeth, that there are an unnecessary number of women attached to her husband. And if I correctly read the undercurrents of last night's conversation, you and Rosebay seem to believe that you both should have been consulted before Tim married Elizabeth."

Janessa opened her mouth to protest, then realized that he was right. Her shoulders slumped. "You've made me feel very stupid."

He put an arm around her waist and guided her toward the hotel. "No need to thank me, honey. Hey—what're friends for?"

The Philippine Islands, late June

Around the time that Frank Blake was beginning to look uneasily homeward, and two days before General Shafter's assault on the San Juan Heights, Frank's father, Henry Blake, arrived in Manila Bay with the first American troops, having stopped only long enough to capture Guam on the way. The troops were regular army, but Colonel Blake couldn't be called that. His orders were to go ashore very quietly and report directly to Admiral Dewey, and to General Wesley Merritt, who was sailing from San Francisco to take command of the land forces at Manila.

Another armed contingent besides the Americans was waiting to attack Manila, and therein lay an uneasy alliance that was no more a partnership than Henry Blake was an army officer.

The Filipinos, like the Cubans, had been in rebellion against Spain for years. They had a national martyr in

José Rizal, who had written two novels of protest, formed the Filipino League to press for social change, and died young before a firing squad, leaving a farewell poem, an ode to his country, to remember him by—all of which added up to a powerful icon.

More dangerous still were the Katipunan, a secret society of poverty-stricken and frustrated men. *Katipunan,* translated from Tagalog, meant "Highest and Most Venerable Association of the Sons of the Nation." Their goal was not merely better conditions but outright separation from Spanish rule. Spain disposed of Rizal the reformer and found itself with a revolution instead.

The Katipunan had more than one hundred thousand members before Spain learned of it in 1896, and full-scale revolution broke out. Spain fought back in much the same way it had in Cuba, with mass jailings and executions—among them, ironically, Rizal's. He had never been a member of the Katipunan; but it was their rebellion that prompted his treason trial and his death that gave power to their movement.

An increasingly savage war went on for more than a year. The Filipinos, like the Cubans, were not noticeably more civilized than the Spanish. They reserved particular hatred for the Roman Catholic priests, one of whose number had informed the Spanish government of their plan to revolt.

By this time the Katipunan had merged with other factions of the liberation movement, and its founder, who had chosen his enemies unwisely, had been shot by his fellow rebels. A dual leadership had emerged—the twenty-eight-year-old guerrilla and soldier, the hero of villagers and workers, Emilio Aguinaldo; and the intellectual power behind him, Apolinario Mabini, law graduate and heir to the poet-statesman mantle of José Rizal. Mabini had been stricken with paralysis in 1895 and was confined to a chair.

By late 1897 both Spain and the rebels were bloody and weary, and very little had been accomplished except death. The Spanish government offered a payoff of

$850,000 plus reforms. Aguinaldo and thirty-four others took the first installment of the Spanish payment and went into temporary exile in Hong Kong, where they proceeded to spend the money preparing for another fight.

The American consul there sold arms to Aguinaldo, while the American consul in Singapore assured Aguinaldo that his country had no intention of becoming a colonial power. As the Filipino exiles stockpiled weapons and printed propaganda, a most unexpected thing happened: America declared war on Spain, and Dewey sank the Spanish fleet in Manila Bay.

On May 20, Aguinaldo returned to his homeland aboard an American revenue cutter and conferred with the American admiral. Aguinaldo believed he came away from that meeting with a promise from Admiral Dewey: After the islands had been taken from the Spanish, they would be turned over to the Filipinos. Dewey maintained that he said no such thing. Nonetheless, Dewey had very definitely given Aguinaldo whatever his men could salvage from the shelled and burned-out Spanish arsenal at Cavite. Whether or not the United States was prepared to recognize Aguinaldo politically, it found his rebel troops, hidden in the islands, extremely useful.

"The damned fellow's completely out of control," Dewey said irritably to Henry Blake over port and cigars on his flagship in Manila Bay.

"We, er, did give him arms, Admiral. We might have expected him to use them." Henry looked across the azure waters at the city surrounded by its dense green canopy, impenetrable and mysterious. Dotted on the bay were the admiral's fleet and the newly arrived troop transports. Aguinaldo was reputed to have thirty thousand men under his command now and was taking Spanish garrisons, regardless of how the Americans viewed his actions.

"He was supposed to make trouble for the Spanish, not set up his own government," Dewey said, then snorted. "He's had the insolence to declare independence—with the Spanish still sitting in Manila, mind you—and proclaim a government, with himself as the head of it, of course. That has to stop."

"I guessed that was what I was here for," Henry murmured.

"Well, not just yet," the admiral told him. "For the time being, the President has chosen not to notice their declaration. We can't give these fellows formal recognition, of course, but we must cooperate with them in prying the Spanish loose. I believe President McKinley has their best interests at heart. Eventually these fellows will be capable of governing themselves."

"They're barely out of savagery, aren't they?" Henry asked.

"The Spanish are to blame for that," Dewey said distastefully. "They've always kept their colonies suppressed, and look what it's brought them. Our job is to let the Filipinos know we're prepared to guide them until they're capable of standing on their own."

"Do you think they will be, sir?"

Dewey sighed. "I believe so. But they're largely illiterate. They have no system of government except on a village level. They have no industry. Worst of all, they have no army!"

"They seem to be building one, Admiral," Henry said.

Dewey dismissed that with a wave of his hand. "A rabble of peasants armed with rifles. Very good for ousting the Spanish, with our help, but not particularly useful for defending against outside aggressors."

"True," Henry said. "I understand that Germans have already visited."

The admiral poured his guest another glass of port. "They're like jackals. They come around when there's been blood to see what's in it for them. We gave them short shrift. But if we pull out—well, the poor Filipinos will be worse off than ever. The Russians and the French will be sniffing around, too. They all have a foot on the China coast already. If we *want* a presence here, of course, then the Philippines are just what we're looking for. Put bluntly, you understand. Frankly, I'm not sure Washington knows just yet *what* it wants. I think it was surprised to get Manila Bay."

Henry chuckled. "Theodore Roosevelt wasn't surprised. Just his superiors."

"That man's a menace," Dewey said, but he laughed. He was a pleasant-faced, roundish fellow with gray hair and a goatee. Largely imperturbable, he looked like a superintendent of schools or possibly an avuncular chief of police. His white summer uniform was wilted and sweat stained, but he managed to maintain a military bearing despite the heat—possibly with the aid of a corset, Henry suspected. But he liked Dewey, and he was far too old himself to make sport, even mentally, of other men's aging.

What he himself would do when he was too old to carry out secret missions was a question Henry avoided considering. He didn't think the War Department could promote him to a desk job or even a field command with any success. What *did* the loners do when they were too old to work on their own?

"Tell me about the Spanish in the city, sir. What am I looking for there?"

"An accurate troop count would be useful," Dewey said dryly. "We've had a report of seven thousand in Manila and five or six thousand elsewhere, but I'm not entirely sure it's reliable. I wouldn't put it past Aguinaldo to inflate the count to make his help look that much more necessary. On the other hand, our people might have purposely underestimated."

"What about civilians in the city?"

"Well, there are the Filipinos, of course, and Spanish civilians. More Spanish are coming in for safety all the time—Aguinaldo's men have been fairly brutal to the ruling class. Can't blame them, poor devils, but still . . . I imagine nearly every priest has fled to Manila—the rebels have a vendetta against them. And then there's the usual smattering of foreigners—Chinese, Japanese, a Russian or two. Mexican bureaucrats brought in by the Spanish. A handful of American adventurers and expatriate Englishmen." Dewey contemplated this tally. "Very much what you might expect in the tropics, in a politically unstable country."

"It sounds similar to Havana," Henry said thoughtfully. "I was there—opportunity and hazard in almost equal proportions. There is a certain type that feeds on that." *Myself included,* he thought.

"True," Dewey said. "I'm told you know what you're doing, so I'll arrange to have you put ashore anyplace you choose. May I ask what you plan to do first?"

"Take a hotel room in the city, I think," Henry said. "I don't plan to act secretively."

"You won't get a very good reception," Dewey warned.

"Oh, I speak tolerable Spanish," Henry said nonchalantly. "I'll be all right, Admiral."

Later, back in his cabin, Henry made a few alterations to his appearance to assure that he *would* be all right. A judicious application of walnut juice and some darkening of his sandy hair produced a face that might possibly have been Filipino, with some European blood. His green eyes would always mark him as part European, one of Rudyard Kipling's half-caste gentlemen adventurers. Or he might have been half-caste Indian or a number of vague lineages, breeds that might be found in an unstable city in the tropics.

Henry looked at his altered visage in the little mirror. He had always had a knack of becoming what he pretended to be. He wondered what would happen if one day he simply stayed in some other skin. Maybe that would be easier than peeling it off again and leaving his true self exposed. Who would care? Who would miss Henry Blake? Except, of course, the army, to whom he was so useful. Certainly his wife wouldn't miss him. She had made that exceedingly clear. Peter was grown and his own master, and he had always been self-contained. There was Midge, but Cindy would never let Henry see her. He listed these facts to himself, his private litany of grievances. And Eulalia? Well, she was his adopted mother, but she was Cindy's natural mother. Then there was Frank. Who knew where Frank was?

Henry set a panama straw on his head. He let the parade-ground stiffness slide out of his carriage, leaving just a touch, the mark of a man who might once have been drilled, a long time before. He adjusted his white linen jacket, picked up his Gladstone bag, and strolled out to the deck. The sun was just going down; the anchored ships bobbed on the fiery bay, tethered in a lake of flame.

The Philippines were born in flame, volcanic peaks that thrust up, breathing fire, from beneath the ocean's surface. They are the northern islands of the Malay chain, which rings Southeast Asia. There are more than seven thousand of them, give or take a few that may rise or sink at any moment. Forty-five islands comprise the majority of the land, most of it on Luzon and Mindanao. It is approximately 580 miles from Manila on southern Luzon to Davao on southern Mindanao—no easy task for a central government to keep this area together as a nation, or for the rebels to coordinate a revolution, either.

The Philippines are warm and rainy, with a twelve-month growing season and a temperature that never dips below sixty degrees, even at the highest altitude. The islands have mountainous, spiny ridges rimmed with a narrow band of coastal plains. Although they are beautiful and lush, they are risky places to call home. Between July and November, typhoons blow in on hundred-mile-an-hour winds and drop twenty inches of rain in twenty-four hours. When a typhoon flattens a village or a volcano explodes, the verdant land covers its own scars almost overnight, burying the damage under a blanket of creepers, bamboo, canes, and finally the tall green canopy of the rain forest.

The ship's boat put Henry ashore in the dark on the

coast between Manila and the ruined arsenal at Cavite. The heat wreathed him with fingers of steam, choked him with the thick scent of the mangrove swamps, called out to him, *Stand still, and we will cover you.*

The place gave him the willies. The night seemed catlike, paws tucked under, watchful, waiting. . . . Bag in hand, he set off up the coastal road and rehearsed the plausible story he was saving in case he couldn't dodge the Spanish sentries.

He covered most of the ground between Cavite and Manila without meeting anyone and was just congratulating himself on that fact when a man dropped out of a tree in front of his nose. It was too dark to see his face, but the machete was noticeable by starlight. He demanded in native-accented Spanish that Henry identify himself.

"I might be the man you're looking for," Henry said in Spanish. But this fellow was no Spaniard and wore no more than a cloth about his waist. Henry sighed. He hadn't wanted Aguinaldo to know he was here before he had seen Manila, though. "I am the one from the admiral," he said, the agreed-upon password to Aguinaldo's camp.

The man peered at Henry. "We were not told you were coming tonight."

"You were not," Henry concurred. "The admiral and I have other matters to see to before I speak with your general."

"The general wishes to confer with you now."

"The general does not know I am here," Henry pointed out.

"The general will wish it when he does know."

They seemed to have reached an impasse. It would be no part of this rebel's orders to murder American couriers. Nor would it endear Henry to Emilio Aguinaldo if he should shoot one of his pickets. Henry didn't care for the idea of shooting the man anyway—it would attract too much attention. The man with the machete had the advantage there.

"I will call on the general after I have concluded my

other affairs," Henry said firmly. He tipped his hat respectfully, watching to see if the machete was going to be involved. It appeared not. The man stepped back and in an instant was gone, having vanished into the black shadows along the road.

No one else dropped out of the trees. Henry felt eyes on him, though. His first encounter had probably spread the word to pass him along unmolested. He found Spanish pickets outside Manila, but they were relatively easy to dodge. They were looking out for attack by Aguinaldo's rebels, not for one man with a Gladstone bag.

There are many ways to enter a sleeping city unnoticed, and Henry Blake knew all the universal ones. After a few days in the city, he would also know the methods that were unique to Manila. He slipped through the outskirts, through the shantytown and the shacks with gardens the size of postage stamps in their front yards. Most of the hovels stood on stilts, long-legged creatures with palm-thatch hair. They were built as Filipinos had always built their dwellings, of materials that grew wild and could be had for the cutting: Bamboo posts and woven bamboo walls, with wide porches surrounding the central rooms. To get in, one climbed a ladder, which could be pulled up if the inhabitants did not want more visitors.

Each house was furnished with a clay cooking stove, water jars, and straw mats and silken kapok-fiber pillows for sleeping. There might be a few modern additions—an oil lamp, a mirror, a crucifix—but these would be more likely in the barrios, the villages, than in the Manila slums.

Manila was a Spanish city, taken in 1570 from a Muslim rajah from the south and made the center of the Spanish conquest. Ironically the rajah, Soliman, had in this century become a hero of Philippine independence.

Native Filipinos who lived in Manila did so only because they had nowhere else to go. Farmers, forced to pay tribute at a ruinous rate to absentee landlords, gave up and drifted to the cities in the hope of finding work. If they found any job at all, it was menial. The only guaranteed work was the forty days of forced labor that every male Filipino had to give the government every year to build churches and prisons and other public works that the Filipinos had not required until the Spanish came.

Henry had been briefed in the States on the Philippines' history from the American point of view and on the Filipinos' culture, insofar as any American understood it. It had made his head swim. There were seven major languages, of which Tagalog was the official one only because the majority of people living close to Manila spoke it. After Henry learned that those seven languages might be split into as many as fifty dialects, he was silently grateful to the Spanish for imposing their own language, which he spoke, on the populace.

The people themselves were a mixture of successive waves of early migrants, beginning with the aboriginal pygmies whose descendants could still be found in the deep forests, untroubled by Spanish rule or any subsequent invasion. The modern Filipinos' ancestors came from the Asian mainland and from Malaysia, with their religion and later additions to their bloodlines from incursions by Hindus, Persians and Arabs, Chinese and Japanese. The result was an unwieldy composite.

The Moros of Mindanao in the south were Muslims, seafaring warriors who resisted "Christianizing" since they already possessed the word of Allah. At their most tractable, they fought like fiends to avoid adapting to Spanish ways. At their least, they raided Manila and the coastal towns of the north, murdered priests and Spanish officials, burned churches, and carried off Christian captives. Mindanao, largely unexplored, was an excellent place to brew trouble.

The Cebuanos, in the Visayas, had their own language, literature, and a tribal loyalty to their own capital city.

The rice farmers of northern Luzon practiced spirit worship and planted their crops on terraces carved from the mountainside, irrigated with techniques brought from

Asia five hundred years before Christ. They, too, were far enough away from Manila to have remained largely impervious to Spanish rule and Spanish religion. Spain claimed a centuries-old ownership of the islands, but the truth was that for all practical purposes it extended only to the coastal and low-lying areas between Luzon and Mindanao. The Tagalog, the majority around Manila, were Christian, although resentment of the Spanish priests was rising.

Henry wondered what exactly his government thought it was going to do with these people once it had liberated them from Spain. They certainly could not be left to fend for themselves. Without some restraint and guidance, they would, he thought, fall to fighting among themselves and slip back into the primitivism from which they had only barely emerged. Henry didn't need daylight to take stock of the poverty through which he was passing on his circuitous route into the city. His nose told him of badly dug latrines, disease, and rain washing the city's filth indiscriminately through the streets.

A pig darted through a hole in a sagging wire pen and ran between Henry's feet, then squealed as he stumbled and accidentally kicked it. A rooster, awakened by the pig, began to crow, and Henry hurried on.

He could hear the lapping of the Pasig River and an occasional sleepy murmur from the canal boats. The shanties began to be interspersed with precarious-looking houses of wood, which leaned over the street. Their lower windows were shaded with wooden lattices, and their upper windows were of shell, thin squares of mother-of-pearl. These houses smelled worse than the palm-thatch shanties of the outskirts. They emanated the smell of salt fish and boiling rice, and of too many bodies crowded into a single room.

As Henry moved farther into the city, he felt saddened by what three hundred years of colonial rule had done to a people who had probably been living contentedly. Still, one couldn't go back. The Philippines would have to go forward now, into the modern world.

He walked toward the Intramuros, the old walled city. The government buildings and the Spanish churches, imposing colonial structures with tropical overtones, were reached by one of eight ancient, tunnellike gates. The Fort of Santiago stood at the northwest angle of the Intramuros, guarding the entrance to the Pasig River. A few feeble electric arc-lights illuminated the dock. Henry stood in the shadows for a long time and contemplated the fort, with its stiffly attendant sentries. Above its main gate rose a stone archway, columned and adorned with bas-reliefs of conquistadores and royal lions, and tropical birds atop its pediment.

The Fort of Santiago, inside two and a half miles of city wall, and the appalling slough of a moat that surrounded it had been built in the sixteenth century by Chinese laborers to keep out pirates. They might still stand off a land army, but they wouldn't be any match for modern artillery unless, Henry decided, wrinkling his nose at the stench, you were worried about the moat. It would probably be possible to decimate an entire army with the loathsome diseases the water must harbor. He supposed the moat had been designed to be filled from the river, but it appeared now to be totally stagnant. Henry, who had American notions about sanitation and proper maintenance, glared at the noxious waters. He wondered if they betokened the entire state of hygiene in Manila.

There was, so he had been told, an excellent hotel of the colonial sort in Manila, which catered to Europeans; but arriving at three in the morning would make him far too noticeable. Accordingly, he retreated to a park and found an overgrown corner in which to sit and doze until dawn. He was not alone. As the sun rose, he watched the Manila police chase other sleepers off the benches.

After straightening his jacket, Henry hefted the Gladstone bag and emerged cautiously from the underbrush to adopt an authoritative stride—no park-bench bum, he. He nodded pleasantly to the policeman on the corner.

Manila by daylight was fascinating, despite the odor, to which he was perhaps becoming accustomed. China-town offered narrow streets, clogged with rickshaws and two-wheeled pony carts. The shops dealt in silk and ivory, porcelains and jade, cloisonné boxes and Buddhist deities, vegetables and strange sea creatures.

Closer to the hotel, Henry stopped to stare at a woman whose delicate face glowed above her fichu and her dress's wide-arched sleeves, which looked like butter-fly wings of starched gauze. Was she Eurasian, he won-dered, or Malay-Chinese? It was impossible to tell, but he thought he had never seen anyone so lovely. She caught him staring and hurried on, clutching her market basket, while he turned away, embarrassed.

A streetcar trundled down the center of the road, drawn by a single pony and announcing its coming with a tin horn. There were carriages for hire, ranging from fairly respectable barouches to the native two-wheeled *calesas*, designed for negotiating the crowded streets. The driver perched up front, expertly dodging mule-drawn drays and wagons pulled by water buffalo. Another form of convey-ance was the *caromata*, a top-heavy two-wheeled native pony cart. They rocketed through the streets with utter disregard for safety, and the driver rode inside, often in his passengers' lap.

Henry chose to walk, the better to inspect the city. It was unbearably hot already, and the air was heavy with mist, which gave the sun a diffuse glow that spilled across the red tile rooftops. Henry noted that each roof had little valleys of green between the tiles, where seeds dropped by birds had sprouted in the permanent warmth and damp-ness.

The Hotel de Europa was an unprepossessing white wooden edifice with verandas overgrown with vines. Small Filipino boys with palm-frond fans kept the flies away. Having given Henry's pesos a thorough inspection, the desk clerk appeared uninterested in his bona fides, which identified him as Señor Victor Vargas from Singapore, an importer of copra.

Henry asked that breakfast be sent to his room. The clerk asked if eggs *pasado por agua* would be acceptable. Henry said yes, assuming that by saying *por agua* the desk clerk had meant boiled, that being the usual thing to do with an egg in water. Then a boy took him upstairs. He gave the child a coin and, wondering if he would get to keep it, locked the door. The room looked somewhat disreputable. The windows were unglazed, with screens of mother-of-pearl that could be slid open to let the breeze through. There did not appear to be any electricity in Manila, but the hotel had thoughtfully provided a pair of tumblers filled with coconut oil and wicks secured to their tops by wire.

The bed's four imposing posts supported lace curtains and a mosquito net, but the base was simply woven cane like a chair seat, overlaid with a thin Malay sleeping mat and accompanied by a sheet and pillow, and a bolster with which Henry had not the faintest idea what to do. The bathroom, shared by several guests, was down the hall. But there were fresh flowers in a vase on the mahogany dressing table and a brass bell by the bed with which one could presumably summon whatever one might desire— providing that it could be found in Manila.

Henry was ravenous. When the tray appeared he took it gratefully and sat by the window. In the course of his travels, he had learned to eat nearly anything. Now he lifted the covers and found a cup of thick hot chocolate, bread, and . . . raw eggs in water. It appeared that the clerk had meant the term *pasado por agua* quite literally. Henry closed his eyes, weighed the trouble and time of persuading someone to cook the eggs, and ate them anyway.

After he had done so, he looked with grave suspicion at the lock on the door. Before he stashed his bag under the bed, he pocketed the second pistol stowed in it, then went downstairs. The hotel bar was where things would be happening, even in the morning.

Henry ordered a gin and quinine from a white-shirted waiter, who brought the drink on a silver tray. The bar was of deeply polished mahogany. Behind it a mirror reflected shelves of glassware and a glittering collection of bottles with mysterious labels. A ray of sun shot through a crack in the shutters and exploded light, which was turned into a rainbow by the cut glass. A punkah hung from the shadowy ceiling, and a Filipino child pulled rhythmically on its ropes.

Henry settled with his drink into a bamboo chair and took stock of the other patrons. Most appeared to be Asians and Europeans, but there was one Filipino in a western business suit, and two Spanish officers were having an eye-opener by themselves in the corner. The drinkers were all men, but they were attended by the bar girls in silk sarongs and *sayas*; the beauties offered admiration for a peso and romance for somewhat more.

A dark-haired man in an embroidered native shirt came and sat in the chair next to Henry's. He unfolded a newspaper and, clucking his tongue, shook his head over the articles. "All fools," he said with asperity.

Henry eyed the newspaper. It would be the official government paper. No others were allowed. He chuckled—softly enough for the other man to ignore, if he chose, but also loud enough for him to hear.

The other man looked over the paper. "What do you make of it?" he asked. "The Americans are sitting out there like corks in a bottle, and what is our government doing?"

"It is a difficult situation," Henry agreed. "I am from Singapore, of course. You and the Americans are making it very hard for me to go home."

The other man chuckled now. "My name is Alberto Rodriguez," he offered. "I am from Cebu. My family grows sugarcane."

"I am Victor Vargas, from Singapore. I have never

been to Manila before. An intriguing city, although I have stayed longer than I meant to."

"We live in exciting times," Rodriguez said happily. "Because I know the area, I shall travel overland, then sail from another port." He sighed. "When all the foreigners have finished fighting with one another over the right to rule us, we shall forget the inconveniences they have caused. They will be gone, but we will still be here."

Henry looked at him closely. "You favor independence?"

"Not out loud," Rodriguez said. "Not at all, to a man I do not know. Particularly not to a man with a Spanish name."

"I see," Henry said. "Hypothetically, if the Americans win, would you favor independence? As opposed to an American supervisory government?"

"To prepare us for the twentieth century?" Rodriguez smiled. "Great civilizations always wish to civilize other peoples, whether or not they wish it. My dear Vargas, look at Britain. Before that, look at Rome."

"Rome?"

"I had a classical education," Rodriguez said proudly. "Here at Santo Tomas University."

"But the downfall of Rome was caused by the people's immorality and decadence. You really can't make a comparison."

"They conquered everyone," Rodriguez said, shaking his head. "France, Spain, Britain. The Holy Land. The Balkans. Everyone became Romans. One was not allowed anymore to run naked and eat fruit from the trees."

"That would seem to be an advantage," Henry commented. "No country has ever progressed until it has been shown western ways. And you can't run naked in Europe in the winter anyway."

They looked at each other, slightly puzzled. A fundamental difficulty existed, which dawned suddenly on Henry. His people were never going to understand Rodriguez's. The Filipinos were simply stuck with the Americans and vice versa.

Rodriguez folded his paper and rose, leaving his empty cup on the table by his chair. "I hope you have an excellent stay." His teeth flashed in a friendly smile. "Remember the Romans."

Henry followed him out with his eyes, still considering, and caught the glance of a young European also drinking gin and quinine at the bar. He gave Henry an interested but quizzical look, and Henry realized with a jolt that they had seen each other before. Where, he had no idea, but odds were Henry had not been calling himself Vargas. He left the bar as quickly as a pretense at nonchalance would allow.

In the lobby Henry wondered if he was going to have to change hotels. He leaned over the counter toward the desk clerk and said confidentially, slipping a peso under the clerk's blotter, "That young man. The British-looking one at the bar with the fair hair. Who is he?"

The desk clerk shrugged. "He comes in to drink sometimes, señor. He is not a hotel guest."

"I see. And how often does he come in?"

The clerk looked at him curiously. "Not often," he allowed. "Perhaps if you introduced yourself, señor . . . I do not see him with any other gentlemen—or the ladies."

Henry's face flushed. "I'm not—never mind." He stalked out, his ears burning. He was almost certain the clerk thought his interest was an intimate one. Beautiful young men as well as young women plied the hotel bars. This one hadn't looked sleek enough for male prostitution, though. He had the rumpled look of someone whose adventures were more wholesome. Henry still could not place him; so he would simply have to stay away from the bar until the young man left.

XII

A daylight inspection of the fortifications along the river seemed in order. Still horribly embarrassed by the clerk's assumption, Henry set out toward the Intramuros. The fellow's knowing stare seemed to follow him down the street. *What do I look like, anyway?* Henry stifled his indignation by reminding himself that he looked exactly as he had disguised himself to appear—a man of uncertain ancestry and habits, one more adventurer in Manila. In the course of his various missions, Henry had managed to dwell on the seamier side of the human condition without ever understanding its denizens or adopting their ways. He could mimic them but not *become* them. Their intrinsic truths rolled off him as if he wore some invisible shield. His army colleagues and associates believed that he was incorruptible. That was also the concept he had of himself. Now, however, in this bizarre and uncertain place, he felt as if the shell might crack. The feeling of imbalance made the space between his shoulder blades itch.

The Intramuros looked even more decrepit in the daytime than it had by starlight. The three-hundred-year-old walls showed the cracks of numerous earthquakes, and Henry thought it a wonder that the Intramuros was still standing at all. Perhaps the constant prayers of the friars living within had something to do with it.

The Intramuros sheltered a cathedral, eleven churches, numerous monasteries, Dominican and Jesuit colleges, and the palace of the archbishop. Government buildings appeared to have been an afterthought, which might account for the lack of upkeep. *God might prevent your walls from tumbling down,* Henry thought, *but He did not polish your cannon for you.* The old bronze artillery, which sat on rotting carriages, would prove more dangerous to the luckless souls firing them than to the enemy.

Below the fortifications along the bay was the Luneta, a carriage drive and promenade that served as Manila's social gathering place. Band concerts were a popular event, according to the American guidebooks. The military musicians were Filipino, drilled by European bandmasters. In fact, Henry had seen very few Europeans not in military uniform or friars' robes. He thought again of the young man in the hotel bar and wondered what *his* business was.

Henry, making his way through one of the dank, tunnellike gates, was forced to flatten himself against the wall to avoid a water-buffalo cart coming over the drawbridge in the opposite direction. He stopped on the bridge to peer down into the fetid water. The moat was even more revolting in daylight, when it could be seen as well as smelled. Henry wrinkled his nose.

Manila seemed to have no drainage system at all. Canals radiated from the Pasig River, and the city simply poured its garbage into them. The canals were thick with dugouts and *cascos,* native cargo lighters, and with houseboats of woven bamboo that often sheltered seven or eight people. Were it not for the fact that a decent waterworks supplied cooking and drinking water, the city would be unlivable. Even as it was, disease was rampant. *The first thing we'll have to do,* Henry thought, *is get a team of U.S. doctors in here.* The situation was bad enough now. Disturbed by a battle, every noxious microbe would rise out of the mud and the muck like evil spirits from a bottle.

He stood brooding over the moat a few moments too long and made himself the target of the street vendors who roamed everywhere.

"Billete, señor?" A vendor stuck a sheaf of tickets under Henry's nose.

"No." Henry pushed the tickets away.

"Billete? Lottery tickets. Perhaps you will be lucky." The native vendor smiled encouragingly and held the tickets out again.

"I will be lucky if I do not die of standing this close to your moat," Henry said. "Why has it been allowed to get in this state?"

The ticket seller shrugged. "The government, señor. They fear to disturb it, lest they release a pestilence." He put the tickets in Henry's face again. *"Billete?"*

"Here." Henry dug in his pockets for money and bought the tickets to get rid of the man.

The seller darted off, dodging traffic, and his place was immediately taken by three more peddlers, hawking mangoes, bouquets of flowers, and boiled eggs. Henry pushed his way through them to the end of the bridge.

"Stick with the lottery tickets," an amused voice said in Spanish, and Henry turned to find the young man from the hotel at his elbow. "You wouldn't care for the eggs." He gave the egg seller a coin and cracked a shell open. Inside was an embryonic duckling, boiled. "They're a delicacy," he explained. His Spanish was fluent but accented.

A Mexican accent, with an American one on top, Henry thought. "For whom?" he asked, despite his growing discomfort at the fellow's presence.

The young man didn't claim acquaintance, however. Maybe he couldn't remember where they had met, either. He put his fingers in his mouth and whistled, and a Filipino girl just passing by turned to stare at him. She was about eight years old and barefoot, with a basket of dried fish on her head. She looked hungrily at the egg.

"For Filipinos," the young man said, presenting it to her. She wolfed it down nearly in one gulp. "I can't eat them, either," he confided to Henry. "There's something about that beak. . . ."

"A man will eat anything when he's hungry," Henry said curtly. He stuffed the lottery tickets in his pocket.

"The Manila lottery's an extraordinary institution," his companion said. "It generates half a million dollars in revenue for the government every year. You can buy tickets for it in Hong Kong."

"Extraordinary," Henry said. He didn't know how to get rid of the fellow.

"I don't suppose you speak English," the young man said wistfully. "Spanish is a strain for me."

"I am afraid I don't," Henry said. The young man showed no signs of going away, and Henry wondered if the fellow was looking for an easy mark or had some idea of blackmail. He'd get a surprise, Henry thought grimly.

They were standing on a small promontory overlooking the Luneta. "Carriages move counterclockwise around the drive," the young man said softly. "Only the governor-general and the archbishop are allowed to drive clockwise. That way no one has an excuse for not recognizing them and saluting. Everyone in Manila comes out to the Luneta in the evenings. On the nights when no concerts are scheduled, the government lines up rebels, or those suspected of being rebels, against the sea wall and shoots them. The citizens come out for that, too."

"Good God," Henry said, appalled. "The Spanish are barbarians."

"You are not Spanish?" the other inquired.

"No," Henry said shortly. "I am from Singapore."

The young man studied him. "I was raised in Hong Kong," he offered. "My people are British."

"No, they aren't," Henry said. "You're an American. You learned Spanish in Mexico." *Let's see what you do with that.*

"And anyone who could peg my accent that precisely isn't from Singapore," the other said, then chuckled. "I've been praying the Spanish wouldn't notice it." He sobered. "If the Americans are going to invade, I would very much like to know."

"How should I know what the Americans will do? But I don't imagine they are sitting in the harbor for no reason."

"I expect not," the other agreed. "Well, poor devils."

"Who? The Filipinos?"

"Oh, them, too. But it was the Americans I meant. They have no notion what they are getting into. There are pitfalls that they dream not of. Look here, couldn't we speak English? This is getting tiresome."

"I told you, I don't speak English." It was a very interesting game they were playing, Henry decided. He wasn't sure of the stakes, but he was beginning to enjoy himself. It was what he did best. "What pitfalls? Surely the Americans can't do a worse job than the Spanish. The Filipinos ought to be grateful for their presence."

"They would be grateful to have the Spanish chased out, I'm sure. But the Filipinos have the oddest notion— they want to run their country themselves."

Henry snorted. "They couldn't run a picnic by themselves. They have no unifying language, they have no army, they have a tribal economy, and they haven't the foggiest notion of hygiene."

"In other words, they're still in the Stone Age," his companion suggested.

"The ones in the mountains most certainly are. There are people back there even the Spanish don't know about."

"I've met some of them," the young man said, surprising Henry. "All of the earnest Americans who want to civilize the savages have yet to explain to me why the savages should be civilized at all. They show a marked disinclination for it."

"Well, there's no turning back for the ones in the cities," Henry countered. "They've been civilized far enough in some regards, and not enough in others."

The man laughed. "You're thinking of the duck egg. The Chinese eat far stranger things."

"I'm not thinking of the duck egg," Henry said huffily.

"I do not judge a country on its native dishes unless they happen to include some other fellow's liver."

"There are a few headhunters left in the mountains," the stranger admitted. "But I'm not certain they actually *eat* them."

"I don't give a damn whether they eat them or not," Henry said. "It just serves as further evidence that these tribes will never learn to get along with one another without some more advanced country's help."

"America being the more advanced country?"

"Some stabilizing influence is needed. These islands are in what may become a very critical spot on the globe. And they have natural resources that the Spanish have been too foolish and the natives too lazy to tap. They need to be carefully managed. Someone's got to step in. This rebellion has been going on for years, just like the one in Cuba. We can't have critically strategic areas existing in constant states of revolution and insurrection."

"You *are* an American," the other said. "Or an Englishman. No other nationality is so certain that it knows what everybody else ought to be doing."

He said it in English, and Henry barely managed to bite his tongue and look blank. Henry shrugged his shoulders, spread his hands. "I can't understand you. And I am afraid that I have business to conduct, if you will excuse me."

The young man smiled. "Of course." He turned down the path that led back into the old city, and Henry watched until the shadows of the gate swallowed him up. Henry set out in the opposite direction, along the Rosario, a crowded thoroughfare mired in mud from the constant rainfall and the hooves of ponies and water buffalo. Rain began to fall as he walked. A sheet of wind-driven water enveloped him. Despite the downpour, the rain was not much colder than body temperature. He took refuge under the overhang of a rickety shop and found himself nose-to-nose with a basket of what appeared to be pork snouts.

By the time the rain let up, the street was a quagmire.

Henry hailed a calesa and gritted his teeth as it careened wildly over bumps and ruts. He resisted the urge to close his eyes when a dray hauled by two stolid and enormous water buffalo loomed suddenly before them like a brick wall. The driver swerved around them with a hairbreadth to spare and exchanged incomprehensible insults with the driver of the dray.

At the hotel Henry saw with relief that there was no sign of his companion from the Intramuros.

Midday dinner was being served and proved to contain an enormous array of Spanish dishes, all flavored with either garlic or sweet peppers. Even with the usual small boys tugging on the punkah ropes, the day was growing hotter by the moment, and Henry was beginning to appreciate the Filipino native dress. For men this consisted of flat slippers, trousers, and a thin shirt, worn untucked, of the same pineapple cloth the women used for their dresses. The Europeans, despite heatstroke, persisted in the notion that an untucked shirttail was the moral equivalent of stark nudity.

As soon as the meal was finished the diners disappeared into their rooms for a siesta. Henry decided to do likewise. It seemed depraved to him somehow; but he knew that no business would be conducted, and no one would be about, in the heat of day. If he were, he would only make himself conspicuous. Accordingly he slid into the bed and wrestled with the mosquito netting. In so doing he had allowed a swarm of mosquitoes in under the mesh. He swore, chased most of them out again, and returned to his sanctuary to rub himself with citronella. He thought he smelled like lemon-flavored coal oil. A mosquito, which was apparently attracted to the citronella, whined past his ear until he slapped the pest between his palms.

Henry lay down upon the bed and discovered what the bolster was for—it was to support the parts of the anatomy that the bed did not—and once he had the hang of it, it proved an admirable invention. He stared at the ceiling for two hours, then got up again.

He spent the afternoon prowling the city and passed the evening observing the promenade of carriages on the Luneta. There was neither a band concert nor an execution that night, but the next evening he was subjected to exactly the spectacle that his young companion had described.

Five Filipinos, with their hands tied behind them, were marched out to the sea wall and lined up against it while the elite of Manila watched from their carriages. A Spanish firing squad raised its rifles, and the sound of the report was not quite drowned out by the cheers from the crowd.

Henry turned away suddenly, lips compressed, and bumped into a Spanish policeman standing on the lawn. Henry retreated hastily.

For the next few days, he roamed both the Intramuros and New Manila across the river and began to acquire the knowledge he had come for. It wasn't difficult to assess troop strength when the Spanish soldiers were paraded to impress potentially rebellious natives. A cursory inspection of the fortifications and the cannon defending the city prompted Henry to wonder why Spain had let matters come to a war with the United States. His own country might have been unprepared, but Spain appeared to be totally impoverished, holding on by its nails to a totally unworkable feudal society.

He reported as much to the contact person the admiral sent ashore on the appointed night, but, roaming the twisted streets of the Tondo market next morning, he could not help but be seduced by the splendid barbarian chaos that was the result. The native quarter was a rabbit warren of shops nearly all run by women or by Chinese. Vats of water lined the rows of the fish market, and vendors pulled out their wares for prospective customers, occasionally chasing a silvery sample that flopped off the counter. The air was redolent of fish—mud fish from the flooded rice fields, ocean fish caught by Japanese fishermen in the bay, little octopi, lobsters, sharks, and creatures Henry could not identify. A live turtle was tied by its tail to an iron stake outside one stall. It was nearly as big as a laundry basket, and it hissed and clicked its jaws at Henry.

He found more of the nearly hatched eggs, known as *balut*, and a cacophony of live birds, from minuscule songbirds in bamboo cages to furiously quacking wild ducks. The meat market offered pork and *carabao*, the water buffalo that was so ubiquitous in the islands, wrapped in banana leaves and tied with rice straw. Eggplant and sweet potatoes appeared to be the main offerings of the vegetable stalls, but the fruit vendors had an amazing array of goods. Pineapples were grown mostly for their fiber, but there were oranges, lemons, and pomelos, plus custard apples, mangoes, and papayas. There were bananas in a bewildering array. Henry tried one and found it had an odd, puckery taste.

For a long time he contemplated the durian—a fruit that resembled a green football covered with spines. It weighed eight or ten pounds and frequently injured passersby when it dropped from its tree. It had an odor more repellent than the moat or a well-aged Limburger cheese. Despite all that, he discovered that its fruit, covering a dozen or more egg-sized seeds, was sweet and nutty and more pleasantly like a banana than the bananas. Who was the first man, he wondered, who had eaten a durian? What desperation or leap of faith had prompted him to cut open that spiny shell and close his nostrils to that smell? To pull out one of those seeds and suck off its pulp? And having done all these things, the eater of the durian could expect great rewards. The durian, he was assured by the stall owner, restored vigor to old men and brought children to barren families.

The next stall offered cigars, tobacco, and betel nuts. Henry watched as a young girl in a green and scarlet dress, with huge gold hoops in her ears, bought betel nuts. She bit into one, and when she opened her mouth, blood appeared to drip from her lips. She smiled, exposing teeth as red as a vampire's.

"Extraordinary," Henry remarked. "Absolutely amazing." He was so intrigued with this beautiful creature with the startlingly scarlet mouth that he said it in English and thus called himself to the attention of a policeman.

The officer laid a large brown hand on Henry's shoulder. The policeman was a *mestizo*, mixed Spanish and Filipino, in a tropical uniform of white duck. "May I see your papers, señor?"

"Papers?" Henry looked guilelessly at him.

"Your passport. Your quarantine papers. Where are you from?"

"Singapore," Henry said. He put his hand into his pocket as if to draw out the requested papers. He withdrew it again and slapped his jacket to indicate the pocket's emptiness. "I believe I have left them at the hotel."

The policeman's nostrils flared. "You must come with me, señor."

"I can't possibly do that," Henry said gently. "You see, I have a most important appointment. If you will call at my hotel this evening, I will be glad to show you my papers." Henry hoped the policeman would assume that anyone naïve enough to make a suggestion like that must be innocent.

Apparently he did not. "No, señor," he said quite firmly. "You come with me now." He pulled a whistle from his breast pocket as if to summon assistance.

Henry took to his heels, and the policeman's whistle sounded a screeching blast.

Henry dodged among the stalls, sliding in the mud puddles that collected everywhere after a rain. He stumbled over the tethered turtle and twisted his way between piles of bananas. His whistle shrieking, the policeman pursued him.

The vendors took in the chase with interest. They did not seem inclined to join it but rather more to cheer the fleeing victim. As Henry ventured a backward glance, he saw an old woman with a stall of palm-leaf brooms stick one between the policeman's legs. The lawman went sprawling into a crate of chickens, which flew clucking into the air as the wood splintered.

Unfortunately the policeman was armed with a pistol. So was Henry, of course, but if he shot a policeman, he would land in a cell in the Fort of Santiago even more certainly than if he did not. A shot rang out behind him, and he dodged around another stall, praying that the gunfire wouldn't hit some innocent granny in her betel-nut shop.

Henry risked another look over his shoulder. The policeman stumbled on, kicking chickens out of his way. Henry knew that if he could just get lost in the maze of streets in the native quarter, he would be safe at least for a while. He turned a corner and fell into a man with a market basket on his arm.

It was the young man from the hotel. "Is that you they're after?" He started to laugh.

"Get out of my way," Henry said between his teeth, abandoning his pretense not to know English.

The young man hefted a huge melon and heaved it at the pursuing officer. It knocked him nearly sideways and splattered in the mud. The policeman's pistol slipped from his fingers, and before he could grab at it again, a Malay fish seller had snatched it up and retreated behind his counter with it. The policeman came after it and found the fish seller armed with a bolo, the long native machete with which nearly anything might be carved—fish, canoes, heads.

The young man grabbed Henry by the arm, and Henry decided to follow him. They dodged and ducked between rows of shops, nearly upending a housewife bargaining for a flounder, leaping the row of vats while the fishwife swore at them. The young man seemed to know where he was going. Behind them they heard a commotion that might be the policeman trying to retrieve his gun.

They ran between rows of native huts that stood on

poles above the mud flats. Henry's companion scrambled up the ladder that leaned from one, indistinguishable to Henry from all the rest. The young man stood on the porch and bowed into the hut, saying something Henry couldn't understand. Henry climbed the ladder and found a middle-aged Filipina smiling broadly at him with betel-stained teeth.

"This is Serafina. She only speaks Tagalog. She'll let us hide out here until the shouting dies down."

"Why?" Henry bowed to Serafina, too.

"Because she's a friend of mine," the young man explained. He ducked inside and sat on the bamboo floor, then motioned for Henry to do likewise. "I'm Paul Kirchner, by the way," he said. "I finally figured out where I knew you from. I met you at the Holts' ranch in Portland. You, er, weren't wearing blackface then."

Henry peered at him in the dim light of the hut. He sat down and scratched his head.

"Henry Blake," Paul said. "You're Toby Holt's brother-in-law."

"Information of which I was already aware," Henry said dryly. "I'm trying to place *you*."

"I was working for the Holts at the time. About four years ago."

Henry suddenly remembered the man. "You were getting ready to go off on some expedition with Teddy Montague! You're Maida Oberg's son! What the devil are you doing in Manila?"

"Still working for Teddy," Paul said. "The pay is dreadful—she's always one step ahead of her next quarter's income—but I've been to some amazing places. She's writing a book about the tropics. We were exploring the outer islands when war broke out, and we've had a hell of a time since. My being American makes it impossible to ask the Spanish for help. We can't think of anything to do but lie low till the war's over."

"Here?" Henry could see no evidence of inhabitants other than Serafina and her family, nor room for them.

Paul shook his head. "Serafina's husband is one of our bearers. We're camped in the jungle north of here. I come into Manila every now and then just to sniff the wind and do our marketing."

"I see."

"You'll notice I didn't ask you what you're doing here," Paul said, his eyes twinkling. "But if you feel that you've made Manila too hot for you, Teddy would be delighted to have company. I, er, think there's a strong possibility we may be camped with a fellow you've come to see."

Henry raised his eyebrows.

"General Aguinaldo," Paul said.

"Now you listen to me! You are not—repeat, *not*—to involve yourself in this war. This is a matter for the military to handle, and I won't have civilians running loose and creating incidents."

"We aren't involved," Paul said mildly. "Except to be hiding from the Spanish."

"If the Spanish catch you with Emilio Aguinaldo," Henry said, "you'll probably be shot in front of the sea wall."

"We didn't go out looking for Aguinaldo," Paul explained. "Serafina's husband took us to him when the war broke out. Neither Serafina nor Mateo have any use for the Spanish. They lost their only son to a firing squad."

Henry looked across the room at the woman. She was pretty; but her face was deeply lined, and Henry guessed that she looked older than she was. She smiled at him, having understood only her name in their conversation. She was boiling rice in a pot on an open fire built on a heap of earth in one corner. The window above her stood open, and she carefully fanned the smoke out, away from her guests. She had a pot of water on the fire, too, and after it boiled, she made coffee and brought it to them with a papaya on a bamboo tray.

"I wish she wouldn't do that," Paul said. "She always insists on feeding me, and I feel guilty about it because I

know they don't have much. But you can't refuse because
that would be insulting. We upped Mateo's wages out of
sheer guilt."

"I'm not happy about your hanging around with
Emilio Aguinaldo," Henry said. "But since you are, I
suppose I'll have to tell you that I *am* here to meet with
him. I was planning to go out tomorrow, but tonight might
be a better bet. I need to get my bag from the hotel,
though."

"I'll get it for you," Paul said. "The police are going to
be paying you more attention than is healthy."

Henry thought about that. "Go straight to the hotel,
pay my bill, and get the bag." *That* would give the desk
clerk something to smirk over, Henry thought, but he was
past his earlier embarrassment. He leveled a finger at
Paul. "Do not do anything else or speak to anyone else. Do
not play secret agent."

"I was planning to tunnel into the Government House
with a knife in my teeth," Paul said.

"What do I do while you're gone?" Henry asked. "I
can't talk to Serafina at all."

"Eat whatever she serves you," Paul said.

Henry sat wondering if he had lost his mind, trusting
this fellow. But he did remember Paul from Portland. And
Paul had certainly proved today to be the capable sort.

Henry still didn't like the notion of Paul and Teddy
Montague running loose with the insurrectionists, however. He contemplated these matters while Serafina sat
and smiled at him. After a while that began to make Henry
nervous, but he couldn't think of a way to get her to stop.

When he tried to speak to her, she immediately fed
him rice and fish and a cup of ginger tea, then sat down,
still smiling, to watch him eat. All in all, he was extremely
relieved when Paul came back.

They waited until dusk and then set out along the dirt
road that led out of the native quarter into the countryside.
Very quickly it turned from a road to a footpath and then

to a goat track in the jungle. Trails branched this way and that, and Paul seemed unerringly to know which to take. *If we have to fight in this,* Henry thought, *we'll need men with special training. This makes Cuba look like a botanical garden.*

They were climbing into the foothills, through a rain forest. The trees rose two hundred feet above their heads and were dense enough to block the sky. Fern, mosses, bamboo, and cane braided themselves into a mat that threatened to swallow the trail with every step. With twilight the trees shimmered mysteriously and formed strange shapes under the weight of the vines that were wound around them. Orchids, some in clusters as big as a carriage wheel, clung to the branches. As the night darkened, the fireflies came out, glittering swarms of them that cascaded through the trees. A monkey chattered at them from the crotch of a tree, and the birds made a constant din, undeterred by darkness.

"A truly magical place," Paul said. "No wonder the natives believe in spirits."

They stopped to rest for a moment and sat with their backs against a tree with a curiously lumpy trunk. Henry rubbed his hand over it.

"That's a strangling fig," Paul said. "It starts out as a vine and grows round and round an unsuspecting host. Eventually it kills the host by shutting out its light, and the fig's stems interlace until they look like a regular tree trunk—only it's hollow inside where the strangled tree has rotted away." Paul pondered the fig's trunk. "This country fascinates me. I envision myself sometimes caught, laced round, barely able to see out through the apertures."

"Let's get moving," Henry said abruptly.

Some distance farther, Paul held up a hand. "Stop a bit." He put his fingers in his mouth and whistled. A moment later, a rebel soldier popped up under their noses. He had a rifle on his back and a machete in his belt.

"Sorry to come back so late," Paul said in Spanish. "We had a little trouble, but no one is following us."

The soldier looked at Henry. "Who is this?"

"I am the one from the admiral," Henry said. "Señor Kirchner is an old acquaintance of mine. I bumped into him in the city."

The soldier turned and beckoned for them to follow. Aguinaldo's camp was a clearing in the jungle that held the tents of maybe five hundred men. There would be more such camps, all ringing the Spanish garrisons. As each outpost fell, the rebels converged on Manila. They were proving far more disciplined and aggressive than Dewey had bargained for, and Henry regarded them with a wary eye.

Emilio Aguinaldo, when he appeared, said that he was glad to see Colonel Blake. He was young, not quite thirty, with thick hair brushed back from his forehead and an intense, mobile face. "Have you brought me the American recognition of our independence?" he asked without preliminaries.

"I have been asked by Admiral Dewey to work with you and your men on how our forces may best cooperate," Henry said tactfully.

Aguinaldo frowned. "I have waited for an answer. It is important that I get this."

"General." Henry gave him the title deliberately. "I possess no authority to make these decisions or grant diplomatic recognition."

"We'll talk tomorrow," Aguinaldo said curtly.

"He's going to be difficult," Henry muttered after the rebel leader was out of earshot. "And we need him, damn it."

"Come on," Paul said. "I'll take you to Teddy. She'll be thrilled."

"I would prefer that Señor Aguinaldo were thrilled," Henry muttered. "I would prefer that you and Lady Teddy were elsewhere." He looked around him at the glow of campfires and the rebels with their guns. "I don't like this at all."

XIII

Lady Theodora Montague was nearly sixty, a brisk and pleasant woman whom Henry recalled as a kind of cheerful windstorm, sweeping about the globe and returning occasionally to America or her native England to lecture before geographical societies. She was generally described in the press as "the noted female explorer," but the truth was that she had taken up her avocation *because* she was female, rather than in spite of it. The other prospects available to a plain, intelligent woman of good family and limited funds had not looked promising.

Now she rose from a folding camp chair and greeted Henry with delight. "Colonel Blake!" Teddy shook his hand forcibly. "Just fancy!"

"I was surprised to find *you* here, ma'am," Henry said.

Teddy inspected his darkened hair and skin with amusement, but she made no comment. "Well, I'm quite aggravated to be here," she informed him. "Your war has put a dreadful crimp in my schedule. General Aguinaldo has been very kind, however, and made us extremely comfortable." She made a vague gesture at their tents, set up on the edge of the rebel encampment. There appeared to be four small canvas shelters, two occupied by bearers. A string of ratlike native ponies was tethered behind them. "We had quite a nice house in the village several days ago," Teddy continued, "but when General Aguinaldo moved on, we thought we'd be safer going with him."

"I'm not sure that was the best idea," Henry said.

"Well, my dear man, you weren't there at the time," Teddy retorted.

Paul was unable to suppress a chuckle.

"Have some tea," said Lady Teddy. "And sit down." She motioned to a Filipino bearer, and he squatted by the fire and extracted a hot kettle from the coals.

"This is Mateo," Paul said. "Serafina's husband."

Mateo looked up at the sound of his name and smiled at Henry. "Good morning," he said.

"That's all the English he knows," Teddy explained. "But he can manage a bit of Spanish. He's an excellent servant—provides you with anything you need. Just ask," she told Henry. Her tone reminded him of the manner in which gracious English ladies welcomed houseguests. She took up her palm-leaf fan and waved it while Mateo brewed a pot of oolong.

Henry studied her. Teddy's graying hair was pinned in a plain pompadour, and she wore a khaki shirtwaist and a divided skirt of tan gabardine. On her feet were serviceable hiking boots, and the only concession that Henry could see to her age was a carved ebony walking stick. She was an earl's daughter, with a modest inherited income that generally ran out halfway through her expeditions, necessitating cables to her brother in England. An advance on the next quarter might or might not be forthcoming— the brother found her an embarrassment—but Lady Teddy took setbacks in good cheer. Henry had heard that she had once made a living reading tea leaves in a Tibetan village after her brother refused to wire her a check. Henry wondered what the brother would do if she was caught up in a revolution and arrested by the Spanish. The man would probably blame the United States, Henry decided.

"I could arrange to have you taken on board one of our troop transports," Henry suggested.

"Wouldn't hear of it," Teddy said. "*Very* kind of you.

But we have an enormous amount of work left to do in the region. We haven't even gotten to Mindanao."

"Just leave until the situation stabilizes," Henry said. "You wouldn't have to give up your expedition entirely."

Teddy looked him in the eyes. "As soon as the Spanish are defeated, you'd put me ashore?"

"As soon as the situation is stable," Henry said.

"No offense intended, Colonel," Teddy said, "but no, thank you. I get aboard one of your ships, and I'll be stuck there until you Americans decide to let me off." She lowered her voice. "I'm not saying I disagree with you, if your government is reluctant to let these islands govern themselves. I myself don't think they're fit for it. But I'm not going to be kept cooling my heels until you've settled it. I have too much work to do."

"I don't set my government's policy," Henry said stiffly. "I am merely concerned for your safety."

"Well, then, I shouldn't worry about it if I were you," Teddy told him. "These fellows here will do me no harm." Mateo set a bamboo tray with teapot and cups on the camp table at her elbow, and she poured Henry a cup. "Sugar, Colonel?"

"Lemon," Henry said irritably.

Paul, who had been silent during this last exchange, accepted the cup of tea that Teddy handed him and smiled into its depths. "I believe Colonel Blake is more concerned about our safety from the Spanish, which you know perfectly well. I'm afraid I didn't bring our groceries back," he added. "So that's the last of the sugar."

"What did you do with them?" Teddy asked.

"Lost them in the market when I bumped into Colonel Blake. There was a row—the police were after him. It was Colonel Blake or the groceries, I'm afraid."

"Oh, well, in that case," Teddy said graciously, "there was no question."

Paul chuckled again, and Henry developed a growing suspicion that they were both having a laugh on him. He did not mind, though. He liked Teddy Montague, admired her grit and her unflappable attitude in the face of all setbacks. He found her plainness and lack of feminine attributes a relief. It meant that he could deal with her as if she were a man. For Henry that was comfortable and comforting.

Paul Kirchner, on first meeting, had seemed to be Teddy's opposite—an irreverent drifter who had abandoned his prosperous family business to chase some dream down endlessly branching paths. He had been working as a ranch hand on the Madrona between one feckless venture and the next, or so it had seemed to Henry at the time. But another side altogether had surfaced in Manila, and Paul's quick thinking and daring claimed a good deal of kinship with Henry Blake. And Paul could keep his head in a crisis. The young man could play Henry's game. In fact, he showed a great natural talent for it.

"I'll go back to Manila for your groceries tomorrow," Henry said to Teddy. "It will be an excellent excuse to scrub my face."

"If you think that returning to your natural coloring will render you unrecognizable," Paul remarked, "then think again. You'll be more conspicuous than you were."

"You *don't* know everything," Henry informed him. "Most people don't look at anything but the features that stand out the most. Why do you think all Chinese look alike to us? We all look alike to them, too. The average person doesn't see beyond the mere fact of being Chinese, or whatever. The police will be looking for a dark-haired man, probably a mestizo. I could probably bump smack into the fellow who chased me and not trigger anything, except having my papers asked for, for looking European."

"Well, you don't want that to happen, either," Paul pointed out.

"I didn't say I *was* going to bump into him."

"*I'll* go back for the groceries."

"I have to go anyway—if not tomorrow, then eventually. I have to monitor the situation there."

"I can monitor it as well as you can," Paul said. "I'm

an old hand at monitoring. And the cops aren't looking for me—not in Manila anyway."

"How do you know?" Henry retorted. "You threw a melon at the policeman. If he got a good look at you, then he's looking for you."

"He doesn't want to let anyone else have any fun," Paul said to Teddy.

"It isn't fun, and you aren't being paid to do it," Henry said.

"To do what?" Teddy said.

"He's a spy," Paul said.

"How exciting," Teddy said.

"I'm an army officer!" Henry snapped, and they grinned at him.

"We're being bad," Teddy said to Paul. "And you, particularly. You go into Manila with Colonel Blake and behave yourself and bring me back my sugar."

"Yes, memsahib."

Henry watched them, amused now. "Do you do vaudeville?" he inquired.

"We've considered it," Teddy said happily. "My brother's suggestion—the little earl. He was terribly affronted after my last lecture in England. He said I ought to stick to geography and stay away from native customs." She pursed her lips and looked less amused. "He felt that I was speaking on matters unsuitable for a middle-aged spinster. He thought I made myself ridiculous. He believes there is something undignified, almost vulgar, in a homely, unmarried woman having any sort of adventurous life, any knowledge."

"He's a pig," Paul growled. "He didn't like me, either. He thought I was her fancy boy."

"If I'd been born a man," Teddy said, "he'd be bragging to his cronies at the club about his brother the famous explorer. Nor would he mind if his *brother* had a fancy boy. Well, bad luck to him."

Henry wondered silently if Teddy had ever *had* a

fancy boy, or anyone else. Being plain did not make one uninterested in love.

"I really can't forgive him for that," Teddy said firmly. "He told me I had made him a laughingstock."

"It's always easier to forgive scurrilous accusations than ridicule," Paul said gently. He put a hand over Teddy's.

She sighed. "I suppose so, dear. Well, there's no point in talking about Vincent. It upsets my digestion. Colonel Blake, I shall bid you good night. I expect Paul can make room for you in his tent."

She held out her hand again, and Henry rose and shook it. After a few moments a large lizard made a hurried exit from Teddy's tent. They heard her muttering as she wrestled herself under her mosquito netting, and then all was silent.

The fires of the rebel camp had burned low, but neither Paul nor Henry felt any urge to sleep. The dangerous events of the day had left them wakeful.

"Maybe I'll hunt tomorrow," Paul said, "instead of marketing. It seems silly to me to buy food in Manila when it grows on the trees out here. Or roosts in them." He shied a rock into the vine-covered canopy, and a hornbill flew up squawking.

"How did you get guns out here?" Henry noted the proliferation of rifles and shotguns in Teddy's camp. No explorer could do without them, but Spanish customs routinely seized incoming weapons lest they fall into the hands of rebels.

"With a great deal of tenacity," Paul said. "It was before war broke out. Between us and Spain, I mean. Teddy had an attaché case full of official documents and credentials. The little earl may denigrate her, but her government is proud of the woman. The British consul here set them all off on the proper channels. Otherwise, the request could have gotten lost on some bureaucrat's desk. 'No, señor, we do not know where your papers have gone.'"

Henry chuckled. "It's much simpler just to smuggle one's guns ashore."

"True," Paul allowed, "but you aren't traveling with eight trunks and a companion. Teddy would have preferred smuggling. In fact, she suggested it when the Customs House and the governor-general's office began shuttling us between them—mostly for their amusement, I suspect. But by that time the Customs House *had* the guns, and we were trying to get them back. The *administrador* of the Customs House couldn't read a word of our papers, but they have quantities of wonderful wax seals. I think he would have approved our request on the seals alone if he hadn't been afraid of the governor-general. And the governor-general didn't want to pass them largely because he doesn't like the British. He sent us on to the civil governor. *He* refused to do anything unless the governor-general ordered him to."

Henry looked at Paul. "Well? How *did* you get the guns?"

"I'm working up to it," Paul said. "You'll like this part. We went to call on the archbishop. Teddy had classified some of the birds in the Jesuit College museum for the padre in charge there, and he got us an entrée to the archbishop's palace. She talked theology and drank sherry with His Grace for half an hour and came away with a personal request for the governor-general. It did the trick. The church here has even more political power than the military."

"I know," Henry said, "and it makes me uneasy. Having the church work cooperatively with the government for the suppression of the people is a perversion, to my mind."

Paul poked the fire with a stick and watched the sparks fly up. They made a cloud like the fireflies, and then they settled again into the red heart of the fire. "These gentlemen here"—Paul turned his head to indicate the rebel camp—"are very bitter toward the church. The church has refused to appoint Filipino priests, and the Spanish ones are very much disliked. They are very religious men. Some kind of native church will come out of the ashes, I think. But I wouldn't like to be a friar just now."

"Will they harm the priests?" Henry asked. "Killing a priest—"

"They already have," Paul said shortly. "All of the friars are essentially spies for the Spanish. Aguinaldo's men caught one yesterday. There wasn't anything we could have done about it, or done for him, so we stayed away. But I'll remember it for a while."

"Stay out of things like that," Henry said unnecessarily.

"You are preaching to the converted," Paul assured him. He grimaced. "Unfortunate analogy."

"What the devil are you doing with Lady Teddy, anyway?" Henry asked him. "I would have thought you had a career all cut out for you."

"So did my mother, unfortunately," Paul said. "It's only in the last year that I can drink Oberg beer without having the sensation of tipping hemlock down my throat. I was supposed to be the next master brewer, the last of the Obergs. I cut and ran."

Henry looked at him thoughtfully. "And you haven't been back since?"

"I tried," Paul said, "last year at Christmas. I think Father was glad to see me, but Mother couldn't help launching into a catalog of my sins. She tried not to, I think, but she just couldn't stop herself. I didn't turn out the way I was supposed to, and she simply can't accept that fact."

"What was the matter with beer?" Henry asked. *What is the matter with the army?* He had the oddest sensation that he might be talking to Frank.

"Mostly that it was more important to her than I was," Paul answered. "I was supposed to learn this arcane specialty, to the exclusion of any other interests, to make certain that Oberg beer continued to exist. That Oberg beer existed was more important than whether I was happy. After I figured that out, I left."

"Didn't your father have any influence?"

Paul smiled. "Not over my mother. No one has a say when my mother's set on something. I'm much more like my father in temperament and interests. But he's perfectly happy because he adores her. He wanted me to be a brewer simply so that Mother would have what *she* wanted."

Henry felt momentarily irritated that Cindy had not adopted that attitude. He brooded into the fire. By rights he should dislike a young lout who had thrown over his parents' plans for a meaningless whim. But Henry had met Maida Oberg—a stiff-necked, impossible, tunnel-visioned woman if ever there was one. Paul probably had a point in not wanting to work with her.

"At least they know where you are," Henry said moodily. "You've had the decency to keep in touch."

"I didn't for several years," Paul said. "I had the irrational fear that if Mother knew where I was, she would swoop down like an eagle and carry me off in her talons. Then I realized that if I didn't shake myself out of that, I would never be an adult. I would be a bad child forever. So I wrote from the Madrona and told them where I was. Father answered, but Mother wouldn't. That was why I went home at Christmas, to try to mend things."

"You couldn't have stayed and been a brewer anyway, despite your mother's attitude?" Henry asked. His voice held a faint note of pleading. "Family tradition is important, in the way that honor is important. It's what links you, grounds you, gives you your place. If you deny that place, you take a slap at everyone who went before you."

"Not unless they choose to take it that way," Paul said. "I didn't feel inclined to play Isaac to my mother's Abraham and her great god Beer."

"That's a harsh analogy," Henry said. "Not to mention sacrilegious."

Paul grinned. "I expect my mother would find it apt.

Assuming, of course, that she had a sense of humor." He stood and yawned again. "I have words of wisdom for you, Colonel Blake. When you have children who are old enough—do you have children?"

"Three," Henry said.

"Ten generations of family tradition will not make the eleventh love it if he doesn't love it on his own. Have one of them paint that in large black letters across a wall in your living room. And now I'm going to bed. Pontificating makes me tired." He crawled into the tent next to Teddy's, then stuck his head out again a moment later to inform Henry that spare bedding and a mosquito net would be found within.

He withdrew again and left Henry staring at the glowing coals. They burned sullenly, and to Henry the coals seemed like red eyes, piggish and malevolent, staring back at him. He emptied the tea kettle on them in a cloud of hissing steam. It was uncomfortably hot already; who would want scalding tea?

In the morning Henry awoke with the instantaneous sentience he had learned to command, aware even before he opened his eyes of where he was and what hazards might be there with him. Paul was snoring gently beside him, cocooned in mosquito netting. The young man was a restless sleeper; his netting had come loose from its framework, and now he was wrapped like a larva in it.

Henry crawled out from under his own net and collected the shaving kit from his bag. The air was hot even at daybreak. As he tried to lather his face with tepid water he realized why he should not have doused the fire—his shaving soap floated like scum in the bowl. He was doggedly shaving with it anyway when the face of Emilio Aguinaldo appeared in the mirror, behind his left shoulder.

"Good morning, Colonel Blake."

"Good morning, General." Henry went on carefully shaving.

"We must confer."

"As soon as I have removed my whiskers." Henry tilted his chin to shave beneath it. The lather was taking the walnut stain off along with the beard. Aguinaldo watched impassively as if Americans always removed their surface semblance in the morning.

After Henry had scrubbed himself clean, he worked shampoo into his hair, then poured a pitcher of water over it, to emerge with his natural coloring. He rubbed his head with a towel. "Ah, much better. Now, then. Good morning, General. I am sorry to have kept you waiting."

"Good morning, Colonel. Have you brought me your government's recognition of Philippine independence?" Aguinaldo asked as if last night's Colonel Blake had been a completely different person, someone who had vanished with the walnut dye.

Unfortunately the answer was still the same. "That is not a matter upon which I possess any authority," Henry said firmly.

"Your Admiral Dewey promised me!" Aguinaldo snapped. "We have been very useful to you, but we will not remain useful if we are treated as ignorant peasants."

"I am certain that is not the admiral's intention," Henry said. "Possibly there was a misunderstanding between you and the admiral." He smiled apologetically. "His Spanish is not very good."

"We spoke through an interpreter!" Aguinaldo retorted.

"Of course." Henry tried another tack. "Admiral Dewey has requested that I present myself to you as an aide-de-camp, to plan how we may best cooperate with your forces in driving these Spanish devils out of Manila."

Aguinaldo's eyes were hard and black. "If America is at war with Spain, then certainly that is to our advantage. But we are not a prize, a booty for the winner. We have proclaimed ourselves an independent nation."

"Yes. Possibly that was, er, a bit precipitous," Henry allowed. "But—"

"That is not the province of the United States

government to decide," Aguinaldo said. "That is for us, for the revolution."

"Frankly, General," Henry said, "I'm afraid your revolution doesn't stand much of a chance without us."

"We have already taken many garrisons, many villages. Next we will take Manila."

"And how will you govern after you have done so?" Henry asked. "With respect, General, governing is different from fighting. Shooting the opposition is no longer an option. One must get all the factions to work smoothly with one another. Perhaps if you were to let the United States guide you, at first—"

Aguinaldo's teeth clicked irritably. "We are not children! We do not require guiding! It is not the business of the United States to guide us."

Henry strove for as much tact as he could muster. "Most of your land is totally unimproved. Manila is a decaying, medieval mess, rife with disease. Your people are scattered throughout hundreds of islands and speak scores of languages. Some are the enemies of others. *How* will you govern?"

"That is the doing of the Spanish," Aguinaldo said. "We will change that."

"Perhaps you are right," Henry said soothingly. It wouldn't do to come to open dispute with Aguinaldo. "Perhaps. But I do not represent my government in diplomatic matters. I, too, am a soldier, and only a soldier, I'm afraid." He heard a rustle behind him and greeted the appearance of Teddy Montague with relief.

She wore a freshly pressed costume of tan twill, the twin of yesterday's, with a strong odor of citronella and pennyroyal against mosquitoes, and a pith helmet. "Good morning, General," she boomed cheerfully. "Will you join us for coffee? I have a sack I've been hoarding."

"Dear lady." Aguinaldo bowed over her hand. "With pleasure." He seemed to regard her as a sort of pet in his camp. Henry had the suspicion that Teddy regarded Aguinaldo in the same way.

"No sugar, though," Teddy said. "Colonel Blake has promised me some today. Good morning to you, too, Colonel. You look somewhat paler this morning."

"Only the natural man appearing," Henry said. "And, indeed, if General Aguinaldo will give me a safe passage, I shall certainly acquire your sugar." He nodded at Aguinaldo. "The general understands that it is my orders from my admiral that I keep a close watch on the Spanish. Young Señor Kirchner has offered to go with me, but I would prefer that he didn't. It is not even moderately safe for Americans in the city just now."

Aguinaldo sucked his teeth. He gave Henry a long, thoughtful, suspicious look while Teddy's bearer rebuilt the fire and Teddy took herself into the woods, the only place that afforded any privacy. "*You* are going," he said finally.

"It is my duty," Henry said. "Young Kirchner is not in the army."

"Then I will send one of my men with you," Aguinaldo said abruptly. "I wouldn't like you to mistake the path." He sat down in a camp chair to await the coffee and nodded dismissal at Henry. Since Henry had no place else to go, he sat down, too, and they kept a not particularly companionable silence.

Breakfast was rice and salt fish—staples of the native diet—and papaya cut from a strange upright tree in the camp. Fruits as big as Henry's head clung to its trunk and were interspersed with five-foot-long, inch-thick protrusions like whiskers.

General Aguinaldo reappeared with a written safe passage scrawled on copybook paper. Behind him walked a rebel soldier with a rifle, who carried a cartridge belt slung across his bare chest. Henry set off down the path toward the city, with his escort, or guard, behind him. He felt like a convict laborer and was happy to say good-bye to the fellow at the jungle's edge.

The soldier had no such intentions, however. He

buried his rifle and cartridge belt in a mass of vines at the base of a lauan tree. "General Aguinaldo says I go with you."

"That isn't necessary."

"I go." The escort and Henry stared at each other stubbornly until finally Henry shrugged his shoulders.

"Have it your way."

They walked through the outskirts of the native quarter and bought sugar and other commodities as they occurred to Henry. His escort packed them into a string bag he had carried about his waist and followed Henry, for all the world like a dutiful bearer.

Henry had no particular business in the old city, but what he did have on his calendar—another rendezvous with an emissary from Dewey—he had no intention of accomplishing with this watchdog in tow. Accordingly, he ventured into the Intramuros, hoping the proximity to the Spanish authorities would unnerve his rebel escort. The escort remained impassive. Henry sighed. Possibly there was not yet a price on the fellow's head. There seemed to be nothing else to do but lose him. Henry ducked into the shadows of a gateway, and while his watchdog darted after him, he sprinted under the nose of a water buffalo dragging a cartful of copra and scooped up a rock from the street as he straightened.

The carabao, the Philippine water buffalo, does not like the smell of white men as a rule, and this one in particular must have been new to the city. It snorted, rolled its eyes, and lifted its heavy hooves nervously. Henry gibbered at it as he passed, and then shied the rock at its underbelly. The carabao is a generally slow and stolid animal until it stampedes, and then it has the force of a runaway locomotive. This one let out a snort of terror and tried to turn around, cart and all, in the tunnel gate, while its driver hung on and prayed, eyes closed. Henry slid from the other end of the tunnel and vanished.

He had to wait until dusk to conduct his business with the boat from the American fleet, and it took longer than he expected. There was news for him, too, of the American engagement at Santiago de Cuba. It was well past dark when he arrived at the jungle's edge and the spot where his rebel escort had hidden his rifle. Henry approached cautiously, unsure of whether the man was there, and if so, where his rifle might be pointing.

He was there, squatting patiently and smoking. "Where have you been?" The anger in his voice was still tinged with a certain deference, but the deference was lessening.

"Where were *you*?" Henry retorted. He managed a tone of righteous indignation. "That beast tried to kill me, and afterward I couldn't find you."

"Carabao don't like white men," the soldier said.

"And what were you doing while I was finding that out?"

"I looked for you," the soldier said indignantly.

"Well, *I* looked for *you*. And you couldn't have looked very hard because I didn't find you. Have you got Lady Theodora's groceries?"

The soldier hefted the string bag and held it out to Henry.

"Good." Henry started up the path, leaving Aguinaldo's watchdog to follow with the groceries.

They reached camp with no further dispute; but the watchdog was not happy, and when they arrived, well into the night, he went at once to confer with his general.

Matters were not improved when Henry, who had learned the path by now, slipped out of camp before daylight and went back to Manila on his own. He stopped to darken his hair and face again, then spent much time in a café in the new city, drinking vile coffee and listening to the talk around him. The patrons were educated Filipinos, mestizos, mostly, the ruling social class. They were schooled at the Catholic universities; their fathers or grandfathers had been Spanish merchants and provincial officials. Spanish rule sat fairly lightly on them: They were the ones who had sat in their carriages and cheered executions on the Luneta. If Spain was to be overthrown by an army of peasants, then the peasants would want to run the government, and one couldn't have that.

Henry drank his coffee and felt gratified. After Spain was defeated, these upstanding citizens would want very little to do with Emilio Aguinaldo. They would embrace the advantages of American know-how and American culture and send Aguinaldo back to his farm.

Feeling reasonably confident, Henry reappeared in Aguinaldo's camp that evening to find the general much peeved, in conference with a slim dark man in a chair. From the army briefing Henry had studied, he recognized Apolinario Mabini. Mabini possessed the bony countenance and wide eyes of an ascetic. He was a law graduate of Santo Tomas University, Henry had been told, and accounted to be the brains of the Philippine rebellion. Even in this heat he wore a robe draped over his lap. He was unable to walk, and when he wished to change his position, two hefty soldiers lifted him, chair and all.

Henry did not get so far as Teddy's camp. Aguinaldo spun around when the soldier who had permitted Henry entrance into the camp shouted at him.

"That is the American!" Aguinaldo snapped at Mabini, who nodded.

A rebel soldier caught Henry by the collar and propelled him forward toward Aguinaldo. Furious, Henry stumbled and righted himself.

"You did not have my permission to leave this camp!" Aguinaldo's voice was no longer conversational, but it was not quite a shout.

"I do not require your permission," Henry said, barely keeping a grip on his temper.

"You require my permission!" Aguinaldo snapped. "As governor-general of the Philippine Republic—"

"I am an American citizen," Henry said. "I do not answer to anyone's government but my own. I have my orders from my commanders, and with all due respect,

General, they do not include informing you of my actions."

Mabini leaned forward in his chair and spoke to Aguinaldo in a low voice.

Henry addressed himself to Mabini. "Perhaps *you* will understand, señor—"

"We understand this much," Mabini interrupted. "Your government has given no recognition of the right to independence of the Philippines."

"Perhaps my government does not feel that you are ready," Henry said.

"And you confer with the Spanish behind my back," Aguinaldo said. "You negotiate with them to betray us! To wipe out our army before they surrender to you!"

"Now, see here," Henry said, outraged, "we are at war with Spain!"

"What my friend says is possible," Mabini said flatly. He looked at Aguinaldo. "In fact, it is likely. The Europeans will all betray us if they can."

Aguinaldo unholstered his pistol and cocked it. "I have had enough. I do not kowtow to the Americans. I do not sit by while American spies conspire with the Spanish."

"You listen to me," Henry began, wondering if the man had actually lost his mind enough to shoot him.

"Colonel Blake!" Teddy's voice boomed behind him, and they all froze in midmotion. She sailed through the camp like a gunboat, her decks bristling with reinforcements. Henry saw Paul coming purposefully through the darkness behind her, moving in and out of the orange roundels of the fires.

"There you are, Colonel!" Teddy slapped Henry chummily on the back. "We were beginning to worry that you might have run afoul of a Spanish patrol."

"Or something else," Paul said pointedly.

"Well, we've held dinner for you," Teddy said. "I'm sure the general will excuse you—won't you, General?— until you've eaten. You must be famished, and Mateo's been keeping it hot."

Teddy and Paul slid up on either side of him, as

smoothly as sheepdogs cutting one beast from the herd, and drew him away through the splashes of firelight. Aguinaldo said nothing as they left.

"That was a near thing," Teddy commented as they reached their own camp. "If Paul hadn't spotted what was happening, I think you'd have been a goner." She shook her head. "Before the poor fool got his temper back and figured out it wasn't a good idea to shoot you in front of witnesses. That *would* annoy the Americans."

"I doubt they would have done it," Henry said, "but I appreciate your help."

"We had no choice," Paul said, chuckling. "If they shot you while we were in the camp, they'd have had to decide what to do about us."

"They may yet," Henry said.

"Not now that they've thought about it," Paul said. "The general tends to be, er, precipitate, but by now I'm sure he's realized that killing you and Lady Teddy would prove fatal to his cause."

Henry managed to get his breath back. "He's got it in his head that I'm plotting to betray his men to the Spanish, to be ambushed, before we attack the Spanish."

"That's disgraceful," Teddy said. "I can't believe you would countenance such a thing."

"*I* can," Paul said. "The government can be appallingly practical. But I will certainly take Colonel Blake's word for it that he isn't."

"Of course I'm not," Henry said irritably. Actually he had thought of it. He disliked the idea, but if the Spanish and the Filipinos killed each other off, American lives would be saved. Fortunately it wasn't his business to suggest it, but if he was ordered to, he would have arranged it. Paul and Lady Teddy, civilians, didn't understand that unpalatable things had to be done for the greater good.

Henry glanced at Paul. The young man was taking the lid off a pot that rested on a rack above the coals. "Wild pig à la Kirchner," he announced into a fragrant cloud of steam. "The salt fish got to my brain this morning. Mateo and I went hunting."

Henry peered into the pot. "You cooked this?" he inquired skeptically.

"Mmm. A little garlic, a little ginger. As it happens, I am an excellent cook. I worked in a Chinese restaurant once. After you have done that, you can make a dinner of anything."

Henry, exasperated, scooped some onto a plate and sat back in a camp chair. "Why the devil haven't you turned your hand to something respectable? You've been more things than I can count, any one of which could have been parlayed into an excellent career. You're wasting yourself. It didn't have to be beer or nothing."

"Possibly not," Paul agreed. "It may be that I just have a screw loose."

"You're perfectly capable."

Paul looked at Henry thoughtfully. "Maybe I don't want to be capable. With respect, Colonel, you're too capable for my taste."

"Then why bother talking to me?" Henry inquired. He raised his eyebrows, waiting for an answer. It was a look that unnerved subordinates.

"I've learned to pick my friends where I find them," Paul said, apparently not unnerved.

Henry gave a bark of laughter.

"I'll tell you, Colonel," Paul said, "if it hadn't been for Mother, I expect I *would* have been quite happily settled somewhere, raising pigs or totaling columns in a bank. You're quite right—it didn't have to be beer or nothing. But Mother thought it did."

"So it's all her fault you're a young—well, *wastrel*'s too harsh. But what have you achieved as Teddy's assistant, except to see the sights?"

"Maybe that's all I want," Paul commented. "And, no, what I've made of my life is my doing, not Mother's. I'm old enough to grasp that. But I'm happy."

Henry felt unreasonably angry at that. There was so

much riding on convincing Paul to turn his life around. He felt as if he were talking to Frank, trying to make *him* see. For two young men of so much promise simply to chuck it—well, he had a personal reason to be annoyed at that, too.

And where—the idea smacked him between the shoulder blades like a hand—was the likeness between himself and Maida Oberg? Did he, Henry, have anything in common with that humorless woman, a woman whose chief characteristic was destructive rigidity? Was that how his own wife and children saw him? Set aside the fact that army service was a far more important tradition than brewing beer. It wasn't in the eyes of Maida Oberg.

How did she feel about it? Henry wondered. How did it feel to be estranged forever from a child? *Was* the beer more important to her than Paul?

Henry looked across the fire. Paul was eating wild pig and apparently contented, happy to be in a wilderness on the other side of the world from the woman who had borne him.

"Do you hate your mother?" Henry asked quietly, a sharp note of pain buried in his question.

Paul lifted his head from his plate. He smiled slightly. "Not really, no. But I can't say I like her. I don't even think I love her anymore."

XIV

Misery Hill, outside Santiago, July 8

William Randolph Hearst had gone to Cuba in a steam yacht chartered from the Baltimore Fruit Company and equipped for a tropical campaign with working darkroom, printing press, two racing ponies for use on shore, and a large supply of ice. He went ashore, interviewed the generals, and judged them all to be heroic. He watched the bombardment of the San Juan Heights, took down a wounded reporter's dictation of the capture of El Caney, and witnessed the big Spanish field artillery make mincemeat of the American batteries. Still, Hearst remained optimistic. "Our troops," he wrote, "have received their baptism of fire, and no army of Spaniards can dislodge them from the ground they have won or stay their steady march toward Santiago itself."

It was Hearst's optimism—rather than the forebodings of Tim Holt and by now of even Richard Harding Davis and Shafter and his aides—that most Americans read over their breakfast eggs.

Tim and Mike Holt sat in the entrance of their tent, under a wilting palm thatch, and stared glumly down onto the roofs of Santiago. Beside them, Hugo Ware was recording in his sketchbook the flood of refugees that streamed out of the city and down the narrow road through the jungle.

The malnourished men, women, and emaciated chil-

dren had been on the move for four days, trying to get out
of the way of the war. On July 4, the Spanish fleet had
made a run for it, but Sampson and Schley had blown it
out of the water. Admiral Cervera, an imposing old
gentleman covered in gold braid and decorations, was a
prisoner aboard the *St. Louis*.

The civilians were afraid of the American guns, not
the American soldiers. Fearing the bombardment of the
city, they retreated past the American lines to El Caney,
where they clamored to be fed. Tim had been down to El
Caney for a look around and came back sick at heart.
Whether it was the Americans' fault or Spain's, he didn't
know; but the sight of children dying while their mothers
begged for food and medicine from soldiers who didn't
have either was too much for him.

The *Clarion* staff was encamped with an artillery
battery on what had already become known as Misery
Hill. The whole encirclement of the siege of Santiago was
called Misery Ridge. Below them was a jungle-filled valley
and then the Spanish trenches outside the city. Tim
counted over thirty Red Cross flags marking hospitals
within the walls, presumably as an inducement to the
Americans not to shell them. Meanwhile, Spanish snipers
were still shooting from the trees at the Americans'
stretcher bearers.

The battery and the infantry battalion next to it had
pitched their tents wherever they could be fastened to the
uneven ground. There were no shade trees, only cacti,
which couldn't be chopped out with a rod bayonet. The
food was failing. The tinned beef, which had been repellent to begin with, was gone, and the sowbelly that had
replaced it would not keep in the heat. The whole camp
reeked of rotting sowbelly. Hardtack was all that was left,
and even that had to be packed on mules ten miles from
Siboney. Tim, who could get Rafe to bring some supplies
from Jamaica, felt guilty eating them. He and Mike and
Hugo ate one of the hoarded cans of tomatoes in their

tent, where no one could see them, then gave the other away.

It was unbearably hot, even when it rained. There was nowhere to go to escape the heat. The afternoon breeze did nothing to relieve the men's misery. There was a truce now, while General Shafter dickered by messenger with the Spanish general Toral, inside Santiago, for his surrender. The men sat or lay motionless in the heat, and sickness was beginning to creep through the camp. Shafter was still ill, although the correspondents' dispatches skirted the outright statement that he was incapacitated. The men were suffering with malaria, typhoid, and dysentery, and there would be yellow fever soon—it was already at Siboney.

The journalists who had refused to criticize the army at Tampa looked on with horror, and Richard Harding Davis filed a dispatch that provoked a flood of attacks in Washington on the War Department. Given Davis's earlier quarrel with Poultney Bigelow over dispatches that lowered morale, Tim felt inclined to congratulate Davis on a courageous about-face; but Hearst's *Journal* and *Harper's Weekly* ran editorials calling him a traitor.

"All very well for them," Mike said indignantly. "They're not here to see it."

"Hearst is," Tim said. "You have to allow him that."

"Self-aggrandizing bastard," Hugo grumbled over his shoulder. "I don't have to give him credit for anything." He wiped his face with his bandanna.

Mike was occupied with using a rock to pound coffee beans, which he then fried in a tin cup, to bits. Hugo had managed to buy green, unroasted beans in Siboney. A drumroll that they at first thought was thunder came dimly through the racket.

"Hush a minute," Hugo said. He peered forward. Mike put the coffee aside and looked, too.

On the slope below them, the army had set up a table with three camp chairs, and as the men watched, three senior officers filed up and sat in them. A company of guards brought two Spanish prisoners up to the table. Their pale blue cotton uniforms were stained with mud and grass.

"They caught those two firing into the hospital at the men on stretchers," Hugo said. "I heard about it this morning."

More Americans had noticed what was going on, and they lined the hilltop to watch. They were too far above the tableau to pick out voices, but what was happening was plain. The trial was short, almost perfunctory, and they watched the verdict being read. The Spanish soldiers didn't react until it was translated to them. Then the two prisoners fell to their knees and wept.

"Oh, God." Mike turned his face away.

A ragged cheer went down the line of Americans on the hill. "Serves the bastards right," someone said with satisfaction. The Spanish soldiers were led away, one of them having to be almost carried. Hugo drew a quick, vicious sketch, which he then balled up and hurled aside.

They heard later that the soldiers had been sentenced to hang. No one, not even the correspondents, wanted to go and see that. Hugo sat down morosely with his sketch pad, and Tim began to write a dispatch—a "color" piece on life in the camp. There was no news.

Mike had film left, which he was saving for the Spanish surrender—whenever that was going to be. If it was to be. Sampson and Shafter were said to be arguing about whether the American fleet should risk its ships to bombard the city from the harbor. With the Spanish naval power gone, it was even uncertain whether anything would be accomplished by besieging Santiago.

Havana and the western end of the island would still have to be taken. It was a mystery to all the correspondents how the Americans could still be holding the advantage in a war this badly run.

"We wouldn't be winning if Spain wasn't practically tottering to begin with," was Tim's succinct reply.

So much for empire, Mike thought. Spain, exploiter of

the New World, had choked herself for centuries with the gold she had taken from it. Nothing else had mattered, and her colonies had rotted out from under her. Nothing was left but gold braid and *pundonor*—point of honor. It was pundonor that had sent Cervera's fleet out to meet the Americans, to be sunk rather than captured. It was rumored that pundonor would demand one final bombardment of Santiago so that General Toral could surrender under fire—honorably.

Meanwhile, the American troops grew sicker. Men sent on water detail lay down to rest every hundred yards. The bloated belly of malnutrition set in. Soldiers whose faces grew steadily thinner had to let out their cartridge belts to buckle them. They soaked their hardtack in water and fried it in rancid sowbelly. Sometimes they traded it to Cuban refugees for mangoes and got dysentery.

Neither mail nor rations nor medicine got through, but the War Department, at great expense, sent a lieutenant of the engineers corps with an utterly useless cargo. The *testudo* was a siege device known since Roman times, a solid oak shield sixteen feet long and six inches thick on wheels. It was steered from beneath by sixteen soldiers whom it would protect from enemy fire. All that had to be done was to push these devices through the mud along jungle trails that routinely mired every pack mule train, then take Santiago with them. The unfortunate lieutenant reported to General Shafter, who swore at him while Shafter's aides fell down laughing. The correspondents in the camp were absolutely forbidden to publish a word about the testudos, which had been personally designed by General Nelson Miles, now on his way to take Puerto Rico.

Mike desperately wanted to see one, but they were never unloaded. Bored, he prowled around the camp while Tim wrote his dispatches and Hugo sketched. It was aggravating to be dependent on a medium that weighed so much and was in such short supply. Any amount of paper could be packed, but film was heavy and expensive and not available in Jamaica. If Mike wanted more, he would have to wait until Rafe could pick up a shipment in Tampa. And with surrender imminent, Tim wouldn't send Rafe to Tampa.

Mike mulled that over some more and decided to take Sal the mule down to Siboney and dicker with Rafe about cabling Tampa and having the film sent to Key West. Mike loaded the camera onto Sal in case anything exciting was happening in Siboney—and because he took it with him everywhere, afraid of what might happen to it if the army moved while he wasn't there.

He and the mule set out down the backside of Misery Ridge, dodging tents, trenches, and spiny eruptions of cactus. Hugo had said that if the heat let up he might be down later with Tim's dispatch. Mike thought the heat was beginning to get to Hugo; he didn't look well. Maybe they would stay the night in Siboney. Do the town. Have a drink at the cantina. Mike grinned. High living. Siboney only had one cantina, and it had a hole in it big enough to walk through.

At the base of the ridge, the trail to Siboney led into the jungle again, along the way they had come before. The dead horses, and men, had been cleared out of Bloody Ford, but the area felt ghostly to Mike, as if something or someone was still there. Sal didn't like it, either. She snorted and stared into the trees.

Mike unholstered his pistol, but nothing troubled them. At Las Guasimas Mike stood and looked at the spots where the ground had been thick with blood. The stains were all washed away now, and the jungle was mending its broken places. Soon no one would ever know a battle had been fought there. He pushed on toward Siboney, pleased with himself for not being tired. So much for his bad heart. He was in better shape than he had ever been. Better than Hugo. He hoped Hugo wasn't coming down with something. Quinine was getting scarce.

Mike heard the Mauser bullet spatter through the leaves at the same instant that his right foot dropped out from under him. Even then it took him a moment to realize he'd been shot. He toppled to the ground, and Sal snuffled at his head. The sniper was still in the trees, but there was no telling where. Mike hadn't dropped his pistol. He took a moment to be proud of himself for that while he tried frantically to think of what he should do. If he got up, the sniper would finish him off. The sensation of blood filling up his boot made his thinking fuzzy.

The sniper would want Sal—to eat or to ride, Mike thought. A Spanish soldier trapped behind the American lines would be hungry and frightened . . . and dangerous. Mike tightened his hand around his pistol without discernible movement. With half-closed eyes he watched the trees and Sal. He could feel the blood running out of his foot. A land crab, eyes protruding, sidled up to him on tiptoe. *Go away*, he told it silently. *Go away*. If it crawled onto him, he knew he wouldn't be able to hold still.

Sal threw up her head and snorted, and the crab backed off. She swiveled her ears and shifted warily. Something was coming. Mike tried to hear the footsteps, a cautious inching forward, almost like the crab's. Sal stamped her foot, and then Mike saw him, peering through the vines. Mike held his breath. *Closer. Come closer.* The crab investigated Mike's hair.

The Spanish soldier took another step out of the trees, and Mike flipped himself up and shot in one movement. The Spaniard's mouth opened in an *O* of surprise, and blood flowered from his breast. He dropped, still surprised.

Dizzy, Mike bent forward, his head on his knees. He could see a hole in his boot through which blood was oozing. Thin bubbles like soapsuds formed in the hole and broke. Mike fumbled with his laces. His foot hurt like hell. The pain took up his whole consciousness. Whimpering, he dragged the boot off and tied his bandanna around the mess that was his right foot. The crab inched forward again, and he smashed it with his fist.

Startled, he looked at the broken crustacean on his hand as if wondering where it had come from. Repulsed, he wiped it on the grass, shaking away bits of flesh and shell. Sal was calmly mouthing grass by the trail a few feet away. She was an army mule, used to gunfire. Mike grabbed a tree trunk and used it to pull himself upright. He hopped on one foot, wanting all the while to lie down and howl with pain, until he got to Sal. She looked at him curiously as he hooked his good foot into her pack saddle and climbed up on top of his camera box. He turned her nose toward Siboney; they were already more than halfway there. As he passed the dead Spaniard, Mike saw that his light blue uniform was tattered and filthy and his boots were worn through the soles.

Sal swayed down the trail, with Mike bracing himself on the camera box. His head felt light, as if it were stuffed with cotton, and his mangled foot was a source of constant pain.

When he got to the shore, he couldn't figure out how to get down from Sal's back. Siboney was a tangle of supplies backed up in piles, waiting to be loaded on pack mules and slogged through the mud to Misery Ridge. Wounded men were stacked almost like supplies along the shore coastline as they waited for transport out to the *Olivette,* which Mike couldn't see. No one paid him any attention.

He steered Sal to the jetty and waved the *Clarion's* flag at what he thought was the *Chance.* After a moment she came steaming in, and Rafe jumped for the jetty.

"What in the hell got you?" was the first thing he said. Rafe, appalled, took in Mike's greenish face and the bloody foot.

"Spanish sniper," Mike said.

"There's a field hospital here," Rafe said dubiously. "Sort of."

"I saw it," Mike said. "I want to go to Tampa."

"Jamaica's closer," Rafe said. He looked at Mike uneasily and half held out his arms as if he expected him to topple from the box.

"Eden's in Tampa," Mike said with gritted teeth. "I'm not going to let them cut my foot off in Jamaica or out here in a bloody hospital ship that hasn't got any medicines left."

Rafe looked from Mike to the *Chance* to the hills north of Siboney, where Tim presumably was. "What if it gets infected and you get gangrene in it between here and Tampa?"

"If I stay here, they'll cut it off for sure," Mike said stubbornly. "I've been in the field hospitals. They're just amputating anything they haven't time to fix. And even if they don't, I'll limp all my life if I don't get to a surgeon who knows what he's doing. Wash it out with whiskey on the *Chance* and take me to Tampa."

"All right," Rafe said reluctantly. "*I* can't figure out what the hell to do. You're as likely to be right as not."

"Good," Mike said. He closed his eyes and swayed slightly. Rafe jumped. He caught Mike under the arms just as he fell off the camera box.

Rafe staggered up to the *Chance*'s ladder with Mike in his arms, as deadweight as a corpse. *"Hey!"*

Leon Duquesne, the cook, peered over the rail. *"Mon Dieu!"* he cried out, then hurried down the ladder. "Is he dead?"

"He's passed out." Rafe gasped as Leon scooped Mike up and put him over his shoulder. "You be careful with him. He's got a bad heart. Oh, Lord."

"I will treat him like a baby." Leon peered past Rafe at Sal. "Must we take the mule, too, Mr. Murray? I am not comfortable with mules."

Mike stirred. "Camera," he said faintly.

"Camera," Rafe said. "Right." He looked at Mike disappearing up the ladder on Leon's shoulder. "Oh, God." What if he died? Rafe looked at the dismal collection of buildings and tents that comprised the field hospital at Siboney. If he left Mike there, he probably would die, and reports had it that the *Olivette* wasn't any better. Charley

Lawrence had said as much, and he was on the hospital ship. In any case, the *Olivette* wasn't available because it had steamed around to the entrance to Santiago Harbor, where a main hospital would be set up just as soon as Santiago surrendered.

He would have to take Mike to Tampa. Rafe un-hitched the camera box from Sal's pack and eased it down. A pair of privates on supply detail were loading a pack mule train down the beach. Rafe gave them Sal and a message for Tim that might or might not get to him. He was turning back toward the waiting boat when he saw Hugo Ware.

Rafe let out a yelp of relief and waved at Hugo. "Over here! Thank God!"

Hugo turned, rather slowly, it seemed to Rafe, and blinked at him. Rafe shouted again. Finally Hugo pulled a handful of dispatches from his shirt. "Sorry," he said fuzzily. "I seem to be sickening with something. They gave me some quinine up the trail. It was all they had. I ought to be better in a bit."

"You look like crap," Rafe said. "You look worse than Mike."

"Mike?" Hugo blinked at him again.

"He got a bullet in his foot on the way down here," Rafe said. "Sniper."

"Oh," Hugo said with vague interest. "I saw the fellow by the trail."

"He's insisting I take him to Tampa," Rafe said, still trying to confer with Hugo. "He says they'll amputate his foot here. I don't know what to do."

Hugo nodded solemnly.

Rafe narrowed his eyes at him. "Oh, for God's sake. Get on board. You're going to Tampa, too. At least I've got quinine on the *Chance*. If I'm going to get into trouble, I might as well go all the way." He towed Hugo down the jetty and managed to get him up the ladder. Leon reached down to pull Hugo up by the wrists. He studied Hugo gravely.

"I think he's got malaria," Rafe said.

"I don't know," Leon said.

They put Hugo to bed in Rafe's own bunk in his cabin. Mike was already in the spare bunk, dosed with morphine and the foot washed out with gin. Leon got the camera on board, and Rafe paced and peered out the porthole as the *Chance* put out. It was nearly dark. It would take more than two days to get to Tampa.

Mike awoke at dawn, apparently feeling much better, which made Rafe nervous. He swung his feet out of bed and yelled at somebody to bring him a crutch. "Where's my camera?" he demanded when Rafe and Leon, who had appointed himself chief nurse, appeared in the doorway.

"Your camera there in the corner," Leon said, nodding at it.

"Oh. Good. What's Hugo doing here?" Mike said, pointing at the opposite bunk. Hugo was still asleep, but he was twitching feverishly.

"Malaria, maybe," Rafe said.

Mike shook his head grimly. "Hell, you got a fine hospital ship. Where's my crutch?"

Leon and Rafe looked at him uneasily. His face was flushed, and his green eyes looked too bright. Leon presented him with a mahogany walking stick. "I sprain my ankle last year, get aroun' my galley with this. She do you fine."

Mike stood up and tested it. "Where's Sal?"

"I gave her back to the army," Rafe said. "Where you stole her from."

"Why didn't you send her to Tim?"

"How am I supposed to tell her where to go?" Rafe said, exasperated. "She's a mule, not Old Dog Tray."

"You lie down a minute," Leon said. "I want to look at that foot. You got the fever."

"I don't," Mike said, but he lay down and let Leon inspect his foot.

"She don't look infected to me, not yet," Leon announced.

"You're a cook," Rafe said. "You don't know."

"My *maman*, she know," Leon said. "She teach me."

"Listen," Mike said to Rafe, "I want to teach you how to run the camera. You have to get the surrender for me."

"Tomorrow," Leon said soothingly. "Tomorrow you teach him. Right now I bring you some nice turtle soup, put a little sherry in her."

Rafe wasn't listening. He was peering at Hugo. Hugo's breath was even; but he had dark circles under his eyes, and the conversation didn't seem to be waking him. Rafe put a hand to Hugo's forehead. "He's hotter'n the blazes," he muttered.

Halfway to Tampa, Rafe was having second thoughts, but it was too late. Was it better to take the time to get to a city they knew would have medicines or to get quickly to a doctor who didn't? Rafe didn't know.

Soon Hugo was awake and hungry, which relieved Rafe and Leon somewhat. Mike got out of bed with Leon's stick and wrestled his camera box open. "Hey, Florence Nightingale, come here and help me with this."

"I help you back in your bed," Leon said. "Mr. Murray he already say he don't want nothing to do with that camera, him. How she work, anyway?"

Mike's eyes gleamed. He cradled the camera in his lap. "You load the film here, see, but you have to do it in the dark. It threads right here on these sprockets—it's easy to feel."

"Let me see." Leon closed his eyes, then brushed the mechanism with enormous fingertips. "She go through here, right? And here?"

"That's it!" Mike said. "Now, when it's loaded, you have to crank the film through while you shoot—here, give me your hand—just this speed, sixteen frames a second. You can't let it slow down or speed up."

Leon revolved the crank with one hand, beating time on the camera's housing with the other. Mike grinned.

Rafe could find another cook. Rafe could try living on hardtack and sowbelly instead of turtle soup. Mike passed a hand over his forehead. He felt chilly, pleasantly cool. That was nice. Maybe the weather was changing. He did feel a little odd, though. He sat down on the edge of the bed.

By the next morning Mike was rummaging in Rafe's trunk for a sweater, and Leon jammed him in bed and put a thermometer in his mouth.

"I feel fine," Mike protested. "It doesn't even hurt."

"That's because you're full of morphine," Rafe said. He looked over his shoulder at Hugo, who was reading a book. At least he hadn't been any trouble.

"He got a fever, him," Leon said. "Hundred and three." He washed the thermometer and took Hugo's temperature. "Him, too."

Leon got a pan of cold water and bathed both men's foreheads while Mike fussed at him. Hugo lay uncomplaining with his book in his hands.

The *Chance* steamed on. Rafe went to the pilothouse and argued with the captain over the *Chance's* top speed. The captain retorted that if he wanted to blow up the boiler, he'd put on more coal—otherwise, get the hell out of the pilothouse.

Rafe envisioned returning to Cuba and telling Tim Holt that his brother had died between Santiago and Tampa, trying to explain that Mike had insisted, that Rafe had been fool enough to listen to him. An alcohol rub helped a fever; that was what Leon's maman said. The only alcohol on board the *Chance* was the drinking kind, so Rafe went and got the same bottle of gin they had used to wash Mike's foot. He fortified himself by downing a glass of it, then applied the rest to his patients. The cabin smelled like a saloon.

Rafe caught a few hours' sleep in Leon's cabin, and as light was breaking on the third morning, the *Chance* turned into the channel to Tampa Bay.

Leon shook him awake. "We nearly there. Mr. Holt, he up and about, I give him more morphine. But you better look at Mr. Ware—I told you he don't have malaria."

Hugo's fever was gone. But his face was clammy to the touch and as rubbery as a dead fish. And it was faintly but unmistakably tinged with jaundice.

XV

Tampa, July 11

"He's got it," Janessa said. "It's yellow fever." She looked at Rosebay's ashen face, which was bent over Hugo's.

Rosebay nodded mutely. She held Hugo's hand, stroking it fiercely, automatically, as if trying to pull him back to her through her touch.

They were in a private room in the Tampa Bay Hotel, with Rafe biting his nails in the hall. Everything was in chaos. Janessa had been at the point of sailing for Cuba on the Red Cross ship but instead had sent Steve Jurgen on without her. Then, after looking at Mike's foot, she contacted a surgeon from St. Petersburg. Eden and Elizabeth were with Mike, who was raving that if any surgeon tried to cut his foot off, he would blow the son of a bitch to hell. Eden had taken his pistol away and hidden it.

Rafe slowly opened the door to Hugo's room. He had a look of hangdog misery. "Dr. Post is here," he said.

Janessa got up and straightened her skirts.

"You're not going to leave him?" Rosebay asked fearfully.

"Just for a few minutes," Janessa said. "There isn't anything I can do by being with him. His body has to fight the disease off. It might help to have *you* with him, though. My husband had yellow fever. I was with him

249

almost every minute. Sometimes I think it was what pulled him through." She laid a hand on Rosebay's shoulder. Rosebay gripped Hugo's hand harder.

The surgeon from St. Petersburg was waiting in the corridor, a nurse in a starched uniform at his side. The doctor was elderly, with a white goatee and flowing white hair. "Are you the sister who sent for me, ma'am? The doctor?"

"Yes, I'm the sister *and* the doctor," Janessa said. She had shed her Hospital Service uniform for old calico and knew she looked more like a scrubwoman.

Dr. Post appeared to digest this and find it barely plausible. "What is the patient's condition?"

"Bullet wound in the foot," Janessa said shortly. "I have no experience with orthopedics."

Dr. Post seemed mollified by that. Janessa escorted him into Mike's room, and he inspected the patient. "How long ago did this happen?"

Mike was gritting his teeth in pain and didn't look capable of a coherent answer.

"Two days and a bit more," Janessa said. "His friends washed it out with gin," she added.

Dr. Post chuckled. "Probably as good as anything."

"Not as good as carbolic," Janessa said.

"Don't see any gangrene, do you?"

"All the same, I cleaned it again myself this morning."

"No harm in that," Dr. Post said cheerfully. He looked at Janessa. "Relax, Dr. Lawrence. I may be old-fashioned, but I'm not prehistoric. I'll practice every possible aseptic and antiseptic procedure. And now, young man, we are going to put you to sleep. And chase the rest of these lovely ladies out of here."

"You aren't going to cut my foot off," Mike said through clenched teeth.

"Not intentionally," Post said. He ordered Eden and Elizabeth out; then he and Janessa transferred Mike to a portable table that Post's assistant had brought with him. His entourage also included a nurse in a stiffly starched apron and cap over voluminous blue- and white-striped skirts. When preparations were to his liking, Post ordered Janessa out as well.

"I'd like to observe," Janessa said.

"This is very finicky work," Post replied. "I don't intend to do it with the patient's sister observing. If you want to watch me operate on someone who isn't kin to you at some later date, I'll be happy to oblige."

"I'll be in Cuba by then," Janessa said loftily, but she gave up and left. Dr. Post was right. She would be incapable of refraining from comment, and a man trying to repair splintered metatarsal bones did not need an armchair coach.

Rafe stopped her in the hallway on the way back to Hugo's room. "Dr. Lawrence—"

"I think he is going to be all right, Mr. Murray," she said gently. "It's too early to say whether he'll have a limp or not, but I'm almost sure he won't lose the foot."

"Almost," Rafe echoed gloomily. His dark, handsome face, usually alight with mischief, was brooding. "And what about his heart?"

Janessa bit her lip. "I told Dr. Post Mike's medical history when I contacted him. *I* don't know what will happen, but I will tell you this: As far as strain on his heart goes, he's far better off here with Dr. Post than he would have been in a field hospital. So please don't be too hard on yourself over your decision."

"But what about Hugo?" Rafe seemed desperately in need of something to blame himself for.

"If you kept him comfortable and fed, and did what you could for the fever, then you did all that could have been done in a hospital. Yellow fever has to run its course. The only cure is not to catch it in the first place."

"That's what Leon says," Rafe said.

"Who is Leon?"

"My cook."

"Oh." Janessa looked at him oddly for a moment.

"How do you get yellow fever?" Rafe asked.

"We don't know. Mosquitoes are one theory. I would recommend taking great care with your netting."

"Right you are."

Rafe went down to the hotel bar for a gin and quinine, in case that was an antidote, too, and then upstairs to sleep. Since the journalists and the army had cleared out, rooms were to be had. It took him a long time to get to sleep, though, and then he dreamed of being in the middle of the Atlantic and burying Mike Holt at sea.

Janessa found a hollow-eyed Eden in Hugo's room. It gave her something to do, Eden said. Elizabeth was with them, too, with an arm around Eden.

Hugo was asleep, but as Janessa came in, he woke, retching. He was bent double in the bed, unable to get up, and was spewing the broth he had eaten for breakfast. "I'm sorry," he said faintly, embarrassed while the women got a basin and cleaned it up. In half an hour he vomited again, and this time there was blood in it.

Rosebay gripped Janessa's wrist tightly in the doorway. "Is he going to die?"

"I don't know," Janessa said, feeling helpless.

After another hour, Dr. Post's nurse tapped on the door, and Janessa and Eden flew into the hall, brushing past her stiffly starched skirts. Mike was unconscious, but his foot was still there, embedded like a sausage in bandages. The room smelled of carbolic acid, and Mike was back in bed, in freshly laundered sheets. He looked frail, nearly as pale as the sheets, his red hair damp and plastered to his skull. His mustache, grown long and straggly, fluttered as he breathed.

"His heart held up like a champ's," Dr. Post said. "He only *looks* half dead."

"When will he wake up?" Eden asked quietly.

"Will he limp?" Janessa wanted to know.

"Let's let him sleep," Post said, putting a finger to his lips. "It's important that he rest."

Eden sat down beside Mike and folded her hands in her lap to keep from touching him.

"He will very likely have some limp," Post whispered to Janessa. "It should not be crippling."

Janessa closed her eyes for a moment and let her breath out slowly.

"You might want to telegraph your parents," Dr. Post suggested, "before they read some garbled account in the newspapers. So far as I can tell, the journalists haven't the slightest regard for the facts." He put his hat on, hefted his bag, and departed, followed by his nurse with a bundle of dirty cloths and his assistant with the folding table.

Despite Eden's best intentions, Mike's eyes fluttered open, possibly under the intensity of her gaze. She clutched his hand.

"Hey, there." Mike smiled at her tiredly. He squeezed her fingers. "I wasn't going to let any doctor chop me up."

"Certainly not," Eden said. She blinked, and two tears slid down her cheeks. "You scared me, though."

"I scared me," Mike said. "But you—you held up fine."

She bent down and laid her head on his chest. "I couldn't come apart until I knew you were all right."

"Quit listening to my heart," Mike said.

Eden lifted her head. "I'm not!" she said, a little too emphatically. She caught Mike's eyes and flushed. "Well, just a bit. Do you really feel all right?"

"Until you get down to my foot," Mike said. "The fever seems to have gone."

Janessa came over to him. "You can have some morphine," she said, briskly professional. "And you're not to try to get out of bed."

"How's Hugo?" Mike asked her.

Janessa bit her lip.

"Damn it, Janessa, tell me. If you don't quit sparing me things, you'll make me crazy. I'll get up myself and find out," he threatened.

"He has yellow fever," Janessa said. "He's very ill."

"Charley had yellow fever," Mike said. "He got over it."

"Yes, darling," Eden said. She stroked his arm.

Janessa slipped out and went down the corridor. Elizabeth and Rosebay were sitting with Hugo. Dark circles rimmed their eyes, and Janessa suspected their weariness was more from strain than exhaustion. She studied them, then selected Rosebay to be ordered off to rest.

"I'm not going to leave him," she said stubbornly.

"He's sleeping now," Janessa said gently. "You should rest so you can be with him when he's awake."

Elizabeth looked at Janessa closely, but Rosebay just nodded and stood up. "You'll call me if there's any change?"

"I will," Janessa promised. "For now, I can give you something to help you sleep if you like."

"No," Rosebay said. "I reckon not. Doctor gave me something one time, and I slept till the next day."

"It might be a good thing if she did," Elizabeth said quietly after Rosebay had gone.

"She knows that," Janessa said. "It's why she won't do it." It was the closest that either of them would come to admitting, in Hugo's possible hearing, that they thought he was going to die. He lay very still now. He had vomited up more blood, almost without waking, and his skin was growing steadily more yellow as the disease ate at his liver and kidneys.

"How is Michael?" Elizabeth asked.

"Michael is fine," Janessa said. "Not a sign of his heart acting up. I think Eden's relieved to have him back here and out of the shooting."

Elizabeth smiled. "A roundabout way but a happy end?"

"Oh, the Holts have a knack for that," Janessa said. She smiled back, a small smile that had to struggle to survive. But it served as a narrow bridge between the two women.

But as the afternoon went by, Hugo's heartbeat slowed, and his fingers, which had lain still on the sheet, began to pick unconsciously at the linen, as if in search of something.

Janessa looked at Elizabeth. "Please bring Rosebay in," she said quietly.

Rosebay was curled like a child on top of her coverlet, her hands crossed on her breast. She breathed in tired, ragged breaths, mouth open. Elizabeth touched her shoulder. "Janessa thinks you ought to come."

Rosebay nodded and followed Elizabeth without saying a word. It was dim in Hugo's room. The day had faded into twilight, but no one had lit the lamps. The palmettos outside the window gave the air an aqueous light.

"Is he better?" Rosebay asked.

Janessa shook her head. "I'm afraid not."

Hugo's breathing did not seem labored; it had merely grown shallower, his heartbeat slower, as if his body were a machine being shut down, switches turned off one by one. His skin was as yellow as old parchment. Rosebay looked at him in horror and wrapped her arms around him. "No! You can't die. You can't go off like this and leave me!" Her voice was fierce. "You got to bide with me, Hugo. I promised to bide with you, and I did. Aw, God, Hugo, you can't leave me!"

Janessa and Elizabeth exchanged a quick look and in silent consent left her alone with him. They stood in the hall, unspeaking, until Rosebay's howl of anguish drew them back into Hugo's room.

Rosebay, her face slick with tears, was sitting on the floor by Hugo's bed, weeping, howling, and hiccuping.

Elizabeth knelt beside her and put her hands on Rosebay's shoulders. Elizabeth couldn't quite define why, but in some way that had to do with Tim, she knew this was her job. Janessa seemed to sense it, too. She drew the

sheet up over Hugo's still face and waited until Elizabeth
had led Rosebay out.

With no very clear idea of what to do with her,
Elizabeth took Rosebay to her own room and rang for
some tea. *Funny how I always send for tea in a crisis,* she
thought. She had no idea how much use the tea would be,
but sending for it gave a structure to the chaos.

Rosebay's face was mottled, blotched, and her eyes
were red rimmed. She couldn't stop crying, and it was not
dainty, feminine weeping but great howling sobs that
shook her whole body. The boy who brought the tea tray
stared at her.

"Oh, God, it isn't fair! You didn't have to take him,
you could've had somebody else!" Intent on berating God,
she pushed away the proffered cup of tea. "I been brought
up to believe you don't do anything without a purpose. But
it's not fair, nobody can tell me *why*! Oh, bring him back,
give him back!"

Elizabeth sat silently in the other chair, sipped her
own tea, and wondered if it would help or hurt to suggest
to Rosebay that perhaps God did not personally choose
who should die at any given time.

Finally Rosebay's sobs abated to an anguished whim-
per. Elizabeth gave her practical comforts—a handkerchief for her streaming eyes and nose, a cup of still-warm
tea with lemon for her throat.

"Oh, I'm sorry," Rosebay said, miserable. "You don't
even know me."

"I know you need someone to be with," Elizabeth
said.

Rosebay snuffled into the handkerchief. "I can't get it
in my mind that he's gone. Every time I think of it, it hits
me like a sinking spell."

Elizabeth nodded, silent. She had not turned on the
light in this room, either, and the darkness crept in.

"This isn't the first time," Rosebay said. She stared
into the dusky garden outside the window. The peacock
was pacing in the shadows. "I lost my first husband. I don't

know if Tim ever told you. I reckon I'm some kind of jinx."

"Don't be ridiculous," Elizabeth said briskly, sure of her ground now.

Rosebay sniffled. "He got shot." Her voice was hoarse with weeping. "Wedge was bad to drink, and jealous. He picked a quarrel with a cowboy 'cause the cowboy was looking at me. They killed each other." She hung her head. "That was how I met Tim. Him and his cousin Peter, they were camped right by, waiting for the land rush to start. That was out in Oklahoma."

"You are not to blame because two men were fools," Elizabeth said. "You'll make yourself ill if you think that way." She couldn't tell whether Rosebay even heard any voice but her own.

"That was where I met Hugo, too," Rosebay said. "He was—he was just on the loose when I met him, writing his stories and making his drawings, all about how America looked to an Englishman. A publisher printed them up in a book," she added proudly, "after he was married to me. So I was some good to him, wasn't I? I kept him from drifting." She put her head in her hands, crying again. "I *tried* to make him happy, I swear I tried to do right by him."

"Of course you did." Elizabeth closed her eyes. How ineffectual she sounded in the face of this woman's grief. And yet there seemed to be things that Rosebay felt the need to tell Elizabeth as well as God—or to tell God by way of Elizabeth.

Elizabeth lit the bedside lamp, and its oil flame, more enclosing than the harsh light of electricity, created a circle that encompassed them both, fixed them in their corner of the room. Rosebay's mourning seemed to move in and out of that circle, first ferreting in the darkness for Hugo, gone forever, then telling about his life in the light. And somewhere between the two was a transient space in which anything might be said.

Night slid on toward dawn, and Elizabeth rang for sandwiches and more tea. She heard Janessa in the hallway, talking with Eden. "Mike's taking it hard," Eden said.

"Peter Blake," Rosebay said, turning to Elizabeth. "Peter ought to know. He was with Hugo and Tim and me in Oklahoma."

"I'll be sure he's been told," Elizabeth said. "Are there others?"

"Tim'll know," Rosebay said quietly. She thought for a few moments, her eyes moving among the garden shadows. "I want his body sent home. Back to England. They wouldn't have him when he was alive, but they'll take him back now, damn them."

A bird in the palmettos woke and sang sleepily to itself, a little four-note trill, repeated.

Without warning, Rosebay began to cry again, deep, heaving sobs that shook her whole body. Elizabeth watched helplessly. Should she put her arms around Rosebay? Try to hold her? How might she be comforted? Under so much duress, her corn-silk hair was sliding from its pins and tumbling into her face. Elizabeth knelt by Rosebay's chair and pulled the strands back. Rosebay leaned her face into Elizabeth's shoulder.

"It's all right. Go ahead. Cry it out."

"It's not fair! I was good. I *was*. I did right by him. It's not fair to take him *now*!" Rosebay gave an anguished wail; her hands dug into the upholstery on the chair.

"You won't have to worry about how to go on," Elizabeth said, wondering if practical assurances might give her balance. "Tim saw to it that everyone who came out here had life insurance."

Rosebay's tears redoubled. "You can't insure against—you can't—how could he *know*?" Strangled sobs choked her. "It's funny enough to make a cat laugh. It was bad enough when *I* was married and he wasn't, but now—"

Elizabeth froze. Rosebay spilled things better left unsaid, things that she very possibly didn't know she was saying, into the starched white cotton of Elizabeth's dress.

But Elizabeth continued to stroke Rosebay's hair, while her right knee developed a cramp from not moving.

"I didn't *mean* to want him," Rosebay howled. "I knew he wasn't interested in me. Some other girl had already jilted him, I knew there wasn't hope. And Hugo was wanting me, and I *do* love him, I *do*. I been everything I said I would be for him, even after Tim and me—"

Good heavens, Elizabeth thought.

Rosebay shook with misery. "Tim never could figure anything out without a floor plan, and that's the truth. But even after, I kept my bargain, and then he got married, and now he—" More strangled sobs. Rosebay bent double and buried her face in her hands while Elizabeth wondered frantically what on earth she ought to do.

"I didn't want it! I didn't want it to happen! Lord Jesus, you got to believe I didn't want Hugo to die!" Rosebay's whole body shook with guilt.

"Of course you didn't," Elizabeth said briskly. This was going too far. "In any case, what you want doesn't have the slightest effect on what actually happens."

"Wicked thoughts," Rosebay said, sobbing. "Wicked thoughts are avenged by the Lord."

"Bunk," Elizabeth said. "He wouldn't have time."

Rosebay lifted her head. "That's downright blasphemous. Oh, I should never have said all this to *you*!" She buried her face in her hands again.

Elizabeth was unsure whether that had to do with her status as Tim's wife or merely with her supposed ungodliness. Still, she had to respond. "Rosebay, if thoughts could kill people, there wouldn't be anyone left standing. Now forget about that right now. Do your grieving and don't get it tangled up with some supposed sin on your part."

"Oh, Elizabeth, how are you able to say that to me?" Rosebay snuffled.

Elizabeth eased back from her knees, now that Rosebay wasn't leaning on her. "Because," Elizabeth said carefully, "whatever went on between you and my husband—or didn't go on," she said hastily as Rosebay took a breath, "whatever, as long as it was before he met me, I do not see that I have the faintest right to complain about it or even comment on it. Hugo," she added thoughtfully, "might have felt otherwise, since it does seem to have, er, overlapped your marriage, but I'm sure you behaved just as you ought to."

"Oh, I did!" Rosebay sniffled. She rubbed her eyes with her fists. "Every time I met a nice girl, I introduced her to Tim."

Elizabeth's lip twitched in spite of herself. "I'm afraid Tim's not very . . . malleable."

Rosebay lifted her head from her hands, her eyes wide and red. "I don't know how to go on without Hugo. It's not money, it's just *him*. He won't ever be here anymore!"

Elizabeth reached for her, gathered Rosebay into her arms, and Rosebay cried, wringing out her grief in deep, wordless sobs as dawn came up in the palmettos.

Elizabeth came stiffly out of Rosebay's room. She had finally led her down the hall and into bed, and Janessa had come along with a spoonful of laudanum. Now, in the corridor, Elizabeth put her hands to the small of her back and stretched. She ached all over and wondered how Tim was going to react to Hugo's death. Would he, like Rosebay, feel anguish and guilt over their affair?

Rafe came into the hall with his bag in his hand, and she straightened up.

"I'm going back to Cuba," he told her. "I'm taking Dr. Lawrence. She missed the Red Cross boat."

Janessa followed behind him, buttoning her Hospital Service jacket.

"So soon?" Elizabeth asked. "Rafe, you just got here."

"Have to, kiddo. There's no one else to run the boss's copy for him. With poor Hugo gone and young Michael out of action, we're pretty well up against it."

Elizabeth's eyes widened in surprise. "You're going ashore? Who's going to run the *Chance*?"

"I'll have to trust her captain," Rafe said gloomily. "I don't like it. He'll hang back as far as he can if any shooting starts."

Elizabeth pushed her hair away from her face. "Take me with you," she said.

Rafe peered at her. "Pardon my saying so, darling, but you've been up all night, and you aren't exactly yourself. I can't take you into Cuba now—there's a war on."

"Rafe, you're an idiot," Elizabeth said. "I don't want to go ashore. I'll run your blasted boat for you."

"I can't do that," Rafe retorted. "Tim would split a gut."

Eden had come out of Mike's room to say good-bye to Janessa, and the sisters-in-law were listening with interest.

Rafe seized on another good reason. "And besides that, you can't just go off and leave Mrs. Holt to take care of Mike *and* poor Rosebay."

"After the things poor Rosebay told me last night," Elizabeth remarked, "I am going to be the last person she wants to see this morning."

"Really?" Rafe's brows shot up with interest. "Rosebay and the boss?" Rosebay was Rafe's landlady, and he seemed to feel that negated any necessity for tact. "There *was* some talk."

"Well, there had better not be any more," Elizabeth hissed at him, "so you just remember that when you've been drinking."

"You're a shrew," Rafe said amicably, "and I'm not taking you to Cuba."

"Do *I* get to say anything?" Eden inquired. Janessa looked content to let them argue it out without her assistance.

"No," Rafe said. "Begging your pardon."

"Certainly," Elizabeth said.

"Well, then," Eden said. "I can take care of Mike, and there's Dr. Post if he has any problem. He's promised to check on Mike again. And I don't think Rosebay's going to want to see anybody for a while—except maybe you, Mr. Murray, and you can't stay. But she doesn't know the rest of us very well."

"Good," Elizabeth said. "I'll pack my bag."

"Will you just wait a minute?" Rafe followed her down the hallway.

"No," Elizabeth said, going into her room. "Argue with me while I pack." She opened her medium-sized bag and began tossing clothes in it.

"Nice touch," Rafe said as she added a pistol.

"I always carry it," Elizabeth said. "Rafe, you've known me for years. You know I can run that boat."

"You could probably run the navy," Rafe said. "But Tim would skin me alive."

"Not until he doesn't need you," Elizabeth retorted. The opportunity to do something useful and to escape from Rosebay Ware had her in its grip. She had begun to feel guilty and mildly exasperated. It was aggravating of Rosebay to be in love with Tim and expect Elizabeth to comfort her for it. She folded a twill skirt into the bag.

"If you get shot or drowned, he won't wait," Rafe commented. "For God's sake, Liz, if you wanted to be Nelly Bly, girl reporter, you should have cleared it with the boss and not put me in this fix."

Elizabeth's dark eyes flashed. "He's not my boss. He's my husband."

"He's *my* boss," Rafe retorted. "He can't fire you, which the poor devil may yet regret, but he can fire me. And he will, too, if something happens to you. God knows what could happen. Raped by marauding Spaniards. Pardon my language."

"In the middle of the ocean?" Elizabeth demanded. "Surrounded by the American fleet? Marauding Spaniards in balloons?"

"Dammit, Elizabeth—"

"Besides," she said, packing, "I met Leon. He's nearly the size of the boat. Any marauding Spaniard who met him would end up served for lunch." Elizabeth closed the bag.

Rafe followed her into the hall again, alternately protesting and trying to carry the bag. She refused to let him, convinced that he would do something devious with it.

Janessa was waiting outside on the veranda. She hailed a carriage to take them to the pier, and Elizabeth settled into it with her feet on the bag. Eden waved to them from the hotel porch.

"I hope you don't get seasick," Rafe muttered.

"I'm a martyr to it," Elizabeth said. "Leon can hold my head."

Janessa was silent.

"I'm sorry," Elizabeth told her. "We're behaving very badly."

"It's quite a normal reaction," Janessa said, "to behave a little strangely after a death. I'm just trying to think how to tell Tim I let his friend die."

They turned to her and said in unison, "*You* didn't—"

"Irrationality affects everyone," Janessa said moodily. "As you can see."

The *Chance* was at the pier, working up a head of steam. The captain was presumably in the pilothouse, and Leon met them on the deck. If he was astonished by female passengers, he was tactful enough not to say so and bowed them aboard with New Orleans gallantry.

XVI

Misery Hill, July 14

Tim looked in disbelief at Rafe. "Dead?" His face said clearly that Hugo couldn't be dead; he had just seen him. How could someone you cared about simply vanish from the earth?

Rafe hung his head. On the way up, he had assuaged the guilt that refused to leave him in a cantina in Siboney, and now he had a headache from raw rum. "I keep thinking if I had taken after the *Olivette* and put him aboard her . . . but your sister said it wouldn't have made any difference."

"If she says it wouldn't, then it wouldn't," Tim said. "Janessa knows." He scrubbed at his eyes, banishing unbidden tears. "Is she still on the *Chance*?"

"We caught up to a Red Cross ship, and I put her aboard it," Rafe said. "Um . . ."

"Michael's all right?" Tim said. "You're sure? I've been having nightmares about him. Some soldiers with the last mule train said he'd been shot, but they didn't have anything else straight. You took him aboard the *Chance*?"

"The doctor says he's all right," Rafe said.

"Thank God. Did you see Elizabeth?"

"Of course I saw her. She's fine. She's, er—"

"Good. Get this back down to the *Chance*. Did you hear the scuttlebutt in Siboney? Toral's surrendered. We knew he was going to, but we just got official word."

"I heard there'd been more shelling," Rafe said.

"All for show. Silliest damn exhibition. We'd fire and be careful to miss them. Then the captain would come out and yell at the battery for laying the guns wrong. Then we'd fire some more. Once we got too close, and the Spanish got mad and started shooting back. Now Toral's surrendered—Shafter threatened him with all of General Miles's troops. Actually, the general's men are headed for Puerto Rico. But Shafter said they were his replacements for sick troops, and Toral swallowed it. I think Toral's been trying to figure a way out for days."

Rafe looked across the jungle and the Spanish trenches at Santiago. "Will Shafter let us in?"

"He says not. We've been ordered to Siboney for transport back to the States. We're not to set foot in Santiago on pain of arrest. He'll put us in irons. And so forth." Tim grinned. "We'll go in anyway, Shafter will have apoplexy, and it will all be drill as usual." His face fell. "I wish Hugo were here to see it."

"He was a good man," Rafe said solemnly. He pulled a flask from a pocket of his field jacket, drank, and offered it to Tim. "A hell of a reporter and a fine boy all around. Rosebay's cut up."

Tim took a swallow and handed the flask back. "Toral's given Shafter all the men in Santiago and another twelve thousand from the rest of the province that Shafter didn't even ask for. No one knows why, but I suppose that Toral figures it's the best he can do for them. They're to be repatriated. Better than more fighting. Spain's used up." Rafe offered the flask again, and Tim took another drink. "Did Rosebay say what she's going to do now?"

"Not to me," Rafe said. "She may not know yet." He looked at Tim with a certain amount of curiosity, and Tim capped the flask.

"Get those dispatches back to the *Chance*," Tim said, "and run them to Jamaica. The cable's working at Guantánamo now; but it's the army's, and I don't want my copy cut. The army's trying to censor dispatches because things here are so awful."

"Right," Rafe said. His eyes scanned the ridge, sweeping over the sick men sweltering in the miserable shade of shelter tents and past the lesser number of well ones, who were merely hungry.

Tim had never seen anything like this, nor could his worst nightmares have conjured up this foul-smelling landscape, with men dropping in their tracks from fever and spoiled food. Although there was no food to spare, a little was doled out constantly to the civilian refugees from Santiago who crowded around the edges of the camps, weeping, holding swollen-bellied children by the hand. So far there were only dysentery and malaria on Misery Ridge, but there was yellow fever in Siboney.

That must have been where Hugo caught it, Tim thought, *on one of his trips down to the boat.*

"Er, boss, I still need to tell you something."

"What?" Tim asked suspiciously. "Is it Elizabeth?" He looked at Rafe accusingly. "You said she was all right."

"She *is* all right. She's fine. Blasted woman's in perfect health. But she wore me down into letting her run the *Chance*."

"*What?*"

That hadn't worked. Rafe rephrased his explanation. "We need someone. She wanted something useful to do. She's sailed all her life. She used to go out on oyster boats with Jack. And anyway, I couldn't stop her." He stuffed the dispatches in his pocket and eased away from Tim, who was still glaring at him. "I'll be back in the morning. You look terrible. I'll try to find some quinine." He picked his way down the ridge.

Tim stared after him. He wanted to shout after Rafe to go with the *Chance* to Jamaica, not to leave Elizabeth alone on her, or to come back and sit on Misery Hill to watch Toral while he himself went down to the boat. Tim opened and closed his mouth a couple of times, but the words didn't come.

What would he say? How could he justify himself—
not to Rafe but to Elizabeth? That she wasn't competent to
take the *Chance* to Jamaica and back? She was perfectly
competent. That it would be dangerous? Not as much as
what he was doing, and he had not given her any
opportunity to object to that. In any case, she had chosen
to take on the responsibility of the press boat. He searched
for some justification but could come up only with his own
stark terror. How could he forbid his wife to lead an
interesting life because he was afraid of losing her? Tim's
marriage to his suffragist, freethinking wife was the prod-
uct of considerable negotiation, a ruthless examination of
his own convictions, and a leap of faith on her part. To
order her off the *Chance* would blow their relationship
sky-high.

Stymied, Tim sat in the entrance to his tent. It was
also maddening to have her so close. He missed her
desperately on Misery Ridge, in the company of mules and
feverish men and the heat-stricken Shafter, whose stan-
dard response to any question from a journalist was
unprintable. And now Janessa was here, too. That was her
job, but apparently Charley didn't know of her arrival yet.
How would they handle it? And how would Rosebay
handle Hugo's death? Tim closed his eyes. It didn't seem
possible that Hugo was gone. He forced himself to think
about Rosebay, widowed. He summoned up a terrible
sympathy for her—and an uncomfortable feeling that
something was wrong, that more might be wanted from
him.

He wished that Elizabeth were here to talk it over
with. Maybe she might know what he could give Rosebay
besides what he was afraid she wanted. Maybe he'd have
rocks in his head to ask her, though. Tim felt oddly
light-headed himself. *Not malaria,* he thought. *I don't
have time.* He should have told Rafe to make sure
Elizabeth stayed on the *Chance* and didn't come ashore.
Lord, he felt like hell. He'd stick it through, though, until
Toral marched his men out of Santiago and the flag went

up there. No paper could be taken seriously if it missed the taking of Santiago.

The generals were still negotiating for peace the next morning when Rafe came back, bringing some quinine from a Red Cross outfit. Just in case, he said. Tim took one of the pills, just in case, and they waited for Toral.

On the sixteenth General Shafter made plans to move in as soon as Toral moved out. The journalists asked if they could accompany him. Said the general, "Not a m—— f—— rod!" He suggested that they go bother General Miles in Puerto Rico—via the United States. To Tim's amusement the docile among them dutifully went to Siboney for passage.

"The man who can't get into Santiago doesn't belong in this business," he said to Felix Runyon of the AP the next day as they watched Shafter and his attendant generals take their positions for the surrender.

General Shafter and General Toral were very splendid. General Toral marched his troops out of Santiago; General Shafter accepted and returned General Toral's sword; the generals presented their junior generals, and the Spanish all marched back to Santiago to wait for Shafter to follow.

Tim gave Rafe a scribbled dispatch. "Take this down to Elizabeth." If she was filing copy in Jamaica, she wouldn't be hanging around Siboney and catching yellow fever. He had a persistent nightmare about the Fates trying to arrange for Rosebay and him to be together by killing Elizabeth with yellow fever.

Tim wondered if he was going a little bit loony. If so, then getting away from the war would cure it. Being in Cuba certainly had caused it. But, by God, he was going to get into Santiago first.

Refugees were streaming back into the city now, a ragged, unwieldy column that neither the Spanish nor the Americans paid much attention to. That gave Tim an idea. A dollar proved enough to buy a hat, tattered trousers, and a homespun shirt. He shucked off his clothes at the edge of the jungle, made them up into a tight roll, and hung them in a tree. They were filthy, but among the bundle was his favorite jacket. He put on his new outfit and scratched uneasily—it was inhabited.

He slipped easily into the flow of miserable peasants who were slogging through the mud and hoping that something of their huts would be left standing.

As they neared the city, a horrible stench rose from the ground. The road was lined with dead, bloated horses, most of them still saddled and bridled. Shallow graves beside the trail had been dug open by vultures and their contents half-eaten. Farther on, the road was encumbered by a barbed-wire construction like a cattle chute, which forced travelers to zigzag across it, while exposed to the guns above. Built by the Spanish, it had been intended for the American soldiers. *We wouldn't have got through this under fire*, Tim thought. *Shafter was lucky*. Sand-filled barrels shielded the trenches, and piles of paving stones blocked the side streets. The thick-walled houses were loopholed, their windows barricaded.

Tim, traversing the cobblestones of the inner city, craned his neck at the sights while the American army, parading in behind him, did much the same thing. They looked more like rubbernecking tourists than a triumphal army. The generals were received by Toral at the governor's palace for a state luncheon and reception while the common soldier loafed and waited.

Tim inquired in his dockside Spanish for the location of the city telegraph office, but he found it empty even of its telegrapher, who was presumably watching the parade. Tim, who could send Morse himself when he had to, sent three thousand words before one of Shafter's aides appeared.

"No nonmilitary messages. General Shafter's orders."

"That's hardly fair," Tim protested.

The aide looked tired and irritable. "You aren't even supposed to be in the city, Holt. I could have you arrested."

"It would be a lot of trouble," Tim suggested. "And such bad publicity afterward."

The aide glared at him. "It would be more trouble than you're worth. Stay out of the general's sight if you know what's good for you. That getup won't fool him."

Tim exited and watched with amusement as the aide padlocked the door and posted a private beside it. The *Clarion* had a scoop; no one else would be able to send copy out of Santiago until Shafter relented, if he ever did.

In the plaza the Americans were preparing to raise the flag. The Ninth Infantry marched in and formed up in front of the palace with the regimental band at the center. Three American officers with a folded flag scrambled over the palace's red-tiled roof. Tim slipped into a crowd of Santiago's citizens to watch it go up. Despite the mistakes and incompetence, despite the fact that he hadn't thought that America ought to be fighting this war at all, he felt the ceremony catching at his throat. He took off his dilapidated straw hat and held it over his heart.

The ceremony was halted momentarily when General Shafter discovered Sylvester Scovel of the *World* on the roof with his officers. Scovel was ordered down, and Tim watched in amazement as Scovel and Shafter shouted at each other and then actually tried to land punches. One does not punch a general. The journalist was removed by two soldiers, and the ceremony proceeded. In a country with a military government, Scovel would have been shot, and Tim suspected that Shafter would have loved to execute the man had it not been for the problem of public opinion. Tim decided to stay out of Shafter's way for the next several days.

Upon Scovel's immediate departure, however, the ceremony picked up where it had left off. As the cathedral clock struck noon, the Ninth Regiment presented arms, the band struck up "The Star-Spangled Banner," and the red, white, and blue bunting flowered out into the wind. It looked fine, Tim thought, just fine, flowing over the city.

* * *

Rafe appeared in Siboney with Tim's account of the surrender to find the *Chance* back from Jamaica and bobbing at her anchor cable offshore. When he signaled her, she steamed up to the jetty. Rafe went up the ladder while Elizabeth leaned on the rail and waited for him.

"You look pleased with yourself," he said.

She wore a dark divided skirt and a white shirtwaist open at the collar. A Panama straw hat shaded her sunburned face.

"I am pleased with myself. We filed your last dispatch last night and turned straight around. Where's Tim?"

"Trying to sneak into Santiago. Shafter's ordered all correspondents barred. What's going on here?" He pointed at the dilapidated rubble of huts on the beach. Soldiers were stacking bundles of brush around them.

"They're going to burn all the shacks," Elizabeth said. "It's yellow fever. They're afraid of it spreading to the men in the trenches."

"Burn the whole town?" There wasn't much of it, but a knot of Cuban peasants stood by disconsolately, their possessions bundled in their arms.

Elizabeth nodded. "I don't know on whose orders. It may be the best thing they can do, but I feel sorry for these people."

As they watched, a soldier went up to the civilians and as gently as possible detached the bundles of blankets and bedding. A woman tried to jerk back a pillow as she protested in Spanish. Another soldier held her while the first one threw the pillow back into an empty hut. A third soldier brought a torch, and the hut, with its dry thatch and brushwood kindling, went up in flames. The mud walls of the hut cracked open in the heat.

"My sister-in-law thinks it's spread by mosquitoes," Elizabeth said broodingly. "If she's right, this is all for nothing."

All along the beach, Siboney was going up in flames. A flat cloud of black smoke sat in the air above it. The civilians, weeping or stone faced, trudged away into the hills.

Rafe stayed long enough on the *Chance* to bathe and change his clothes and let Leon feed him. "You take care of Mrs. Holt, you hear?" he said under his breath to Leon.

"She don't need so much taking care of," Leon said. "The mate, he want to go ashore, find himself some trouble in the cantina. Miz Holt, she say if he go ashore, he stay ashore, so he don't bring no sickness back. She tell him all 'bout yellow jack, he don't make no more noise about cantinas."

"You're having too much fun," Rafe told Elizabeth as he left. "Kindly remember that war is hell."

"I'm sure it is, up there," Elizabeth said somberly. "Is Tim really all right?"

"So far as I know," Rafe said. That didn't sound very heartening, but with the way things were outside Santiago, it was impossible to say with surety that anybody was all right. "I expect he'll pull out soon," Rafe said encouragingly. "There won't be much more excitement going on. The Spanish are just about done for all over the island. The next action's going to be Puerto Rico."

He departed, leaving instructions for the *Chance* to anchor in Santiago Harbor after her return from Jamaica, if the navy had cleared it of mines.

The *Chance* steamed off to Jamaica again. It was like a cruise, Elizabeth thought guiltily. The weather was quite nice as long as the boat was moving, and it was fun, vying with the other papers' reporters for the cable at Kingston.

This time the *Chance* arrived neck-and-neck with a boat from the Chicago *Tribune*. The *Tribune*'s man was hefty and suffering from the heat. He clambered woefully over the side of his boat.

"Are we going to let *him* beat us?" Leon demanded.

"Certainly not," Elizabeth said. She raised an eyebrow at Leon. "'We'?"

"I thought I come ashore, do a little shopping," Leon said. It was what he had said the last time.

Elizabeth laughed at him. "Then you'll have to catch me." She took to her heels, overtaking the startled *Tribune* man.

Leon caught up to her in two strides. She wished he wouldn't play watchdog, although, in truth, she found his large presence comforting. He left her at the cable office door and went to see about a chicken and some greens in the Kingston market. The telegrapher recognized Elizabeth, and by the time the *Tribune* man arrived, she was translating the illegible parts of Tim's lengthy dispatch for him.

"Madam." The *Tribune* man huffed to the counter. "I must ask you to delay your transmission. I have urgent copy from the fighting front in Cuba."

"I'm with the San Francisco *Clarion*," Elizabeth said. "So I am afraid you will just have to wait."

"Impossible." The *Tribune* correspondent glared at her.

"Try," Elizabeth said. "You'll find that you can."

"You can't be with the *Clarion*. The army doesn't allow females." He looked as if he considered that an admirable viewpoint.

Elizabeth debated arguing and certainly would include the fact that she had outrun him to the cable office. But it would be an awful lot of trouble, and he probably wouldn't listen anyway. She contented herself with pointing out that she did seem to be there, didn't she?

After another few minutes, Leon poked his head in the door, with a string bag of greens in one hand and a plucked chicken by the neck in the other. He took note of the *Tribune* correspondent, who was now attempting to argue with the telegrapher. "Miz Holt, you want me to get rid of this nuisance fellow, out of here?" He loomed over the *Tribune* man.

"No, that's all right," Elizabeth said hastily.

The *Tribune* man eyed the swinging chicken with dislike. "We're nearly finished," Elizabeth added. The telegrapher, who was trained to be undistractible, continued to click his pad. Leon leaned against the whitewashed wall and waited.

"That poor man," Elizabeth said, breaking into chortles after they left. "I think he was afraid of your hitting him with that chicken."

"This chicken she's very good for lunch," Leon said. "When I hit a man, I hit him with my fist."

"You aren't going to have to hit anybody," Elizabeth said. "Leon, I really can get by without a nanny."

"Who knows what kind of thing go on in a foreign country?" Leon said suspiciously.

Elizabeth surveyed the cobblestoned streets and whitewashed houses of Kingston. The faces around her were mostly dark, but the accents were British. If you closed your eyes you could imagine yourself in London—or at any rate, an American could. It seemed to her far less foreign than New Orleans, where people still spoke French. It didn't seem useful to put it to Leon that way, however.

The *Chance* returned to Cuba to find Santiago Harbor open and the Red Cross ship *State of Texas* anchored there. The Santiago Yacht Club had been turned into a hospital, overseen by Fighting Joe Wheeler's daughter and Clara Barton. Tim, very thin and scraggly looking but clean, came out to meet the *Chance* and flung himself into Elizabeth's arms. He was grateful to have escaped Shafter's notice; Sylvester Scovel had spent a night in a moss-grown and rat-infested *calabozo* in Santiago and was so grateful to be released the morning after the surrender that he went without protest to Siboney to be shipped home.

"Are you all right? Are you really all right? What have you got?" Elizabeth pulled away and inspected Tim's face intently.

"Well, I don't seem to have malaria," Tim said. "Even Janessa doesn't think I have it. I can't help what I look like. I'm apparently healthy except for the fact that heat and hardtack don't agree with me. We're going to Puerto Rico tomorrow."

"That will make a nice change," Elizabeth said demurely, then waited expectantly.

Tim laughed. "All right. I admit it. You've done an ace job with the boat. Rafe says you're absolutely unflappable."

"Leon and I fought off rival journalists with a dead chicken this morning," Elizabeth told him.

"I don't think Leon's a good influence." Tim nuzzled her ear. "I do have an almighty itch to go below deck with you. I think that's what's wrong with me."

"It's the middle of the day. We'll be a scandal. Where's Rafe?"

"In a cantina, no doubt, with three Cuban señoritas on his knee."

"All right, then." Elizabeth gave him her hand, and they went below. Tim was pulling off his clothes, and hers, alternately, before she had even bolted the door.

"Oh, Lord, I missed you!"

"You're thin!" She felt his ribs.

"Good," he said with satisfaction. "I was getting a little pudgy. Too much soft living on our honeymoon, lolling around in gondolas."

After a while, they lay still, sated from their lovemaking. Her head was tucked against his shoulder when Tim mused, "I wonder if anyone running this war has had the foggiest idea of what it was like to be a soldier in it. Do you know the YMCA sent a tent with reading material, writing paper, and envelopes?"

"That seems useful," Elizabeth said.

"The chaplain took over the tent, declared it for the use of officers only, and wouldn't so much as let the poor fellows get out of the sun in it. There isn't any shade in the trenches up there. The chaplain gave the troops the tracts, then sent them back to the trenches."

"What tracts?" Elizabeth asked drowsily. The sun, bright off the water, came through the porthole and pooled on the sheet that covered them. She stretched, pushing one arm above her head.

Tim chuckled. "Carefully chosen reading material, uplifting clean stories for our fellows in the trenches. *Sailor Jack's Homecoming*—lucky Sailor Jack—and *Little Susie's Prayer.* The men are using them in the latrines, paper being in short supply, so I suppose you could say they're doing some good."

"How many of the men are sick?"

"At least half. They've stopped blowing taps and firing funeral volleys at burials—the sound never stopped, and I think Shafter just couldn't stand it. Anyway, an order came down saying it was demoralizing to the troops. There isn't any sick call anymore. Anyone who can stand up to report sick is considered well enough for duty. The truth is, no one is completely healthy. Orders came down to boil all the drinking water, too. Pretty late in the game, but it doesn't matter; none of the outfits have anything to boil it *in.*"

Elizabeth closed her eyes and winced. "That's a disgrace. I'm selfishly glad to have you out of there."

"To give Shafter credit, I was told, sub rosa, that he's made it clear to Washington that he has to pull these men out and that replacements had better be forthcoming."

"And what has the War Department said?"

"The War Department is far more interested in invading Puerto Rico, where there aren't so many trouble-some Spanish troops."

"Why do we want to invade it?"

"Because it's there, I suppose. Oh, Lord, you feel good. Come here again."

"Are you sure you aren't going to Puerto Rico so you don't have to see Rosebay Ware?"

Tim jumped. "What?"

"Got your attention, didn't I?" She smiled and kissed his nose. "You've been wearing a sort of hunted look, and I agree that it's not malaria."

"Well, it isn't Rosebay," Tim said. "Not the way you mean, anyway."

"You don't know what I mean," Elizabeth said, "but all in all, I think Puerto Rico's a pretty good idea." She slithered down in the sheets. "You feel nice yourself. Very lively. No, you don't have malaria."

In the morning the *Chance* steamed toward Puerto Rico, in the opposite direction from Tampa, and arrived in time to report on the textbook campaign. The Spanish troops in Puerto Rico were few, and the Puerto Rican volunteers were reluctant soldiers. The city of Ponce, two miles inland, surrendered enthusiastically on four different occasions. Wrote Richard Harding Davis, "Indeed, for anyone in uniform it was most unsafe to enter the town at any time unless he came prepared to accept its unconditional surrender."

When General Miles arrived, Ponce surrendered again, then celebrated with a parade. Casualties occurred only when a fire engine ran over several of its volunteers, thus finally providing the local Red Cross with someone to carry on stretchers. This was accomplished with zeal, four men to a stretcher, despite protests from firemen that they could walk.

The roads in Puerto Rico were excellent, and the Puerto Ricans were embarrassingly fond of Americans. Small skirmishes were encountered on the advance to San Juan; but the Spanish invariably retreated, and the towns threw themselves into American hands. One village surrendered to Tim and Richard Davis when they stumbled into it by mistake, ahead of the American troops because they had been trying to outmaneuver each other and be the sole man there for the surrender. Tim relayed this news to Elizabeth via Rafe and told her she might address him as mayor, or possibly governor-general, from now on.

The triumphal march was halted only when word came on August 12 from Washington that the United States and Spain had declared an armistice. Spain had ceded Guam and Puerto Rico to the United States, abandoned all claim to sovereignty in Cuba, and essentially told America that it could have Manila if it could hang on to it.

In Cuba, Shafter's sick soldiers had finally been sent home, and Charley, with his yellow fever experience (and immunity) was reassigned off the *Olivette* to the yacht-club hospital in Santiago. Leonard Wood, commander of the Rough Riders, had been appointed the military governor of Santiago, taking over from Shafter, and his first priority was to stem the tide of disease before it decimated the newly arrived troops as well.

Charley arrived at the yacht club in a state of advanced aggravation because for the past week Shafter had refused to allow Janessa aboard the *Olivette*. Nor for that week would Shafter allow Charley to go ashore. Charley greeted his wife in the same fashion that Tim had, by taking her to bed first and asking questions afterward. He had questions saved up, however.

"Why didn't you tell me you were coming out here? And what about the twins?"

Janessa sat up in the rumpled bed and fished on the floor for her chemise. "Because I knew you would say not to come. And then we would have had a lengthy, expensive argument by cable, and I would have come anyway, so it seemed more economical just to do it." Janessa pulled the chemise over her head and got out of bed.

"Your logic never ceases to astound me," Charley said gravely.

Janessa was hooking her corset. "Steve Jurgen is here. Have you seen him?"

"Not yet. What if you get sick?"

Janessa turned around so she could look directly at him. Her hair fell around her shoulders in rumpled waves. "I can get just as sick in New York. I could catch anything, anytime."

"Probably not yellow fever."

"You're immune to yellow fever. Even if I get it, you won't—if you're worrying about the twins."

"Of course I am." Charley looked uncomfortable. "I suppose I'm not allowed to worry about *me*. About my losing you."

"Nope," Janessa said. "You're not. I need to work, Charley. And I need to work with *you*, when I can." She sat down on the bed.

"All right." Charley put an arm around her shoulders and leaned forward so that their noses nearly touched. "I used to like it when we were a team," he said wistfully.

"I know," Janessa said. "And we need to do it sometimes. *We* need it. Us. Our marriage."

"And you were restless," Charley went on.

Janessa gave him a thoughtful look. "Maybe. And maybe it's important for us that I not be restless."

From that understanding, if that was what it was, the Lawrences pitched into the task of trying to clean up Santiago. The Hospital Service doctors and the Red Cross cleared drains and flushed water supplies. They scrubbed the barracks of the evacuating Spanish, boiled all the army's drinking water, and saw to it that there were pots to boil it in. They ordered the Cuban civilians' water boiled and got curious stares in return. The Cubans were hungry. They would eat anything, spoiled or not. Why, they wondered, were the Americans worried about water when there was nothing to eat?

The Hospital Service doctors and the Red Cross burned palm-thatch huts suspected of harboring infection. They dosed sick soldiers and lined them up in row after row of cots, each with its own tent of mosquito netting. The head nurse had a team of orderlies specially detailed to collect the patients found half-naked and delirious, crawling on the floor. They had dysentery; they had typhoid; they had malaria or yellow fever. Some had more than one disease.

°   °   °

The Hospital Service doctors were quartered with some Red Cross nurses and a handful of army doctors at the yacht club. The doctors' accommodations there proved to be palatial after the *Olivette*. The club was tile floored, with vaguely Moorish-looking arches that gave Janessa the feeling that the harem had just left it. But it did get a sea breeze that helped to keep the insects down. Nobody had proved anything about yellow fever and mosquitoes, of course; but Charley held firmly to his belief that there was a causal relationship between the two, and he was convinced that the breeze and the netting might at least keep the hospital staff from catching it. They all had orders to douse themselves in citronella and swat mosquitoes on sight.

"They'll begin to think you're as big a crank as Finlay," Janessa warned. Carlos Finlay lived in Havana and had proclaimed the mosquito theory for years, while the medical establishment laughed at him.

"If we ever get *into* Havana, I'm going to go and sit at his feet," Charley retorted.

"Yes, dear. I am wearing my citronella. Unfortunately, I find that it repels more than mosquitoes."

"It doesn't repel me," Charley said. "I can't smell it anymore."

Unfortunately, it didn't repel tarantulas, either. They were native to the island and of a comparable size with the land crabs. When Janessa found one shifting from foot to foot on her dressing table, she fled screaming into the hall.

"How any medical school graduate could be afraid of spiders—" Charley said, smacking it with a stack of tracts provided by the YMCA.

"I'm not afraid of *spiders*," Janessa said. "But they aren't spiders when they're more than eight inches across."

"This one's not more than six," Charley said, inspecting the mangled corpse. "And that's when it's flat."

"Don't *measure* it," Janessa said through gritted teeth. "Just get *rid* of it."

She never got accustomed to the bugs, including cockroaches as big as her fist, but her horror of them was soon overswept by her horror of the general conditions in Santiago.

Janessa found the Cuban street children who trailed her skirts the hardest to deal with. They were hungry all the time and were convinced that all Americans had food in their pockets. They were barely more ragged than the American soldiers—only the Spanish troops, awaiting transport home, looked like a proper army—and gladly traded stolen Spanish insignia as souvenirs to the Americans in exchange for sowbelly. There were better rations for the soldiers in the trenches now, unloaded from the ships into landing sheds on the waterfront and packed by mule train and then by wagon on a newly built road. For reasons no one quite knew, at least not at the hospital, the men stayed quartered on Misery Ridge.

An exception was the Ninth Infantry, which had marched General Shafter into Santiago for the surrender. They were quartered in the Santiago opera house, diagonally opposite the palace of the archbishop, behind whose grilled gates a priest stalked up and down in his cassock, glaring at them. Whether he represented the archbishop or merely his own opinions, no one was sure.

Janessa was appalled by Santiago. She had seen dirt and misery before, certainly, but Santiago seemed to have hit a level she wouldn't have believed possible. War, famine, and pestilence had galloped through its streets, leaving a desolation that made her cringe.

"Isn't there some way to clean this up?" she demanded of Charley. "We'll never make any headway."

"You can't just get a new broom and sweep clean," Charley said. "Not the filth of ages."

"We got *this* place clean," Janessa said. "And you should have seen it." The yacht club had been relatively easy to scrub, compared to mud and palm thatch.

They were in the dining room, eating tinned peas and biscuits from the Red Cross stores. Steve Jurgen came up with a tray and sat down. "Tell her about the opera house," Charley said.

"They're using the cellar for a latrine," Steve said. "Our own army, bless its heart. I went on a rampage when I saw it, but the officer in charge seemed to think it was an excellent idea. So convenient."

Janessa put her head in her hands.

XVII

Slowly the family straggled home. The fighting was over, and some things would never be the same. Word came from Manila that the city had surrendered to the Americans on August 13; but before that, Emilio Aguinaldo had declared himself dictator of the Philippines, and no one knew where Henry Blake was.

Theodore Roosevelt, in command of the Rough Riders after Wood was appointed military governor of Santiago, went home a hero, and forever after popular imagination held that he had personally led a charge up San Juan Hill and captured Santiago. The soldiers of the Fifth Army Corps were sent to a quarantine hospital detention camp in Montauk Point, Long Island, and were left there for weeks in tents to die of malnutrition and medical neglect until the secretary of war heard enough scandalous reports to visit the camp and order the survivors furloughed. The Rough Riders fared somewhat better in Montauk because they were not so sick to begin with; Roosevelt had personally seen to it that his men in Cuba had had rations and medicine, buying them out of his pocket when he had to.

No one could say that the treatment of the American soldiers of the Cuban invasion was malicious. It was simply incompetent, shortsighted, and delivered from afar by men in Washington who hadn't thought things out and who had never been rank-and-file soldiers. The war, which had started so gloriously with speeches and drawings of

283

flags on the front pages of all the papers, came home coated with muddy reality and spitting up blood.

Mike Holt returned to New York from Tampa, with Eden in solicitous attendance. On Janessa's orders, however, they went to Washington immediately to see Cindy.

A tentative telegram brought a response assuring them of their welcome, but Mike nearly chickened out at the last minute. "What if Uncle Henry comes home? I'm a sick man. I'm not up to Uncle Henry."

"If Uncle Henry was there," Eden said practically, "your aunt wouldn't have invited us. I really don't think she's ever held us to blame."

It was in the somewhat bohemian household of the Michael Holts that a seventeen-year-old Frank Blake had mingled with socialists, reformers, freethinkers, and other incendiary types and had decided that there was more to life than a career in the army. The result had been his departure from home.

Mike approached his aunt's house in Alexandria with some trepidation as a result; but she appeared genuinely glad to see them, and Midge attached herself to Eden with the passionate devotion of an adolescent for an adult not that many years older than she. Janessa's twins appeared at a dead run, like a pair of kittens dashing through the parlor. They knew Mike and Eden and fixed themselves firmly in their laps as soon as they sat down.

"Where's Mama?" asked Lally hopefully.

"Oh, dear," Eden said. "She'll be home soon, darling."

Cindy's eyes widened. "Is Janessa coming back?"

"Well, not immediately, I don't think," Eden said. "She hasn't told us. We haven't seen her since she left for Cuba right after Mike got hurt."

Cindy let out a slow breath.

She doesn't want to lose these children, Eden thought.

Midge was sitting on a hassock at Eden's feet. "We're taking good care of them," she said. "Aren't we, sugar bun?" She poked Lally's tummy, and Lally giggled.

"Have you heard anything from Dad?" Mike asked.

"We contacted them from Tampa. They wired us back, saying that Mother was horrified I'd been shot and that Dad had told me so. But no letter yet."

"Your father's not much of a letter writer. Janessa's always been the one who kept people up with one another." Cindy's mouth tightened. "I don't know what's happened to this family. Everyone's unhappy and estranged."

Midge flushed, possibly remembering the reason for their departure from the Madrona, which everyone knew about by this time but had strict orders not to mention.

Eden was flabbergasted by Cindy's remark. Didn't she realize that the family's awkwardness had all started with Frank's leaving and her quarrel with Henry? "It's the war," Eden said. "It's got everyone overwrought."

"It's the date," Mike said. They stared at him, and he said, "I mean it. We're almost at the turn of the century. People don't know what to do with that. There's supposed to be some wonderful new world, some modern paradise when we get to 1900, but it all looks just as messed up as it always has. Maybe worse in some ways. It makes people resentful."

"I had a postcard from Frank," Cindy said abruptly.

"You did? Oh, that's wonderful!" Eden leaned toward her, cuddling Lally in the crook of her arm. "Where is he?"

Cindy's face relaxed for just an instant. "In Dawson City. The Klondike," she added when her answer was met with blank looks. "Not getting rich, so he says. But that's *all* he says. I—" She waved her hands helplessly and let them fall back to her lap. "I told my men not to pursue it."

Mike and Eden were aware that Cindy had hired detectives to look for Frank after he left home. "I think that's wise," Mike said carefully.

"At least we know where he is," Midge said hopefully. "Mama's afraid if she sends the Pinkerton men, he'll leave again."

"That's not—well, perhaps it is," Cindy said. "I don't . . . I thought maybe, with this war, he'd come home."

"And enlist, you mean?" Mike asked.

"He *was* planning a career with the army," Cindy remarked stiffly.

"Be glad he *didn't* enlist," Mike said. "Wait until you see my film."

"We'll have prints made and distributed as soon as we get back to New York," Eden said. "Mike thinks it will pay for the cost of the trip and then simply bring in money."

"I wish I'd got Toral's surrender, though," Mike said. "And after I taught Leon to use the camera, too."

"He's been grumbling about that surrender ever since Tampa," Eden explained. "Mike, darling, I don't blame Mr. Murray for leaving it behind. It weighs sixty pounds."

"Hmmph," said Mike.

"I wouldn't worry too much about Frank," Eden said gently to Cindy. "I mean, if possible. His going off on his own that way must have been terrifying for you, but I've noticed that the Holts make a habit of it. Look at Peter. And Tim. And Mike. Well, goodness, look at me."

"Peter isn't a Holt," Cindy, his stepmother, said. "He's a Blake. And he left home in that wonderfully orderly Blake fashion, with his father's permission."

"Well, Frank's a Holt," Mike said, chuckling. "Through and through. The only problem is he has a Blake for a father. Pardon me."

"That's disrespectful," Cindy said automatically. "And untrue. Your grandfather Lee wasn't like that."

"Grandpa Lee was in the army all his life," Mike said. "It suited him right down to the ground. I don't mean he was a martinet. But look at the difference between Grandpa Lee and Grandpa Whip Holt. I wish I had known him—a wagonmaster and a frontier scout! And from what Dad says, he was an individualist and a loner. He used to drive the army commanders crazy. Don't worry about Frank. He's just a throwback to your side of the family."

"Is that supposed to be comforting?" Cindy groaned, but there was a faint curve to her mouth that hadn't been there before.

"Absolutely," Mike said placidly, in spite of the fact that Brandon was bouncing like a ball in his lap. "Uncle Henry made a big fuss over Frank's refusal to follow in his family's tradition. But he didn't take into account that there are two sides to the family. I probably shouldn't tell you this, but I've always wondered how you and Uncle Henry got married in the first place."

"I loved him," Cindy said bitterly, and Mike knew he had gone too far.

"It's getting late," Mike said contritely. "I don't suppose Kathleen will ever get these two in bed if we don't go." The little boy appeared to have run out of steam. He lay with his head against Mike's chest and was sucking his thumb, but his eyes were determinedly open. "No bed," he said.

"I'll take them up." Eden's look at her husband indicated that he was to stay here and make things right with his aunt.

"I'll help you," Midge said eagerly.

After they had turned the babies over to Kathleen, Midge followed Eden to her room and lingered hesitantly in the doorway.

"Come in, sweetie," Eden said. "Mike won't be up for a bit."

Midge sat on the edge of the bed. "I wish I were a Holt."

"Well, you are. Your mother's a Holt. You don't suppose that only the men count, do you?"

"No, but I'm afraid I'm a Blake anyway," Midge said sadly. "I look just like Peter, very dull and stuffy. It's all right for him, I suppose, but I hate it." She looked gloomily into the mirror at her brown hair and her ordinary face. "The only time I ever had an adventure, it caused so much trouble we had to leave the Madrona, and I loved it there."

"Maybe your mother just felt it was time for you to come home," Eden said tactfully.

"No, she's still mad at me for what I did." Midge

looked dolefully at Eden. "Sally was glad to see me go. The only reason I don't mind your being pretty is you're so *nice.*"

"Sally will be much nicer when she's grown up," Eden said. "It's a terrible age to be, where you are right now. I remember it."

"Did you ever want . . . well . . . did you ever think about boys?" Midge blurted out.

"Heavens, yes. I fell in love with Michael when I was twelve, and I never thought about anything *else.*" Eden sat down at the dressing table and turned the bench so she could face Midge while she pulled the pins out of her hair. "We had everyone in the family worried to death because we were so young, and no one wanted us to marry because of Mike's heart. They were all afraid we'd run off together. And of course I did exactly that. I ran away from home to marry Mike as soon as I was old enough." Eden smiled mischievously. "I had a few adventures of my own, believe me."

Midge's eyes widened with interest.

"Not," Eden remarked, brushing her hair, "that you are to construe that as encouragement from me to do the same."

"Nobody ever encourages me to do anything," Midge said gloomily.

Eden chuckled. "You don't *really* want to run off with this boy from the Madrona, do you?"

"No, I guess not," Midge said. "I just wanted to— to—"

"Experiment a little?" Eden suggested. "Have an adventure Sally hadn't had?"

Midge nodded. She looked at her fingers and twisted them in the blue serge folds of her skirts. "Is it wicked, to kiss a boy you're not in love with?"

Eden thought about that. "No, not wicked, at least *I* don't think so. But it might not be a good idea. Boys tend to, well, assume things when you kiss them."

"I know," Midge agreed. "And everybody else assumes things, too."

"Poor Midge. You really stirred up a hornet's nest, didn't you?"

"I *liked* kissing him," she said defiantly.

"Well, I should hope so. Why on earth would anyone want to kiss someone if they didn't like it? But the thing is, you don't want people to think you're fast."

"If only fast girls kiss boys, how can I ever kiss anybody without people thinking I'm fast?"

Eden thought. It was evident that Midge, reassured that she wasn't wicked, had decided not to give up kissing. Eden hadn't ever wanted to kiss anyone but Michael, although one young man had tried to force himself on her while she was traveling cross-country. There were other people whom it would have been interesting to kiss, but the reward would not have been worth the resultant trouble. "Well, you don't want to kiss just anybody. For one thing, it's beneath your dignity, and for another, boys talk." Her bachelor friends discussed their love lives freely in her presence, and Eden had made a note of that fact. "They talk just as much as girls do, and they aren't a bit nicer."

Midge pleated her skirt between her fingers. "I don't think Finney would have talked about me. He was—he was nice, Eden."

"I'm sure he was. You wouldn't have wanted to kiss a boy who wasn't nice. But you don't want to get caught doing it, either. If people see you kissing someone, they always feel as if they have to do something about it. And you absolutely, positively, never want to do *anything* but kiss him. That last part's important. That's how things get started that you can't stop."

Midge nodded. "I know about that," she said with nonchalance. "I wouldn't do anything like that with *anybody*."

Eden shuddered to think what Cindy would say if she could hear this conversation. Michael came down the hall, and Midge popped up at the sound of his footsteps.

"I'll go to bed now," she said. "Thank you!" Her cheeks flaming, she ducked past Mike as he opened the door.

"What was that all about?" he inquired.

"Woman-to-woman advice," Eden said airily. "About men."

"Oh?" Mike closed the door behind him.

"She has a very healthy attitude about men. She likes them. I hope no one comes along and spoils it for her." Eden shook out her folded nightgown.

"I'd lay even odds on Aunt Cindy's ruining it for her as on some faithless fellow," Mike said. "I don't like it here at all. This house is giving me the creeps."

"Me, too," Eden said abruptly. "I thought maybe it was just because I don't know your family very well."

"Generally, to know us is to love us," Mike said.

"Oh, Mike." Eden's eyes widened. "You don't think your aunt is getting to be like Mama?"

Mike turned the lamp down and started to undress for bed. "It was losing a child that finally pushed your mother over the brink," he pointed out. "Franz *died*, Frank's just—"

Eden shivered. "I wish their names weren't so much alike."

"Now *you're* getting silly." He limped over to the window and raised the sash a few inches. "It's always stuffy in here. Aunt Cindy used to be a fresh-air fiend."

"She's hanging on for dear life to the twins," Eden said. "If I were Janessa, I'd come and get those babies before Aunt Cindy decides they're hers. I have the oddest feeling she's trying to replace Frank. You mark my words. I know what I'm talking about. *I* was supposed to replace Franz. Only I never could, because I wasn't a boy."

"Damn and blast the woman." Mike crawled into bed and held out his arms for Eden. She quickly undressed, pulled her nightgown on over her head, then got into bed and snuggled next to him. "Now, you listen to me—"

"I don't think about Mama much anymore," Eden said. "You don't have to pamper me."

"I like to pamper you."

"I know." Eden buried her face in his chest. "That's why Mama's neglect doesn't hurt me anymore. I've got you."

"Aunt Cindy ought to have Uncle Henry," Mike said. "And vice versa."

"Well, they don't." Eden yawned. "Love is very mysterious. I used to think the tangled loves were all between lovers, between men and women, but there's a wider web than that." Eden's eyes closed. Her arms tightened protectively across Michael's chest. "I'm lucky," she said sleepily.

The preternatural cycle of love, past, present, and possibly future, continued to hound the Holts, the Blakes, and their acquaintances that summer, as if they exuded some attractant that mired the hapless in unexpected complications. Rafe Murray found himself the object of the attentions of *two* Puerto Rican señoritas and nearly became the press's first Puerto Rican casualty after the women found that he was planning on taking neither of them back to the States. Leon met a woman who, he said, had once jilted him in Bimini. She was married now, to a jealous Puerto Rican, and Leon took to singing doleful French love songs in the galley. Possibly spurred on by that, Tim finally had to admit there was nothing worth staying for in Puerto Rico, gritted his teeth, and he and Elizabeth went back to Tampa. He knew he had to confront Rosebay. He couldn't in good conscience lurk in Puerto Rico and wait for her to go home. But he had no idea of what to say to her.

Tim approached the Tampa Bay Hotel with trepidation. He felt as if it were his fault Hugo was dead, and that made him feel queasy. And he missed Hugo. While he checked into the hotel, Elizabeth settled herself in a white wicker chair in the lobby and picked up a book. "I think

you had better go make your condolences solo," she told
him. "I'll meet you later in our room."

Tim paced a couple of quarter turns about the lobby,
not quite ready to face Rosebay. He was a little startled
when a feminine voice, a Spanish-accented voice, hailed
his wife. He turned to see a señora hurrying toward
Elizabeth. The woman had a pretty girl by the wrist. The
young beauty was wearing a white mantilla over her raven
hair and clutching a bouquet. They were trailed by a
younger girl, wearing a wreath in her hair, and a Cuban
boy, who looked maybe seventeen.

Tim walked over quickly to find out what was happening.

"Señora Holt! I hear from the carriage driver that you
are back. We are on the way to the church, but we stop to
tell you! Lupita, she is getting married—a good Cuban
boy. That way I don't have to cut nobody's liver out
anymore."

"That's wonderful," Elizabeth said, and cast a glance
at the bridegroom. He looked torn beween passion and
apprehension. "Congratulations and best wishes."

Had Mama threatened to cut the boy's liver out? Tim
wondered, shuddering.

Elizabeth made introductions all the way around, but
all the while Tim couldn't help but feel like a playgoer who
had walked in during the middle of the second act.

"Thank you, señora, for all your help," Lupita said
decorously, then smiled at her groom meltingly, eyes wide.
He swallowed hard and smiled back.

Elizabeth gave Tim a quick look, opened her pocket-
book, and pressed a twenty-dollar gold piece in Lupita's
hand. "This is a wedding present from Señor Holt and me.
To help you get started."

"Gracias." Lupita tucked it down the front of her
dress.

"Jorge will make sure she spend it on pots and pans,
not on silliness," Mama assured everyone. "Lupita is too
old for silliness now, *si?"*

"I suppose so," Elizabeth said regretfully, then looked at Rosie. "*You* stay silly for a while."

"Would you care to fill me in?" Tim asked as soon as Mama and her charges had departed—noisily, through a small knot of gawking hotel staff—presumably for the church.

"Later," Elizabeth said. "Tonight. After you see Rosebay," she added. "I'll meet you in our room."

Tim nodded glumly, then went upstairs.

Rosebay was in her room, sitting by the window. She was dressed in black, a shade that washed all color out of her face. "Oh, God, did you dye all your dresses black?" Tim groaned.

Rosebay looked at him curiously, as if trying to find some deeper meaning in the question. "Of course I dyed my dresses," she said, sounding shocked. "I couldn't go home in colors."

"I know," Tim said. "You just look so awful in it—no, that's not what I meant. You always look pretty, but that black thing is—"

"You want some tea?" Rosebay asked. She had a pot and two cups on a tray by the window. "Sit down. You look awful yourself."

Tim sat. He wished he had worn a hat so he would have something to do with his hands. He could have balanced it on his knee and twiddled the brim. But he had decided to leave his things in the room before going to visit Rosebay, so he wasn't wearing a hat. "I—are you all right?" he blurted out.

Rosebay poured him some tea, whether he wanted it or not. "I'm—I got to the point where I'm not yelling at the Lord every night, telling him how he did me wrong. I don't know much else. I sent Hugo's body back to England. I paid the freight myself."

"Are you sure you wanted to do that?" Tim asked gently. She wouldn't have any grave to put flowers on. "We could still bring him back to San Francisco. Sometimes when we make decisions in a hurry—"

"He would have wanted to go back to England. He always kind of yearned after it, even though he said he didn't." Rosebay's lips compressed.

"What did his family say?" Tim asked her.

"I don't know. I cabled them after the boat sailed, but they haven't answered yet. It doesn't matter what they say. I sent him home." Her eyes filled with tears. "He didn't really belong to me. I didn't deserve him." She reached forward and clutched Tim's wrist. "Tim, I *tried* to."

"Of course you did," Tim said uneasily. "And I think sending him to England as some kind of penance is just—"

"It's not penance!"

"What do you call it? I never knew a woman more inclined to self-flagellation."

"I don't even know what that means," Rosebay said.

"Never mind. I just think you may regret it."

Rosebay closed her eyes. "I got plenty to regret. One more thing won't matter until I get it all sorted out." She opened her eyes again, cornflower blue, as wide as the skies, and turned them on Tim. They made him feel wistful, but no longer as if he might fall into them and drown.

She must have seen that in his face, for she sat straight in her chair, her chin up. "I'm going home, too, Tim."

"We're all going home," Tim said. "It's time. This war's pretty well done."

"Home to Mossy Creek, I mean," Rosebay said. "Home to Virginia."

"What?"

"You heard me. And don't you tell me no. I've been thinking about this since Hugo died. I've thought a right long time, and I know I can't go back to San Francisco with you."

"You've got a house there," Tim said. "And a job." He was beginning to feel extremely guilty.

"You can rent the house out for me," Rosebay said. "Find some woman to run it, to look after my boarders."

How did I get into this? he wondered, feeling as if he had stepped in glue. She wouldn't come back to San Francisco because of him, but she was perfectly willing to stick him with running her boardinghouse. And he couldn't find a way to tell her no, not the way he was feeling. "Rosebay, I don't know what to say. You know I—"

"You're married now," Rosebay said firmly.

But she was looking at him sideways, and Tim, feeling queasy, knew that she was waiting for him to say he would leave his wife for her, waiting to see if he *would* say it.

"Maybe that's a good idea," Tim said. "Home is a good place to think. I go home to Portland when I need to sort things out. I spent two weeks there before I proposed to Elizabeth," he added deliberately.

Rosebay nodded, the question answered, the door closed. "I got Hugo's insurance money—I thank you for that—and that's enough to keep me on for a while, even without the house rent and the royalties from his book. You can find another bookkeeper."

"Not as good as you," Tim said evenly.

"Just as good. And I got kin I haven't seen in near ten years."

"Because you didn't want to see them," Tim pointed out. "You told me your father wouldn't let you come back."

"That was for marrying Wedge. The Bashams always were a bad lot. He'll let me come back now." She smoothed the folds of her black taffeta dress. It was more elegant than the best Sunday dress she'd ever owned in Mossy Creek. "He'll be right glad to see me, is what."

Tim nodded silently.

"I got brothers and sisters," Rosebay continued. "If I don't go back now, I'll turn into somebody that can't. And then I won't ever have a place. Maybe I'll let you know in a while what I'm going to do."

"Take all the time you need," Tim said, and fled.

°   °   °

As promised, Elizabeth was back in their room, sitting by the window, when he came in. She looked up from her book, but Tim wasn't convinced she had actually been reading. He let out a long, ragged breath and looked at her.

"Are you all right?" she inquired.

"I didn't know you then," he blurted out.

Elizabeth closed the book. He saw the cover: *The Collected Sermons of the Rev. H. Q. Ashworth, Privately Printed.* She didn't seem interested in marking her place. "Are you trying to convey that you didn't know me when you had a fling with Rosebay Ware—but if you *had* known me, you would have been far more interested in me and would never have had a fling, and therefore I don't need to be jealous? Or are you trying to reassure me that you aren't going to run off with her now?"

"Both," Tim said. "Neither." He sat down opposite her. "How do I know what I would have done if I'd known you then? If we'd been fighting, I probably would have had the fling. If it was after we got engaged, of course I wouldn't have strayed. You know I'm not going anywhere now, and I don't want to. But talking to her was awful, all the same."

"I know." Elizabeth put a hand on his. "I shouldn't have prodded you like that, but I'm feeling a little prickly about it myself."

Tim turned his hand over and gripped hers. "Look. I won't tell you I never cared about Rosebay, because I did. It's a part of me. I don't want to pretend it was never there, any more than I want you to erase pieces of your own life. We *are* our memories. She was a powerful force in my life." He twisted his head to peer at the book on the table beside them. "The reverend have anything useful to say?"

Elizabeth smiled, relaxing. "Not about that. His writing is incomprehensible. I can understand why he's privately printed. I found him on a table in the lobby while you were at the desk checking in."

"Why would anyone bring a book like that on a holiday?" Tim asked, diverted.

"Possibly he whiled away many golden hours for someone," Elizabeth said. "On the other hand, the book might have been brought here for the expressed purpose of being left behind. But you're changing the subject. Or aren't you?"

"I don't think so," Tim said. "We may never know why we or other people did certain things or behaved in certain ways. But I know what I want now. I know what makes me happy. I know where I intend to be." He took her other hand and cupped it in his. Their rings touched and made a faint silvery click. "Was I the first man you were ever attracted to?"

When Elizabeth smiled, it began with a faint twitch of her lips, then spread into an outright grin. "No," she said, relieved.

"And you don't have any desire to go run off with any of them now, do you?"

"No, of course I don't."

"Well, what's contentment for the goose is contentment for the gander. Men aren't natural sexual rovers, not once they get old enough that their bodies can't shout louder than their hearts. I have you. I love you. Why would I ever want anyone else?"

"I don't know," Elizabeth said. "I'm such a paragon." She laughed ruefully and held her arms out to him. He laid his head against her shoulder.

"That was a horribly uncomfortable visit with her," he said. "I hate it when people want something I can't give them. I feel indecently relieved that she's going back to Virginia. I didn't tell you that."

"Well, I feel indecently relieved myself," Elizabeth said frankly. "I can't help feeling, well, invaded."

"I know." Tim lifted his head. "What a year it's been. You didn't even have time to set up housekeeping before I dragged you off to this war and stuck you in a hotel with my past. I didn't mean to make life quite that interesting."

"It's been enthralling." Elizabeth rose, and when he looked up to see where she was going, she settled herself in his lap.

Down the hall Rosebay Ware packed layer after layer of black dresses into a trunk. She had already packed Hugo's clothes. They would fit somebody in Mossy Creek; there was no use in wasting them. Where Rosebay was going, very little was wasted, and still there was never enough to go around. It had been a long time since she had lived like that. She wondered if she could still do it or if she had already crossed some unbridgeable gulf. Would she seem a foreigner, like the visiting nurses who came from Richmond? Or could she be Wedge Basham's widow, who had come home where she belonged? It was Wedge, comfortably dead, whom her mind kept turning to. She had even dug his grave herself; but it was a long time before, and all the blisters had faded. Wedge's was a loss she could talk about dry-eyed.

XVIII

Santiago

The Fifth Army Corps had been pulled out, replaced by fresh troops, including Hood's New Orleans regiment of "Immunes," who were supposed to have had yellow fever already. Quartered in one of the open, iron-roofed storage sheds that lined the waterfront, the men were nervously aware of being in "enemy territory." The first night, under the impression that Santiago was about to erupt with Spanish soldiers attempting to retake it, their officer addressed them sternly. He ordered them to be on the alert and to load with ball cartridge. Hearing this, the doctors in the hospital on the bay front put their mattresses on the floor.

All night the Immune sentries jumped at noises and arrested hapless Cubans who strayed into their lines. By midnight they had frightened themselves nearly to death, and chaos broke out in the storage sheds.

"Turn out the guard! Where's the corporal? Turn out the guard!"

Rifles clanked on the cement floor, Immunes stumbled over their cots, and the guard ran into a stack of crates of canned goods and sent an avalanche of tinned peas rolling into the street. By the time the officers had it sorted out, one of the Immunes was in the hospital with a self-inflicted bullet wound in his foot, and another was admitted with a lump the size of an egg on his head from

falling peas. In the morning, to Janessa's relief, the
Immunes' officers received an explanation from headquarters that Santiago had been captured already, and please,
they were not to try to take it again.

The wounded Immunes stared curiously at the yellow
fever patients in the hospital and offered Janessa useful
advice.

"You put a bag around the neck, she got three onions
and a clove of garlic, *hein*? And a picture of Saint Rosalia."

"Coatgrass tea."

"Nah, that don't do no good. My tante Bébé, she die
quick like somebody chop her off with a hoe—whack!"
The first soldier made a slicing motion with his hand, and
the second one winced.

"Why for hell you so superstitious? You make the
doctor think we are stupid, us."

"Not me, just only you."

They glared at each other as Janessa motioned for a
nurse to escort them out, one with his head in a bandage,
the other on a crutch. The next week the soldier with the
bandage was back, having proved not to be as immune to
yellow fever as had been thought. Hood's troops did better
than most, but a number of them still fell victim to malaria
and typhoid if not yellow jack. And the other replacement
troops fared worse.

Janessa had signed on for the duration of the war,
assuming that as soon as the Spanish were defeated,
Charley would be sent home. Now, however, he received
orders to stay on with the occupation.

"And exactly how long is the occupation going to go
on?" she asked him fretfully. She found herself torn daily
between wanting to stay in Santiago, to do *something*
about the city, and wanting never to see it again.

"Lord knows," Charley said. "If we pull out now, half
the island will starve. The war has burned all the farmland.
The farmers evacuated, and the fields are being swallowed
by the jungle. If we're going to keep our troops here, we
must have American doctors. Anyway"—he looked at her

a little guiltily—"it's a first-rate chance to study yellow jack. If we're going to build a Central American canal, we have to eradicate the disease before we send work crews in. If we find what causes it in Cuba, we can wipe it out in Nicaragua. I'd give a lot to be responsible for that." The guilty look turned wistful.

"I know," Janessa told him.

"There's talk of a special task force to work on the problem. It's just talk so far, but they'll choose the doctors with tropical experience."

"I know," Janessa said again. She stood on one foot, uncertain, the other scratching the back of her ankle under the heavy folds of petticoat. "Maybe I ought to stay during the occupation, too."

Charley raised his eyebrows, but there was a quick light in his eyes. "What about your hospital?"

"They'd *love* it if I stayed," Janessa grumbled. "If I go home, I'll just get my name in the papers again, as Kathleen says."

"What about the twins?" Charley couldn't help looking hopeful, though, as if somehow Janessa would find a way around all of it.

"I don't know," Janessa said fretfully. "I miss them dreadfully. But I miss you, too, and I miss being in the field, and I *don't know.*"

"Go up to Washington and have a think," Charley suggested. "See how they're getting on with your aunt."

"I suppose," Janessa said.

Washington

She didn't feel any more certain boarding the Red Cross ship that was steaming back to Tampa for supplies. What if the army wouldn't let her back into Cuba? What if the twins were miserable in Washington? What if they *weren't* miserable? What if they liked Cindy better than her? What if—?

"Janessa," Charley demanded, handing her aboard, "do you have any idea what you want?"

"No," she said plaintively.

"Well, that's an answer." He kissed her. "Give the babies my love. Wire me when you know what's what." He stood on the dock and waved until the ship was well down the harbor.

Several days later they docked at Tampa, and Janessa stepped off the spur line that ran from the dock to the hotel to find all her relatives gone and the Tampa Bay Hotel wearing the unswept air of a schoolhouse just closed for the summer. She took a train from Tampa north to Washington. Cindy's carriage, with Midge as official greeter, met her at the station. Janessa looked around for her children.

"It was more than our nerves would stand to bring the twins," Midge confided. "They're so slippery. Hard to keep a grip on, I mean. And there are too many trains."

"How are they?"

"Well, *we* think they're fat and sassy," Midge said. "We hope you do, too, because we hate to part with them. I think they do Mother good."

Janessa took stock of Midge. The girl seemed considerably more cheerful than the last time Janessa had seen her. She wore a wonderful straw hat with a silk rose that was appropriate for her age but was still very elegant. Her frock was less like a schoolgirl's than the sort she had been wearing before. Janessa complimented her on her outfit.

"Mother's been taking me to her dressmaker," Midge said proudly.

Cindy was waiting for them with tea. The twins, scrubbed and brushed, hurled themselves at Janessa and clung to her, but after the first ten minutes they climbed down again, distracted by little cakes and apparently quite happy.

"Are you going to take them back to New York with you right away?" Cindy asked carefully.

"That's the difficulty," Janessa said. "I need to stay on in Cuba for a bit, but I don't know if I should."

"Oh." Cindy looked hopefully at Janessa, while Janessa inspected Cindy as unobtrusively as she could manage. Cindy looked better, too; but with Cindy that was relative, since she had looked so terrible the last time Janessa had seen her. Now she seemed more relaxed, her movements more fluid, but the taut look was still there. It was just deeper under the surface now.

Lally, with a box of paper dolls under one arm, marched over and sat down between the black kid toes of Cindy's boots to open her box. Cindy brushed her ringlets with one hand. "Do let them stay a little longer with us." It was almost a plea. "We love having them, and you can see they're thriving."

"What will Henry think when he comes home?" Janessa ventured.

"I haven't the faintest idea when he is coming home," Cindy said. "It's possible he won't be staying here if he does."

"Mother!"

"I do not have any intention of severing your connection with your father," Cindy said, "or of subjecting you to the humiliation of a divorce. You'll have to be content with that."

Midge lapsed into a silence that indicated that they had had this conversation before.

Janessa wished she had kept quiet. Brandon crawled into her lap, and she hugged him. "Are you sure they won't be too much trouble for you?" And how could she bear to leave them? She hugged Brandon tighter.

"Ow, Mama!" The little boy squirmed loose.

"Of course not," Cindy said. "I've been dreading your

taking them back. And New York is *so* unpleasant in the summer."

Janessa chuckled. "While Washington is so delightful." She fanned herself with one of the numerous paper fans Cindy kept everywhere. Even though the old stone house was relatively cool, the air outside was hot and still and felt humid enough to bathe in. "Although I must say it *is* delightful after Cuba," Janessa conceded. "You have no tarantulas, for instance."

Cindy shuddered. "I suppose that's some compensation for all the politicians."

"Well, I'll think it over," Janessa said. "I'll stay with you a few days, if I may, and spend some time with the twins, then decide."

After three days Janessa was reasonably sure that the thing to do was to leave the twins with Cindy. It was a joy to watch her aunt with them. Cindy doted on Lally and Brandon, let them follow her everywhere, and was willing to read them their favorite poem, "The Owl and the Pussycat," a dozen times without complaint. Maybe, Janessa thought dubiously, kissing them good-bye and feeling that the whole world was pointing its collective finger at her, stigmatizing her as an unnatural mother, the twins would give Cindy a handhold back into stability, something to hang on to besides her anger.

The carriage rolled away with Janessa leaning from its window to wave one last time, the twins on the lawn waving back. Then they returned their attention to the daisy chain Kathleen was teaching them to make. Cindy swallowed hard, dislodging the lump in her throat. She had been fearful up until the last moment that Janessa might change her mind.

"I'll mind them now," Cindy told Kathleen. She took a lap robe from the hammock that hung between two oak trees and spread it on the grass to sit on. The lawn was wide and gently sloping, starred with white clover and the tiny yellow blossoms of wild strawberry. Cindy watched the twins fumble with the delicate flowers, trying to knot them into the chain. Mostly they fell out, but sometimes they stayed.

Both the twins could tie a knot. It was an accomplishment they were proud of, and they knotted everything they could. They had knotted the cook's bootlaces once, and she had to use a knife to undo them.

Cindy sat on the blanket, propping herself on one hand, and gazed lovingly at Brandon's pale curls, dreaming away the fact that he wasn't hers, dreaming away Janessa, and remembering Frank at that age. She had sat with Frank on this same lawn, watching his first baby steps, watching him sit still for minutes at a stretch, intent on a worm or bug in the grass. She remembered Midge learning to walk while Frank held out his arms to her and called, "Come on, Baby!" He had been jealous only sometimes. Once he had hit her in the head with a wooden mallet. It had never mattered to Midge; she adored him regardless.

It had always been just the babies and her, exactly as it was now. Henry had always been somewhere else, on duty in the army. And when he was home, it was Cindy he wanted to see, until the children got older. Henry had no patience with babies.

A fat bumblebee, furred in black and gold, hummed and hovered just over the surface of the grass. His drone gave a deep bass note to the birdsong, a somnolent midafternoon lullaby in the heat. Cindy watched the twins contentedly through a haze of memory and soft summer air. The postman came up the walk with his mailbag on his shoulder, and she waved at him.

"Over here, Mr. Atkins! Good afternoon."

"Good afternoon, Mrs. Blake. It's a fine day, isn't it?" Mr. Atkins handed her a small bundle of letters. The twins stared up at him solemnly and exhibited their daisy chain.

"They're going to stay with us a while longer," Cindy informed him. "We're so pleased."

Mr. Atkins regarded them fondly. "You tadpoles take good care of your aunt. She's a fine lady." He tipped his cap at Cindy before he left.

Cindy sorted the letters in her lap. One was from an artist who wanted to exhibit in her gallery. His work would revolutionize the art world, he assured her, as soon as he found a gallery that could appreciate it. *We'll see,* she thought. A second envelope held a dressmaker's bill. And a third was from Henry, posted in Hong Kong. She opened it slowly and took out a sheet covered in his familiar, decisive handwriting.

The contents were as close to an apology as Henry was probably capable of. He didn't actually admit he had been wrong about anything, but he did manage to concede that *she* might possibly have been right. On that sentence he had dug the pen nib deep into the paper and left a blot of ink behind. It was easy to envision him gritting his teeth as he wrote. He was sorry he had hurt her feelings. And he wanted to come home.

Cindy stood up slowly with the letter in her hand. She felt as if she were detached from everything except the babies on the lawn as she walked through the hot, wet air toward the house. She called for Kathleen through the front door and kept her eye on the twins until she came.

"Sit with them for a minute, dear. I have to go inside." Cindy stepped through the relative coolness of the front hall and into the parlor. She stood in front of the unswept fireplace and, reaching for the matches on the mantel, clucked to herself over its untidiness. She knelt to set the letter on the andirons. The paper flamed up golden, the color of oranges, and the fire ate away at the envelope.

Kneeling, hands in her lap, Cindy watched the paper until it was completely burned. Only a ghost shape remained, frozen in the ash, limning the corners of the envelope, the address still readable across the front. Cindy took the poker and cracked the ash envelope open, then stirred it into powder. She got up, dusted her hands, and rang for the housekeeper.

"See that the fire in the parlor is swept out. I want to put flowers in there."

XIX

Dawson City

While his family, estranged parents and cousins, were extricating themselves from the war with Spain, Frank Blake was swatting mosquitoes and digging six inches a day through the permafrost. He was going after a tantalizing lateral vein that held just enough gold to lure him on.

"I don't know why I'm doing this," he said to the dogs. "Do *you* want to be rich?" The dogs lolled their tongues at him. Frank shook his head. He knew what the dogs preferred—they wanted to go hunting.

Frank hauled another bucket of mud and gravel out of the shaft. He set it down without bothering to wash it, then sat on the edge of the shaft, swinging his feet over the hole, twenty feet deep, that he had personally dug into the frozen earth. What was he trying to dig up? Lately Frank had been trying to figure that out. Money? Some justification for having run out on his family and his education and all the plans everyone had made for him?

He felt no urge to fold himself back into his father's envelope and doubted that he would fit now; but he knew he wasn't going to want to be on the loose all his life. Now, while he was young, it was an adventure. But when he was forty, if he had cut all his ties . . . He was glad he had written his mother. He wondered what he should do about Peggy.

Frank looked at the bucket of muck beside him. He

had been back to his cabin for only a couple of weeks, since the beginning of July, and already he was looking for some excuse to go to Dawson. He had deliberately avoided the Fourth of July festivities (most of Dawson's population was American), feeling peevish and reluctant to watch Peggy making sheep's eyes at Rory MacKenzie. Now, perversely, he felt as if there had been a party he hadn't been invited to, and he wanted to go to town and make them take notice of him, "they" being Peggy. Possibly.

Frank grabbed the last bucket of gravel, sluiced it, and found just enough gold to encourage some other damn fool. He kicked the bucket into the bottom of the shaft and whistled to the dogs without bothering to set a fire for the next day's digging. He saddled his horse and put his rifle behind it in his pack, along with his small accumulation of gold for the Dawson Bank and a sack of dirty laundry. Frank still had a change of clothes at Peg's, and if MacKenzie didn't like that, it was too damned bad.

Frank stopped first at the Daybreak Saloon for a drink and the news—or maybe he was just reluctant to go to Peg's, after all. Heartache Johnson had a newspaper.

"Bought it off a fellow from Skagway," Heartache said. "Had it read in the town hall last night."

"Well, what's it say?"

"Cost you a dollar, same as anybody else."

"For Pete's sake, Heartache, you already had it read out loud. All I have to do is go ask somebody."

"Go ahead, then. It's a dollar if you want to read it personally."

Grumpily Frank gave Heartache a dollar. He spread the newspaper out on the bar and began to read, sipping his whiskey. It was a San Francisco paper, a copy of Tim's *Clarion*, delivered through who knew what circuitous channels. There were reports of the Fifth Army Corps landing at Daiquiri in Cuba over a month before, but maddeningly, there was no way to know what the outcome had been.

Frank read and reread Tim's account of the voyage

from Tampa and the chaos of the landing, and tried to imagine what it had been like to be there. He guessed at what had happened next. The only clue he had was this small, isolated piece of news, frozen in time, a journalistic fly in amber.

After he had finished with the war news, Frank read the city articles and the editorials, and even the fluff of the society pages. He turned the pages slowly and held out his glass for another shot.

"Don't spill anything on that," Heartache warned anxiously. "And you don't get to take all day with it."

Frank ignored him. He was going to get his money's worth. Reading matter in the Yukon was scarce, a high-priced commodity. After he had read the paper from back to front, including the advertisements for Carter's Nerve Pills and Allcock's Porous Plasters, he turned to the front page again.

"Hey!" Heartache protested. "You already read that!"

"I want to read it again."

"Then you owe me another dollar," Heartache said.

"Oh, for— Listen, you old skinflint, my cousin wrote this. I don't want to miss anything."

"No foolin'?" one of Heartache's saloon girls asked. She peered over Frank's shoulder. "Which one? This one here?"

"That's right."

"I don't believe you," Heartache said.

"Well, what did you think, I sprang up out of the ground? I've got family, and Tim Holt's my cousin." Frank finished reading while the saloon girl watched him with interest. She had a round, painted face that made Frank think of clothespin dolls. He folded the paper neatly, then handed it to Heartache. "There. Thanks for your benevolence. I think I'll move on before you charge me for the barstool."

Heartache looked at the bag of laundry at Frank's feet. "Been to Peggy's lately?"

"Not in a couple of weeks," Frank said.

The saloon girl clucked in sympathy and patted her hair. She gave Frank a hopeful look.

"Why do you ask?" Frank inquired.

"No reason," Heartache said. "None whatsoever."

Frank glared at him with distrust as he departed with his laundry.

The first thing Frank saw in Peggy's yard was MacKenzie's horse. He knew it by the Northwest Mounted Police brand and regulation saddle. Frank tied his own up next to it and stalked to the door, which bore a new sign: Closed. Laundry and Bathhouse Open 8 A.M. to 5 P.M. Daily. He started to knock, and then for some perverse reason changed his mind. He knew he *should* knock, he just wasn't going to. He'd be damned if he would.

Frank pushed the door—and discovered that it was bolted. For some reason that made him furious. He banged his fist on it hard enough to rattle the hinges. There was a flurry of movement inside.

"Who is it?" Peggy sounded cautious.

"It's me!" Frank shouted back. He heard a click behind him and spun around to see a window opening across the street, presumably for a better view. Face flaming, he pounded on the door again.

The bar rattled, and Peggy opened the door, not wide enough to let him in. "I'm closed right now, Frank," she hissed. "This isn't a good time to drop in."

"Uh-huh," Frank said. "You boarding MacKenzie's horse for him, or is it okay for *him* to drop in?"

His dogs started to slip past him, and Peggy pushed them back. She looked ready to cry. "Please, Frank. Come see me tomorrow. I can't let you in right now."

"Bed too crowded?" Frank inquired. Immediately he wished he hadn't. Peggy's face fell, and she put a hand over her mouth. "Ah, Peg, don't. I'll come back later. I just—"

MacKenzie loomed in the doorway behind her. He seemed even larger than usual. His scarlet jacket filled all available space. "It's late in the evening for calling, friend," he said equably.

"What brings you out, then?" Frank inquired. "Selling subscriptions to the Policeman's Ball?"

More curious faces appeared in the window across the street.

"Frank," Peggy said. "*Please* go away."

He had been about to, until MacKenzie appeared. Now he glowered at the Mountie. "You're out of uniform, General. Your jacket's not buttoned."

MacKenzie lifted a large hand, approximately the size of a melon, and clamped it on Frank's shoulder. "Go home," he said.

"Rory, don't. Don't you, either." Peggy pushed Mac-Kenzie back a little until he let go of Frank.

Frank looked at him pugnaciously, then changed his mind. "I shall call on you in the morning," he said stiffly to Peggy, and tipped his hat, a gesture particularly unsuited to the dilapidated felt object on his head. He left, taking his dirty laundry with him. As he rode past the interested faces in the window opposite, he tipped his hat again.

"Back again?" Heartache Johnson took note of the sack of laundry and, with some caution, Frank's glowering expression.

"I want a bath," Frank said. He refused to mention why he hadn't bathed at Peggy's. "And I want a room for the night, and don't tell me you're full up. Those girls upstairs don't use those rooms for more than half an hour at a time, and you know it, so don't get pious with me."

"Never thought of it," Heartache said. He poured Frank a shot of whiskey. "It's on the house." He seemed to feel sympathy for a kindred spirit.

Frank downed it, to the accompanying frowns of the other patrons of the Daybreak, all of whom had paid for their whiskey. "You boys leave him alone," Heartache said. "He's crossed in love."

The saloon girl sat down beside him hopefully. "I'm Nancy," she said. "You want to buy me a drink?"

Frank didn't want to much, but there didn't seem a

polite way to say so, either. Heartache poured it, and she sipped delicately. Frank paid for it, aware that it was cold tea. Saloon girls spent their whole day letting someone or other buy them a drink. They got a share of the take, and sometimes they struck a private bargain. Nancy leaned against his arm.

"I used to know a fellow wrote for a newspaper," she volunteered. "Like your cousin."

"Mmm-hmm?" Frank mumbled. If Peggy was so worried about what people would think, then why did she let that galoot tie his horse up outside her cabin after hours, with the police insignia as bold as brass on its saddlecloth?

"That was in Vancouver," Nancy continued. "He used to do card tricks. All us girls thought he was a real gentleman, but it turned out he was married. I was real sorry, though, when he got run out of town. Are you married, hon?"

If Peggy thought Mounties were so respectable, she had another think coming. "Huh?" Frank asked.

"I said, are you married?" Nancy winked at him. "You ain't got a wife back in the States?"

"I haven't got a wife anywhere," Frank said.

"Aw, good." Nancy wrapped her arm around his and butted her round doll's head against his shoulder like a cat cozying up. "I don't know what you'd want with a girl who spends all her time scrubbing clothes for anyway, ruining her hands. How about another drink, hon?"

Frank ordered it. There didn't seem to be any reason not to.

Nancy sipped her tea, little finger stuck out. When she had finished it, she snuggled against him and played with his shirt buttons. "We could go upstairs," she suggested. "You don't want to spend your time frettin' your heart out over *her*."

"I don't have money for that," Frank said. He hadn't had *that* much to drink.

Nancy looked disappointed. "Aw, they never do. Not

the nice ones." She leaned her head against his shoulder again and breathed a deep sigh. After a while, she said, "We could go anyway." Her smile was inviting and hopeful.

There didn't seem any reason not to do that, either, so he did, with the expectation that if Peggy found out, she would feel bad. He hoped she would, and he was mildly ashamed of that. The dogs waited in the hall outside the door.

Nancy seemed to Frank desperately eager to please, and he thought, even while he was making love to her, how dreary it would be to love only those people who paid you for it. But he was young, and neither that thought nor thoughts about Peggy got in his way much. Afterward, Frank went downstairs for a bottle of champagne, which was more expensive than paying for Nancy's favors would have been, but she had made a gift of herself to him, and he wanted to do something nice to reciprocate. Nancy and he stayed up late giggling and finally fell asleep just as the brief Arctic darkness faded into light again, with the empty bottle on the floor and the sheets untucked and balled into a tangle in the middle of the bed.

Frank woke in full daylight, sun streaming through the ratty curtain. Nancy had spent the night with him. She didn't work for Heartache; it wasn't his business if she wanted to take a night off, and Frank had already paid for the room. She was sleeping silently beside him, the comatose sleep of one for whom days are the customary hours for slumber. Her makeup was smeared in streaks and blotches of red rouge and black mascara. Frank rubbed his chin, wondering how much of it was smeared on *his* face.

He washed in the single bathroom at the end of the hall and shaved in the cracked mirror. The dogs weren't around, and he wondered vaguely where they'd gone. He kissed Nancy on the forehead as he left, for form's sake, and to stave off the nagging feeling that he had not been kind, either to her or to himself, in accepting her offer. Then he picked up the champagne bottle and took it downstairs with him, knowing that if he didn't, nobody else would. Frank slunk out past Heartache, who was morosely polishing the bar.

MacKenzie's horse was gone from Peggy's yard, but Frank's dogs were there. They greeted him with wagging tails and the happy expressions of creatures who had found their way home.

"They showed up last night," Peggy said, "and barked till I let the durn fools in."

"Well, I don't know how they got away from me," Frank said. "I'm sorry." He looked embarrassed. "I guess they think they live here."

Peggy seemed embarrassed, too. "I guess. Uh—" She glanced around the cabin as if for someone to tell her what to do now. "You want some coffee?"

"Yeah," Frank said. "Thanks." He hesitated, unsure of himself now in Peggy's cabin, suddenly on alien ground. "You want to tell me about last night?"

"What about last night?" Peggy asked evenly. "I spent the evening with a gentleman caller."

"*I* spent the evening with a tart!" Frank flared. "After you made it clear who *you* wanted to see!"

"Well, I hope she was nice," Peggy said. "You don't sound like you had any fun."

Frank looked at her unhappily. "I don't know whether I did or not," he admitted.

She poured him a cup of coffee from a pot that was already hot on the stove. Frank could see two cups and two dishes in the sink. Copper cans of water were heating on the stove for the first wash. Peggy studied them intently, as if they had to be carefully watched. "I got to talk to you," she muttered.

A miner was singing, lugubriously and off-key, in the bathhouse next door. His voice punctuated their conversation.

> *"Amazing grace, how sweet the sound*
> *That saved a wretch like me."*

"How can I talk with that yahoo mooing in the tub?" Frank demanded.

Peggy sat down at the table. She didn't pour herself any coffee; she folded her hands tightly in her lap as if she were holding on to something inside them. "I'm going to marry Rory," she said.

Frank took a sip of his coffee and seared his tongue. Peggy always served it nearly boiling. He didn't answer. He couldn't figure out what he was supposed to say.

The bather next door heaved himself about in the water with a splash and started the second verse.

> "'Twas grace that taught my heart to fear,
>   And grace my fears relieved."

"Oh, for God's sake!" Frank jumped up and pounded on the wall with his fist. "Shut up, you moron, or you'll get a lot closer to God than you bargained for! Do you hear me? *Shut up!*" Even to himself he sounded as if he were raving. Peggy looked at him warily, and the singer in the tub fell silent.

Frank took a deep breath. "Is that why you wouldn't let me in last night?"

"It didn't seem like a real good idea," Peggy conceded. "And I wanted to tell you myself, without Rory around."

Frank sat down again and stared at her. He kept his mouth stiff, but he knew his eyes betrayed his hurt. "Okay," he said finally.

"That all you got to say? 'Okay'?"

"What do you want me to say? Old Constable Mac-Kenzie's a fine, upstanding Mountie, a credit to the force." Frank's mouth twisted. "Nice uniform, too."

"That's not it," Peggy said. Nervously she swept the toast crumbs on the red-checked tablecloth into a small pile. "Rory's a good man, Frank. He'll stay by me; we can build something together up here."

"And I wouldn't." It was less a question than an admission.

"You really think you would?" Peggy asked him. "Oh, come on, Frank, you got itchy feet already, talking about Nome. I'm going to expand this laundry. I ordered me a real boiler, so I don't have to lug all these cans. I told you about it last month, and you went to sleep while I was talking to you."

"All right. I guess boilers don't enthrall me." Frank shuffled his feet on the floor, stared at the toes of his boots, then at Peggy's kitten picture and her Hawaiian maiden.

"You always hated those," Peggy said. "You know you did. Rory likes them. He likes the things I like. He's going to take me down to meet his ma in Winnipeg."

"That'll be a treat," Frank said.

"Don't you be snide!" Peggy snapped. "You aren't in no position to."

She glared at him, and he shrugged. "I'm not on visiting terms with my family, alas."

"Wouldn't make any difference if you were," Peggy said. "Your ma's not speaking to you now, but you wait and see what she'd have to say if you brought *me* home. And you know it."

Frank didn't answer. He *did* know it. His first thought was to offer to marry her anyway, and he almost did. But the words didn't come.

"I love Rory, Frank," Peggy said. "I don't want you to think I'm taking second best. I'm flat in love with him, and I invested a lot of time in *not* falling in love with you, 'cause I knew it would turn out like this."

"What makes you so sure you don't love me?" Frank demanded, perversely eager to prod at the wound.

Peggy smoothed her pile of bread crumbs out with her fingers into a little circle. "I said I wasn't *in* love with you—I'm not because I say I'm not, and that's going to have to be good enough for both of us."

"Oh. Mind over matter."

"Yeah. I do love you. I'll never forget you. But I'm in

love with Rory, in a way that makes me think I could spend my life with him and be comfortable and happy. We fit, Rory and me."

Frank put his elbows on the table and put his head in his hands. "I'm sorry, Peg."

Peggy gave him another wary look, perplexed now. "For what?" she asked quietly.

"For not treating you right, I guess," Frank said. "For not being what you needed."

"I never saw a man worry at himself as much as you do," Peggy said. "Honest to God. I didn't say you hadn't treated me right. I'm not some simpering ninny. It's just time for me to move on now, that's all."

"Oh." Frank took a sip of his coffee. It was cool enough to drink now. The morning seemed to have tilted; everything was askew.

"What are you going to do now?" Peggy asked. They both knew that she had cut him loose from Dawson as well as from herself. There was nothing to keep him now.

"I don't know," Frank said. "I don't really want to go to Nome, you know. Not honestly."

"You don't want to stay here, either," Peggy said.

"Yeah, I know." Frank peered into his coffee as if there might be a very small oracle in it. "I think I have to go home."

"You worried about the war?"

"I've been worried about the war." He looked up from the coffee. "I have this dream where I keep getting this telegram that my father's dead. They're supposed to give it to my mother, but they keep giving it to me."

"So?"

"I think it means I think he's going to get killed," Frank said. "If he does, Mother and Midge will need me. I can't keep on ducking that." He kept on saying "if," but for some reason the idea had got stuck in his head that his father *was* dead. He couldn't shake the notion. Maybe that was why Peg had cut him loose. "Peg?"

"Yeah?"

"Have I been getting weird? Creepy lately? Is that it?"

"No! You mean all that talk about graveyards, or what? No, you haven't been stranger than usual. You know you got an odd kick in your gallop to start with. What are you getting at?"

"I thought maybe that was why you were giving me the push," Frank said helplessly.

"No." Peggy reached across the table and took both his hands in hers. She had to tug on them before he would let her. "You're just like you always were. You're a fine man. But you're not ready to settle down, and I am."

"Oh." No list of grievances, no failure on his part, nothing to correct. "I don't know what to do with the dogs," was all he could think to say. "They came over here when I was staying at the Daybreak."

Peggy let go of his hands with a small squeeze. "Leave them with me, then."

"You don't even like them," Frank said.

They stuck their gray noses in her lap, and she scratched their ears. "They're all right. Rory thinks I ought to have one, Dawson's got so big."

"I can't drag them clear to Washington," Frank said.

"Leave them, then. They'll remind me of you." Peggy flushed. "I'd sort of like that."

Frank stood up. "I'm going." He looked at the dogs. They wagged their tails at him. "You stay. You live here now."

He thought maybe Peggy was going to cry, but she didn't. She walked him to the door and stood in it. He thought about kissing her good-bye, but he couldn't make himself do it. He lifted his hand in a vague gesture of farewell, then walked up the street. When he turned to look back, the dogs were still sitting in the doorway with Peggy.

XX

"How come you're bailin' out?" The cheechako stuck his head above the edge of Frank's mine shaft and peered at him suspiciously. "If there's pay dirt like you say, how come you're leaving?"

"I want to go home," Frank said.

"I didn't just get into town yesterday, you know," the other man said. "I can tell if a mine's been salted."

"Well, this one hasn't," Frank said. "And if you don't want to buy it, I've got some offers."

The head disappeared into the shaft again. Frank could hear the man rummaging in the horizontal drift that Frank hoped he personally never had to look at again. The thought of digging any farther into the frozen earth held, for Frank, all the futility of trying to tunnel to China.

The head popped up again. "Two thousand," the man said.

"Three," Frank said.

The cheechako scrambled out of the hole. "Don't have three," he said. "And I bet you ain't been offered three by anyone else."

"If I had, I'd have sold it to them," Frank said. "But I've been offered more than two." He was lying, but so was his prospective buyer. If the fellow knew the first thing about mining, Frank would eat his hat. The man would be lucky if he did buy Frank's claim before someone took him for a ride.

"How much more?" the cheechako asked cagily.

"Twenty-four hundred," Frank said. When he saw the cheechako's brow furrow in thought, he added, "I'll sell it to you for twenty-five. I'd hate to see somebody get it that's already got more gold than he needs."

"Why you want to go home?" the cheechako asked again.

"Look." Frank squatted down and bent over so that his nose was just above the man's. "If you think this claim is salted, go ask around Dawson, and you'll hear that I've been taking gold out of it regular—not a lot, but enough to be promising, just like I told you. I've got better things to do than waste my time digging a twenty-foot hole just to cheat the greenhorns. And my reasons for going home are personal and private and none of your damned business. If you don't want to buy this claim, then climb on up out of it and beat it. I've decided not to sell it to you."

"Now hold on. Move back so I can climb out. Let's not be hasty."

Frank didn't budge.

"I didn't say I didn't want it."

Frank sat back on his heels.

The cheechako licked his lips. "I reckon I could go twenty-five hundred." Frank thought the fellow had talked himself into it as soon as Frank had told him he couldn't have it. "The cabin goes with it and everything? The horse?"

"Everything but my bedroll, clothes, and pistol," Frank said. "And you'll have to pick the horse up in Dawson."

The cheechako thought. Frank waited. This was the only dwelling he had ever had of his own. It was oddly untroubling to leave it. He wondered if something was wrong with him that he could build a cabin and furnish it and then so blithely abandon it.

"You got a deal," the cheechako said.

"Good." Frank waited for some pang to assail him at the parting, but it didn't. He shook hands with the cheechako. "I hope you get rich, friend."

°   °   °

Frank stood on the muddy banks of the Yukon, his bedroll on his back, his cap pulled low over his eyes. He hadn't stopped to say good-bye to Peggy. He knew that despite the fact that she had sent him away, she would be hurt if he didn't say good-bye. But he just couldn't make himself do it. He had had several conversations with her in his head so far, explaining why he couldn't.

The river rolled wide and muddy toward the Bering Sea. It was congested with incoming flatboats, rafts, scows, anything that would float. The big river steamers that made the run to St. Michael were going out. They were as crowded as herring cans, and it had cost Frank a good part of what he had been paid for his claim to get a passage on one of them.

The riverbank was crowded with disgusted miners looking for any way home. *Home*. This time Frank was going home, not just somewhere else. He felt oddly purposeful, almost relieved, as if an aching homesickness could now be acknowledged. He had never thought that he would be homesick, never thought at the time that he *was* homesick; but it sure felt like it now. He examined the sensation, trying to decide if he was just missing Peggy. The thought made Frank flinch a little. How much did he care for her? How much of her was he taking away with him? How often would she come into his thoughts this month? Next month? Next year?

"Passengers for the *Yukon Darling*!" The steamer bumped against the dock while its purser bellowed over the crowd. "Ticketed passengers only!"

August found Frank in St. Michael, on Norton Sound, his money nearly gone. To hold on to what he had left, he decided to work for his passage south, and so he began to haunt the waterfront saloons where the steamer captains drank. The urge to go home had taken him by the throat. Having left behind Peggy, the dogs, and even his horse, he felt naked and vulnerable. He did not miss any of his possessions, just the living beings. On a sunlit night, when nothing had turned up, he stood sipping the single drink he allowed himself and watched the man who swept up the floor. The sweeper looked to be about thirty; but his face was almost unlined, so it was hard to tell. He did a kind of dance with his broom, a series of motions that contained a rhythmic exactitude that caught Frank's interest.

The bartender appeared to feel otherwise. "Damn it, Farley!" he shouted past Frank's ear. "I told you to quit that! It makes me crazy. Just *sweep*!"

"Sure, Bob," the sweeper said. He began to push the broom, plodding behind it. But after a moment his feet stepped sideways. His arms curved around the broom handle, hugging it to him.

"Farley!"

"I'm just sweeping, Bob."

"You're not just sweeping. I don't know what you're doing, but it ain't just sweeping. It makes you look like a goof. Now quit it."

"Okey-dokey."

"He's simple," the bartender growled in Frank's ear. "He gets into these things, and he won't quit. I don't know why I keep him on. He keeps saying he wants to go home, but how the hell can I turn a loon like that loose to get back to Nebraska?"

"Nebraska?" Farley stopped sweeping. "Are we going to Nebraska?"

"No!" the bartender said, exasperated. "I didn't say that. Go sweep." He poured himself a shot, possibly to deaden the effect that Farley seemed to have on him. "I came up here with his brother and him," he confided to Frank. "His brother was okay, but he must have had rocks in his head to bring Farley along. Their ma didn't want him to, but Farley was hot to go. I must have been crazy to agree to it." He shook his head.

"What happened to his brother?"

"He got caught out in the open last winter and froze

to death, the poor bastard," the bartender said. "And left me stuck with Farley. We were all greenhorns then, but I knew better than to go out with nothing but an overcoat like I was in Omaha."

Farley tapped Frank on the shoulder. "I want to tell you something." His round face was earnest.

"What is it?"

"Are you from Omaha?"

"No," Frank answered. "But I've been through Omaha."

"You go to my house?"

"Quit it, Farley," the bartender said. "He's never seen your house."

Farley looked sulky. "I was just asking."

"Could *you* find your house, Farley?" Frank asked.

Farley's face lit up. He nodded.

"I've got a proposition for you," Frank whispered to the bartender. As Farley tapped him on the shoulder again with two fingers, he wondered if he was going to regret it. But the Bering Sea would freeze in another month, and that was his route home.

It took some negotiating. "And how do I know you won't just take the passage money and leave him somewhere?" the bartender demanded.

"You don't, I guess," Frank said. "But I won't. I was sheriff of Dawson City for a year," he offered by way of bona fides.

"That just proves you're crazy," the bartender said. "You'd have to be dumber than Farley to do that." But he looked reassured. He obviously *wanted* to be reassured. "I buy the tickets to Vancouver," he said. "You get cash for the rest of the trip. And you got to swear you'll do right by him. He makes me crazy, but I don't want him on my conscience."

"Farley can carry the money if you want," Frank said.

"God, no. You carry it yourself."

"I like to carry the money," Farley said.

"Well, you ain't gonna."

"Frank?" Farley said. "What time we get to Omaha?"

"I don't know," Frank said. "But come on, let's go buy our tickets."

Farley's large presence at his elbow was oddly comforting, companionable. It might be nice, he thought, if you could be like Farley, some of the time, anyway, and ignore the things you didn't understand or that frightened you.

The latest newspaper to be found in St. Michael detailed the Spanish surrender. There were beginning to be reports of sickness in Cuba. And fighting was still going on in Manila.

Manila, August 13

Frank wasn't the only Blake who wanted to go home. Colonel Henry Blake wished vehemently to be elsewhere, but he was a man who knew his duty. He was preparing to watch what he knew was a sham: The "taking" of Manila by the American forces of General Wesley Merritt. Oddly, it wasn't the Spanish who were the problem.

He hadn't stayed long in Emilio Aguinaldo's camp. He left just after Aguinaldo, with Mabini's urging, proclaimed himself dictator of the Philippines. After that, it had seemed prudent to go elsewhere, taking Teddy and Paul Kirchner with him. Paul had protested at first, but Teddy had said nonsense, there was a war about to start now, and the best thing that civilians could do was stay out of the way until the thing was settled. She declined, however, to go aboard an American ship. Instead, they moved in with Serafina, in the Tondo district.

"We're about to start shelling the city," Henry said, exasperated.

"Nonsense," Teddy said again. "Spain's sued for peace. There will be a little formal ceremony, and that will be the end of it. It's Aguinaldo you're going to be fighting, as soon as Manila surrenders."

Henry did not dispute that. It was becoming obvious, although still diplomatically unspoken. Teddy's bearer Mateo, Serafina's husband, had abandoned the expedition members and joined the rebel army, which was, with the American troops, besieging Manila. Plans for the capture of Manila had hit a stumbling block almost immediately after General Merritt's arrival: The insurgents in their trenches outside Manila and the Americans in theirs were neither allies nor enemies, although they counted Spain as a common foe. It made matters difficult.

On August 7, Admiral Dewey and General Merritt, warily eyeing the actions of Aguinaldo's troops, had sent an ultimatum to General Don Fermin Jaudenes y Alvarez in Manila. The Spanish commander was warned that he had forty-eight hours in which to remove the noncombatants from the city before the Americans attacked it. General Jaudenes replied politely that he thanked the American excellencies for their warning, but because the city was surrounded by insurgents, its citizens had nowhere to go.

On August 9 Dewey and Merritt sent another message, simply demanding surrender. Jaudenes asked for time to consult with Madrid, a request that would have required much time, since Dewey had cut the cable from Manila to Hong Kong. The Americans refused that. All the proprieties having been taken care of, serious negotiations got under way through the offices of the Belgian consul. By this side door, far more private than formal messages, it became understood that Spain would offer only token resistance to the Americans entering the city.

In much the same fashion as the surrender of Santiago, this saved face for the Spanish generals, but it also served another purpose. It would keep the Filipino rebels out of Manila, and for that reason it had Henry Blake's blessing. In a peaceful surrender and a formal entry, he informed General Merritt, "You will have the place full of armed natives and Aguinaldo setting up shop in the governor's palace, and then we'll have to throw him out."

Accordingly, General Merritt wrote a memorandum to his officers that effectively scripted a fine performance and let them know exactly how the Spanish would surrender under fire. As an afterthought, he added that if the weather was unfavorable, they would postpone action. One wouldn't want it to rain on the spectacle.

It didn't rain, but neither did the show come off entirely as planned. While Admiral Dewey paced and fidgeted on the *Olympia,* field glasses in hand, the American land forces fired on the Spanish positions. No Spanish fire came in return. As called for by Merritt, the warships had bombarded the fort at Malate, a mile and a quarter down the coast from the city, and the American troops had moved through it with ease. But now where was the white flag?

Henry, outside the fort of Santiago with the soldiers, was wondering the same thing. The troops proceeded through Malate and approached the walled city, having encountered no other resistance than gunshots from the windows of houses, and those had quickly stopped. Henry's horse picked its way along a muddy road beside General Francis Greene's, the officer to whom he had been attached. They were trailed by Greene's staff and a herd of journalists, of whom Henry disapproved. He had put on his uniform in keeping with the official nature of his assignment, which was, as Teddy Montague irreverently put it, "to stop slinking around and be a proper soldier for a change." And he hoped Teddy was lying low. Scripted engagements had a way of getting loose from their authors.

Henry looked at his watch, then upward at the walls of the city, upon which numerous Spaniards could be seen. A shout came from somewhere ahead. "They've raised a white flag!"

The flag was held by a Spanish officer, with a Spanish private in attendance, just outside the city walls. Greene put his heels to his horse, with Henry beside him and the comet's tail of aides and correspondents behind.

"Has the city surrendered?" Henry asked.

The Spanish officer looked doubtful. "I do not know. I was ordered to put up this flag."

"One generally displays a white flag for a surrender," Henry said, looking warily at the Spaniards on the walls. He could see more Spanish troops coming along a road that intersected the route the Americans were on. Henry had an uncomfortable feeling that something was horribly wrong.

The Spanish officer looked ill at ease, too; but before anyone lost his head and started shooting, a carriage dashed through the tunnellike gate from the Intramuros, and a Spanish soldier flung himself out of it, saluting everyone in sight. He handed a message to Greene.

Greene read it, muttered, and climbed off his horse. "I am supposed to go inside and 'assist with negotiations,' Colonel Blake."

Henry smiled. "Possibly by relating to the Spanish exactly how many troops you have waiting outside their walls."

"Possibly. Our representatives and the Belgian consul are conferring with General Jaudenes. You will take over here until I return."

"Certainly, sir."

They waited. The Spanish flag continued to fly over the Intramuros. Henry had no idea what was going on in the surrender conference; but the noon sun was getting hotter and hotter, and his men were beginning to keel over. He let them sit and ordered water brought. In the harbor he could see the international signal flag for "Do you surrender?" flying from the *Olympia*.

"Colonel, there's a native who wants to see you."

Henry confronted an excellently armed Filipino officer in a ragged shirt and pants. "General Aguinaldo wishes to know when he will be able to enter the city," he told Henry.

"I am afraid the general will not be able to bring his men in just now," Henry said.

"The general wishes to meet with General Merritt to transfer the government into Filipino hands."

"Well, son, we haven't quite got the government out of Spanish hands yet, so I'm afraid you'll have to wait for a while."

The Filipino stiffened. "Are you refusing to allow the government of General Aguinaldo to be seated?"

"That's not my department," Henry said. "I just take orders from my general. But *your* general is going to have to realize that proclaiming himself a dictator does not make it so. You can be sure that America will do what is best for the Philippines."

Aguinaldo's messenger turned on his heel and walked off. Filipinos were a touchy, prideful lot, Henry thought, rubbing his chin. They were going to be the devil to govern. But heaven knew that the American government couldn't just turn them loose. There was the matter of the Philippine Islands' usefulness as a coaling station. German warships were in the bay, claiming their privilege as "observers." The British had already voiced concern about it. Henry looked at the moat around the walled city and shook his head again. The Filipinos ought to be grateful to have the Americans move in with some proper engineering know-how. After their streets were clean and they had a decent system of drains, they *would* be glad.

Eventually the Spaniards on the walls lost interest and moved away. The Americans waited and sweltered. In the negotiating chamber, the Americans and the Spanish agreed among themselves, and in early evening the gates were opened. The Americans, but not the Filipinos whom they had come to liberate, were allowed into the city.

The Spanish flag came down slowly, sinking majestically on its pole. A moment later an enormous silk American flag, presented for Admiral Dewey's use by the New York *Journal*, rose up the staff. Appropriately, the cloud cover that had hung all day like a steambath over the city broke, and a shaft of sunlight illuminated the flag. A cheer erupted from the American troops and spread to the citizens of Manila. *"Viva Americanos!"* they shouted.

Henry smiled. The flag always made his heart skip a beat. He loved it as a symbol of the country he adored, and he felt inspired by the spangled glory of its stars and the jauntiness of its stripes. It was a powerful representative, one that spoke to the world.

The roaring celebration continued around him as the sun sank slowly behind the flag. Henry's head was beginning to ache from the noise and the heat. His back and chest were soaking wet inside his uniform jacket. A mestizo girl flashed him a betel-stained smile and tucked a scarlet flower in his buttonhole. Henry managed to smile at her, but she looked as alien to him as if she were some kind of exotic flower. He wanted to go home.

He had begun to dream of it—strange, disjointed dreams in which he walked up a familiar street and felt the cobbles melt, or he found that his house had vanished. If he was home, he could make Cindy understand, could make her respond, could beat down the barricade around her. His throat tightened with fury that he was in Manila, instead. For possibly the first time in his life, Henry didn't *want* to do his duty, didn't care about it. He would do it anyway, but the old, glad willingness was gone.

Vancouver, September

Frank stepped off the British coaster that had brought them from St. Michael to Vancouver and purchased a paper from the first newsboy he saw. The papers were full of the news: Emilio Aguinaldo's insurgents had dug themselves into fortified trenches opposite the American outposts. Frank kept a good grip on Farley's arm. He had discovered that Farley had a tendency to drift off if not watched.

"What's for dinner?" Farley wanted to know.

"We'll go to a restaurant," Frank said, his nose in the paper. "You can order what you like."

"I like steak," Farley said.

"Good." Frank steered him into a chophouse and sat down. The paper reported, in a fairly restrained Canadian fashion, that the city of Manila had been turned over to the Americans and that discussion continued as to the proper disposition of the Philippines. Frank noted that the Filipinos who had been referred to in previous stories as "allies" had now become "insurgents." Some casualties were reported.

"I can read," Farley told Frank proudly. He tapped him on the shoulder. "I can read a menu."

"I know you can," Frank said gently. He looked longingly at the paper, the first one he'd seen that wasn't a month stale. He knew he wouldn't get to read it in peace until Farley was eating. As a baby-sitting job, escorting Farley had proved to require constant attention, mostly because he liked to talk. There was something endearing about him, though, something galumphing and sweet. And he could sometimes entertain himself, building fantastic machines in the air with his hands. When he fitted an imaginary pipe into an invisible socket he provided an audible click and hiss and engine noises for accompaniment.

Frank was beginning to see why he had got on Bob's nerves. Right then, though, he would have been happy if Farley would build something, noises and all, and people could stare if they wanted to.

Frank ordered him a steak, and when it came, Frank read the rest of the paper. He decided he'd buy another one after they got to Seattle. A stateside paper would have more war news. When Frank pulled out his wallet to pay the waiter, Farley looked at it wistfully.

"I like to carry the money," he said.

"Sorry," Frank said, "but I am the official money carrier."

"I *like* to carry it," Farley said stubbornly. He folded his arms.

Frank got them a room at a waterfront hotel that wasn't quite a flophouse. It was redolent with the scent of fish from the canneries, but it was clean, and Frank saw the mate and the engineer from their ship checking in. Farley attached himself to them, but Frank decided not to intervene. They were used to Farley by now. He had developed a passion for the ship's engines and had spent every minute he could in the engine room or watching the fireman stoke the boilers. Frank thought maybe it was a steam engine Farley was building.

"Come on, pal, early to bed." He pulled Farley up the stairs. The mate and the engineer looked as if they were settling into a poker game in the saloon. Frank was too tired to join them. "You wear me out," he told Farley. "Don't forget to brush your teeth."

He drifted off to sleep, thinking that he sounded like somebody's dad. What would it be like to have Farley for a child? A child who never grew up. Certainly a child who would never fill all your ambitions for you. *Is that how my father feels about me? That I might as well have been like Farley? Was that why he was so angry?* Things got mighty complicated once you started trying to see the other fellow's point of view.

Farley climbed into bed beside Frank. He folded his arms and stared at the ceiling. Frank twitched and began to snore. He was used to sleeping with Peggy or the dogs, so Farley's weight on the other half of the bed didn't disturb him. But he never noticed when Farley got up again, either.

"You *what*?" Frank slapped at the empty pockets of his trousers, held them up, and shook them. Farley stood before him, downcast.

"I like to carry the money," he said.

Frank glared at him. "What did you *do* with it?"

Farley's face flooded with confusion. "I forgot."

Frank hitched up his long johns and ran a hand through his hair. He caught sight of himself in the flyspecked mirror. He looked crazier than Farley. He probably was. "Where did you go with it?" he asked as evenly as possible.

Farley's face creased with concentration. "Vancouver!" he said suddenly.

"We're *in* Vancouver," Frank said. "Vancouver is the city we are in. When you left this room, where did you go with the money?"

"They don't know."

"*Who* doesn't know?"

"Mr. Barrows."

Barrows was the engineer from the ship. "You went to see Barrows." Frank felt that maybe he was getting a handle on things. "And then what happened?"

"I like to carry the money," Farley said.

"What did you do with it?" Frank shouted.

"I can't remember," Farley said. "I want to tell you something. What time do we get to Omaha?"

"It's going to be a while," Frank said grimly. "Let's try again. Where was Mr. Barrows when you went to see him?" *And where is he now, the thieving bastard?*

"Downstairs," Farley said. He remembered something. "They were playing cards."

"You didn't play cards with them, did you?"

"I don't like to play cards." Farley looked uncomfortable. "Playing cards makes me get nervous."

"Good," Frank said. "Did you have the wallet in your hand?"

"I like to carry it," Farley said.

"And you showed it to them, didn't you?"

"I'm sorry, Frank."

"And you showed them the money, didn't you?"
Farley nodded.

"Then what did you do with it?"

"I forget. They couldn't find it."

Frank got a grip on himself before he blew up. He

had learned that anger only confused Farley more, to the point at which he would answer every question in the affirmative, trying to be helpful. He started over again, with Farley and Barrows and the mate, trying to walk Farley through it step by step, and finally he deduced that Farley had set the wallet down somewhere after showing off how he carried the money, and it had inexplicably vanished.

"Uh-huh." Frank pulled his trousers on and jammed his hat on his head. With Farley in tow, he went down to the front desk and found that Barrows and company had mysteriously disappeared, too.

"When do we eat breakfast?" Farley asked.

"Later," Frank said, feeling sadistic. "If at all. Come on, you're coming with me. I don't want to turn my back on you even for a minute."

They went back to the dock, although Frank figured it was probably hopeless, and it was. The ship was gone. Frank dug in his pockets. "I have three dollars and sixty-seven cents," he informed Farley. "Do you know how far we can get on that?"

"After breakfast?" Farley reminded him hopefully.

Frank closed his eyes. "If it wasn't so much trouble, I swear to God I'd take you back to St. Michael."

"I want to go to Omaha," Farley said.

"I know." Frank took Farley by the arm and headed him back up the street. He might as well feed him. The money wasn't enough to do anything else with.

"Frank? I don't like to do this."

Frank stopped shoveling. He wiped his forehead with a coal-stained forearm. "I don't like to do this, either," he informed Farley. "But if you want to get to Omaha, you'll have to. So keep up the good work."

"I just like to ride."

"Boat rides cost money," Frank said. "We lost ours, remember?"

The firebox's mouth glowed a sullen red, but outside

it, every surface was black with coal dust, including Frank and Farley, who were paying their way to Seattle. Of the various occupations that Frank had tried, one of the few that he truly loathed was stoking coal. But the *Seattle Belle*'s fireman had jumped ship in Vancouver, and the captain was ready to give passage to two men with muscles. Frank had assured the captain he had stoked coal all his life, and Farley had been threatened with going without dinner if he contradicted that.

"As long as you're Americans," the captain said. "I don't hold with foreigners. Won't have 'em, 'specially in wartime." He peered at Frank. "You boys going to join up?"

"Yes, sir, that's what we're going home for," Frank said. He squeezed Farley's arm as he started to say something.

"Ow," Farley said.

"Will you just let me do the talking?" Frank hissed after the captain had gone.

Farley appeared to have been thinking that over, while he shoveled coal. Now he said, "I don't want to join the army."

"Nobody said you had to," Frank told him.

"You did," Farley said. "I don't want to."

"I just told the captain that," Frank explained, exasperated. "So he'd take us on."

"You told a lie," Farley said accusingly. His round face betrayed a certain triumph in having caught his companion in a transgression. Most people told him what *he'd* done wrong.

"Farley," Frank said, "do you want to go to Omaha?"

Farley nodded.

"Then sometimes, when you have lost all your money—because somebody lied to you—then you may have to tell a couple of lies, too, particularly to people like the captain, if you don't want to walk. And that is a true philosophy of life, so I would suggest you just don't worry about it and go on shoveling some coal here."

Frank dug his coal shovel into the pile and threw a load into the firebox. He was dripping with black sweat, running with rivulets of coal dust. The box's interior offered a fiery landscape of orange hillocks, black mountains, and deep red chasms that fell in upon themselves. As he threw coal on it to burn and ultimately vanish, he thought of Peggy, washing clean all the dirt. He wasn't sure what the connection was, but when she stepped out of the closet of his mind, in her white starched apron and a cloud of soapsuds, she wasn't an angry apparition or a sad one. He felt that she might be someone he could just say hello to up there, once in a while, and whose fond memory might tide him over the next few months or years.

"I don't want to join the army," Farley said again, leaning on his shovel. It appeared to have been preying on his mind.

"You don't have to," Frank said craftily. "As long as you keep shoveling coal, they won't make you join."

"I don't like the army," Farley said earnestly. "They make you get up early."

"I didn't like it myself," Frank muttered. He chuckled. "You hit the nail on the head, pal. No army for us—just adventures, all the way to Omaha."

"I'll like that," Farley said.

Frank smiled. It was hard to stay mad at Farley for long, even if they were going to have to get to Omaha in a boxcar. Maybe he could provide Farley with an adventure that he could keep in his mind, one that would last him while he spent the rest of his life on his mother's farm. That seemed to Frank to be something worth doing, something that would somehow justify his own homecoming.

Frank shoveled more coal into the box. And if his father wasn't dead—why did he keep feeling he was?— then Colonel Henry Blake could tell Frank how the army could match that.

Manila, October

"My dear man, we do thank you for your assistance." Lady Teddy Montague, resplendent in a solar topee and a khaki shooting jacket with numerous pockets, pumped Henry Blake's hand with her usual vicelike grip. "We're off to Mindoro to study the Mangyans, and then we shall sail for Mindanao."

"I wish you wouldn't," Henry said. That seemed to be his stock answer to whatever Lady Teddy had on her agenda. Her plans generally struck him as fraught with menace.

"Pish tush," Teddy said. "The Filipinos have been very well behaved. I'm quite impressed with the way they have handled the situation. I understand they are all in Malolos, hard at work on their constitution."

"The Mangyans aren't," Henry pointed out. "They're not even civilized. If they get mad at foreigners, I won't answer for what happens to you."

"I've never met a native I couldn't tame," Teddy said. "All you have to do is respect them. And that's a talent my government and yours would both do well to cultivate. I'll leave you with that thought, Colonel."

Paul Kirchner kept silent. It struck him that if he were a Filipino of *any* tribal affiliation, he would definitely be mad at foreigners. Lord knows the Filipino had seen enough of them. And to get rid of the Spanish friars only to find you had traded them for a bunch of condescending Americans didn't seem like a bargain. The Americans were running Manila and blatantly taking no notice of Emilio Aguinaldo's congress, convened in Malolos to write a constitution for a Philippine Republic. Over a hundred delegates were there, including hereditary chieftains and the Filipino intellectual elite as well as Aguinaldo's army of the poor and dispossessed. So far they had refrained from shooting at the invaders and were counting on their constitution to demonstrate their ability to govern themselves. How much longer that resolve would last was debatable, since the Americans were inadvertently being as insulting as possible.

No Filipinos were involved in the peace commission negotiating with Spain in Paris. The commission simply relayed President McKinley's decisions as he made them, and the President was swayed by feelings at home. There was a great deal of talk about Manifest Destiny, and the Kipling poem was much quoted.

In August President McKinley had demanded a naval base for the United States in Manila. By September he felt the need for sovereignty over the whole island of Luzon. And by October the peace commission was ordered to demand cession of the entire archipelago.

The antiexpansionists (including Grover Cleveland and Andrew Carnegie, along with Toby Holt) were vocal, too, but they were outnumbered. The cry continued to annex Cuba and Puerto Rico, along with Guam, the Philippines, and anyplace else no one was watching closely. One San Francisco paper even carried an editorial calling for the annexation of Spain. Tim Holt had a fine time responding to that, but it didn't dampen anyone's enthusiasm for empire building. The Americans weren't going home.

Paul thought that over as Henry shook his hand in turn. "I hope you don't have too long a stay here, Colonel."

"As long as it takes to clean up the mess," Henry said. He straightened his back as if prepared to wield a broom himself.

Paul and Teddy and the expedition's gear were being loaded into a calesa that seemed as if it might tip over at any moment. Paul, his knees under his chin, looked with difficulty past the driver as the calesa turned into the street. Henry Blake stood stiffly on the flagstones outside the Hotel de Europa, but his eyes stared at nothing that

Paul could discern. He had no idea what had caused the look on Henry's face; he just knew it had made him think, horribly, of the strangling fig.

On impulse, Paul stuck his head out of the calesa. "Go home, Colonel!" he shouted at him. "Go home *now*!"

XXI

Wichita, Kansas, November

"I want to tell you something." Farley prodded Frank in the shoulder.

Frank grasped Farley's hand and folded the two outstretched fingers down. "I'm right here. You don't have to do that. I don't like it when you poke me."

"Aw." Farley, penitent, put an arm around Frank and tried to hug him.

"And don't do that, either, okay? Not here."

They were standing in dry, cold grass in a ditch by the railbed. A barely visible trail ran along the other side and into a scrubby woods. Frank took Farley's arm and pointed him at it.

"Are we in Omaha?"

"Not yet," Frank said. "But we're getting there. You did just fine." He had taught Farley to jump for a moving boxcar, but it had taken all of Frank's nerve. They had tramped for weeks, heading from Seattle down the coast toward Sacramento, working for food when they could find a housewife who wanted wood chopped or a back stoop repaired. Frank had liked being on the road again (now that he had admitted he was, relatively speaking, nearing home, he found himself perversely slowing his steps), but finally Farley had complained so much that Frank decided to try the trains. They couldn't walk all that distance anyway, and winter was coming on.

All the same Frank had been scared practically to death, beset with visions of Farley's falling or sliding under the iron wheels of the train. He insisted on waiting for an unlocked boxcar and refused to let Farley on the rods under the cars or the "death woods," the narrow plank above the couplings, or even on the top deck, where he knew he would have to hold on to him every minute. Frank had ridden them all, but he wouldn't take a kid along. Farley was a kid. So they waited for an open, empty boxcar, and whatever deity looked out for hoboes provided them with one on a freight headed for the stockyards at Wichita.

Even then Frank woke from a doze and found that Farley had pulled the sliding boxcar door open—he didn't like the dark—and was sitting with his legs hanging over the edge, admiring the view of the Rockies.

Frank hurled himself at Farley and dragged him back just as the train highballed around a curve. The sliding door slammed closed like a sideways-moving guillotine.

"You want your legs to stay up here," Frank asked, gasping, "while the rest of you goes to Wichita? Don't you ever do that again!"

By the time they reached Wichita, Frank had just about decided he didn't ever want to have children. Parenting must be even worse, he decided, if the youngsters were too young to understand. At least with Farley, if you told him not to do something, he usually didn't do it. All you had to do was stay ahead of what you ought to be telling him.

Farley looked around wide-eyed at the Wichita hobo jungle. Deep in the woods, hidden from the railbed, the yards, and the water tower on the other side, was a city of packing crates, corrugated tin roofs, pieces of abandoned boxcars, anything that could be salvaged and cobbled together. A whimsical signpost had been nailed to a sycamore in the center of the camp, and it pointed the way to New York (1424 miles), San Francisco (1698 miles), and Hell (26 feet). At least fifteen hoboes were clustered around half a dozen fires. They glanced briefly at Frank and Farley and then away. Frank had bought a tent with a day's pay, earned packing chickens for market on a chicken farm in Newcastle, and it was compact enough to carry on his back with his bindle. He set it up while Farley stared at the jungle.

"Don't stare at anybody," Frank said, tent pegs in his teeth. "It's okay to look around, but these folks are real private."

"Okey-dokey," Farley said. He sat down and craned his neck to look at the lines of drying clothes strung from the canopy of the trees. The Wichita jungle was a main stopping place for the 'boes who followed the work season in the stockyards, the orchards, and the oil fields. When the first snow came, the men would be gone, south and west; but for now the jungle was a city in its own right, with a communal washtub and a relationship with the railroad guards compounded partly of bribery and partly of laissez-faire.

Wichita was a friendly town to hoboes, as towns went. No one shot at 'boes riding the rods or the tops of cars, or burned out the jungle for fun on Saturday night. The water tank, the hoboes' post office, was scrawled with messages from one to another: *Big Joe Jospey's gone north to Spokane; Fresno Pete was here, looking for Alley; Divvy heard in Texas there's work in Oregon.*

It seemed a fairly safe place to bring Farley. Until now Frank had found them enough work to pay for a bed in a flophouse in whatever town they passed through. Farley was strong, and under proper supervision he could shuck corn or clean chickens with the best of them. But now, closing in on Omaha, Frank wanted to give Farley this, a hobo adventure he could recount to the fellows at the feed store. Although his mind would always be a ten-year-old's, as his body grew older he would have some status among others as a man who had had an adventure.

"Come on," he said to Farley. They walked to the nearest fire, and Frank pulled a piece of beef and a handful of onions out of the pockets of his greatcoat. Mulligan, the communal stew of the jungles, was bubbling in a dented pot on the fire. Frank set about peeling the onions.

"I know you?" one of the hoboes asked.

"I doubt it," Frank said. "Haven't been this way in a while." He tossed the onion in the pot, then hacked at the beef with his knife. It was gristly and pale, a grudging backdoor handout, but anything was welcome in the pot. He felt strange all of a sudden, as if with his new tent and new boots he were playing hobo. It had been over two years since he had been on the road. "I'm Fritz," he said. It was one of the road names he had used, a nickname his brother, Peter, had once devised to annoy him. He could always remember to answer to it. There were reasons not to use Frank, going back to a dead man whom Frank hadn't killed and a jungle full of hoboes who thought he had. Frank jerked a thumb at Farley as he dumped the meat into the mulligan. "This is Farley. He's my pal."

"I'm Red Dog, and this is Apple and Clem."

"I want to tell you something," Farley said. "You ever been to Omaha?"

"Sure, kid," Red Dog said. He seemed to know instinctively what Farley was and how to talk to him. He glanced at Frank measuringly.

"I'm taking him home to his mom," Frank said. "He got kind of stuck, up in the Yukon." His look dared Red Dog to imply anything more. He was big and muscular and no man's easy mark. The things he had learned on the road he hadn't forgotten.

"Sure," Red Dog said. "Sure. I been to Omaha. Used to have a girl there I'd go and see. Used to work in the stockyards some."

"You ride the trains?" Farley said. "I *like* the trains."

"Ride 'em all the time," Red Dog said. "That's a hobo's life, highballing along all for free, your feet on a mail sack, your bindle under your head, just smoking a big cigar and watching the world go by."

There was a note of sarcasm in Red Dog's voice that escaped Farley entirely. Farley's eyes glowed. Sensing a willing audience, Red Dog elaborated. Apple got a battered guitar from the lean-to that tilted under an elm. He strummed an accompaniment. Yarn spinning was welcome entertainment.

They told of riding the cannonball mail clear from Chicago to San Francisco, of dodging railroad bulls, of brakemen outrun and outsmarted. Of the time that Nine-Finger Jack earned his name and his fame in a fight with a Mexican girl in a cantina in Sonora. Of trying to get a stake together on the Indian Valley line, where all the pay was beans and company scrip. Of John Arable, meanest man on the county work gang, who could pull a chain apart with his bare hands. They sang of the Red River Valley, and of Brady and Duncan as if they knew them.

Farley grinned broadly. He ate mulligan stew and drank bitter coffee boiled in a can and listened, soaking it all up. Frank even let him have a nip of whiskey from the flask the men were passing around, then he went to sleep, happy in the tent, his arms wrapped around his chest.

They got to Omaha in December, by the first snowfall. Frank took a slow route, the easiest trains. They jumped out of a slowing boxcar just south of the stockyards as flakes started falling, large, soft puffs looping out of the sky. Frank had memorized Farley's address so that he could ask directions, convinced that Farley would have no notion of how to get there; but he was wrong. Farley, in utter certainty, made a beeline for his farm, towing Frank behind him. It was five or six miles outside town, down an unmarked country road that sliced through unidentifiable wheat fields, now winter bare and fuzzed with stubble.

"Come on," Farley urged. "We're almost there."

Frank looked dubiously at the endless vistas of wheat. "You've been saying that for miles."

"*You* said it since we left," Farley pointed out. "This is Omaha, Frank."

And it was. They came finally to a rural route mailbox at the end of a rutted dirt road. Hand lettering on the side of the box read: E. Johnson. Beyond the mailbox the road curved up a slight hill to a red barn and a weathered house with lathe-turned columns on its porch.

The woman who opened the door was angular, with muscular forearms and a faded gingham dress and apron. Her face had the lines of one who had not always been patient with life but had managed to cope.

"Oh, Lord," she breathed. "Bob wrote me you was coming, but I didn't dare believe." She held her arms out to Farley.

He enveloped her in his embrace and lay his cheek down on the top of her head. Then Farley's mother drew them in, exclaiming over Farley, thanking Frank, patting them both.

The house was crowded with knickknacks and framed prints from subscription magazines. A picture of Abraham Lincoln hung over the fireplace. Farley's mother sat them down in the parlor, gave them hot chocolate, and asked Frank where he came from and what his family did, as if he were some nice boy who had come courting her daughter.

"Well, I'm on my way home, too," Frank said. "Kind of by the long way." Now that he was getting closer, he felt uncertain about his decision. He didn't know what he would find there and was uneasy about being engulfed, the way this house had wrapped itself around Farley. Farley sat there with a big grin, drinking his mug of chocolate and tipping back in the rocking chair.

"It's December," Farley's mother said. "You stay with us for Christmas."

"I wouldn't want to impose," Frank said. The house, upholstered everywhere in red plush and plaid wool, its tables crammed with miniature china dogs, wax flowers, and paper cutouts of the Statue of Liberty, made him claustrophobic.

"No, you stay," Farley's mother said. "You stay. It's the least we can do. If you want to help, that's fine. But you stay with us and have a proper Christmas, not out on the road somewhere." She seemed to know that he had been planning to drag his feet until January, to duck Christmas at his father's house. "These things are important," she said firmly.

Farley's father came in from the barn for supper. He was a little round man with a head like a marble, thatched with thinning blond hair in a bowl cut. "Well, Son," he said, patting Farley's back. Farley engulfed him in a hug. "Now don't do that. Grown men don't do that."

Farley went and leaned on Frank instead. "This is Frank," he said happily. Frank staggered a little from the weight.

They sat down at the table, and Farley and his father enthusiastically applied themselves to fried pork chops and applesauce.

Farley's mother smiled mistily at her son. She dabbed at her eyes with her napkin. "I'm just so glad to have him back," she said to Frank. Perhaps she saw Frank's eyes stray to Farley's father. "Mr. Johnson did talk about going up there to fetch him," she said carefully. "But he never felt like he could make it up north. Not after he'd been so disappointed in losing Ronny and all."

"Of course." Frank tried to keep his voice uncritical. Mr. Johnson had probably never been out of Nebraska in his life and couldn't see the use in going. He suspected that Mr. Johnson could have done without Farley, too. Frank's mouth tightened.

Mrs. Johnson saw it. "It's been a disappointment to him," she whispered. "It's harder for a man." It was clear she wasn't going to elaborate further. Instead, she brought up Christmas again and insisted on Frank's staying.

So Frank remained, despite the asthmatic feeling that all the knickknacks and homeyness gave him. At four in the morning, he milked cows with Farley's father in the icy December air and let Farley proudly show him the pigs, a fat, supercilious sow and her new litter. But he wasn't a hired hand this time; he was a member of the family, and they tried to take him in. Mr. Johnson talked to him about the price of hogs, and Mrs. Johnson so plainly expected him to go to church with her on Sunday that he couldn't say no. He lay in bed at night with the fine scorn of the rebellious young and wondered at himself for putting up with it all.

On Christmas Mrs. Johnson discovered that Frank had no shoes, only his boots, which were heavy and serviceable, but certainly not dressy. Farley's mother decided that they were not appropriate for the Christmas dinner table. She felt that wearing them to church had already been straining propriety. Farley's father had little feet, and despite his hulking frame, so did Farley. At last a pair of the dead brother's carpet slippers were unearthed from the attic, the only footwear of the proper size available.

"You wear these," Farley's mother said. "You wear these to dinner." She looked at him in the way she might look at a wild horse.

Frank balanced the carpet slippers in his hands. Made of worn red leather with a sheepskin lining, they were metaphorical hobbles to hold him to respectability. "Sure," he said seriously.

"There's something you need to know about us, Frank." Farley's mother looked up at him. Her round blue eyes were serious. "We're small people. We don't cast a very big shadow in the world. And small things are important to us."

Frank looked down at the slippers as if they had suddenly opened themselves insole from uppers and spoken to him. "I understand," he said. He wore them dutifully at Christmas dinner and for the rest of the evening. After dinner, Farley's mother gave him a woolen

scarf she had knitted herself, and he felt hot tears slide
down his cheeks.

Manila, February 4, 1899

It was one of those jumpy, twitchy nights that Henry
Blake had learned to associate with a full moon. He didn't
care what anyone said; as far as he was concerned, a full
moon made people crazy, and he had had the experience
to prove it. Actually, it was just coming off full, waning into
a blunted circle, pouring light off its flat side.

In Washington the Senate was debating ratification of
the treaty the Paris peace commission had signed with
Spain. In Manila the American troops were edgily waiting
for the Philippines' reaction. In December President
McKinley had simply ignored the Malolos Constitution,
adopted by the native delegations in November. He
extended the military government of Manila, under General Merritt's replacement, General Elwell Otis, over the
entire archipelago without bothering to wait for ratification.

Emilio Aguinaldo's ragged insurgent soldiers were
still in their trenches outside the city. They had been told
they would be fired on if they attempted to come in, but
it was Henry's considered opinion that Aguinaldo would
launch an attack if the Senate ratified the treaty. It was an
opinion shared by the Americans inside the city, too. The
American sentries on the Luneta were nervous and seeing
ghosts in the hot night. The cable to Hong Kong had been
repaired, and Henry had been baby-sitting for it since the
debate started. He was now attached to General Otis's
staff as head of intelligence with an office in the Fort of
Santiago. Inherited from the Spanish, its thick stone walls
enclosed a verminous rabbit warren of barracks and
prison cells. The soldiers quartered there swore it was
haunted.

It's the moon, Henry thought again. He watched it riding over the Luneta. When would it rise over Washington? he wondered. Would his wife look at it? Would it inspire her to sit down in its light and write to him? He had sent letter after letter, half a dozen at least, but never got a word back. The chaplain, when Henry finally mastered his humiliation and asked for help, had found out that Cindy was indeed back in Washington and that she and Midge appeared to be well. But the army chaplain from the War Office who had approached her had been told in no uncertain terms that his counseling services were not wanted.

Or would the moon's influence only make her more angry, Henry wondered, and lock her into her bitterness? It would be cold in Washington now; there might be snow. Henry envisioned Midge skating, her fingers buried in a fur muff. It was always hot in the Philippines, sticky and as clinging as the vines. Even in the middle of the night, the air was sweltering. Henry loosened his necktie. He was prodding at his collar button when shots crackled in the thick air, close enough so that he could smell powder through the open window.

Henry flew down the old stone stairs. The threadbare carpet nearly sent him headlong. Lights were beginning to come on in houses, and anxious voices spread across the city. There was more firing, and a bugler's call-to-arms split the night. General Otis would be at home in the Malacañang Palace just up the river. Henry thought about heading there, but instead he turned toward the Luneta. General Otis had plenty of aides to tell him people were shooting.

An excited sentry passed him through the gate onto the Luneta. Troops were pouring from the barracks.

"What's happening?" Henry demanded of the sentry.

"It's the rebels, sir. They tried to get past our lines. We fired on them, sir," the sentry said proudly.

"Good man."

"Yes, sir, we've got them on the run."

Henry went out on his horse to see what was happening. The rebels had again retreated to their trenches outside the city, but they stopped there and returned fire.

Now the shooting spread. A warehouse went up in flames on the dock. A knot of insurgents slipped through, hidden in one of the decrepit houseboats that plied the canals, and fired on the palace. The Americans were driven from one of their outlying posts, which was promptly occupied by the rebels.

By morning General Otis had ordered troops sent from house to house to search for insurgents, and an American patrol had been ambushed in a barrio north of Manila.

The United States Senate, hearing of the engagement, voted to ratify the treaty and annex the Philippines. An influential minority had opposed annexation, but now American troops had been fired on. It was America's duty to uplift and Christianize these people . . . and besides that, America couldn't be made to look ridiculous. The treaty passed the Senate with one vote to spare.

That merely made official what had been fact in the islands since the first shooting: America was at war—not with the villainous figure of Spain but with a native population America was supposed to be protecting.

The fighting continued. The native rebels took to the jungle. The Americans followed, trying to hack their way in and beginning to die of heat and the endemic conditions of the tropics. Emilio Aguinaldo was declared an outlaw, and the Americans, in their efforts to keep the disaffection from spreading through the barrios, even resorted to the *reconcentrado* camps about which they had howled in such outrage when the Spanish general Weyler had tried them in Cuba.

Nothing worked. It would take years to learn Aguinaldo's whereabouts, Henry thought, listening to a patrol interrogate a prisoner. The jungles simply opened and swallowed him up, and then he reappeared in the rear, encouraging another barrio to turn on the Americans. They would have to find him, dig him out of the jungle, and then put out his rebellion fire by fire.

General Otis began almost immediately to plan the cleaning up of Manila, the installation of drains and pavement, but the native Filipinos were unaccountably not grateful. A few of the wealthier, the intellectual elite, were wooed from Aguinaldo; but still the rebellion went on, and citizens at home in the States began to ask themselves how they had gotten in this mess in the first place. Rafe Murray grew tired of hearing Kipling quoted, and he wrote, in a story picked up by other papers:

> *We have taken up the White Man's burden*
>   *of the ebony and brown;*
> *Now will you tell us, Rudyard, please,*
>   *how we may put it down?*

America had never had a colony before and was a little uncertain what to do with it. A feeling of embarrassment, of having caught one's foot in wet cement, began to take hold. Henry felt it, felt the jungle closing in on him like the arms of the strangling fig. He had sent an American cutter to Mindoro with orders to get Teddy Montague and Paul Kirchner off the island, with or without their cooperation, and they had gone, protesting. But there was no way to cut himself loose.

Henry went back to his office in the fort and stared fixedly at the damp stone wall where soft plaster was peeling away in chunks. For the first time in his adult life, self-doubt and loneliness threatened to overwhelm him. He bit down hard on his lower lip. By the time

he had bitten through to blood, he had mastered the urge
to cry.

Alexandria, Virginia

There was snow on the ground in Alexandria. It had
started in early January, as Frank was leaving Omaha, and
blanketed the Midwest. Shivering, he had found shelter on
a ranch in Iowa, trading room and board for splitting wood
and replacing rafters in a bunkhouse. When the sun came
out, he resumed his travels and had made it to Louisville
before the next storm and finally up to the tidal lands
around the Chesapeake Bay, where snow didn't take itself
seriously. Glinting and silvery, it powdered the cobbles of
the old street. It lay in pillows on the branches of the pines
and sparkled in the gutters.

His father's house gleamed icily like a fairy-tale castle,
and Frank wondered self-consciously how long he was
going to stand in the street, hating his own uncertainty,
before some neighbor grew uneasy and called the police.
Or before his own mother looked out the window and saw
him scuffing his toes like a bad child. Or his father. What
could he say to his father?

Finally Frank hefted his bindle onto his back again
and started up the walk. It was longer than he remembered. The house wavered and retreated from his
approach—or it seemed to Frank that it did. It slid away as
if it were afraid of him, also. Frank lunged the last few
steps up to the porch and grabbed the door handle, cold
brass in his hand, and hung on. He would face his father
if he had to.

Frank yanked the bell, and the door flew wide open
before him. His mother's face was framed in light, eyes
round, mouth open, in a look of complete disbelief.
Behind her shoulder Midge's face hovered, startlingly
older, features changed, rearranged, superimposed on the

baby sister he had left. He looked beyond Midge, but there was no one else to be seen. His mother took him by the arms and drew him in, into the warm depths of high-ceilinged rooms and the graceful shadows of the firelight.

Author's Note

This book owes a special debt of gratitude to my son, Jefferson Crowe, who provided the foundation for the portrait of Farley Johnson.

For the reader interested in further information on the war in Cuba, I recommend *The Correspondents' War* by Charles H. Brown, an account of the notable journalists who first promoted and then reported the Spanish-American War. *The Little War of Private Post* by Charles Johnson Post provides a private soldier's candid view of the proceedings and is enlightening, to say the least.

Many thanks to the Book Creations team: Marla Engel, chairman of the board; George Engel, president; Laurie Rosin, project editor. Thanks also to Danelle McCafferty and John Marcus.

The Holts: An American Dynasty
Volume IX: **TAOS HOMECOMING**
by
Dana Fuller Ross

The year is 1899, and there is a feeling of expectation in the air. A new century awaits, and with it the promise that humankind will be remade, will right all wrongs, will provide prosperity for all.

India Blackstone senses only tension when she arrives at the Washington home of Cindy Blake, where the Blake children, Midge and Frank, are staying, along with the three-year-old twins of Janessa and Charley Lawrence, who are in Cuba providing medical assistance in the aftermath of the war. Henry Blake, Cindy's estranged husband, is in the Philippines on an army mission; the longer they are apart, the more bitter she becomes. Cindy discovers that India has tremendous artistic talent and suggests that she hone it in the Southwest, where the landscape would offer more unusual challenges. To everyone's surprise, Frank escorts India there.

Janessa returns to Washington, and while she is there Midge contracts diphtheria, a highly contagious disease. They must get word to Henry, but no one knows his exact whereabouts, and a frantic search is made to find him. Will the threat of his daughter's death be enough to bring him back to his unhappy marriage?

Mike and Eden Holt are in Taos, New Mexico, shooting a movie about the passing of the Old West. When they stumble upon a secret Anasazi cliff dwelling, they also land in the middle of a gunrunning scheme, and their film—as well as their lives—is in jeopardy.

❏ *California Glory* (28970-5 $4.99/$5.99 in Canada) Riots and strikes rock America's cities as workers demand freedom, fairness, and justice for all.

❏ *Hawaii Heritage* (29414-8 $5.50/$6.50 in Canada) Seeds of revolution turn the island paradise into a land of brutal turmoil and seething unrest.

❏ *Sierra Triumph* (29750-3 $5.50/$6.50 in Canada) A battle that goes beyond that of the sexes challenges the ideals of a nation and one remarkable family.

❏ *Yukon Justice* (29763-5 $5.50/$6.50 in Canada) As gold fever sweeps the nation, a great migration to the Yukon Territory of Canada begins.

And now
WAGONS WEST:
THE FRONTIER TRILOGY
From Dana Fuller Ross

❏ *Westward!* (29402-4 $5.50/$6.50 in Canada) The clock is turned back with this early story of the Holts, men and women who lived through the most rugged era of American exploration.

❏ *Expedition!* (29403-2 $5.50/$6.50 in Canada) In the heart of a majestic land, Clay Holt leads a perilous expedition up the Yellowstone River.

❏ *Outpost!* (29400-8 $5.50/$6.50 in Canada) Clay heads to Canada to bring a longtime enemy to justice.
